MY

YEAR

ABROAD

Chang-rae Lee

WITHDRAWN

RIVERHEAD BOOKS

NEW YORK

2021

RIVERHEAD BOOKS
An imprint of Penguin Random House LLC
penguinrandomhouse.com

Library of Congress Cataloging-in-Publication Data

Names: Lee, Chang-rae, author.
Title: My year abroad / Chang-rae Lee.
Description: New York : Riverhead Books, 2021.
Identifiers: LCCN 2020009507 (print) | LCCN 2020009508 (ebook) |
ISBN 9781594634574 (hardcover) | ISBN 9780698407046 (ebook)
Classification: LCC PS3562.E3347 M9 2021 (print) |
LCC PS3562.E3347 (ebook) | DDC 813/.54—dc23
LC record available at https://lccn.loc.gov/2020009507
LC ebook record available at https://lccn.loc.gov/2020009508

International edition ISBN: 9780593332535

Printed in the United States of America
1   3   5   7   9   10   8   6   4   2

Book design by Amanda Dewey

For my teachers

Without heroes, we're all plain people
and don't know how far we can go.

—BERNARD MALAMUD,
The Natural

He who truly loves the world
shapes himself to please it.

—THOMAS MANN,
Confessions of Felix Krull, Confidence Man

Music in the soul can be heard by the universe.

—LAO TZU

MY YEAR ABROAD

1.

I WON'T SAY where I am in this greatish country of ours, as that could be dicey for Val and her XL little boy, Victor Jr., but it's a place like most others, nothing too awful or uncomfortable, with no enduring vistas or distinctive traditions to admire, no funny accents or habits of the locals to wonder at or find repellent. Call it whatever you like, but I'll refer to it as Stagno, for while it's definitely landlocked here, several bodies of murky water dot the area. There's a way that the days here curdle like the gunge that collects on the surface of a simmering broth, gunge you must constantly gunge away.

Still, Stagno serves its purpose. It's so ordinary that no one too special would ever choose to live here, though well populated enough that Val and Victor Jr. and I don't stand out. And we ought to stand out. For it would be natural to ask what a college-age kid was doing shacked up with a thirtysomething mom and her eight-year-old son, and why neither of us worked a job, or why the boy didn't go off to school. Do we ever leave the house? For a brief period, we did, but not much anymore. We stream movies and shows. Val is ordering everything online again, including groceries, the only item she regularly ventures out for being a grease-soaked foot-long hoagie named the Widowmaker that is the carrot for Victor Jr. when he reaches his daily tolerance for our homeschooling. There is no stick. Val handles social studies and arts and I cover math and science, but all in all we get a C+ for conception, execution, and effort, which Victor Jr. is well aware of and is undoubtedly banking on using against his mother someday. He's an exceedingly smart, cute kid, if notably hirsute, something genetically cross-wired for sure because a kid his age shouldn't have arm and leg and back hair and definitely not the downy mustache, the nap of which the boy caresses whenever he's noodling his human child's plight.

In the future Victor Jr. may strategically deploy my name, but we still can't predict the full extent of my presence in his life. What we know is this: Val and I have a good thing going. We try to see our roles as limited in scope and intensity. We aren't aspiring to all-time greatness, whether in homeschooling or partnering. We aren't each other's stand-ins for the world-as-it-should-be. My stated obligations to Val are to treat Victor Jr. better than the sometimes unruly pupster that he is, and to be, as she says, her reliably *uberant* fuck buddy (*ex-* and *prot-*), and finally to pick up around this cramped exurban house so it doesn't get too skanky. In return, I have her excellent company and a place to stash myself for however long we mutually wish. I require nothing of her at all, except that she not ask after my family, or what I was doing before I met her several months ago, or why my only possessions were the very clothes I was wearing, a very small Japanese-made folding knife, and a dark brushed-metal ATM card that until recently magically summoned cash every time I used it.

I know something about Val because she basically told me her recent life story right after we first met in a food court of the Hong Kong International Airport. She was ahead of me in line with Victor Jr., who was as usual gaming on his handheld, and found that her credit cards weren't working, and she had no cash. When the boy heard this he immediately started wailing about the depth of his hunger, which I have come to know as bottomless. My impulse was to jam a duty-free baton of Toblerone between his oddly super-tiny teeth. But Val, even with her laughing, narrow eyes, the kind certain Asian girls can have, with that wonderful hint of an upward lilt and dark sparkle when they gaze at you that says in a most generous way, *Really?*, looked like she wanted to don a crown of thorns and climb atop a Viking pyre, so without a beat I paid for their food and was heading off with my own steamer basket of *xiaolongbao* when she asked if she could meet my parents to say what a gallant young man I was. She actually used the word *gallant*. When I told her I was solo she hooked my elbow and plunked us down at a table. While her son destroyed his mound of hot and dry Wuhan noodles, Val began telling me she was kind of solo, too, not counting Victor Jr., and then casually mentioned how her husband Victor Sr. was disappeared and probably dead. Maybe because I was freshly adrift myself, smashed to raw bits by circumstances too peculiar to recount, I matched her nonchalance and asked if he was in a kinder place. Something fell away from her wide, sweet face and she proceeded to tell me how some months earlier she had detailed for federal agents every last facet of her husband's dealings with a gang of New Jersey–based Tashkentians that involved Mongolian mineral rights, faux sturgeon eggs, and very real shoulder-mounted rocket launchers, which were supposedly part of an ISIS-offshoot-offshoot's plan to enrich themselves and arm potential client cells in Western Europe. All this was substantial enough to predicate Victor Sr.'s sudden absence from this life and worth a witness protection setup for Val when they got back to the States, a good deal considering she was the legal co-owner of her husband's trading business and faced money laundering and tax evasion charges plus the prospect of having to give up her dear little Victor to foster care.

She said she was certain she could trust me with her story, and that I had an "open and welcoming face," which I must admit that

I do. People trust me when they ought not to trust me, which these days is more often than they imagine. She talked about her and Victor Jr.'s visit with a relative in Kowloon, and I gave the much-expurgated tourist version of my own visits to Macau and Shenzhen, and how we were both heading back to the drab life of the US Eastern Seaboard. I told her I was from New Jersey myself, a few counties south of where she and her husband used to live. She asked for my email—I didn't have a phone anymore—and said she would connect with me in a couple weeks, when things got more settled. She didn't ask what I was doing out in this part of the world, which is just like Val. Since then she's asked, received my basic answer, and not mentioned it again. This is one of the many reasons I have quickly grown to cherish her. Val encounters life and persons as they come to her, this total acceptance of the fact that you're here, that you belong to the space you're taking up, that it's all and only yours. A rare thing, IMHO. If you think about it, most persons, including many of those who say they love you, can't help but question your particular coordinates in whatever you're doing or thinking or hoping for, then want to realign you to function more smoothly in their eyes and thereby calm their fretful souls.

Val's soul seems to me a crock of honey set on a warming plate, its flows exchanging imperceptibly from top to bottom so that there's hardly any gradient within, one example being that even when Victor Jr. is at his petulant, grating worst Val will bat her eyelashes twice, very slowly, while expelling the lightest of sighs, and then try to reason with the beast. Normally if her attempts with Victor Jr. fail she flags me, and I automatically fix us a snack. A couple Shin Blacks for us ravenous boys, grilled salami-and-cheeses. I watch him eat in his dainty Victor Jr. way, his thumbs and index fingers pincering the food, the other digits splayed out, and then wink if he's especially pleased. His micro-teeth furiously snip and grind and pulverize. Even if he was my own issue I couldn't deny that he might very well end up a charming and effective sociopath, one immensely successful, snarfing my offerings with warbles in his throat while picturing his foes and beloved alike in hot fat, deep-frying like chicken wings.

But at some point we're all extra hungry, aren't we, if not necessarily for grub? And if not it's probably because we've too much of a fill. Take me. I'm on the other side of feeling I was about to burst, having skipped out on this last semester to hit as many tables and stations and taps of life's grand buffet as I could, which I had no idea could be so available, so glorious and miserable, so heroic and lamentable at once. Sometimes Val senses me going funny and intuitively gives me space to sit by myself on our splintery back deck with a blunt, or to veg out when we're eating whatever we've ordered in. Sometimes Victor Jr. will bark at me, *Yo, Tilly! Wake up!* Val would likely have no trouble believing the things I've done and seen in this past year and maybe only wonder how I ever returned after being in so deep. I would say to Val that I don't know. I don't know how it was that I came back, because I didn't want to come back, ever, until I did.

Though now that I am back, I'm grateful to be with her and nobody else. Would I die for her? That's a weird question to bring up but I know I would. It doesn't mean I love her or value her most. I do love her and that's that but sometimes I think I love the world more. I'd die for the world, if this makes any sense, just because Val is one of the many remarkable phenomena in it. And this means I'd die for Victor Jr., too. Am I totally messed up? If you're willing to die for too many things, does it mean you care way too much or too little? Does it mean you'll break down very soon?

Maybe. I'm cleaning up the dinner dishes while Val gives Victor Jr. his bath (which he still insists on her doing and probably will until he's in college), and once we both have a go wrestling the little porker into his pajamas, Val and I will climb into the frilly canopied bed that came with this rented place and fire up the flat screen and watch until our pupils start vibrating, when we'll fall asleep or else get busy. We leave the screen on so I get to see Val in my favorite way, her nakedness strobed dusky blue, the cold flame of her body flashing on and off above me. She's always ready, if you know what I mean, which she tells me is not always the case for women at her older young age. Sure, she's got a lot of years on me and probably before this last year I might have gagged on noticing any dustings of gray in the hair of a woman I was getting with, but then I would have caused Val to swallow back the bile, too, for how painfully unfledged I was. My twee neat goolies. If they're no fatter now at least they've got an educated hang, like the bags under old soldiers' eyes, each drape an unsung but unforgettable campaign. Val got this about me, right there in the airport food court, she somehow understood I'd been away on a harrowing journey and that I should receive some sheltering for a while. Sometimes the plush tide of her hair on my belly, my chest, my face feels so good, tears come to my eyes and she'll rub her eyes with the wetness. Our lashes interlace. Our noses rumba and slide. And we taste the salt from ourselves, which is the tastiest salt there is.

R ECENTLY, I did a good thing for Val. I'm still thinking about it. I haven't told her about it yet and hope I never have to, unless she's really got to know. I was actually out shopping for some mini-barbells for Victor Jr. and when I was driving back into Val's neighborhood I noticed a shiny black SUV cruising very slowly down at the far end of a street parallel to ours. I pulled over and pretended to make a call. The SUV was creeping forward like a limo might, but something about the way it was moving was sketchy, it wasn't really pausing long enough to be checking house numbers, more like pretending to check but being lazy about it, as if the numbers didn't matter. An older lady was walking her dog and the SUV stopped beside her and she warily went over to it, her Pekingese yapping. The person in the SUV must have said something funny or charming because the lady smiled and tucked her dyed reddish hair behind her ear. Then she craned in slightly, clearly examining something the driver was showing her; then she shook her head. I made a quick U-turn and from the opposite direction sped to our place. I slipped the car inside the garage and without pausing grabbed a baseball cap from the rack and doffed it bill-back and borrowed the neighbor kid's BMX lying in the grass and pedaled out as fast as I could so I wouldn't be seen leaving our house. When I saw the black SUV turn onto our street I hooked in earbuds and ran over evening papers on the driveways, tightroped the curb, tried to bunny hop an ornamental yard stone, and fell on my ass but popped right up again like any kid would. The SUV—I could make out the driver now, white guy, dark sunglasses, short cropped dark hair—accelerated ever so slightly and drifted over to the wrong side of the street to where I was doing a wheelie on the sidewalk.

The smoked window rolled down. The driver was muscly in the neck and shoulders and arms but must have been a shrimp otherwise because his seat was pitched high and forward, very close to the steering wheel, just the way my tiny grandma used to have hers while she drove, her knuckles practically grazing her chin. This guy was maybe late thirties at most but had a receding hairline and was rocking an overmanicured five-o'clock shadow plus oversized mirror-shade aviators and stippled black leather driving gloves and I almost asked him how long he'd been driving Formula 1, but instead recast myself as goat-faced and sleepy-eyed, as dim as the fescue I imagined myself chewing, and just stared at the dude like he was an endless plains vista, a portrait of beige.

I was pleased to see a diffident teenaged reflection of me in his sunglasses.

"S'up, little bro?" said the guy, super mellow and friendly.

I shrugged. He had the faintest foreign accent to the West Coast vibe he was fronting, this pitchy Highlands timbre funneled through a Balkan gruffness that sounded folksy and aggressive all at once.

"So you loving that Sapient?"

"It gets me around," I said.

"I used to ride an '89 GT Performer, until I trashed it."

"Yeah, what happened?"

"I cracked the frame jumping a shopping cart. Fucked up my nose, too. See?" He turned straight on and I could see the nasty dent and skew in his bridge, which really made it seem like he'd kick-boxed some asphalt with his face.

"Cool."

"You got a smoke?"

I did, even though I don't smoke, for I have come to learn that having a ready pack and light is often worth more than a wad of cash. Most situations, as someone once instructed me, depend more on the style of entry than escape. In this case, though, I decided not to smoke with him and keep my stance as disinterested as possible. But I had to ask him what he was doing there, because he was obviously not hiding the fact that he was doing something, and it would be suspicious if I didn't ask.

"Can I help you, mister?" I said, having lit his cigarette.

He took a big drag, though I could see he made sure to exhale out the window, like it wasn't his vehicle.

"I doubt it," he said, a reply I expected. "I'm Todd Brown, by the way, with the VA. You know what that stands for?"

"Veterans Affairs?"

"That's right. You're a smart kid. What's your name?"

"Tiller."

"What kind of name is that?"

"I don't know. My mother gave it to me."

"Was she a boat person?"

"You mean like a refugee?"

"I'm making a joke."

"Right."

"So you know what we do, Tiller? At the VA."

"Look after old soldiers?"

"Soldiers, sailors, all servicemen and -women. They don't have to be old, either." He flashed me an ID card but not long enough for any inspection. "We take care of their families, too. That's my department. We're trying to do more outreach these days. I was supposed to meet with the widow of a recently fallen hero, to make sure she knew about all the benefits and support that she's entitled to. Unfortunately, she wasn't home."

"Maybe she was too bummed to answer the door."

He weakly smiled, on the fence about whether he should appear offended.

"Yeah, maybe. Anyway, it was a long drive here for me and I thought before I left I should try to connect with any veteran families in the area. I can't connect to the department server, so I can't look up who's around. I guess you're not part of one. A veteran family, that is."

"Nope," I said. "Both my folks work at the Chicken Hut."

"Good for them. But you don't happen to know of any, do you?"

"War widows?"

"They could be widowers, too. But we don't like to call them that. But yeah, mostly families, that, well, have a dad away on duty, or is deceased."

"Single-mom households."

"That's right."

"That's like half the houses in this neighborhood."

"No kidding?"

"But there aren't dead army dudes that I know of. Just deadbeat dads."

Todd Brown laughed. He bummed another smoke. Then he asked me if the high school girls around here were cute and I told him if they liked me they were cute, and then even cuter if they didn't. He laughed like he'd been there and smoked some more and then gestured for me to lean in.

"Listen, you seem like a knowledgeable kid. A smart kid. So I think I can trust you. In fact, I know I can."

"I wouldn't know why you'd want to."

"See, that's exactly what I'm talking about. You're no dope. Besides, I know I'm not fooling you. I'm not fooling you at all, right?"

I shrugged like it didn't matter whether he was or not, which only satisfied him more.

"I'm sort of with the VA," he said, letting his cigarette butt drop to the curb. "I do contract work for them, to be honest, as an investigator. Can you guess what I'm looking for?"

"Nope."

"I bet you can. Come on, Rudder, take a guess."

"My name's Tiller."

"Sorry. *Tiller.* I think you already know."

"I really don't."

"Try."

So I took an earnestly trying breath.

"Fraud?" I ventured.

"Bingo!" he shouted, and I could tell just by the way his voice instantly and lethally sharpened that Todd Brown (or whatever his real name was) was schooled in the ways of hurting people. Sometimes snuffing them, too, *Bingo* being the last dumb word they'd hear.

"People take benefits they're not eligible for, like saying they were married to a serviceperson when they weren't, or getting remarried and hiding it, or falsely claiming dependent children. I'm looking into a number of people in this area. I got a whole book of them."

This is when Todd Brown showed his hand, which he might have only done to some random bored teen or bored lady with a Pekingese, for despite how blatantly lame his whole deal was, guys like him can depend on most of us being indifferent to everything, totally not caring if something isn't directly affecting us *right now*. Before this last year I was like that, maybe I'd say I gave two shits about the plight of others or the doomed planet but my genuine condition was that there was no way I could do anything about it, because I had no clues about how.

But I have some now.

"See?" he said. He had a thin ring binder of clear plastic folders inset with pictures of various people, most of them obviously downloaded off the internet and home-printed, each sticky-labeled with a bogus address—there were way too many streets with tree and presidents' names.

"I have locations, but many keep moving and we don't know where they went. Take a peek."

"Nobody likes a snitch," I said.

He winced, something stirred muddy at the core of his perp morality. He pushed his sunglasses up the crooked bridge of his nose while his other hand gripped the steering wheel, the leather of his glove getting shiny as it stretched. I could feel how angry he suddenly was, lasers shooting out from his eyes and getting greenhoused behind his shades, building up all this pissy heat. He wants to bring me pain, is how I read him, and had we been in a nighttime urban alley instead of an exurban development on a bright spring afternoon, I'm pretty sure he would have tried.

Instead he tightly replied, "Just say if anybody looks familiar."

I flipped through the pages, two or three headshots per, pausing for effect whenever someone had curly hair, just to keep him in limbo. I went through the binder, viewing several pages twice, and then gave it back to him.

"Sorry, Todd," I said, instructing my lungs to flatten, my heart to slow, "but I don't recognize anyone."

He grunted *Fine* and tugged the folder back and rather rudely powered up the window. I saluted him but before he could pull away I quickly pedaled in front of the SUV and then around the passenger side toward the back, where I pulled out the faithful companion to the smokes I always carry, the little folding knife with a blade I keep razor sharp. As I drifted by I flicked it out and made a shallow foot-long incision in the SUV's rear tire, deep enough to compromise the sidewall but not enough to let out any air. At least not just yet. Temperature and speed and pressure would take care of that.

I gave a tap to the back window to send Todd Brown on his way. He couldn't know that later on he'd end up being a filler item on the local eleven-o'clock news, a nasty one-car wreck on the interstate. Driver transported to regional hospital. I admit I don't want Todd Brown to recover. I am almost certain he is a bad fellow. He squealed a little rubber as he shot down the street, swerving out of the neighborhood and onto the county road, heading north toward the highway. I pedaled back to Val's the long way, just in case he decided to double back, but he didn't, and as I rode up the driveway the neighbor kid, Rafe, was standing there with his hands out in a WTF splay. Rafe's a junior-high stoner and normally we would have bullshitted for a while but I just coasted his bike to him and shaka'd and went into the house. My chest was busting back and forth like a woofer. I wanted to be with Val. Seeing that tinty picture of her and Victor Sr. in Todd Brown's loose-leaf, both of them mugging for the camera with their hair windblown and with the Golden Gate Bridge in the background, taken in no doubt happier times, somehow crushed me. Not because I was jealous but because I wished for Val that she could go back there, I wished she could have stayed in that moment forever. Of course she couldn't. No one can. They tell you to live in the moment, not to constantly look ahead or backward or try to add it all up but to taste the full ripe fruit of the now. But if you really did you'd stay there, stringing yourself along like some kind of addict, jacking yourself in until all that sweetness couldn't do anything else but turn rotten.

So what should we do?

Inside, I found Val pedaling on the stationary bike—we have a mini-gym setup, so we don't have to leave the house too much—and I surprised her when I touched my forehead to her back. I held her slowly pivoting hips—her pace is more a river bike tour in Europe than a shouty spin class. Still, her sport top was damp but smelled good anyway and Val, just like she would, only barely paused and then kept on going, the blendering whirs of the machine tuning through her densely fleshy body. Her steady rhythm quelled most of the leaping inside me. It amazed me how she always generated just the right amount of delicious heat. Soon enough she dismounted and plucked out her earbuds and turned to me with a flag of worry in her eyes and she said, "What's up, kiddo?"

"Not much," I told her. "I just missed you."

"Well, I missed you," she said, gently squeezing my earlobe. "Should we think about ordering some dinner?"

"Sure," I said.

"What do you feel like? Vito's? Phoenix Garden?"

"You decide," I said. "My treat." I was already thinking about what Victor Jr. might enjoy, his fingertips shimmery with grease, when Val kissed me, not just a peck, her lips warmed from the light exercising.

"What's that for?"

"I don't know," she said. "There's something going on with you."

"Is it a good going on?"

2.

So where was my home before this home of Val's in Stagno? Technically it was my dad's house in the historic town of Dunbar, New Jersey. The historical part has to do with the Revolutionary War, a famous battle taking place in a huge field that's a quick traipse through the woods from my parents' backyard, and where I used to do tequila poppers with my high school semi-friends on the limestone plinths of the ruined classical-Greek-style monument that's perennially sticky and stained because of partyers. It always smelled pretty nasty, too. When I was young I often peed behind the weather-worn Doric columns, having sprinted there for what seemed forever from the other end of the open pasture. The grass was irregularly mowed so it was often tough sledding for a little kid, like running knee-deep in shredded office paper, and I remember once tripping and falling hard on my face and letting out a draft of whiz that made a creeping blot on my tyke's overalls. I got up with grass in my mouth and was crying with self-revulsion as I ran again for the monument, the shameful warmth down there an oddly comforting sensation as it marinated my mini-junk.

My mother was still around then, and though she scolded me for holding it in too long when I got back to her where she was reading on a tartan-plaid blanket, I remember how she lifted the blanket up and curtained me so I could peel off my soggy underpants, then fan-dried the overalls with a magazine before sending me off to play again. She was always reading something, piles of novels and magazines littering the kitchen and the screened porch and the car, and she was always sipping water from a refillable sports bottle that I'd take feverish gulps from between my rounds of play, the muddy, oily taste of her lipstick on the nozzle staying with me for a long, long time.

I can still taste it.

At some point I'll say more about her and my dad Clark and how our nuclear family all kind of precipitated out and got scattered and blown away. But for now let's just say that up to last year, I pretty much always lived in Dunbar. I was home again for the summer after attending a second year at my small expensive college, which small expensive college in particular doesn't matter, and was set up for a semester abroad program in another place that doesn't matter, except to say that the college and the semester abroad program were one and the same in terms of people and anticipations. Namely: we were generally well-off and generally bright and generally interested in the things worth being interested in like sustainability and creativity and equality and justice, but also generally keen on hooking up and cool beaches and cheap authentic-enough ethnic restaurants and making connections with people who might offer opportunities for cultural and professional experiences that were life-changing but hopefully not too much. We would return to the rest of our junior year and bear down and party that much harder in reward but also for being deeply anxious about the future, a future others before us have definitely ruined but that we would be responsible for, whether we wanted to be or not.

I never wanted to be responsible. Even if it meant freedom, even as I grew up with my single-parent dad Clark, who didn't get home until the early evening, stepping into the house from the back door after his walk from Dunbar Station and calling out in his commute-weary croon, *Hey, Til, I'm home.* Which is when he'd heat us a quick frozen pasta dinner from a box or take us out for a burger or burrito. We made the rounds around Dunbar like a lot of other lonesome father-child duos, there were plenty of our kind in our divorce-rife town, and when I was younger I could sometimes score a free soda or a side of fries with a glum overbite, the waiter or waitress feeling sorry for me. I never made dinner, nor cleaned the house, just stayed up in my room doing homework or playing games online. A nice lady from Poland came twice a week to vacuum and do laundry, a landscaping crew weekly to cut the lawn, but otherwise I was reposing solo. Clark's one rule was that I never unlock the front door, that I never open it unless there was something like a fire or child molester drooling after me and it was the only way out. None of this makes any sense, you'd better lock the back door first, if not all of them, but he was fixated. This was obviously more psychological or metaphorical than anything else, which even as a middle-schooler I understood to be important to him. And so this was the prime directive for me, not that I not have friends over or that I stay out of the liquor cabinet or not try to cook anything on the stove. I didn't do any of those things, even though I sometimes wanted to. It's not that I was afraid of something bad happening, or my dad finding out. As noted, he wouldn't have freaked out. It was that I had zero interest in being the presiding party, because being the presiding party means you have to retain order and sometimes holler at people and keep an eye out for trouble and be the responsible one, all of which is a total drag.

The thing is, I am responsible now, and in a way I never imagined I could be. Not just by taking care of things, not by way of being the type who's steady and maintaining, but by understanding the need to alter the moment, whether directly or indirectly, and then decisively doing so, and not worrying about what the future might bring. For example, I don't know for sure if it was Todd Brown's SUV that was involved in the crash, and if it was, whether another person associated with him will soon be loitering in the neighborhood again. I don't know what would have been a good, better, or best action for Val. I don't know how any of this will ultimately affect me. All I know is a video of me slicing that tire wall kept popping onto the screen of my mind and I gave myself over to it like the most enthused bride, a response I can only credit to my time away, which was most definitely abroad, if not so wide.

But I'll explain.

It was midsummer and I had a few weeks to kill in Dunbar before I was to fly off for my official study abroad program and as usual I had to make money to help cover the room and board for the year. Clark has been a salaryman for a well-known global financial services firm and we live in Dunbar Village and not sprawly new Dunbar Crossing just on the other side of Route 111, so people assume we're just as One Percenty as most of the other folks around here but really he's one of the countless midlevel managers in a huge back-office facility that's not even in NYC but in postindustrial New Jersey though right on the train line, which is why we can live way out here. Clark prefers not to drive. He earns just enough that he pays almost the whole tuition for my definitely not selective enough liberal arts college but because his sister, my beautiful aunt Didi, is the way she is, and will reside for the rest of her life in her nearby group home for autistic adults, and has no one else but him to look after her, we have to be careful about our spending.

So while my Dunbar friends rode air-conditioned coach buses to sleepaway camps in Maine and then in later years flew to summer enrichment programs at Oxbridge and Stanford, I've worked every summer mowing neighbors' lawns or walking their dogs and then, from the time I was old enough, scooping ice cream and bussing tables in a number of the many town eateries. I didn't mind not going away. I would've despised summer school and felt sorry for the zombie instructors burnt out from the regular year but desperate to make extra bank. I would have enjoyed camp, for sure, because most kids do, but even a totally gross job like dishwashing can be worthwhile, if not for the usual reasons. Sure, you can't help but develop some grit in the face of being shat upon hour after hour, and come to realize how exploited most people are, but the main thing you learn about yourself and everyone else toiling away is how much of your mental activity and chatter is about dreaming of doing something else, whether noble or debauched or downright silly.

Most Dunbarites, adults and kids, are already doing what they imagined, or at least believe they are. Growing up in Dunbar and attending a private college where the kids might casually say things like "I feel like treating myself to a snowboarding and spa weekend" and actually mean it, you'd think I'd be inured to this kind of privilege. Truth is, I never much cared about the swank life. It did bug me that I never got off the waitlist to be a tagalong for a friend's family trip to Cozumel, or to some dad's corporate box at MetLife Stadium, or the Sweet Sixteen birthday bash at a Michelin-starred sushi place in the city. I *heard* details so exhaustive of said junkets that I could practically feel the powder spray of the off-piste at Vail, wipe my chin of the buttery Wagyu grease they kept jawing about, but never actually went on anything special unless you count getting invited by Isaiah Pan and his family to Six Flags and getting those skip-the-line passes, which made the day great. Clark was too old-school sensible and frugal and dad-clueless to offer hosting any such outings, and it never occurred to me to ask.

At the dishwashing job we worked in threes, and I partnered with different guys depending on the shift, but none of them could stop talking about their imminent trajectories; take Pikette, an ex-con who for some reason wanted to open up a chain of mani-pedi studios, or Clay Weinberg, a stout, filthy-mouthed teen who wanted to write and direct sci-fi pornos, or the gray-haired former acid freak whose real name we didn't know so we just called him Jerry (after Garcia), who was studying tax accountancy at the community college so he could do people's returns.

"Hey, Jerry, you could do my dad's taxes next year," I shouted to him, after he told me his final term was almost done, this through the din and the fetid searing steam of the washers. I was in the clean-out position, clearing the leftover food off plates and emptying glasses and letting the conveyor take them to Jerry, who'd slot them as fast as he could into a tray and then push it through to the double-doored washer, which after thirty seconds was clawed out on the other end by a guy wielding a hook.

"Does he have self-employed income or foreign investments and limited partnerships?" Jerry yelled back, though he actually never yelled, just sort of intensely whispered.

"I don't think so," I said. "He just works for a company. I think he has a 401k."

With great prudence Jerry shook his big nose at me. "Then he should just get one of the popular computer tax programs. They're really very thorough, and so easy to use."

"Okay. Hey, check out these scallops."

Jerry never wanted any of the leftovers like Pikette or Weinberg would, and I plucked them off with tongs and set them aside on a big platter just for edibles, which we called the Toilet. This was the most important part of the job when you worked clean-out, to make selections for the Toilet. I was more discerning than others, but the one basic rule was that the food item could have no bites taken out of it. So whole raviolis were always Toilet ready, but not linguini, which could have dangled from a diner's lips. Never mixed salad, but definitely a clean spear of pickle. Fries were always fine, except if they were smudged with catsup or cheese sauce. The exceptions were any remainders of cocktails or wine, which were immediately gulped down. We picked at the Toilet all night like it was green room catering. You'd be amazed what Dunbar diners left on their plates, especially the older ones and the 2-iron-thin ladies, who might eat just two jumbo shrimp out of five or take one cut out of a perfectly good strip steak that was slightly too rare for their taste. I'd eat off a plate if I was super famished, often after a couple tokes out back with Jerry or one of the bussers, and then only if it was something the diner couldn't possibly have spit out.

I might have worked at the restaurant the rest of the summer had I not last-minute subbed one day for an acquaintance of mine at the local country club where he caddied. I knew pretty much nothing about golf except for playing a golf video game once and watching *Caddyshack* multiple times stoned but he said it was a member-guest tournament and all I had to do was forecaddie, which meant positioning myself in the area where people would hit their shots and helping to find errant ones and raking the bunkers and holding the flagstick during the putting. Because the caddie master knew I knew nothing he put me with a foursome none of the regular caddies wanted. I guess nobody wanted them because the member was a beginning golfer and his shots went all over the place and because of the assumption that his three guests would be no better.

The member was a cardiologist named Patel, a big, strong, chatty lefty who indeed hit his shots long but very wrong and sometimes dead sideways and once even backward, an amazing unintended trick shot that he accomplished by just barely undercutting his teed-up ball with a ferocious swing, creating such wicked backspin with the top of his metal wood that the ball went almost straight up in the air, landed a few feet in front of him, and then spun back to where the rest of us were standing.

Dr. Patel's guests were two of his colleagues, another tall Indian guy and a chubby Jewish lady who was actually quite good, as she'd played some high school golf, plus a friend of his named Pong Lou, who was a chemist at one of the big pharmaceutical companies headquartered nearby, and they all broke up like crazy after the shot, with Dr. Patel helicoptering his club into the bordering native grasses and raising his hands in victory. I retrieved it for him and he let me have one of the cocktails studding the cup holders of his cart. The whole day went like that. After the first nine holes I was totally beat, running back and forth from the woods that framed every fairway, searching for their tee shots, stepping ankle-deep into streams to retrieve dunked ones, and raking the sand after they basically strip-mined the bunkers trying to blast their balls out.

The chemist, Pong, was the worst at the beginning but not by the end. He had never played before, not having even once gone to a driving range or a putt-putt. For the first six or so holes he pretty much whiffed on half of his swings, and then the ones he did strike often didn't fly as far as the massive pelts he'd excavate, these lush, beauteous mini-islands of sod. On one green he needed seven putts before holing out, putting clear off the green not once but twice. And he almost brained his host when he shanked a fairway wood, the shot whizzing past Patel's ear so closely that the cardiologist swore it nicked his earlobe. Patel laughed about it but absently massaged it the rest of the round, and then touched his fingers to his lips, as if tasting the haunting liquor of oblivion. But that was Pong's last really awful shot. His swing was certainly funny looking—imagine a pirate sabering himself free from a knotty mess of rigging—but he began making solid contact, and if they weren't majestic, his shots started landing near the fairways, then near the greens, then sometimes on them, and he suddenly got a feel for the speed and slope of the surfaces, holing a few long putts. He even chipped in. He actually made a legit par on the last hole, which Dr. Patel said was the toughest on the course.

As I was loading the group's clubs onto a golf cart to ferry them to the bag drop area in the parking lot, Pong told me to take his clubs back to the pro shop, as they were rentals. I said he ought to buy his own set now, for how well he was already playing, and he said no way, joking that his "brilliant career" was over. I could hardly decipher "brilliant career" because of his peculiar pronunciation, which I could tell right away was because he was a native Mandarin speaker. I sort of took Mandarin 1 and 2 my first two years of college and the instructor, Ms. Wu, had the same way of speaking English, with all those gargly *shur* and *wur* and *toe* sounds. Anyway I said some of the final shots he hit were freaking amazing, and he admitted that he'd spent the entire night before studying instructional videos on YouTube on every aspect of the game, including dress and etiquette.

"But watching a video and playing are totally different things," I said.

"They are not so far apart if you try to focus on something fundamental."

"What is that?" I asked, curious as to what he'd gleaned.

"To follow through with fullness," he said, sweeping his hand forward and upward, right up to the sky. "This sport is fascinating but it takes too long to be useful for someone like me. I would prefer if only nine holes were played. Just long enough for enjoying the game, and for doing business. There would be more time for camaraderie afterward as well."

"We have an eternity for camaraderie now," Dr. Patel announced brightly. "Time for some serious drinking, my friends."

When I returned from the bag drop they paid me for the day—I was supposed to get $100 total for the afternoon but each of them happily gave me that, they said for my slavelike effort and game attitude—and I was heading off to where I'd parked my bike when they insisted I accompany them to the awards ceremony and banquet. I didn't know any better so I just went along. We sat at one of the round tables on the side and Dr. Patel ordered two metal mini-steins of beer per person (the toy glass-bottomed steins were a club tradition, apparently, and all the other tables were messy with them) and ordered us to down both quickly before heading to the buffet of hot hors d'oeuvres and a raw bar and a carving station of prime rib and rack of lamb. Though I hadn't realized it until that moment, I was starving, as I'd not had any lunch or snacks while traversing every square yard of the golf course for the last five and a half hours. There must have been a beastly look or stance to me because when I mounded a plate with food Patel tapped me on the shoulder to indicate that I should load up two for myself and when we sat down again I didn't see or hear a thing for several minutes, nourishment-locked as I was. When I looked up the doctors were staring at me with a certain horrified awe for my snarfing performance but before I could apologize—I wouldn't apologize for such a basic human thing now—there were two fresh beer steins set out for each of us plus a shot glass of a cloudy, piss-colored liquor, a special tequila that Pong himself had brought along and was intending to import and distribute in the Northeast as a hobby business.

"This is made from an extremely rare variety of blue agave that only occurs in a very dangerous area of the Mexican state of Michoacán. Very expensive but very smooth. It is said to have aphrodisiacal properties well beyond the typical effects of the alcohol."

"Given the great beauty of Dr. Raskin," Patel said, winking at his colleague, "it would seem terribly risky to serve us this now, Pong. Plus, we're all married people, except, I assume, our forecaddie Tiller."

"Keep your cart of cowshit, Bags," Dr. Raskin said to him. Patel's given name was Sahbagya but they all called him Bags. "Everyone knows I've been after your mocha ass since the group started. But you just can't love me."

"Untrue, untrue!" he protested. "Tell us, Pong, does it enhance male stamina? Because I can see Deborah will be an unrelenting mistress."

"I don't care about stamina," Dr. Raskin said. "Just length and girth."

"Luckily I'm the perfect man for you."

They clicked steins a bit too hard, sloshing out beer foam.

"What's the name of this, Pong?" the other doctor asked. He was sniffing at his shot glass. "Smells like sweetened dirt."

"You're very perceptive, Sam," Pong said. "The maker inoculates the desert sand with a secret mineral mix. He's a former drug dealer who wants to create a legitimate brand. He calls his liquor 'the Mule.'"

"I like that," Sam said. "The Mule. Grow Some Hair Down There."

"Burro a Tunnel," Deborah chimed.

"Don-key O-D'd," Bags added.

"'Cross All Borders' is the test-marketing slogan," Pong said, taking a stein in one hand and a shot in the other. "But we will see. Why don't we try it now? It'll go very well with this lager. Let's have beer, tequila, beer. All in a row."

"You got it!"

"Ichi, ni, san!"

"Kombei!"

We threw down a stein, then the shot, then a stein, rapping the table with each. Except the last of us to finish, Dr. Raskin, who didn't usually drink heavily and had flushed pink with the insta-binge, unwittingly brought down her emptied stein right onto the shot glass, which smashed through the stein's thin glass bottom. The sound drew looks from the surrounding tables, every last one of them highly disapproving sunburnt white guys (though more for her gender—Bags didn't know it was a men's member-guest tournament and it was too awkward for the tourney chairman to send her away). Soon enough one of the assistants came over looking more than a little miserable and sheepishly said, "I'm very sorry, Dr. Patel . . . ," but before he could finish Patel sharply countered, "Listen. We're simply enjoying ourselves and the club traditions!" But the assistant then glanced at me and whispered, "I'm sorry, Dr. Patel, but the banquet is only for the golfers."

Patel was about to get all pissy anyway, slinging his arm around me like I was his favorite heir, but I decided it would be better for everybody if I got out of there, which I did only after Patel blustered and fussed and had me do another stein and shot with him and Pong in full view of the head pro. I biked back into town with some serious wobbles from shots of the Mule, which I kept tasting. It wasn't exactly sweet but funkily dirtful for sure, tectonically alive on my tongue. And definitely smooth—very smooth, so much so that I was feeling something like a loving, if not toward anyone or anything in particular. Like my heart was outside of me, beating and warm, but no longer only mine. And it wasn't until I got home that I remembered that as I was exiting the banquet room Pong gave me his business card, saying I should call him if I wanted more summer work.

"I have some opportunities that may be interesting for you," he said, a phrase you hear a lot when you're a kid in summer in a town like Dunbar and that usually means the very opposite.

But not this time.

3.

A COUPLE DAYS LATER while I was loading the washing machine, I almost tossed Pong's business card. It was propped up in the waste bin among waddings of dryer lint and receipts and butterscotch candy wrappers (hard sweets are Clark's primary addiction). It caught my eye only because of the tiny graphic beside his name, this pie-shaped embossing of red and white and green with microscopic flecks of black, which I realized was a wedge of watermelon.

What that meant to Pong I'd learn soon enough, though I think now that the graphic was meant for me, a colorful lure that would compel you to reach out one more time and take an extra, crucial look. Pong was the kind of person who naturally understood all such possibilities, and by all I really mean all, from the grand to the trivial. He wasn't some OCD freak or super-cautious nerd who had to run through every scenario and its branching scenarios and then come up with preparations for each, though I'm pretty sure he could have explained such things and PowerPointed such a chart if he had to. No, I think it was all just obvious to him, maybe the way it was for me when I played point guard on the JV basketball team. I was a mediocre shooter and wasn't fast or tall or strong enough but I could handle the rock and more than that I sensed *what could be done* with a clarity I had in no other area of my life, for example, like when a play broke down, I could see how a certain penetration or pass would collapse or open up the defense, which another, better point guard would have exploited to full advantage but I mostly muffed. What I'm trying to say is that Pong had that court vision, plus the talent, but of course his court was unfathomably wide, and long, and deep.

The first time we met after that golfing day was in Dunbar Village, at one of the frozen-yogurt shops in the main square. Dunbar, to describe it a bit more, is one of those remaining American towns that look like a classic American town in the way people would like to picture such a town, with lots of little nonchain shops for everything you'd ever need plus a few in-town educational institutions (one of them famous) and an arty movie house and a commuter train station, the whole place quaint and prosperous and not too unfriendly. Of course there are way too many coffee shops and beauty salons and pet-clothing boutiques. People from the surrounding area like to drive in and hang out in Dunbar, have a casual dinner in one of the many restaurants and then an ice cream or gelato afterward while strolling the town square or the paths of the maple- and oak-shaded grounds of the elite university, which owns much of the real estate in the downtown area, and is thus Dunbar's biggest landlord. You'd think the town would be bedbuggy with its hard-driving, self-overscheduled students, but they almost exclusively stay on their idyllic campus because there's no time left for them to do anything else. They're not engineered to wander. Otherwise it's just the mostly fancy locals: families bike together and handsome singles walk even handsomer dogs. The seniors look aggressively vigorous and contented. There is a quorum of colored people, including a long-standing black community that's steadily disappearing, a fast-growing Central American population, and then the Asians and

South Asians like Pong and Bags Patel, plus a smattering of hapa halfies and quarters and a few one-eighthers like me.

The rest is how you'd figure. Lots of overcharming, overarticulate children. Exhausted-looking young dads, at least when they appear on the weekends. Apex MILFs, married and divorced and about to be. Certain rebellious or artistic or asocial types who grew up here (like my mother) think it's a purgatorial shithole (something she actually said) because it's perfect in its way, and they may be right, there's a stink of bourgeois misery that doesn't easily die once it gets up in your head. *Is it from outside or just in my nose?* But to most it's pretty fucking nice here, period. I guess for the growing minority of basic almost white boys like me and basic totally white guys like Clark, Dunbar is a solid place to live while we can still afford to live there, which he often said was something we shouldn't count on. It's funny that he said that, because I never gave him any sign or vibes that I would want to keep living there, especially after going off to college, or that I would ever consider it his duty to make it so if I did.

A word on my near whiteness. If I were fractionally black it would be entirely different but being twelve and one-half percent Asian is no big deal except when somebody wants it to be. I guess you could call me Low Yella. Plain truth is it doesn't come up because aside from my dad and some psychically/geographically distant relatives, nobody could know anything about what's helixing inside of me. If I'm asked, sure, I'll say what I am, but nobody asks. Nobody thinks to. It's like the situation my high school friend Wendell Chung found himself in when he went skiing once in Aspen or Deer Valley or wherever rich Dunbarites go to schuss and shred with other richies who don't fret spending two or three large per day/night for the family so they can pose for glorious mountaintop shots and fireside Instagrams with their skewers in the fondue pot. I went skiing once—a last-minute invitation by a different Dunbar friend whose number-one choice got the flu—and I completely sucked at it and literally froze my ass off because I didn't have ski pants and I'll tell you it's a retro white world there in every way, with the rare contrasting dot of color, this fantastical dreamscape of unexamined, untroubled surplus in which the rest of us were not even known to have existed.

Anyway on one ride on the lift Wendell was the odd family member out and shared the next chair with a kindly retired couple who chatted him up about Dunbar (most everyone's heard of it because of the university), and his academic interests of computer science and engineering, and his college aspirations for Caltech or MIT, and whatever else you talk about in the eleven minutes of dangling wind-chill hell, and by the time they were approaching the off-ramp they were practically exchanging emails, the nice old lady exhorting him to keep up the good work, for which he instantly thanked her in the gracious android way Dunbar youth do, when her husband cracked, "Have fun with all the slopes!"

Wendell at first thought he said "on" all the slopes, but the old dude was grinning too archly, baring his gin-bleached teeth, and Wendell realized that with his mirrored ski goggles and balaclava covering his face this affable pair had no idea that he wasn't a high-end whitey like they were. He wanted to say something mean or slide up his goggles but the wife cooed, "Oh, Tom," and he just couldn't pull the trigger. They went their separate ways, Wendell pushing up his goggles the rest of the day whenever he rode with strangers, and we decided it was sort of like that for me all the time, Tiller the Ski-Goggled, stealthily pizza-ing down the groomed green runs of Dunbars everywhere.

I doubt I'll ever live in Dunbar again. Of course I'll visit Clark at some point. It seems impossibly distant now, and the thought of strolling those neatly cobbled alleys feels like it would be dimension-ally disappointing, like going from 3D to 2D. Clark believes I'm still away on my study abroad program, now extended another semester, slow-burning time and cash and brain cells somewhere in a gamey young people's nest in the EU, so I was thinking I'd just tell him to meet me sometime in Barcelona or Edinburgh or another place I ought suitably to be, and that might also be a fun visit for him. But not back in Dunbar. Dunbar now haunts me, if mostly because of Pong. I have to exhale and reset when I think of his friends and associates who are wondering where he's been, all the various enterprises and employees of his that have had to cease operations and work, not to mention his bereft family, his wife and his young daughters, the sight of whom would be crushing to me.

I'm sure they're desperately trying to go about their lives, with his wife, Minori, shuttling the girls to their swim and cello lessons and in between Candy Crushing and Bejeweling while waiting in their Mercedes wagon, keeping as idly busy as possible on apps and websites, which may be the best inventions for not mourning when you're mourning. It seemed to me like she was a typical fancy suburban mom, but Pong told me she was also obsessed with multiplayer shooter games and used to be a top-class pianist in her late teens and early twenties, guest-featuring with symphonies before quitting cold turkey one day, totally burnt out. Supposedly she'd not touched the keys since. But maybe she's playing again now. She and the girls can't be doing great, even with the pile of money I'm sure he left them. For Pong, I know, it was never about dough. People probably assumed he was the kind to have a mad dream of being a world-choking tycoon, some imperial billionaire with a private staff of traders monitoring screens in the command module of a megayacht, its whirlybird fueled up and ready on the aft deck, but he didn't care about any of that.

Pong just liked having many pots on many burners, things always developing, with the scheme I got caught up in being the most special, but I think it was the everyday stuff that brought out his resourcefulness and entrepreneurial talent. Take where we met, WTF Yo!, which turned out to be one of several shops he owned in Dunbar. Again, his regular gig was as a bench chemist at the global pharma-giant BaderGarth, but he could treat it like a part-time job because the work there was effortless for him, just mindless maintenance that he could do in the background, his foreground taken up with constant meetings back in Dunbar or the abutting towns and wherever else he had something brewing.

When I walked up he was sitting on a stool at the counter in the front window of WTF Yo!, checking his phone, and when he saw me he gave a shaka sign, like Hawaiians and surfers will do, which seemed kind of funny coming from someone who was an adult emigrant from China. Like everything else Pong did there was an explanation for it, some seed of a reason or purpose that ended up spreading through all the other layers of his person, until it was just another element that was as ingrained and natural as any other once you got to know him. This is the way with all people, I guess, but with Pong it was exponentially scaled; he hoovered up whatever likable thing he saw or heard or tasted and assimilated it with such delight that you couldn't help but grin, because isn't it always a happy moment when something good about the world isn't wasted? Which is why I felt instantly compelled to shoot him a quick shaka right back.

"I would like you to do something for me, Tiller," he said, immediately directing me toward the back of the shop, where the yogurt machines were built in to the wall. Again he had that thick accent that you should hear from now on and that I won't point out too much again. WTF Yo! is one of those places where you self-serve your preferred flavor of frozen yogurt (mine is Super Euro Tart, which tickles a couple ways) and then hit the toppings bar and load up your cup with sweet and savory shit like crushed malt balls and mango chunks and wheat germ and then have it weighed to calculate the always shocking price; I've seen little kids plop their cup of encrusted yogurt mountain on the scale and their parent had to produce a $20 bill to cover it. Anyway there was an employees-only door beside the machines and Pong led us through it, which is when I realized it was his place, and sat me at a metal table. He rarely explained anything contextual, instead training your attention on whatever was at hand. I was impressed by how clean the room was, all the humming machines sparkling and the buckets of yogurt mixes neatly stacked, a line of smocks hanging on hooks, the concrete floor mopped and buffed to a high shine. There were measured beakers and flasks, just like in a lab.

"Please try these and tell me what you think." Before I could ask, *Try what?* a total honey of a high school girl appeared in a clingy pink WTF Yo! T-shirt and white short shorts with a black-and-white houndstooth-patterned vinyl belt, her tanned feet shod with furry white flip-flops. Racially she was mixed white and black and probably lots of other things, an electric streak of silvery purple running the length of her long heather hair. I realized that the employee at the register, also super cute (a big-booty Goldilocks), had been outfitted the same basic way, both of them at a level of hotness so far beyond my reach that it didn't even hurt, like how a geezer might get a fuzzy warming in the back of his neck when he marveled at some drop-dead sunset in gratitude for his center orchestra seat on existence. Miss Purple set down a tray of five paper sampler cups, each filled with a fat dollop of white yogurt. There was also a glass of water.

"Anything else, Mr. Lou? I know your friend is tasting, but would you like a latte or Italian soda?"

"Not right now, Gabby, thank you very much."

"Well, just buzz me when you do."

"I will do so, yes, thank you."

"You're totally welcome, Mr. Lou!"

Gabby smiled broadly at him, really kind of beaming, and then micro-winked at me as she went back to her post, though it was crystal clear that the wink had nothing to do with me and everything to do with Pong. A cynic would have said she was being brown-nosy or mercenary, pretending to be into him so he'd pay her more or give her the best shift, and if you asked me right there and then in my still-ignorance of the man, I might have agreed, despite the evidence of her genuine enthusiasm. For why the hell would a tight young hottie like Gabby show such naturally unabashed fondness for a sort of funny-looking fiftysomething Chinese guy who spoke English like he'd stuffed bread clods in his mouth, and whose lightly muscled five-eleven frame seemed barely capable of holding up his oversized skull crowned by the strangest hairdo you'd ever want to see?

His hair, for sure, was the one vanity he indulged, the irony being that he executed it so badly, even as he was so winning at everything else. The strands were straight but sort of kinked, too, and to tell the truth it was hard to say if any or all of it was his own hair or, more accurately, his own hair actually growing out of his head and not otherwise planted there. Regardless, as I spent time with him, it was never consistent. Sometimes it looked pluggy and thin, other times much denser in its weave, and then periodically, particularly if we were going to be out for the night, he would slick it back with plenty of product into a smooth, hard-looking shell, and because of his faint widow's peak and slightly jutting canines he could come off like an Asian Count Dracula, if one who sported nerdy squarish black-framed glasses. The deal was all pretty ridiculous, but I never heard anyone mention Pong's hair, or make fun of him about it. It was like with your best friend or sibling or even archnemesis who had some prominent mole or tic that you couldn't see anymore because you were so used to it, for one of Pong's qualities was that from your very first encounter he could make you feel like you'd always known him, that he was to be as he was to be, and how that was that.

"Okay," he said, with a wave of his hand, "if you would please sample these, going from your left to your right."

"Should I finish each?"

"Not the first time through. If you would like to finish any of them after, no problem. Please take some water in between."

I did as he said, giving each a good lick, cleansing my palate, then trying the next. I took my time, as it was clear that's what Pong wanted. When I had tasted all five I took another sip of water and then went through them again, in the same order.

"Which was the worst one?"

"I sort of liked them all."

"Okay, good to know. But which would you choose *least* often?"

Without hesitating I pointed at number 3, even though they were similar, all creamy and, well, yogurt-flavored.

"Can you say why?"

"I don't know. Maybe too sweet?"

"And your favorite?"

"What do you mean by that?" I asked him. "The one I'd choose most often? Or the one I'd want to eat the most of?"

Pong's eyes lit up, like I'd confirmed a trait he'd somehow seen in me. "Please describe all distinctions!"

"Well, like I said, number 3 is definitely the sweetest, which is nice at first and maybe little kids would go nuts for it but I wouldn't want to have too much. Number 1 is probably the most ordinary— really clean and healthy tasting, but maybe a little dull? Numbers 2 and 5 are both intense, but in different ways, number 2 definitely for milk lovers, number 5 for those who are maybe actually craving ice cream, something fatty and rich."

"Very perceptive, Tiller! Please tell me about number 4."

Number 4 was confusing, and I told him why: at first it didn't seem to have anything going on in particular, and if he had asked me right after the first time through I might have said it was my least favorite. It wasn't too sweet or too creamy. But when I tasted it the second time I got a funny vibe, a kind of hollow feeling, but not a *sad* hollow. It didn't taste like it, but it must have been the slightest bit salty. Or not salty exactly but kind of bready, or yeasty, like there was something extra alive about it. I know yogurt has "active cultures" but this was a thorough proliferation. I told him it seemed to get to every part of my mouth, though not in a gross or gluey way, just satisfying and full. I told him that the second time the taste seemed just right, it was what I wanted; actually, more like what I wanted again and again and again.

Pong was grinning and nodding and excitedly pushing up the bridge of his spectacles, and he asked if I was willing to try some more and I said sure and he buzzed Gabby and had her bring out a full suite of samples, which ended up being many more sets of five, in other flavors. I still didn't know what he was angling for, or why I was so easily floating along with it. I had never thought of myself as someone with a keen sense of anything, taste or otherwise. But in the sparkly clean back room of WTF Yo!, with Pong peering at me expectantly, like he was the audience to someone who not only knew what he was doing but was in fact an expert, I could believe I was. I'm not a big person or big eater, just your slightly-below-average guy in all categories, and though I hardly knew him I wanted to please him, and impress Gabby, too, who was being equally attentive as she stood brimming with gorgeousness beside him. I wanted to satisfy our enterprise of the moment, fulfill its every hope and possibility.

I tasted each sample twice, ultimately finishing most of them, and fueled by all those lipids and sugars busting around my system I was driven to comment exhaustively, surprising myself with how many layers I could peel away, hold up and twist about in the light, sort and collate, until the two of them actually fist-bumped me. It would turn out that I identified most all of Pong's preferred versions, and those I differed on he made notes about on his phone. He was obviously fiddling with the standard mixes he received from the supplier, using his chemist's expertise to tease out certain desired attributes with the various compounds and additives he used, all of them, he said, natural and nontoxic, if not FDA-approved for the application, the critical formulation being the one that would compel you to come back for more, as I experienced, again and again and again.

But suddenly I felt dizzy and I pictured myself spewing all over Gabby's lovely butterscotch calves. Pong saw my distress and quickly retrieved a vial from one of the metal cabinets. He said, *Say ah,* and squeezed a few intensely bitter drops onto my tongue, which itself almost put me over the edge. But within a minute I was myself again.

Or more than myself.

"Whoa," I gasped. My breathing was easeful and shallow, my belly magically lightened, like there were only diaphanous high clouds between my lungs and my junk. "What was that?"

He shook the little brown dropper bottle. "Tincture of opium, slightly modified."

"Really?"

"Would you like some more?"

"Do you think I need it?"

He nodded. So I opened wide, the liquid not too bitter now.

"I was wondering if you would like to visit a couple of my other establishments. There could be more tasting, if you wished."

"I doubt I'll eat any more, but I'd sure like to see them. It's just that I have my dishwashing shift at the restaurant."

"When?"

"In thirty minutes."

"Do you like the job?"

"Well, I wash dishes."

"Very serious work. I did that for a time, when I first got to this country."

"You moved on."

"To other tasks, yes. All very necessary. You must know fulfillment can find many forms."

I thought of the overganja'd firm of Pikette, Weinberg, and Jerry G, the simultaneously revolting/piquing bouquet of the leftovers-cum-steamy-slop, the incomprehensible idiocies we'd shout to one another over the typhooning machines, the forlorn charms of the Toilet, and I had to say that yes, I sort of did.

"This is not to suggest you quit your job, but could they manage the shift without you tonight?"

"I guess so. After a while they probably wouldn't notice, but I'll call in."

"I'll make it worthwhile for them," Pong said, rising and ushering us out. I didn't ask him how exactly. Somehow I already trusted his every word. It turned out that he sent Gabby over with a tray of fro-yo for the crew, each cup rubberbanded with a $20 bill. But I had already forgotten about them and my work shift. As we strolled the village I felt like I was treading on the most welcoming substance, an invisible cushiony layer overlaying the sidewalks of Dunbar, overlaying the shops and the vehicles and the trees as well as the other pedestrians, and I welled with a happiness for how snugly sealed they were without their even knowing it, which made me think of the figures at a Madame Tussauds that Clark and I visited in some touristic city, and how maybe they weren't fake, lifeless versions of the famous and infamous but instead were genuine forms of those people existing in a freaky dimension of super-slo-mo time, at least as we perceived it. They couldn't see us—we were moving too fast—and were living out their legendary lives without a clue of being observed or a care for what we'd think of them, like they were welcoming an unavoidable destiny. And maybe I felt comfortingly encased in such a layering, too, and not just because of the cooling glow of Pong's tincture. I hardly knew him but there was a fidelity in his tone, his movements, a sureness in the way he strolled through the town like it was his own backyard and he possessed every branching crack in the patio, every new hydrangea bloom, like it was all fused into his being, with nary a stray leaf or pebble.

And I liked being drawn along in the curling wave of his wake as we inspected his other shops in Dunbar. There was Gnarly Gnoodle (which served various Asian soup noodles), and MadMad Maki (all kinds of rolls, some with crazy fillings like BLT, and pickles and peanut butter), and You Dirty Dog (hot dogs with luxury toppings), with each eatery, like WTF Yo!, wholly designed by Pong alone from the flooring to the light fixtures to the sexy outfits of the employees (with not a male among them). He wasn't a creeper, you could already be sure of that, just long past the idea that some pimply dirty-socks-smelly teenage boy wasn't anything but a liability, saleswise. After introducing me to his personnel we sampled menu items and although I didn't feel I needed to eat for another month I ate everything the young ladies put before me, tempura udon and dynamite rolls and links of Maine Red Snappers et cetera, while responding to Pong's rolling queries about flavors and textures and which items I found the most surprising, the most memorable, the most addictively compelling. *And not a microgram of MSG!* he added ironically, which of course to him was quaintly old-school, FOB, a blunt analog instrument compared to the laser guidance of his palatally/synaptically targeted boutique additives, which he told me he had formulated in a lab in China for a fraction of what they'd cost here. He didn't need all that much in the way of additives but was selling them to smaller and midsized enterprises, and was in negotiations with some conglomerate-scaled frozen food producers. For Pong this was both pastime and serious business, a way to exercise his tireless mind and draw stout profits to boot. Like at the golf club, it was eating that initially linked me to him, and for the next months we ate and drank like lusty kings. But it was everything else that made my time with Pong so gorgeable, if I can make up a suitable word; I guess there's something about stuffing oneself and experiencing certain physical responses that makes you deeply vulnerable to the suggestion of those with a special plan.

There was a hiccup of sorts that sampling day. At You Dirty Dog, where a second platter of a stoner's hot dog fantasy was spread before me, I looked down at myself and noticed a mounding as pronounced as a baby bump. I began to catalog the feed program I'd undertaken, and while I still wasn't nauseated I couldn't help but think I should be, which initiated a string of emetic images that soon enough condensed in a mouthful of wildly flavored spit. I actually leapt over the counter and bolted outside and pushed through a group of tweenies hanging out with their iced caramel mochaccinos before epically barfing on the front wheel and fender of a parked Dunbar Township police cruiser. One of the kids shouted, *Fuck yeah!* and I weakly gave them a thumbs-up from my bent position, my eyes all teared up. Sometimes booting can seem like a genuine achievement. The cop, who was coming out of the coffee shop with a latte and scone, also caught the finale of my vomit aria, the cruiser's tire and the drab concrete curb glittering with some of the finest speckling you'll ever see. None of it was much digested and I could tell that even the disgusted cop was half amazed by the galaxial variety of my spew soup full of fresh chunks of hot dog and rice grains and dark green flecks of nori, a tureen of which could have been served as is at a summer camp. He grabbed my shirt collar and ordered me to stand up, clearly assuming that I was just another underage binge drinker.

"Where are you from, loser?" he barked, his crew cut spiked with a mixture of gel and sweat, his scalp angry with a fresh sunburn. He was typical of most Dunbar cops, meaning overmuscled (lots of time to work out), overreactive to any perceived slight (there being very few bona fide threats in a place like Dunbar), and loaded to the nuts with military-grade gear and weaponry and vehicles (courtesy of the endless war on terrorism), which they could never deploy to even minimal satisfaction. So they took out their frustrations on us younger citizens who might thrill-shoplift or smoke weed by the high school or relieve ourselves in public, and on older folks who drove home from the restaurants under the influence, and then on pretty much every black or brown motorist, whom you'd see always pulled over on just this side of the township borders. Otherwise they were familiar and chatty with Dunbar's rich and influential and bossy to everyone else. I had no chance, as he could instantly tune in my *You reek like swine* vibe. It didn't help that scone crumbs were clinging to the corners of his plump, bassy, mustached mouth, the sight of which made me gag. I would have heaved again but I was all poured out. I mumbled that I lived in Dunbar.

"Where?"

I took out my wallet and showed him my driver's license.

"You're not twenty-one. Who bought you the alcohol? Who were you drinking with?"

I said I hadn't drunk anything but he didn't believe me and reached into the cruiser for a breathalyzer, which of course didn't worry me, but then I wondered if/how something like liquefied opium might register on the machine. He shoved the mouthpiece in my face.

"Blow."

"I wasn't drinking."

"Don't fucking lie to me."

"I'm not a liar," I said, which is true. I don't lie. Maybe I don't always disclose everything, but I've never lied, which I'll say shows almost nothing about my character except that I'm willing and able to endure any consequences, whether my doing or not.

"You're a punk is what you are. You're on something, and I'm writing you a citation. Are you refusing the test?"

I knew it was my right to refuse, and that because I wasn't in the act of driving (this the one nugget of wisdom gleaned from a Dunbar High friend who'd been busted multiple times for public drunkenness), there was no automatic penalty like loss of license, which I told the cop. My doing so didn't please him. He stiff-armed my chest, poking me hard enough in the softish lower Y of my sternum that I felt like a fragile baby bird—his fingers alone were mega-strong—and I instinctively scrunched up, sure that he was going to sock me. Had it been late at night and deserted he might have really roughed me up, maybe not liking something about the subtle angle of my eyes. But just then the chorus of some diva pop song rose up around us, and we both turned to see Consuela, one of the You Dirty Dog employees, emerge from the shop bearing a freshly laden platter of bite-sized samples, a miniature retro-styled Wi-Fi boom box dangling around her like some rapper's necklace. Another YDD girl lugged a sudsy five-gallon bucket and went right to my leavings, sloshing out half of it to clean the cruiser fender and tire, then poured the rest over the splatters on the curb. I felt bad for her and tried to help but she said she'd be right back with a refill and skipped inside the shop. Meanwhile Consuela had drawn a crowd with the free food and music, the tweens and some Dunbar University summer-sports-camp lax bros pinching in all around us in an instant street fair. Pong was now out there, too, already handing half of a truffled mac 'n' cheese dog to the cop.

"You will love this new item, Scotty," Pong said to him, "if you favor real black truffles."

Schutzstaffeler Scotty sniffed at it, inspecting the dark flecks in

42

the macaroni topping. "But the truffles are straight from China, right?" Even the cops in Dunbar have fancy tastes.

"Please!" Pong cried. "Not a chance! I have a partner in the Périgord who brokers the pieces that are too small for restaurant use but too high quality for paste. I must charge nineteen dollars for this hot dog but I think you'll agree it's worth it."

Officer Scotty took another sniff, nodding approvingly, then easily popped the mounded half dog inside his wide, fat-lipped mouth. "A spray of truffle oil, though, right?"

"Not a drop," Pong replied. "You should know we don't take shortcuts. But sometimes supply can be a problem. In fact, I see you have met my new assistant, Tiller, who will soon be scouting other suppliers for me. Plus his other duties, like reviewing our menus. I fear we went overboard today. It's all my fault!"

"No sweat, Mr. Lou," he said, accepting a different dog from Consuela while trying to lather her with the lovey eye, to which she smiled broadly but emptily.

"Let me reimburse your department for a proper car washing," Pong offered.

"If he's with you, it's all good," he said, though flashing me the glare of a thwarted rodent exterminator. Of course I figured Pong was just blowing smoke when he called me his assistant, which was fine with me. I was actually feeling good, having cathartically emptied myself and maybe still riding some of the little brown pony from the vial. The officer fist-bumped Pong and grabbed another couple pieces of hot dog before getting into his cruiser and pulling away.

I still don't know whether Pong had prior plans for the sidewalk sampling or simply improvised it. Either way it just naturally expanded into the rest of the evening, with the cook pumping out tray after tray, which I and Consuela and Pong busily served. The sidewalk got jammed up and in the street a few cars double-parked illegally to check out the commotion, passengers scooting out to grab a taste. Consuela and I mostly just stood with our samples amid the buzzing but Pong waltzed about with his tray, half dorkily and half winningly chin-wagging with the youths about some nasty TMZ story, and commiserating over local property tax rates with some grayhairs, and outright cackling with a pair of moms about a soft-core beach novel they'd happened to have all just read, the ladies pinching his arm whenever he referred to something salacious. Guys were of course boxing one another out to get close to Consuela so I was pretty much ignored, which was okay by me. It was a ducal feeling, to give all that awesome food away. I'd never had much of an interest in business—I know this is naive and exposes my economically comfortable upbringing but selling things always seemed a bit sneaky to me, because it only really worked if someone was paying too much. But then barter led nowhere, at least in the capitalist scheme of constant growth, if I gleaned anything from Intro Macroeconomics sophomore year.

Anyway, I'm sure we didn't sell a single hot dog inside the shop that night. But it was no worry of Pong's. The business was already very popular and he didn't need to be offering freebies, so I suppose you could think he was doing some goodwill marketing or something purposeful like that. As savvy as Pong was, that wasn't the deal at all. He was simply doing what he felt like doing, and was now on to the next moment, not a cell of him lingering on how he got there or what else it might lead to, and I have to say that we were right there with him, unaware of how long we'd been on our feet, right up to the time he wound down our impromptu street fair. Afterward we swept the sidewalk of our litter and tidied up the shop and he let Consuela and the other YDD employees off early, closing the shop from the inside. I figured I ought to head home, too, and so thanked him for showing me his stores.

"You are made too tired?" Pong said, his speech immigrantly

altering for the first time. I would notice that it sometimes shifted when he wanted to be more intimate, avuncular.

I shook my head. We'd worked ourselves hard for sure but it was still barely past nine.

"Come then and have a refreshment at my house, and meet my family. I can give you a ride home later."

Before I could answer he'd rolled in my bike from the alley, propping it next to the walk-in freezer. After he locked the back door of the shop he tossed me his key fob.

"Would you drive? I have a conference call with Shenzhen scheduled and I would prefer not to be distracted. My house is in the Cloister at Dunbar Crossing. You know the development?"

I did. I took the wheel of his car, a massive but shapely and extremely low-slung sedan that smelled like a huge new baseball glove. I didn't recognize the badging but later I realized the *B* was not for Batmobile, which I mention because Pong would never make a big deal of having a $200,000 car. I don't think he cared about brands at all, and drove it not to impress potential business partners but because he couldn't pass on the deal he got on it from a shady New Jersey mortgage company owner who ended up leaving the country after the financial crisis; the car also provided a tasty return as an ultra-luxury rental for weddings and rich-kid proms and for a certain kind of douchebag heading to his twenty-fifth high school reunion. Pong got on the call and other voices came on, two men and a woman. I don't know if it was the car's audio system or the cell service but the sound quality was eerily perfect, as if they were sitting directly behind us and not on the other side of the planet. Pong informed them of my presence and introduced me and when I said *Ni men hao* to greet the group (*ni hao* is for one person), a chorus of appreciative aahs crooned from Shenzhen. Pong gave me a look of pleased surprise. Two years of scrappy B minuses in college Mandarin were just enough for me to mildly impress in restaurants and taxicabs and social situations like this, if little else. After a round of greetings everyone immediately began sawing away, the woman especially animated, her voice high and keen but not at all shrill, focused and powerful like a singer's; you could tell she had a lot more revs before redlining. I pictured her a slender, long-throated beauty. I kept wanting her to talk, but the others butted in. You might have thought they were all pissed at one another, thoroughly frustrated, but I could tell that they weren't angry, or even being contentious. They were discussing something about a warehouse, or maybe a factory, and if there was any anxiety it was coming from the Shenzhen people, who seemed stressed about a bunch of newly hired workers, or maybe it was some newly sourced raw materials. I couldn't be sure; B minus in both Mandarin 1 and 2 only gets you somewhere in the ballpark. Regardless, Pong was unfazed, he lazily twirled his hands as he assured them that all would work out, this while directing me on turns inside his swanky new neighborhood. He'd reclined his seat ever so slightly and perched his ankle over the opposite knee like he was being interviewed onstage at a business conference, holding forth affably and confidently. Soon the folks on the line got chattier and the woman made a joke. Everybody laughed. I didn't get the joke but I couldn't resist her tractor beam of a voice and said it was funny, which made Pong laugh some more, and then Shenzhen did, too, the woman even slipping in, *See you, Teerer,* before all parties signed off. I blurted back some unintelligible endearment as the line cut out but still I felt just a little bit newer, a little bit shinier, for being included, even if I couldn't see why. A brightness was coming. And as I pulled us up the driveway of Pong's massive cruise ship of a house, it looked in fact as if a righteous day had dawned, every last window beaming out max wattage.

"Come inside," Pong said. "I want everyone to meet you."

4.

I T'S TAKEN ME a long time to appreciate the full measure of the things that Pong said. He was a person whose words aligned too well with the facts, his talk the kind of primary, rigorously descriptive speech that most of us don't much encounter or can't even conceive of anymore. These days we can't help but consciously or unconsciously market ourselves, and mosh opposing truths until they are unrecognizable, and hyperbolize for the purposes of entertainment and vanity. It's how we are and will be from now on, barring a civilization-ending asteroid strike. Pong was different. Maybe it was because English was his third or fourth language, maybe it was the style of his mind, but he had a way of unsettling you with how accurate he was, so that he often seemed to be engaging in profound understatement, which made you reexamine the world and see it as not so ordinary a place.

Take when he said, *I want everyone to meet you,* that first night I drove us to his house. What Pong meant by *everyone* turned out to be something of a surprise. At that middle hour of the evening, even if it was summertime, I figured it would be his teen daughters in the great room poking at their devices, or a couple domestic workers sanitizing the countertops, or a visiting grandfather at the center island in the grand kitchen, munching a few prunes before slumber, all of whom were indeed present beneath the firmament of blazing can lights. They were pleasant and welcoming to me, enthused but with an amazingly easy casualness; they were clearly accustomed to visitors entering their orbit throughout the day and night. Pong's father, Ye Ye, offered to make me something to eat and although I declined he insisted on showing me his own private kitchen built behind the main kitchen, this while Pong checked in with his daughters on how their days had gone. The setup was like in a tiny studio apartment, with a smallish fridge and a short run of counter with a sink and a half-sized dishwasher. But where the stove should have been there was a large cast-iron burner on cast-iron legs and an equally immense exhaust hood above it. A wok the size of a car tire hung on the wall. Ye Ye noticed my interest and fired up the burner for me. The flames blasted up like a smelting furnace and then he switched on the hood and I swear my hair started to rise from the strength of the draw. It was loud but it must have been a typhoon outside, as the blower was on the roof.

"My son like my cooking but not smells," he said, feigning insult. "So he build extra kitchen."

Pong appeared and shut off the hood and he and Ye Ye conversed for a moment. I couldn't follow what they were saying, but I gleaned it was about money. Pong rattled on and the old man listened patiently and Pong muttered some final order, to which Ye Ye grumbled an assent and padded away in his hunched-over shuffle.

Pong opened the packed refrigerator and began removing plastic bags of leafy green vegetables and placed them on the counter, followed by packages of bean sprouts, knobs of ginger, various other gnarled rootlike things, baggies of herbs, and spiky red peppers.

"My father is so stubborn. I keep telling him no more shopping at the Surplus Cutter's market. I tell him to go to Whole Foods, or even ShopRite, but he won't stop. For ten years in this country he was a cook so we like his food but it is very messy and Minori doesn't like the greasy smell in the house so I had this second kitchen built. But he won't change. Whenever he comes to stay he takes Uber to the Surplus Cutter's every morning. He fills the shelves with canned food from Poland and Mexico. And you know where this comes from?" He shook a netted sleeve of garlic bulbs.

"California?"

"How I wish!" Pong said. "I would be okay if they grew these in Elizabeth, New Jersey! They come from China. This ginger and these mushrooms, and probably this bunch of shallots, are all from there."

"Isn't that . . . a good thing?"

"In the era when Mao was alive, perhaps. I can tell you from personal experience, we had only the most *natural* fertilizer." He winked. "But I know what the situation is in China now. You know I'm a chemist at BaderGarth, yes?"

I nodded, if not sure what that exactly meant, idiotically picturing him testing the composition of cold medicines, athlete's foot spray . . .

"As you know, I also have an LLC that makes chemical compounds for various midsized businesses. Everything from food additives to chemical reagents for plastics manufacturers. I have these compounds produced in China for sixty percent less, but sometimes there is a drawback."

"Bogus ingredients?" I replied, having heard scary stories about tainted Chinese products like baby formula and radioactive Halloween glow sticks.

"Good guess, but not quite. Here's an example. I have a reputable production facility in Suzhou, which synthesizes some analytical reagents for a company I deal with in Australasia. But this company didn't want to pay for a recent order, almost a quarter million dollars' worth!"

"Shite!"

"You said it, my friend. So they sent me some samples and I tested them myself at my lab at BaderGarth, and I discovered that there were trace amounts of arsenic and chlorine, which effectively rendered them worthless. So I flew to my production facility in Suzhou and the manager walked me through their clean labs. We inspected every aspect of the operation and watched the entire production cycle. He showed me the purity levels of their base components, which we then assayed together at his bench. They were perfect."

"But I don't understand," I said. "What was wrong?"

"Nothing!" Pong replied excitedly, the glints of his weird shell of hair as twinkly as his expression. "Nothing at all! It was very mysterious. The manager and I decided at the same time that we should test the facility itself, including the water filtration and air systems. He had an advanced chemistry degree, so it was a pleasure investigating the situation with him further. It reminded me of my early university days, when we were all so purely curious. You can probably guess, but we eventually discovered the environment of the building was compromised, particularly the air, and we suspected a nearby pesticide manufacturing plant that had recently opened."

"Did they get that shut down?" I asked, remembering when Clark and our neighborhood association sued the local pool club for its secret yearly pool draining into the brook that snakes through the properties.

Pong chuckled. "That is not how it works. That pesticide plant was approved in many rounds, by many different bureaucrats. Not to mention the paint factory next to it, and the fertilizer plant next to that. A densely rooted system. Plus, the pollution there is wide-scale, and will be for another two decades. When it is clean, China will be the world's top power. Until that day, the best path for someone like the manager is to replace his HVAC system, which was very costly but at least effective. This is why I don't want my father to use foodstuffs from China. Never eat anything from there, if you can avoid it. See what can result?"

He pointed to his hair, and I dumbly nodded, unsure whether he was joking, and he said, "Tiller, you are a tough audience!"

He fist-bumped me to say everything was okay, and proceeded to show me around the various stadium levels of his custom-built home. It was designed, I would learn, by a team of architecture and interior design grad students in Shanghai, using Pong's rough drawings and photographs of the lot. They drew it up and furnished it exactly the way he wanted from cabinet and furniture makers in China, and at a fraction of the typical fee, although even now there was sledgehammering coming from belowdecks; there was some renovation work going on in the basement. The girls were getting older and wanted a more sophisticated look to their hideout/lair, upgrading from a tweenie romper room to something more like a first-class airline lounge, at least as I saw from the magazine photos and fabric swatches plastered on the ideas board they'd made up for their father.

Pong wanted to check on progress, and when we got down there the crew saluted us gruffly but enthusiastically. They were, I would learn, all from Fujian province, undocumented and of course unlicensed, and drove out nightly from NYC. One pair was doing the demolition and the other loading five-gallon buckets filled with shards of shower tiles, chalky wallboard, and nail-encrusted studs, and ferrying them out of the walkout basement to their cube van parked near the back corner of the house. Where they would Hoffa the detritus nobody would ever know. I noticed one bucket for their food containers and soda cans and another for cigarette butts and piss, as they knew not to come up to the house proper. They worked here nights because they worked days back in the city, plus this way Pong could employ them without a local construction permit and skirt the tax bump from the property reassessment that would inevitably result. Plus, it was better for avoiding ICE. Win-win-win. They'd done a number of similar moonlight jobs in Dunbar, and on some genuinely historic houses, Pong setting them up with friends seeking decent work done off the books, at two-thirds the cost and in half the time.

"Renovating attics and basements is their sweet spot," Pong said, he and Bai, the husky foreman, showing me the emptied space of what would be a new basement powder room. "Perhaps redoing a study or baby room, but you would not want them for anything that requires high-end finishes and detailing, like kitchen cabinets or the master bath. They know their capabilities." Bai grinned at us with his grizzled nine p.m. shadow, obviously understanding the gist of what Pong was saying and not caring one bit.

Pong went on, "Because of the good price, my American friends who hire them want them to renovate the rest of the house, but I have to tell them, *No, you better stop.* People are successful when they stick with what they do best. One friend did not listen and he contracted with them on his own to install a steam shower with very expensive English fixtures and handmade Italian tile. His wife and her designer said the work was subpar and after a couple rounds of poor fixes he had to hire a full-price crew to redo the whole thing. He spent more than double what he would have and for six months he had to shower downstairs. He is still angry at me but I am not angry at him. However, he is not a friend anymore."

Before we went back up, Pong peeled bills off the thick money roll from his pocket and gave them to Bai ($100 each, plus an extra Franklin for the foreman), who heartily made a play of refusing the dough with bows and bluster before palming the bills into the back of his dusty jeans. They were doing the project at cost, in appreciation for the numerous jobs Pong set up for them and essentially general contractored; they spoke minimal English and Pong explained that he sometimes had to slip away from BaderGarth and pop in on a project to translate and/or smooth over some misunderstanding. He didn't take any cut; he was just being helpful and useful to his circle in his comprehensive and effortless Pong way, the circle being larger than I imagined even here in crusty old Dunbar, where Labradoodles outnumber the ethnics and mayonnaise is still the number-one sauce.

Back up on the ground floor, in a low-lit home gym piped in with a chill EDM playlist, the coolish air zapped clean by a tower ionizer that was also misting a floral tropical scent, Pong's wife, Minori, was being tutored in a yoga pose by not one but two instructors, a woman and a man; the woman was demonstrating the position while the man adjusted Minori's cut arms and legs. Her instructors wore semitranslucent black body tights and were possessed of the most perfect physiques I'd ever seen, at least that close up, a bristling display of delts and lats and glutes.

"This is Tiller," Pong said to her. "He was a big help today at the yogurt shop."

"Nice to meet you," Minori crooned, her Japanese accent as stout as Pong's Mandarin brogue. She was a cat-eyed fireplug of a beauty and so fit and youthful-looking in her silvery spandex that I wouldn't have blinked if she'd leapt right into a J-pop number. "Will you work for my husband on his new drink venture?"

I glanced at Pong, who while typing away at his phone shaka'd her midtap but didn't specify what the venture was. Minori and her instructors shifted to a lunge position but I kept quiet, not wanting to presume anything despite the dawning idea that it would be utterly cool to be counted as one of Pong's associates/friends, even if that meant being a chronically indigested taster.

"Careful," she said to me coyly, one hand raised high while the other tagged the back of her knee. "You will have too many stories to tell if you do. Everyone who comes to know Pong Lou cannot stop talking about him."

Without peering up from his keystroking, Pong said: "My wife oversells and mocks me at the same time."

"Someone must," she said to me, smoothly transitioning to the mirror-image position. "Otherwise he will fly off and never come back."

"Someone needs to fly, to keep all of this floating."

The instructors blankly stared into space like Bernini statues, trying to stay inconspicuous.

"Someone likes the floating as much as we do."

Pong finished up his messaging, admitting to me: "Yes, I do appreciate nice things." He pronounced *ap-PRE-ciate* with a most satisfying, if slightly tortured, warble. "I enjoy it more when I can share. But if it all disappeared tomorrow, I would be fine. As long as I had my girls."

"I wonder if his wife is one of his girls," Minori said.

"First and last," Pong said, moving alongside her.

"He does not talk about the ones in the middle," she sighed to me, if with a wink. Pong didn't say anything to this and struck the same pose with an easy limberness, and they held it until the instructors murmured the next one, and they shifted in unison. Pong waved that I join in and I wasn't going to but Minori nodded her head, too, and so I attempted to trace their next few positions. I wasn't even half their age and in my supposed physical prime but I needed girding by both instructors, my limbs shuddering with the unusual angles. It's times like these that you realize that eighty percent of your body, maybe like your brain, is on reserve mode most of the time. Soon enough I was breathless and sweaty. I almost lost my balance with my head down between my legs, and was scared to death that I was going to either fart from the strain or get a boner from the point-blank sight of the female instructor's splayed and barely covered patch of crotch as she did a deep forward bend. I snuck some sleazy looks at Minori, too, which I felt particularly gross about because her shapely modest breasts and longish torso and narrow hips reminded me of my mother, or what I could remember of my mother. Pong caught me gazing but didn't seem to mind, maybe tuning in to my thoughts as we shared a reverence for the inexorables of this life.

After a while Minori said, "Okay, gentlemen, you can please leave us alone now. We want to work on some new sequences. Your new friend looks like he needs a cold drink."

I nodded vigorously and Pong kissed her on the cheek and led us out. We went down a different endless corridor, presumably heading back toward the kitchen, but he stopped at an ornately carved wooden door framed by an equally ornately carved doorway, the wood some tropical variety like teak or koa. There was a large and flowingly scripty *L*, I supposed for his surname, overlaid in the center.

"Nice work, yes?" Pong said, looking at the letter. "I did not ask for it but the woodworker offered to do it for another couple hundred, so I let him, even though I suspected he had the letters made in bulk in Indonesia, where he is from. Maybe thirty dollars each, at most. But I cannot help but appreciate someone who pushes his business. We have to keep pushing, pushing, all of us. Then the world will be fine."

"What if you don't have a business?" I said, picturing myself watching videos of dogs wearing velvet smoking jackets and puffing on Churchill-length cigars.

"You have a business," Pong said to me quite seriously. "You just don't know what it is yet."

He swung the heavy two-inch-thick door into what was a grandly scaled room that could have been the reading lounge of a blue-blood men's club but was in fact Pong's home office, judging from the Lucite slab top of the workstation and the multiple monitors and webby ergonomic chair, which were the lone modern items. Otherwise the decor and furnishings could have been straight out of some colonial outpost of the East India Company, right down to the central artwork, a spotlit oil painting of a steep-roofed Tudor cottage set in a blooming pastoral landscape in some idyllic place like Surrey, a sentimental window onto a long-departed, distant home. The funny thing about the painting was that it was super big, Pop Art size, and not at all the modest scale of those we studied in my sophomore year art history class that was deceptively titled "Dreaming EuroScapes," which I had hoped would feature Greek and Italian island beach scenery, tanned bodies included.

The lighting in Pong's office was buttery and dim and Pong poured out two lowballs of a similar-hued whiskey over perfectly formed spheres of ice. I didn't love whiskey but I kept mum about it, feeling like I ought to let Pong guide me, plus I'd never seen such ice globes, nor tasted a liquor as smooth, this savory grainy liquid that you had to hold back from quaffing.

"No surprise to me that you're enjoying it," Pong said. "You have a superior sense of taste, for such a young man."

"What is it?"

"A rare Japanese whiskey, older than you are." He poured me another healthy glug, though only a tiny splash more for himself. I asked him if this was the new drink venture that Minori had mentioned.

"Oh no," he replied, regarding the bottle. "There's not enough of it left to sell. This in fact may be one of the last dozen bottles in existence! Minori was talking about a very different drink. Have you ever heard of *jamu*?"

Of course I hadn't, and Pong told me it was an Indonesian health tonic, which he and a new business partner were planning to sell around Asia in a mass-market version. He gave me some quick background on jamu, which I learned you got from street vendors everywhere in the many-islanded nation, the jamu hawker touting her or his special blends of juices made from fruits and herbs and roots. They were custom-made for each person, depending on what ailed you or what you felt your body/spirit needed, and then were mixed up right there on the top of the hawkers' rolling carts.

"My partner is a man named Drum Kappagoda. He's a part–Sri Lankan, part-Chinese Chinese national who resides serially in luxury hotels when not at his base in the hilly outskirts of Shenzhen. He is perpetually jetting to and from his many various enterprises, including one that owns high-end yoga studios in every continent but Antarctica, with the fastest-growing segment in Asia. This is the business that he and I are seeing as a natural outlet for our mass-market version of jamu."

Pong poured himself some more whiskey, and then topped me up, too. We were officially getting our drink on now and his speech got smoother, or maybe it flowed more freely, his accent simultaneously more pronounced and less foreign to me; or maybe it was no different and I was more receptive, more literally attuned, but regardless, it was as if his brand of English was the one I'd be hearing all my life.

"I first met Kappagoda last winter at something called the Eat-Ceuticals conference in Scottsdale, and then recently again in Tokyo, where we happened to sit next to each other in the audience for a panel about the future of genetically altered livestock and other foods. I immediately liked him, as he's one of those people who must learn everything possible about a particular subject or person of interest. This is probably because he is an autodidact, without any formal schooling past the elementary years. Plus, he goes with his gut, much like you. I think you'd like him."

"I'm sure I would," I said, listening to the strange new surety in my voice like it was somebody else's. It was partly the booze talking, for certain, but mostly, I see now, it was that I was tucked in a new groove, this easy-time mixtape of apprenticeship and comradeship and partnership, of being happily equal and unequal at once, which I guess is as good as any definition of being comfortable with someone, which in turn makes you feel like you belong in the world and kindles the idea that a little part of the world might someday belong to you.

"I was there for my role at BaderGarth, at least nominally." Pong winked archly, jiggling his glass. "You probably are aware that the current science has long enabled the development of animals that reach maturity more quickly and with less feed, or are resistant to certain mass-production-related ailments and diseases, but this panel was about creating livestock and produce that are naturally supercharged with a desired profile of essential vitamins, minerals, et cetera. You could have omega-3 beefsteaks for people who don't like fish. Antioxidant-rich chickens for kale haters."

"Or protein-loaded broccoli for all those steadily starving vegans."

"Exactly, my friend! Ultimate superfoods. This next level of biofortification is still in its speculative phases, but Drum and I talked late at the hotel bar about nutritive engineering, which then led to our discussing our jamu venture."

"Maybe I should meet him!" I cheekily said, carelessly overstepping. But Pong, maybe a bit unbounded himself, clicked my tumbler hard. We both took big slugs, both slightly grimacing—clearly neither of us was a natural boozer.

Pong said, "Drum and I want to bring jamu to the masses, but never for it to be cheapened. Literally watered down."

"You want everybody to think it's special, like an Apple computer."

"Precisely," Pong replied. "A premium offering that has no real equal, at least as perceived. Have you taken an economics course?"

"Not yet." This was technically true, as I dropped Intro Macroeconomics two weeks into the semester after compiling eleven points out of forty-five in three quizzes.

"Do not bother," Pong advised. "You have good instincts, Tiller, to go along with your keen sense of taste. What is most valuable in real-life business is understanding what people want and then doing your best to give it to them."

"That sounds so simple."

"It is simple. What is complex is that what people want is often difficult to figure out. Sometimes they don't know themselves, until they see it."

"Or maybe drink it."

"Yes, for sure." Pong laughed, and we drained the last drops of the liquid amber. He yawned, which made me yawn, too, at last feeling sodden and wearied from the surely unholy accumulations of boutique fro-yo and gourmet hot dogs and Japanese whiskey. Pong said he'd get me an Uber back home and I accepted, realizing I might have already overstayed my welcome. I didn't want to ruin a good day and evening, and maybe something more. I was just tame Clark Bardmon's tame son, in the dull tumble of another infinity loop of a hazy Dunbar summer, and had no energy to act out the usual suburban idiocies, nor the luck to have a berry-breathed girlfriend to knot up with in the sheets. I was not looking forward to my study program abroad. I don't think this was the festering malaise of an otherwise suitable young man, the kind that gasses out of gentlemanly southern novels or existential tales of terminal Europa. Or maybe it was and I couldn't smell it. I just knew that there was something very curious cooking in the airy warrens of Pong's *Nimitz*-class mansion, here in fast-densifying and fast-rising

Dunbar Crossing, where at the NYC express bus stop you mostly hear the strong yarns of Hindi and Russian and Mandarin, this simultaneously full-bore yet casual activity that beckoned me blithely around every corner, whether blind or not.

"I think you really should meet Drum Kappagoda," Pong said, while ushering me into the rideshare car out on his massive circular driveway. "Let's make that happen."

"Sure," I said, giving a thumbs-up. Normally I'd let any such offer from an adult simply glance off me, especially one coming from someone like an entrepreneurially winning immigrant with a ginormous house and a broad portfolio of investment vehicles, but with Pong, I believed him, my hope stoked. You could say it was some clichéd Chinese thing about him, some patronizing Western bullshit about harmony, or that it was just my pathetically needful core being, when the truth of the matter is that it was an expression of the deeply seated inclination Pong had toward all of us in his circle, an inclination that was fundamentally charitable. Charitable not because of morals, or for greasing the gears of commerce, or for psychic expedience or ease. Simply put, Pong was generous because he had a bottomless wonder for our multitudinous human family, this perpetual appreciation of how people are.

And maybe: can and will be.

Which might explain why I, Tiller Bardmon, so *okay* through and through, was accepting being invited along. Normally I'd be skeptical that anyone would be interested in me, I'd focus instead on my mediocrities, all the reasons why I shouldn't be. But for once, at last, I didn't.

5.

V AL AND I HAVE BROKEN an original vow, the tacit one about not asking about more complicated life stuff, you know, background on blood relations, pivotal moments in early childhood, relationship issues, the sort of info you'd normally get into after sleeping together maybe the third or fourth time, and started matching each other's socks from the dryer and replenishing rolls of toilet paper. It turns out that Val is also an only child, though with the profound difference that she briefly had a sibling, a younger brother who died before he turned two. A typical awful avoidable thing, phone ringing in the kitchen, unlatched gate, neighbor's swimming pool, you get the horrid picture. Val was only a couple years older so she could barely remember him, and then sometimes forgot he ever existed, I guess because it was one of those deals where instead of leaving his things to gather the dust of a sad and spooky majesty her parents dismantled the crib and rocking chair and boxed away his toys and clothes and all photographs of him and then didn't have another child, and whether they tried to or not Val didn't know. He was called Leon, middle name Yong (both signifying, along with Val, strength and courage), and when I asked what their background was, she said her mother was one-fourth Chinese, which made Val one-eighth Asian, just like me.

Which seems so little, given how Asian her eyes can sometimes look, and I took an unconsciously intense gander at her, to pick through the genetic runes of her face, her hair, her body, and retroactively analyze whatever thing she'd said or done through this new spyglass. But this new spyglass is a trick, you actually have to peer through it the other way and back onto yourself to understand that it's all about you, and always has been, particularly if you're a semi-diasporic postcolonial indeterminate like me (this courtesy of my favorite and fearsome college professor, Raquel Aquino-Mars).

Naturally I wonder what Clark would think of my having hooked up with such a lady. The other day when I was out with Val and VeeJ (my occasional nickname for the boy) at a diner I temporarily commandeered one of the workers' cell phones charging up near the register, taking it into the bathroom and calling Clark anonymously. I wanted to hear his voice was all, because he's a kindhearted soul and I missed him, but I guess I was also thinking how he'd take the news of my living arrangement, not to mention the fact that right after meeting Val and VeeJ in the food court at HKG I decided not to go back to Dunbar. It's not that I don't love him, but I didn't want to weigh him down with the mountains of everything that befell me, make him cringe and want to bury his face even deeper into one of his thick Great Man biographies. Of course, most of all, I knew my choice would pincer him with a sadness, doubled across time, for his long-disappeared wife and now absent son.

On the phone call his *Hello? Hello?* was typically gentle, even yearning.

I wonder if after my journeying with Pong I was unconsciously searching certain frequencies, however jumbled or faint. I latched on to Pong for probably lots of unexamined reasons but let's face it, it was because he was who he was, a bizarre-haired immigrant and entrepreneur and Asian man-about-town in a historically classic haole town that couldn't help but wink at him, with the self-satisfied pride of a benefactor, even though he needed zero benefaction. Maybe I was the one hoping for a lifeline, maybe I was the forlorn Pip, unknowingly awaiting a patron whose mere presence would fire up this rusted piston of a world and rocket me forth on its newly struck axis.

And what, of Tillerdom, did I tell Val? Most of the tale, I guess, up to my time with Pong, with naturally some emphasis on my folks, on my mother's deeply untroubled troubles, the instantaneous maternal void, the freeway of an affable in loco parentis laid out by Clark the Dad, my Pixar-ready high school sexploits with a couple quirky, whimsical girls who were much smarter and more interesting than I was, the socio-academic cul-de-sacs of my unfinished college daze. What I didn't handle, when Val inevitably circled back, were any details of my mother's own background or where she was or what she might be doing. I had omitted stuff before (a frosh fall semester bout of crabs, for instance, or how I sometimes let Victor Jr. drink straight from the chocolate milk jug) but never dissembled or intentionally misled her. But when the final disposition of my mother came up again I lost myself in the ice of time and I barely exhaled, "She's not around."

"You mean . . ." Val groaned, reaching out for my hand as we sat in the back booth of the Pita Patter while Victor Jr. was reveling in the live-action delights of the old-school pinball machine, never letting up on the paddles. Now, in contrast, a primordial heartbreak had drained Val's face.

"No, nothing like that," I mumbled, looking down into the messy yawn of my ground-lamb shawarma and not keen on introducing any misery to our mostly excellent and winning days. Val was as solid as any person would be in her singularly weird situation. Why go into the unalterable reality of my family's obliteration, as well as the natural black hole of the effortless accommodation that ensued on our part? Ever since, I have been extra sensitive to the transit of other viable planetary bodies, drawn forth too quickly, and maybe always will be.

Victor Jr. rumbled over to ask for more quarters, proclaiming like a Transylvanian mad scientist, "I *LIKE* those *SIL-VER* balls!" He shoved a fat cord of garlic fries in his mouth and took enough of a slurp of his cola to cheek-blend the mass into a smoothie he could feed on through the next couple rounds. Lucky for him the other kids in the Pita Patter preferred the more typical mass-shooter games.

"I've been wondering lately about how he's going to see things," she said after a long pause, watching the boy furiously rap the side buttons and bitterly nudge the console with his chest. "You know, fatherwise. The last time he saw his father was almost three years ago now, and I know Victor Jr.'s already probably forgotten what little he can even remember. I was thinking, would it be funny if I framed a couple pictures of his dad and put them up in the TV room? Would you mind?"

"Of course not."

"Really?"

"I think it's a good idea."

She smiled and squeezed my hand. "But what about the cognitive dissonance for him? It's a confusing message, isn't it? *Your daddy is dead and he made us hide out but I still want you to respect him.* I know we're talking about Victor Jr., but you think it could mess him up?"

"There's something to be said for his having a solid set of images now," I said. "Stuff he can always instantly access. He can keep them up and running in RAM, and not stashed deep in storage."

Val nodded, though she was clearly unsure of what that meant, tech- or metaphorwise. I wasn't sure, either, though I was already screening the one random picture of my mother that my dad left up for a while. He and my mother didn't have many photographs on display anyway, and most of those were just of me. This one of her was on the kitchen desk for a while after she split, a shot of her solo, taken during my first couple years. (I know because you can see the front part of a stroller, with a sky-blue-socked pixie foot at the corner of the frame.) One day it was gone and I hardly missed it, like what happens when a huge tree comes down after a storm; you think the bright new hole in the sky is never going to get filled, but then a few days later everything has somehow recalibrated and it's as if the tree never existed.

Anyway, in the picture she was kneeling, as if she was retrieving a rattle I had dropped beside the stroller, and for some reason Clark thought this would make an interesting shot. Which, to be honest, it is: she's wearing jeans and a slate-gray blouse with the sleeves rolled up, and her hair is wrapped in a blue-and-white-checked bandanna, which I don't recall her otherwise using, and she's got these huge round dark sunglasses on though it's clearly not a sunny day, the backdrop more like the color of her blouse. She's not looking at the camera but gazing errantly past the picture taker, maybe to the horizon, and the funny thing is—this even when I was staring directly at it—it was tough to be sure it was truly her. In fact, you could wonder if this person was trying to veil herself in the way a person in witness protection (ha ha) would, not just with the obscuring costume of the glasses and bandanna but with an expression to the world that wasn't gleeful or glum, keen or disinterested, and only remarkable in that it was thoroughly, totally null. And although I can conjure her in various moments, those moments have steadily melded into one another to the point that the whole has become this mash, she's become a woman made of her woman-versions stacked in ghosted layers, this final misaligned image that flickers in and out, in and out, in a self-perpetuating cycle.

I guess we each construct our own purgatory, so this must be mine.

Victor Jr., a personality I'm betting will end up with the keys to multiple such properties, has been actually showing some heartening signs of a humanity. Val followed through on one of her domestic initiatives to shake things up a bit in our routine and signed us up for a family cooking class at the Stagno YWCA. I figured it would be either a snoozefest (churning cream into butter, making cookie dough) or a catastrophic event (whining, hollering, bloody digits), but it turned out to be a serene, relaxed session, as a tiny, elegant older lady from Thailand led us through the production of a three-part meal: papaya salad with shrimp, massaman curry chicken, garlic fried rice. I mention these only because you would think Victor Jr., aka Sir Chicken Nugget, would pinch his nose and beg to flee from the intense fragrances, but instead, as we were grouped at our stations before little bowls of prepped ingredients (this was a family session, after all, though we did have to slice some chicken breast), he got kind of loopy while taking fierce sniffs of the lemongrass, the spiky purple basil, the homemade curry paste (which I had my own initially severe reaction to, given what I went through during my time with Pong, but much more on this later). Victor Jr.'s face got so weirdly bent and screwed up I was afraid the little porker might stroke out but then he took an even deeper sniff of each, guffawing like a crankhead jacking into the white-hot splendor of his crystalline stars. After that he got real focused and Val and I, while following the steps ourselves, were dumbstruck by how closely Victor Jr. mirrored Mrs. Parnthong's pacing and movements, right down to the way she patiently shook drops of fish sauce on the shredded green papaya and massaged the threads with her fingers. All the other kiddies lost interest at various points, but *our boy*—I may have actually uttered those words—he was riding as if on rails; he stayed locked on Mrs. Parnthong and made no complaints whatsoever except after she gave us a micro-slice of a fresh Thai chili to try, when he gasped like some dark superhero, "I'm dead!"

But he wasn't, and by the end, when we were all rotating about the room sampling one another's versions of the dishes, he came quietly alive in the way a shyer, gentler child might come alive, complimenting our classmates with *yums* and accepting kudos for our efforts with an easy and generous humility, and without a single sly boast, and I thought, *Whoa, maybe this could be a form of him we should try to keep forming.*

"We must make food together again, young man," Mrs. Parnthong said. We were the very last to leave. "Until then, will you keep cooking?"

Victor Jr. practically wagged his tail, and she drew him to faceplant in her aproned bosom. She sent us off with a sheaf of recipe printouts, plus some stalks of lemongrass and a fingerling of galangal and a baggie of dried red chilies. Val and I both assumed the aromatics would be forlorn and steadily desiccate in the fridge drawer, but the next day, after a surprisingly productive homeschool session, Victor Jr. insisted we go to the supermarket and we came home with bags of ingredients that he immediately partitioned into regiments on the counter, just as Mrs. Parnthong had, and before we knew it Val and I were measuring and peeling and mincing as our chef de cuisine directed us from the recipes, reading aloud with a confidence and energy that were woefully absent when he read from the books on our online syllabus, even the ones about hunting deep-sea treasure and killing alien predators. We succeeded in making a splattery mess of the kitchen and banging up some fingers but I have to say that the pad Thai we ended up with wasn't at all shitty, and the spicy, limey, minced-pork salad that we wrapped in lettuce cups actually kind of rocked, if you didn't mind some oversalting, and as I was cleaning up the dishes I fancied the notion that on this particular evening we were the proprietors of the finest (if maybe only) Thai restaurant in the tri-counties.

There was nothing stopping Victor Jr. after that. Through Mrs.

Parnthong we learned of an Asian market in the next county and for a couple weeks he had us work through her recipes, and we all got better and better in our techniques and timing, Val and I doing the postmortem in bed each night and wondering which dishes Victor Jr. would select for the next day. The dishes themselves got better, too, sharper and more intense and, by the end of the recipe sheaf, plain damn good, at least to us grown-ups; it was hard to say if Victor Jr. "loved" the food, or even liked it, for he was just a kid, with a kid's often touchy palate, and after the first bite of something funky he'd sometimes look as though he might spit it right out.

But maybe a sign of maturity is interrogating your first impulse, and I think this is what Victor Jr. was learning, his innately agile mind engaged in a taxonomic cataloging of all the unusual flavors, their phenomena suddenly and genuinely delighting him. I began to wonder if he was something of a savant; he could describe what he was tasting like he was a wine-snob-cum-sick-puppy-epicurean, saying, about the sour soup: "It's a fishy lemon tea that I already drank and then threw up in my mouth a little." Val and I agreed we should keep him cooking, not just Thai, because by the end of the long day he was fully spent and weary, done through to a level of placidity and unfettered well-being that a monk on a mountaintop perch might even covet, such that there was no more chasing him around at bedtime, no pleading that he pull on his pj's and not forget to pee, the boy just letting his powered toothbrush glide over his teeny razor teeth while his eyes drooped back at him in the mirror. He even let us read to him without a complaint because it took more energy than he had left, as he went flutter-eyed and openmouthed in about eighteen seconds.

He also started watching the cable cooking shows, quickly settling on the ones that featured kids his age in competitions in which they had to make a dish featuring a challenging ingredient such as cauliflower or fresh sardines. Val and I watched with him and, like probably everybody else, wouldn't have believed how deft and knowledgeable these munchkins were if we hadn't already witnessed Victor Jr.'s chopping and sautéing skills busting out big league in a matter of days, this courtesy of Coach YouTube. He had no fear of flame or popping, crackling oil. He'd rattle away at half an onion he'd already sliced into vertically, going *chock-chock-chock-chock-chock*, and before you knew it he had a pile of tiny white onion squares that matched the squares of carrot and celery for his "meer-pwah," one of the many new words and terms in his vocabulary, like *flavor profile* and *pan reduction* and *brine*, my favorite being *caramelization*, which is about staying the course to just this side of burnt, sweetly seared. Lesson to us all.

Anyway, we pretty much stopped eating out or ordering in, though it probably cost us more to buy ingredients than to stuff our maws with the low-grade takeout. I loved it, my taste buds as dazzled and alive as they've ever been from that day at Pong's WTF Yo! shop, or the other times I had while abroad, which I'll eventually describe. Val and I soon began serving as procurers and sous chefs to Chef Vic, who roped wildly from Thai to Moroccan to Italian to Chinese-Korean (his *jajangmyeon*, with homemade sauce and noodles, was epic stoner grub), and somehow possessed the savvy and confidence to cross-fertilize, as in a Peking duck risotto finished with black truffle butter (one of the many specialty ingredients we had to order online), which Val couldn't get enough of, using her fingers to mop up the last starchy streaks from her plate, and afterward torching me in our Thunderdome bed like I was one of Victor Jr.'s cardamom crème brûlées before cracking through the candied shell to my whipped-custard core.

Val, though, went easy on me, compared to certain other times I had while I was abroad. I haven't shared any details of those experiences with her, and never will. Not for propriety's sake, or because I'm ashamed of anything. I'm not ashamed of anything anymore.

Or more to the point: I realize now I've never truly felt shame, but simply pretended to. With Val it's about recognizing that even if the past is always present, snuffing it as much as you can keeps things rolling.

But I'll say this for now: I know how a special savor can stoke madness in a woman.

A consequence of cooking all the time is that you end up with a ton of leftovers that are too good to throw away and that you can't quite ever finish. This led to the idea of sharing the bounty, so one night we invited Mrs. Parnthong over, who brought along her even tinier husband, Mr. Parnthong, who didn't say a word beyond hello and thank you and just ate and ate and ate (where it all went could be a great mystery of science), the four of us (Victor Jr., as cooks will after slinging hash for hours, merely sampling the dishes, more intent on observing his customers) killing the tureens of Provençal-style chicken stew and potatoes au gratin and the herbed cucumber salad. We played card games after dinner and Mr. Parnthong delighted us with his ability to deal someone blackjack whenever he wanted (it turned out he once worked in the casinos of Macau), which he showed Victor Jr. how to do. In fact, Val and I caught each other watching them work their respective decks, Victor Jr. attentive and awed, and the picture of these two (maybe not so) different-looking little people triggered something in us that certainly I, as a college-aged kid, hadn't before registered: a gleam in the veins, that radiant flow, which comes from seeing the passing of wisdom between generations. That it was a primer on cheating didn't ruin it for me, ditto for Val, who I could tell was mulling vignettes of a family life that might have been.

However, the following night, with just the three of us again, went over like the first morning mass after St. Pat's, this despite the fireworks of the righteous gumbo Victor Jr. had us all make. Somehow there was this tang of lonesomeness in that good stew. We ate, cleaned up, watched half an episode of *Kitchen Kiddie Masters*, mumbled good night to one another. The next day Val happened to chat by the mailbox (only full of junk mail for us) with the widow three houses down and before you knew it old Martha was in our living room pulling off the lid from a prepackaged tub of queso dip she'd brought over, to go along with the fajita beef Victor Jr. was marinating and would grill *en plancha*. The dip had the consistency and flavor of a melted Wiffle-ball bat but we all scooped into it anyway as Martha regaled us with neighborhood gossip, ticking off the restraining orders at this house or that, the DUIs, the adult children dead from opiate overdoses, and how the neighborhood used to be filled with lively lunch-pail people who only abused beer and cigarettes and on Memorial Day threw a communal picnic right on our street, with grills and flags and shined-up pony cars. She thought she knew all about me (Val had told her I was cougar-crazy and did "tech stuff" from home) and she complimented us for taking in our garbage bins the same day as pickup. She was good-hearted, though, you could tell by the way she spoke with utter tenderness to her almost blind mutt of a dog, Sleeves, who ended up licking the queso tub clean, along with the leavings from Victor Jr.'s fajita platter.

Martha and Sleeves must have spread the word, because Val and I started getting corralled by other folks on the street about our resident prodigy, the lady pastor and her man-bunned husband asking if he ever did gluten-free, the trucker family with twins *and* triplets wondering if he had a master recipe for Indian butter chicken, the next-door stoner/BMXer Rafe and his scary, muscly much older half brother we called Hardtime wandering over while Victor Jr. and I were slow-smoking a fatty brisket out back. Their parents had left for a Puerto Vallarta cruise without leaving them any groceries or cash, so Rafe and Hardtime ate with us that night as well as the following two, bringing as a hostess gift the only thing they could, a few sticky fat buds called Night Vision that dispatched Val and

going to dissolve, and no fucking way your tender ass is getting lowered into this, but what seems extreme and impossible is very soon survivable and endurable and maybe even pleasurable, until it fully is. Sure, it was socially basic stuff to chat about the cruddy weather, the gnats, the particular Stagno disease of long-unfilled potholes, the new discount superstore that was replacing the old discount superstore, and then, inevitably, what our next steps would be re Victor Jr.'s insanely tasty output. Every last person insisted that we should get him on one of the cooking shows, that we ought to open an eatery in one of the many vacant commercial spaces downtown, that we could peddle his cheddar-and-bacon scones online, that we could start a website. All perfectly semidelusionary red-blooded American ideas that we might have entertained had we been typical citizens. But we're typical citizens in atypical circumstances, and we have to conduct our lives as if someone is reading the lifestyles section of the Stagno *Gazetteer* with Talmudic fervor or scanning the local cable-access channels late into the night with bird-of-prey eyes.

We should have, anyway. Instead, during one of our dinners, Martha of the queso dip along with Sleeves (our first repeat "guests") blithely mentioned through her mouthful of miso-marinated sablefish how there was this long thread on an online local bulletin board about the Superboy Chef of Whetstone Street.

"What?" I practically shouted. "People know where we live?"

"Don't worry, hon, about getting huge crowds out front," Martha said to me, naturally misinterpreting. "You won't have to feed the whole town. People are just curious about Victor Jr.'s special gifts. Just hoping we original fans get waved through the velvet rope!"

She winked at me and beamed at Victor Jr. but he didn't notice, as he was intently peeling flakes from his fish. He grimaced slightly, perhaps determining the fillet was slightly overcooked.

"It's my fault," Val said. "I've been posting some pictures."

"And beautiful ones, too!" Martha added. "The one yesterday of the roasted yellow and red beet salad could be in a magazine!"

Val tried to change the subject but Martha wouldn't let her, because why would she, most parents/guardians would be ecstatic that their (otherwise ADHD/OCD/possibly sociopathic) boy had so keen an interest and demonstrated talent and would have nonstop blabbered it all over the web. That it was for something as fundamental as food made his pursuit all the more wonderful, universally relatable, as opposed to that of some scary-brilliant boy, say, like the sort of kids I grew up with in Dunbar, who'd design and build their own version of a Geiger counter from items in the family basement. But everybody knows there are a few key commandments for witness protection, primary among them being no social media, celebrating your kid or not.

Anyway, after Martha and Sleeves loped off, each with a doggie bag, Val and I went about cleaning the kitchen, pursuant to our new deal with VeeJ, who agreed to use as few pans as possible and put away all the leftovers in containers and get dressed for bed before planning the next evening's meal, which he did while watching DVR'd cooking shows, crouched with pencil and notepad at the coffee table and "smoking" one of those bubble-gum cigarettes laced with powdered sugar. He'd studied pictures of his hero chefs chilling with a smoke after the last covers, and in place of the whiskey and beer back we let him fix himself a lowball glass of tepid sweetened green tea, neat, which you'd think might crank him up but in fact throttled back his RPMs after the hours of intense concentration and execution.

Val and I weren't talking as we worked, forgoing the usual postgame analysis of tickled awe, and maybe I was clanging the pots a bit too loudly in the sink because she came up behind me and crossed her arms in front of my chest and squeezed me as tightly as she ever had. It wasn't a hug of *I'm sorry* or *Let's get it on* or *I know I'm difficult to understand* or even *Please trust me, we'll be safe, totally all right, I love you.* This was a different kind of grip, a force that seemed to come from Val but also from beyond her, superconducting through her flesh, directly and only to me, to say that there was no place else that we belonged.

And okay, I don't care what it suggests about me, so I'll say it: it was a mother's hug, if a mother existed outside of time, and was eternal, and was as wide and unjudging as the universe.

I guess that's why I didn't berate her for publishing our coordinates. When you feel rooted enough, it can feel like nothing can unroot you. Plus, to be honest, it seemed like Val needed to make a statement, if mostly to herself: *This is my only life, and I'm going to live it.*

I don't know how long we stood there letting the hot water run. We'd have failed the words floating around us so didn't risk their ruin. At some point we finished up with the kitchen, I peeled off the red rubber gloves, and Val and I perched in the threshold to the TV room, half spying on Victor Jr., who was bent over like any old-school hash slinger, scribbling down the ingredients he'd need for tomorrow. He peered up at us, squinting past the butt tilted in his mouth, and gruffly murmured: "We got saffron?"

Val and I nodded and he returned to his planning with hardly an acknowledgment. It was sheer focus rather than rudeness, which still stung me at first but scarred instantly over to what I guessed must be parental pride. Was I really here? I was dumb for a moment until Val tugged at my apron and made our sign for burning one, a flick-flick of the thumb. We promptly stepped out to the deck. Once done I figured Val would hustle up VeeJ to brush his teeth, while I fetched the salted caramels, and then we'd reconvene in our bed for a slow and beauteous tarantella of naked sweet 'n' savory. But Val just told Victor Jr. he could watch longer if he wanted and then she headed to the front door, and when she toed into her Keds, I asked where she was going.

"I just feel like a walk."

"A walk?"

"You know, what you do with your feet."

"Around *here*?"

"Uh-huh."

This struck me as odd. As usual we'd eaten college-dining-hall early so it was just getting dusky around the neighborhood, which you'd think would look picturesque and homey in the flattering blood-orange light but sadly didn't, just radioactive instead. Of course I said, "Fine, see you soon." She shut the door. But the second it clicked I diverted from my plan to take a shower and went back to the freshly sponged and disinfected kitchen. We try to stick to higher than Health Department standards. Anyway I was just standing there kind of bereft and looking around at nothing in particular when I drifted to the knife block and unsheathed one of the chef's knives we used, this sturdy and dense high-carbon German model. I let the light play off the burnished blade and realized I'd caught sight of Val doing just the same earlier when we were cleaning up, remembering now how she'd dried the carbon steel with a washcloth and stared a beat too long at the hilt, the point, along the superfine edge, and gripped the heavy knife with a mesmerized emptiness, like it was making her disappear. I slid it back into its slot and without thinking went out of the house, in my bare feet, down the short driveway, and looked in both directions. The street was empty. I had to choose so I started running up the road, the macadam still warm and almost cushy on my soles, and I couldn't help but think this could be a fine stroll otherwise, a legit constitutional like olden-days folks would take to get their lower tracts moving and release pressure out-of-doors, and I pictured Val and me hand in hand and not minding the warm late-spring breeze that carried whiffs of diesel exhaust from the nearby thruway interchange as well as from the huge adhesives plant that each night released intoxicating chemical belches that smelled of burnt sugar.

I got to the higher end of Whetstone where it met Limerock Road and thought I saw a figure moving out of view in the twilit distance. I went up the hill on Mica Way past the edge of the development where the street meandered and finally dead-ended at a turnout that was bordered by a short stretch of steel roadway divider. No one was around but judging from the pox of beer cans and ripped chip bags and an accordioned used condom this was the garden spot for under-age partyers, and why not, for it was at the high point of the neigh-borhood and looked out over what was basically an immense pit, a former stone quarry that was hundreds of yards wide and long and maybe three stories at its deepest. It was kind of majestic, actually, with the new moon rising above the young trees sprouting on the far side's plateau, where a housing development had once been staked out and had since been abandoned. I walked up to the divider conscious of the broken bottle glass and when I looked down saw Val hopping onto a stone ledge. The quarry floor was filled in with bushes and scrub where it wasn't veined with ATV trails but the cutaway cliff-sides were still pretty much bare and now turning bruise-colored with the night coming on. I was about to call out to her but Val looked seriously lovely in that purplish light and I didn't want to disrupt the moment, like she was the heroine of some indie film on the brink of its moody, F-minor ending, everything that had happened so far gath-ered in her sloped shoulders, her neck and face aglow with a sudden illumination, as if something were just now emerging.

But then she stepped forward like a high diver, to the very edge, the toes of her sneakers poking out over the abyss, her arms stiff-ened at her sides, hands balled into fists. The most chilling thing was when she didn't look down at the potentially lethal drop, but instead craned upward, as if to check in with some ward in the sky.

"Hey," I blurted, my chest turned to lead. The sound echoed off the stone cliffsides with an eerie clarity.

Val turned her head and for a long, awful second didn't seem to recognize me (or anything else); she didn't budge.

"Hi," she said. She casually took a step back.

"What are you doing?" I said, which is what everybody says when they know exactly what's going on. I had swung my leg over the metal divider.

"Nothing much," she answered. I thought she shivered slightly, even though it was warm. She lifted her foot onto the next ledge up, and I hopped down and reached for her hand, pulling her to me.

"It's kind of nice here," she said, glancing back at the quarry. "Maybe we could picnic here sometime."

"Sure," I said, ushering us back over the steel barrier. "VeeJ can make us banh mi. We'll bring white wine. I think there's a cooler we can use . . ." I could hear my voice going breathy, flowing over itself. All I wanted was for us to get back to the house.

It was then that she kissed me. I kissed her back. We mashed some more but chastely, easing into a low-voltage hum. Something huge and murky was vortexing about us but instead of calling it out I focused on the unmistakably beatific cast to her face, which was more like a silent music, and I roughly said, without a clue that I ever could: "I love our life together," a phrase that I realized I had heard before, and knew too well.

She stared at me as if wounded, and suddenly she was caressing the back of my neck and drawing me toward her and I was afraid she might cry but I realized, nope, it was actually me; I was the one tearing up. I was the one sniffling and burbling, I guess with what tears of joy really are, which are tears of overwhelming gratitude. Because I did love our life, no joke, there was nothing else I wanted—it didn't matter that there *was* nothing else—and I kept letting the idea freely replicate through me without hesitancy or fear, which only deepened my knowing.

Val sopped my cheeks with the shoulder of her T-shirt. She handled my jaw like I was a puppy, and pecked me on the forehead. I didn't care that she didn't say it back, and not because I knew she felt the same way. I didn't know. What I was certain of was that neither of us was going anyplace in the foreseeable future, whatever that means.

"I want to tell you something about me," she said.

"You already did," I replied.

"I did?"

"You're a little bit Chinese."

Val smirked. "You kind of dig that, don't you?"

"Nope," I said, better now. "I really dig it."

"Victor Sr. liked that about me. I know you're kidding, but he couldn't help but see it in me, mostly because of my mother. He often brought up my mother's beauty. I think I seemed prettier to him, after knowing."

"C'mon."

"I don't blame him. She was especially beautiful, like mixed people can be. Even in her last moments she was stunning, when the rest of us were looking like death by her bedside. Whenever we had a really bad fight Victor would say, 'You should be more like your mother!' even though he didn't know her well. What he meant was that I should be more dutiful and supportive of whatever he happened to be doing, like he assumed my Chinese mother would be."

"Is that what Chinese women are like?"

"I don't think so," she said. "Victor didn't know me, either. Which is what I want to tell you."

"Okay," I said, afraid now.

"I snitched on him."

"I think I know that."

She shook her head. "You remember how I said the federal agents found me and Victor Jr. having an ice cream and showed me all the evidence they had about his bank accounts in Cyprus? Well, they didn't *find* me. We had an appointment. I had to tell Victor Jr. the nice lady and man were my friends from college, and he actually asked them to buy him a smoothie, which they did. It was the second time we met, and they hadn't even threatened anything the first time, only mentioning the range of unhappy possibilities. But I didn't wait. I made them copies of his bank statements. I gave them a zip drive of his laptop. They asked if I would wear a wire and without much hesitating I said okay, but I didn't end up doing it. The next week Victor went on a trip to Riga and he never came back."

"So you don't know if giving them that stuff even mattered."

"But I knew what I was doing," Val said bitterly. "I knew what could happen to him. I loved him. But I'm not a good person. I never have been. I couldn't be loyal for more than a few fucking seconds."

"You were loyal to your boy," I said. "You had to protect your son. He's a total innocent. Now a good part of him always will be, because of what you did."

Val's face almost broke up with that idea, even given the outlandishness of the last part. For who, especially an übermensch-in-training like VeeJ, would ever choose to be an innocent all his life, when there was so much complicated living to be done? She began shaking her head, the way you do when nothing can at the moment mollify, and for the first time I could fathom the constant high energy she'd had to marshal, since everything in her prior life fell apart, to keep things trucking. I pressed into her and got small and made her hug me, told her to squeeze as hard as she could. Crush me, if you need. Her strength surprised. And that's when I realized that loving someone was basically, simply, this: to be the fuel for her depletions.

6.

THE OTHER DAY Val and Victor Jr. and I left the house for some rare fresh-air PE in a newly built playground across town. We were the only people there, as the nearby elementary school hadn't yet let out. Victor Jr. had the run of the place, and even though he had a newfound sense of self from all the cooking, he was still way out of shape. I had to help him ascend the trestle of stiffened thick roping attached to the side of the play ship he was trying to board. The ship was molded in curvy plastic after a Spanish galleon, complete with main mast and boat wheel and a couple fixed cannons poking over cutouts in the railing, though it was actually just half a vessel, as the other side opened out onto a series of slides, on which children chuted down into a tropical lagoon setting, with an oval of blue waffly rubber matting as the water and what looked like extra-high, old-stadium-style turnstiles for palm trees. Your more agile kids might run and leap and grab the "branches," twirl like crazy little chimps, but VeeJ just stared at the tree like it was the Eiffel Tower. There were other elaborate romping and play areas: a mastodon you could climb inside of and peer out through its toothless mouth, a mini-kitchen where you could play house (VeeJ regarded this with haughty disdain), as well as a frighteningly large tortoise whose smooth shell was fitted with climbing-wall footholds so could you crawl forward and backward and sideways.

Victor Jr. could manage the tortoise but not anything else if it was too weight-bearing, boat rigging included, and so I had to place each jittery foot on the roping for him as he made his way up, what meager muscle there was straining someplace deep inside his juicy bubble-tea calves. He'd been working hard at the stove and cutting board but he was eating a ton more, too, and I was afraid we'd doomed him to becoming one of those chefs who got so ginormous that they had to cook while sitting in a custom-made wheelchair. He got panicky whenever he had to let go and reach for the next rung, and I had to assure him I was right there, keeping a hand on his leg, though for a long second I thought the big little dude would bust an artery, for all his sudden knifing wheezing.

This is when I glanced over at Val, who was on a bench by the entrance gate, the grounds deserted except for us and now an emo couple clearly AWOL from high school sharing a forty and a black-cherry-flavored vape as they sat cross-legged beneath the shade of the pachyderm. The emo boy kept looking at me, toggling between pity and consternation, no doubt seeing me as a baby poppa whose miserable trajectory was just now heading into free fall, and I couldn't help mouthing, *Go back to class,* whenever his girlfriend looked away. Of course I wasn't miserable, even when using the crown of my head to steady and boost Victor Jr.'s rump and then foot. Val wasn't poking at her phone or listening to music or sipping a takeout coffee, which at this point are pretty much the compulsory modes for any First World human being. She was sitting comfortably hunched, just watching us, hands quiet in her lap, her naturally feathered '70s-style bangs framing the sort of expression you might get savoring the last residues of a sliver of dark chocolate, which got me thinking I was doing something right. Since the weird business at the quarry last week, which we haven't pipped a syllable about—the next morning we hopped directly onto our homeschool-to-meal-planning-to-kitchen-prep bullet train—I've been drifting around the house with my sensors set on high, alert to any electron of Val's that might be veering off, plus cataloging the numerous ready-made options for self-harm around our place. Domesticity is a chamber of horrors, looked at in a certain way. There is the knife block, of course, which maybe is too obvious and scary to be viable, and the shower-curtain bar for stringing oneself up, and the bottles of drain opener and ibuprofen and rubbing alcohol, not to mention the snug, windowless garage for a CO sauna, the one relief being that ours is a ranch with a roof that you'd have to swan dive from to do real damage. But I guess that's where the quarry is a handy annex, and whenever she steps outside for whatever reason I make sure to follow.

Anyway, I finally got Victor Jr. up and over the pirate ship railing, and to celebrate he started slashing at the air with the jagged end of a discarded broken light saber he found on deck, this mere inches above my head, which I was ready for (I keep my head on a swivel around him) but prompted Val to stand up and snap, "Victor Jr.!," her palms beseeching the heavens. For Val this qualified as a deep-core meltdown. I went to her, nanorips of concern going staticky in my chest, my alarm apparent enough that she kept hold of my hand as we watched Victor Jr. sentence a treacherous imaginary associate to walk the plank. He's a good little actor, as many conscience-lacking personalities are, even pausing with rich facial expressions as he dialogued with the doomed man: "Nobody touches my buried treasure! Least of all you, old grape!" Where he learned this last bit, I can't say. With a vicious backhand slice, he administered the coup de grâce, the sorry sack going plop into the waters. His bark of a laugh even startled the emo pair, who looked at each other a bit creeped out.

"He's a raging little god," Val said, with no hint whatsoever of veiled pride.

"Maybe he is God," I ventured, which induced us both to chuckle nervously, for the shared realization that if our cosmic ruler was an overindulged brilliant child-beast like Victor Jr., then everything about our screwy world made sense.

"I guess that makes me the blameworthy party," Val groaned.

"Don't forget me," I said brightly, though clearly failing to take on any more of the load. It seemed of late that she was getting more anxious about VeeJ, even as he was billowing with confidence and gaining maturity via the kitchen work. I'm just a kid in these matters, but maybe it was his incipient selfhood, and thus the lengthy look-in of how he might be when he was grown up, that was unsettling her. I'd been taking pains to highlight all of our tangible positives to Val, like reminding her how our rent was paid by the feds, how her checking account was infused monthly with a stipend for groceries and internet and lawn care, how my unflagging ATM card would continue to keep our mini-Zeus well provisioned and outfitted.

I said now: "I can take care of us forever, baby."

She pecked me on the cheek for my grand and sentimental offering. I liked to lay one on her each day, winkingly of course, for even though she knew what I was doing she liked it anyway. Plus, I'm no longer shy about openly cherishing what I cherish. I'm a comet of devotion hurtling straight into the loam of her goodness, I'm her ever unemerging seed, and what I know is of the darkest primeval satisfactions.

Somehow she understood all this because she grinned freely and girlishly, lighting me up with a spell that buzzed every one of my cells. Her hand grazed an unexpected uncoiling in my jeans and I latched on to the lobe of her ear and nibbled with my pouty lonely-boy lips, when we heard Victor Jr. hollering at us; I wanted to wave him off, not caring that we might freak him with some Oedipally charged how-to, when we realized what he was clamoring about was that the school across the street had let out; the neighborhood moms and maybe one or two Mr. Moms had appeared in droves to pick up their grade-schoolers, many of them with infants and toddlers in tow, and they were all now headed to the playground as they must surely do every afternoon, which to any other couple and child would be welcome company but to us was still faintly threatening, this despite our serving hot meals to a few neighborhood folks.

Although neither Val nor I had ever spelled things out to him, Victor Jr. instinctively sensed that we should skedaddle, already disappearing to slide off the other side of the ship. I hooked our tote bag of his snacks and aimed myself toward our utterly bland sedan but Val said, "Let's stay a little," to which I and now Victor Jr., huffy and damp from his motoring, both gave her eyes.

"It's become such a beautiful day." She beamed.

This was true, even here in Stagno, for brilliant white rays were bolting through widening gaps in the scrum of clouds and lighting the particulate-rich atmosphere with this diffusion that flashed me back onto a scene when my mother carried me out of the house on a blistering July afternoon in Dunbar while I was wracked with a high fever, saying the heat would draw out my own.

Before I could remind Val about witness protection best practices, such as engaging in only casual friendliness and circumspection if not reticence, she was already thickly chatting up a definitely too-young mom named Courtney who had a slash of hot magenta dyed into her dyed blond hair about how instantly grungy their boys would get (not true about Victor Jr., as he rarely trooped about in the elements), and the countless things they wouldn't eat (ha!), and how grateful they were about this great new park (despite its being clear across Stagno for us, Val actually naming the development where we lived), all with Victor Jr. and Courtney's boy, Liam, debating the merits of the tread patterns of their sneakers and animated feature films.

Val introduced me as her live-in boyfriend, which elicited a down-home *Ye-ah* from Courtney—she was definitely commenting on my youth rather than looks—and then laid bare our home-schooling challenges and current jobless status, which would have invited all kinds of wonder and scrutiny from most people but luck-ily just gobs of sympathy from Courtney, who then introduced us around to the other youngish moms, all of whom already looked like they could use a stiff drink. Val entered their circle and started yapping and squawking with an exuberance that would have made me jealous if it hadn't been totally obvious how pleased she was to be back in a certain demographic, talking clearance sales and vac-cination conspiracy theories and K–5 standardized testing and other parental arcana that had fallen off her radar but that she could clearly jabber about with what was a startling level of knowledge and authority.

Before long—I was pretending to supervise the kids but was ac-tually listening—it was time to rustle the kids and collect the scatter of half-drunk juice boxes and unfold their strollers for the walk or else fold them up for the short drive home. As noted, Stagno is not a well-off town, but because it's super inexpensive to live here it still almost functions like a traditionally middle-class place, a place where the moms who aren't yet single-parenting don't all have to work day jobs and can look after the kids and fix an old-time three-food-group dinner for a dad who won't have to change smocks and then do a night shift at the big-box store, as there are just a couple of those around (you probably know which). There's the nearby air force base and the community college that's blessed/cursed by overenrollment and then the corporate park where a couple national payroll-service companies have set up back offices that require not only employees but also cafeteria workers, office-furniture dealers, building man-agers and cleaners, landscapers, et cetera. These companies were probably enticed to the area with unconscionably rich tax-abatement schemes (therefore the shitty public education infrastructure, as well as the gesture of the high-end playground donated by the corporate park–management company, a plaque commemorating which Courtney pointed out to us), but at least they are filling the void left from the manufacturing apocalypse of a few decades ago, or so the story line goes. Whatever the truth is, Stagno isn't (totally) overrun by meth heads or in the throes of an opioid crisis (yet), so something must be going at least half right.

"Hey, you guys," Courtney said, "wanna grab some pizza? Have you been to Vito's? Keefer just texted to say he won't be home for dinner, so I'm probably stopping by there anyway . . ."

"We go there all the time!" Val answered. This was news to me; we'd ordered in a couple times, as it was supposedly the best pie in the tri-counties, but had never dined there. "But how about instead we go back to our place and have them deliver? This way the boys can play longer. And we can open some wine."

"I'm down, if you're sure!"

"We're sure!" Val piped, and although I definitely wasn't on board I could do little else but go along, corralling Victor Jr. and Liam and giving directions to Courtney in case we got separated. Courtney was already sparkly with the prospect of a BFF, pushing Liam into the backseat so we could caravan out of there before everyone rushed out, and then practically riding our bumper as she tailed us to the other side of town. To VeeJ, Val said, "Looks like you got the night off," and without hesitation he had her order two large multimeat pies and a chicken Caesar salad and a dozen mini-cannoli as well as a two-liter orange soda, items that would seem many rungs below us now but that prompted his not yet vestigial junk gizzard to start clucking.

I wondered aloud about the soda because I didn't want to say what I was really worried about, namely, inviting someone outside our home's two-block radius, which made her even more of a stranger than our neighbors, which was precisely the reason why Val was excited.

I guess I knew before we went to the park, maybe even from our first days domiciling together, how life at its most complete and comfortable can feel like you've suddenly discovered yourself sous-viding in a plunge tub set exactly at your body temperature. One day the water's no longer fine, which is when you crave a chill in your gut, a fresh sear on your chicken-tender ass, something to pep you the fuck up.

Or maybe the gleam of a new friend.

"Courtney is totally cute, huh? And she's sooooo young! What do you think, like twenty-three?"

"Not even that," I said. "She must have been a middle-school mama."

"Yikes," she said, her eyes bugging. She added: "She's doing something right. Liam's a very sweet boy. He talks kind of funny but he seems like a real angel." This was true, the boy was thoughtful and kind, and spoke with a nasally twang, if a bit too ri-gid-ly and prop-er-ly, like a Stephen Hawking voice. "Did you see how he collected his toys by himself without her saying a word? And then put them in the net bag in what looked like a definite order?"

"Kind of impossible not to notice."

"It must be just how he is," Val said. "Courtney doesn't seem to be any disciplinarian. You wonder what nature does for us, I mean right down to the tiniest details."

Just then Victor Jr., earbudded into his handheld, belched a monstrous direct-from-Hades growl of "Die, peasant!" at whatever innocent he had just obliterated on his screen. It must be comforting to be able to count everyone and -thing as collateral.

"Nature isn't everything," I said, if not sounding so convincing.

"Let's hope," Val said.

When we got home Val jumped out right away and told me to

keep Courtney, who was just turning onto our street, occupied for a few minutes outside so she could tidy the kitchen and dining room. So with Victor Jr. along I toured Courtney and Liam around the fifth of an acre that we didn't much use, showing them the lava rock garden/pile the owner had laid in probably twenty years before and that had come to look like some ancient Micronesian burial ground, the elaborate swing set we bought for VeeJ but that so far his rear had graced only once, and the empty hot tub that I was thinking I'd sanitize and fill and get bubbling for when the nights turned cooler, to enjoy some starry relaxation and maybe lovey sessions with Val. All the while Courtney was overrunning with gushy praise for our tired patch, amazingly polite Liam acting as her foil whenever she asked him what he thought ("It is pret-ty nice, I feel . . ."), and saying how she and her husband would love to install the same, if it weren't for "all the usual shit." I knew what she meant, because if you lived in Stagno you lived in a pretty narrow socioeconomic band, other-wise you'd definitely choose a community higher on the ladder, if not on the top rungs like Dunbar, where people have egregious surpluses and the endless choices/decisions that come with them, and where the complaints are essentially about being psychically exhausted. Pong was loaded, too, but to me his thing wasn't One Percent com-plaints or associated neuroses but inextinguishable yearnings, the kind that come maybe from having your family ground down to this side of nothing. What did Pong once say? *Dirt dust on the heel of a shoe.* Anyway, I didn't know what Val might have fronted about our present circumstance, job- or moneywise, so I was ready to commis-erate about how hard it was to get ahead, remind ourselves that we should focus only on the important things, and hope that despite its lingering problems Stagno was not so bad, when Courtney said: "It's awesome that you guys are getting helped out."

Whoa.

I wasn't angry; I will never get angry at Val. I was more, *Are you serious?* Getting friendly is one thing. I couldn't believe she would ever disclose her situation without some bona fide world-class torture (something I know too much about, unfortunately, after my time abroad), and definitely not during some playground klatch with a gaggle of naturally nosy moms. I ought to mention that Courtney, while friendly and attractively upbeat, also struck me as distinctly curious, maybe because she saw little mystery in store for her in the rest of her very long life.

Lucky for me that Val slid open the glass patio door right then and waved us inside with a bottle of wine, and I made some lame comment about this being my kind of help after a full afternoon of child-rearing, to which Courtney practically screamed, "Sign me up!" Her sudden exuberance was alarming, but not as much as what followed, namely that Courtney, all five foot three, one hundred ten pounds of her, was a certified animal when it came to drinking, that freaky specimen who didn't chug or gulp but simply kept sipping, and sipping; I was constantly replenishing her ever-draining wineglass with the white and then the pink and then the red and then the generic vodka from Martha and Sleeves that Martha would drift over to the cabinet and tipple from for a postprandial digestif.

Val and I don't drink much, keeping just enough wine or beer on hand for refreshers between tokes after our nightly Burning Man operation of breaking down the kitchen and settling in Victor Jr. for bed, but with Courtney visiting, Val went deep, not able to keep up of course yet staying in the hunt until she appeared to flag but then she got a secondary boost from the sugars flooding her system and she wrested the booze from me and poured three brimming shots, saying, "We ought to celebrate," to which I raised my glass and muttered, "To the end of days," the downer tone of which surprised even me. Courtney obliviously blurted, "You got it, honey!" and Val clinked and knocked back her shot, although the language of her shoulders to me was like, *Is there a reason to rain on the parade?*

And I was like, *Okay, but do we need the biggest float?* To which her eyes signaled something like *Go big or go home, buster.*

The doorbell rang with the delivery—the instant scent of it the only thing that could dislodge Victor Jr. and by default Liam from gaming mode—and I paid and the boys and I dumped our meal on the dining room table. I was going to get plates but both the boys and the ladies simply tore into the grub, no method to their frenzy, everybody just poking at the salad with their plastic forks between bites of cannoli and pizza and then bare-handedly fishing in the tub of buffalo wings that was mistakenly included in the order. Soon the table was a nursery-school-art-time explosion of lettuce shards, flesh-flecked wing bones, batons of chewed pizza crusts, the Olympian-level feed magically commemorated by the orange soda rings left by their cups, at least until Victor Jr. reached too far across the table for another wing and pretty much belly-flopped into every-thing. Nobody seemed to mind the mess, not even Liam, who had tucked a napkin into the neck of his T-shirt and was busy repattern-ing the pepperoni rounds on his slice into a more even distribution. Courtney refreshed the upset drinks and Val peeled the cheese from Victor Jr.'s shirt.

Courtney was finally getting a little drunk; you could tell by the bump in volume of her voice and the tinge of pink about the tips of her dangly pear-shaped earlobes that the bulk imbibing was now seeping in. Val was plain soused, all smiley and shiny-faced like she can get when drinking, and loudly aye-ayeing each of Courtney's complaints, most of which were about how her husband, Keefer, had recently decided that he preferred hanging out after his shift with his coworkers instead of coming home for dinner, and was often staying out even longer, meeting former Stagno High School buddies for two-for-one pitchers and brats at Humpteez (a newly opened breastaurant near the interstate) and not rolling in until well after she and Liam were in bed.

"Then all night it's hot dog burps and beer farts under the sheets," Courtney rasped. "It's like the Oktoberfest tent from hell. But he doesn't care. This is on top of the snoring. I bet Tiller's not a snorer. Is he?"

Maybe it was her buzz that had Courtney acting like I wasn't there, or maybe it was the bubble of female solidarity, but what got me was that Val didn't skip a beat and replied that "Tiller" whirred like a ceiling fan, which is funny, because the other morning I noticed her staring up at the one in our bedroom, a not-too-stoked look on her face.

"Shit, we should come live with you guys!" Courtney cried.

Liam's eyeballs kind of bugged out, while Victor Jr. gave Val a hopeful double fist pump, which was a shock, for until now I couldn't see how Victor Jr. would ever willingly share the marquee, but maybe he was already slotting Liam as his galley slave. Val said neither yes nor no nor maybe, just chuckling drunkenly like drunk people have through the ages. This wasn't unattractive. In fact, even with big dots of sweat on her nose and the bloat in her cheeks she remained thoroughly appealing to me, maybe I even liked her getting bombed, for it felt like there was a lifting of whatever cloud had crept up on her. I wanted to kiss her right then, kiss her deeply enough that she would feel my gratitude for her right down to her lungs, her cushy belly, her blocky-toed feet, which only made me want to bring this evening to an even prompter close.

"But what about Fa-ther?" Liam said, if more theoretically than with much emotion. I realized now that Liam was maybe one of those people who can total-recall license plates and bar codes.

"Fucker can stay out all night. He wants to spend his free time watching UFC and shooting pool with even bigger losers than himself instead of being at home with his family, fine. Liam, did you know that every chicken wing your daddy buys for Vesty and Squirrel comes straight out of your college fund? Though I'm not sure you can call it a college fund when it's just breaking into the hundreds. More like a let's go to Red Lobster fund. But you don't actually want to go to college, do you, Liam?"

Liam shrugged, not sure how to respond to his mother's sarcasm. He glanced over to me and Val, intuiting that our presence was the critical difference.

"And you know what? I don't even care that he's partying with high school sluts."

"Really?" Val said. "Not sure I'd be into that."

"I don't care. But c'mon, dude, do you have to post so much? He thinks he blocked me but I changed his settings a while back and he still doesn't realize."

She tapped at her phone and passed it around to us, including the boys. We swiped through the pictures and videos, which were your basic house-party series, overexposed and slightly fish-eyed shots of Keefer (in the baseball cap, Liam indicated to Victor Jr.) and his buddies in a poorly lit den, blowing smoke from a bong or doing a linked-arms shot with a heavily eye-shadowed girl, who despite her nose ring and ample cleavage looked barely legal. Same with her two girlfriends twerking ass-to-ass in their clingy softball uniforms and backward caps, one video featuring them kneeling in front of Keefer while they gripped a bat positioned between his legs, their tongues flicking and tantalizing the mud-encrusted butt end, Keefer's mouth guppying wide.

"They are go-ing to lick that dir-ty stick!" Liam output in his geek-robot speech function.

"Dirty is right, baby," Courtney replied, finally taking back her phone. She grimly considered her husband. "Fucking idiot."

Okay, it was dopey stuff, but it looked kind of excellent, too, though I kept thinking about how the softball girls had come straight from their game. Had Keefer and crew cheered from the stands? Regardless, I guessed homework could wait. I expected Courtney to go on cataloging the rest of Keefer's defects, not to mention all the ways he was betraying and disrespecting her and their marriage, but instead she plucked a fat cannoli from the takeout container and let out a sound that was seismically primal, unwound from the darkest seam of her innards, something like an *Ooo-upp!*, and then crumpled the *dolce* in her hand, the crème filling squeezing out from her fist like surplus grout.

Oh boy.

Val pushed back from the table and I thought she was maybe shocked straight by this but then stood and *Ooo-upp*ed, too, and crushed her own cannoli. Immediately the boys followed suit, Liam wincing like he was handling a dead mouse, with of course VeeJ going double-fisted, striking the pose of an action hero detonating the triple-airburst-mushroom-cloud finale. Ba-ba-ba-boom! At this point the evening was going to end quickly or else veer in an even more unusual direction. Desiring the former, I started cleaning up the table confettied by bits of cannoli tube and crusts and splooged with crème and Caesar dressing and pizza grease and sauce, sending the boys off to go wash their hands. But Val and Courtney weren't moving, they merrily wallowed in the mess before them, sampling the sugary crud on their fingers, and at one point stared at me and then looked at each other and cracked up like the popular seventh-grade girls used to at my expense. I rolled with their antics, despite my surprise at how easily Val had slipped into girls' night mode, as if she'd been craving other kinds of communing all along. I guess I believed that a resourceful, solicitous kid like me could provide or otherwise arrange for full satisfaction for her, but I guess I was wrong.

The doorbell rang again and I heard the boys run for it from the hall bathroom; I suspected Victor Jr. had called in another volley of eats, something he used to do often before we started to cook, junk food arriving at any hour, that Val would bemoan but that we ended up clawing into with the boy, especially if she and I had smoked some of Rafe's hybridized Humboldt County Prime. But when I came out to collect the rest of the dirty plates there were three new people standing around the table, including Keefer, who was in fact much bigger and more built than in the photographs, and a tatted-up early-thirties couple I didn't recognize from the posts. I instantly screened Todd Brown's homely face against these new folks, seeing if they gelled as mates.

But these were total locals; Keefer and the other guy (as big but huskier) wore death metal T-shirts and stained, loose-hanging denim, the woman a camo tank top and crevice-seeking jeggings. Unlike Courtney, whose sensible sandals and simple tan leather handbag gave an aspirational tilt to her skanky underpinnings, they were old-school townies, the kind that had dwindled to a tiny, near-extinct sliver of a demographic back in Dunbar but was still a substantial wedge of the Stagno pie, the sort who too many years after high school still partied to blackout, regularly got in bar and post-bowling league fistfights, and had a bad habit of bedding one another's partners and siblings and sometimes even folks. They were at least shaking every drop of stale beer from their dinged keg of life, which is more than you could say for a lot of Dunbarites, who just sit around mainlining designer vodka and faux complain about their latest fabulous vacations.

"How'd you even find us?" Courtney sneered, suddenly crisp and sober.

"Find-a-Phone," Keefer said, flashing his. "You weren't answering your phone. Led to this neighborhood, and I saw the car."

"So what do you want?"

"We had a date with these guys, remember?"

"Oh shit, I forgot."

"You were supposed to get a sitter."

"Shit, I forgot that, too."

They both smiled sort of murderously and Keefer glanced around, lingering a three-quarter beat on me. Courtney clearly knew the other guy, Tommy, well, but not his girlfriend, Sienna, and they shook hands stiffly. I marked Keefer and Tommy as ex-teammates, halfback and split end, shooting guard and power forward, and I thought they were subtly shaking out their limbs like they were gearing down from a war footing, ready to rain big hurt on whatever dude Keefer imagined Courtney was fucking. For me it was hard to ignore how Keefer hardly acknowledged Liam, and how Liam seemed perfectly fine with it, like he was some random kid in our neighborhood. I wondered if Keefer was his natural father, for as far as I could see, nothing about them was in step.

"Looks like the end of the party," Keefer said.

"We're still having a great time," Courtney replied. "Aren't we, Liam?"

"In-deed," Liam said, though he was now fixated on me as I was clearing the rest of the plates. "I thought there was an a-*dish*-o-nal dessert."

Tommy lamely suppressed a chuckle. Courtney glared at him. Meanwhile Keefer was regarding his son like he was some extraterrestrial with one huge eye and hands for ears.

I said, "Sorry, little man, my mistake. We've got a tub of Rocky Road in the freezer if you want something else."

"Roc-ky Road?"

"That's my favorite!" Sienna gushed. "You haven't had it? With the marshmallow and nuts and chocolate chunks?"

Liam shook his head.

"You got to try it!"

"Why don't you bring it out, sweetie?" Val said brightly to me, her face flushed. So I retrieved the tub and some bowls. I'm a world-class scooper, this from my first summer job at one of the many ice cream shops in Dunbar, and scooped camera-ready mounds of ice cream for the kids and ladies, and even for Keefer and Tommy.

Everything was moving along, some friendly conversation even beginning between the women, with Val not getting into anything more that she shouldn't. I decided to pour some shots for our guests, figuring it was best at this point to keep everyone in a pickled state of détente, and it was looking like the evening would dwindle to an unremarkable close, at least until I got the idea in my head that Keefer was a shit. He was actually perfectly acceptable as far as we all went, not the totally humorless ignoramus I expected him to be. He did a spot-on impression of Tommy, who spooned the ice cream into his own mouth like he was feeding an infant (extra wide open), and joked about skipping a grade in shop class so he could go pro early at Wheels Plus, and even served the next round of shots for everyone, with a special high-altitude pour for Val (which doubled as a passive-aggressive dig at his wife). I could only dawdle at my shot glass, though, letting the cheap vodka burn the tip of my tongue. Who knew how he treated Liam at home, but in front of us complete strangers he couldn't help sighing and shaking his head and acting like this utterly harmless gentle child was a nuisance, or worse, an embarrassment. Sure, Liam was going on dorkily about how this was the most *un-YOU-zhoo-al* ice cream he'd ever had, because he loved chocolate ice cream except *YOU-zhoo-a-lee* plain because plain was just like his favorite furry blankie, but this was even better, "like my blankie with pom-poms," which tickled every-body except for Keefer, who audibly poked at his bowl. Liam kept on talking and finally Keefer snapped, "Hey, buddy, we get it."

Courtney flashed him a weary look and everybody else was mum except Val, who in her numbed state—her lower lip was drooping enough that I could see her bottom teeth—clearly missed the flare of tension and said to Liam, "I love your descriptions, because I know exactly what you mean by pom-poms," to which he quietly said, "Thank you."

People went on chattering but I kept my eye on Liam, who went back to his bowl but just absently grinned down at it instead of diving in with abandon, as kids rightly should.

"You want more, Liam?" I asked.

He shook his head, no doubt feeling like he shouldn't say too much more. My heart flooded right then with what felt like melted ice cream, this cold and dense sopping, and I imagined dunking Keefer in a vat of used 10W-40 and holding him down until he had to open his mouth and drink its nasty syrup.

"What about you?" I said to him, aiming the scooper a bit too directly at his face.

"I'm good," he said, and unconsciously shifted in his chair.

"It's the last scoop," I said.

"Give it to one of the ladies," he said, and not graciously. "I mean it."

"Have mine!" Victor Jr. cried. His voice was strangely babyish, not his usual rascally Stitch. He waved his bowl in front of Keefer's face, his offering basically flecked brown mush. "I had too much. My tummy hurts."

"I believe that," Courtney said. "You eat like a grown man!"

Keefer glanced around in wonder as to why he was the one having to deal with this.

"C'mon, try," Victor Jr. said, raising a drippy spoon of it. "It's still good."

"I think he might not want any, honey," Val cooed, intently working through her own bowl.

"But I *wanna* share," Victor Jr. whined.

No part of Keefer did, that's for sure, but that was when Victor Jr. niftily vaulted himself onto Keefer's lap, grinding his Snickers-built ass right on the dude's junk. *My boy.* I flushed dizzily with pride, for he'd found the precise thing that would gross out Keefer most. Keefer stood abruptly, sloughing VeeJ off and sending him to the floor, his plastic bowl clattering in a gunky mess.

"Hey!" Val said, now woke.

It was then I couldn't help myself. You unleash whatever you have, and what I had was Rocky Road: I carved out a perfect scoop and without thinking flicked it, hitting him at the base of the neck where it met the clavicle, the ball sticking there for a long half second. Then it fell off. Before I knew it he was angling toward me, henchman Tommy right behind.

"Keef . . ." I heard Courtney say, her up-tone the thing that suddenly made me scared.

And that's when we heard a funny noise—curiously not unlike an *Ooo-upp!*—and VeeJ, on his knees, barfed right in his path. *Plash.* Before anybody could react it smacked us, hard. The stink. In a word, it was bad, like a durian-shake shampooing could be bad, a cheesy and bilious lathering that made you want to behead yourself and pickle your skull in paint thinner and torch it until it was a shrunken ball of tar.

Or something like that. Liam calmly informed us he felt sick, too, and promptly upchucked, if more elegantly, adding to VeeJ's unholy spew. Courtney, green herself, tugged him out onto the back deck, where Sienna, still clutching her bowl of ice cream, was already gasping for air. We men stood astride the studded puddle, all holding our noses, and although I was gagging myself I had to admit that the boy had a world-historical genius. He ran to his bedroom, crying as a kid will after puking. Val ran after him, though not before hotly glaring not just at Keefer but also at me.

7.

HONESTLY, I'm not afraid of death anymore, or at least my own death.

This can liberate you in some amazing ways. One of them is being able to see and understand that every person on this earth is in a state of disequilibrium—ranging from mild to severe—and that at certain critical times the artist of opportunity must identify the nature of the imbalance and quickly rejigger. Momentarily setting aside Val's clear irritation with me, I focused back on Keefer. I took his disdain for Liam's nature as deriving from a masculine panic, which included anxiety about slipping from his sexual apex (thus the partying with eleventh-grade chicks), the interminable-seeming sentence of his parental responsibilities, and maybe even his own Aspergery tendencies (I noted how he scraped his ice cream bowl in precise three-to-six-o'clock and then nine-to-six-o'clock motions to fill the well, then licked the spoon clean and set it exactly perpendicular to the table edge), all of which rubbed his Stagno-stud mentality raw. So I said something about how being a dad means always having a slop bucket ready, and I happened to keep a dustpan in the corner, and on both knees began sweeping the hot stomach gruel into it with a little hand broom. This was light duty, BTW, compared to what I'd had to do abroad. Unfortunately, the hand broom wasn't up to the job, the bristles too soft and long, so that I was more spackling than collecting, and I had to start using my bare hand to squeegee the stuff into the pan. Tommy had to go outside, seeing that. I figured Keefer would split, too, but the OCD-curious part of him made him grunt, "Ah fuck," and he went in the kitchen and returned with a metal pizza peeler—Victor Jr. had recently gotten into flatbreads—and actually began helping out.

"You shouldn't have to be vomit maid for someone else's kid," he said, and we both kind of chuckled, knowing it was their literally pooled efforts. Soon enough we had cleared the slop and while I washed my hands in scalding water Keefer broke out the disinfecting wipes and Febreze and the half-dozen other spray cleaners under the sink and we bombed the spot so thoroughly we practically got down to bare wood. By this time Courtney and company had come back inside, having smoked some of their skunky local Caracas, and were amazed by our cleanup, but when Val, along with Victor Jr., appeared we could see she was in a different place entirely and I ushered everyone out, promising a more normal redo the next time, and meaning it.

Afterward I figured Val and I would powwow but once I shut the front door I turned to see her disappearing down the hallway to the bedrooms. Hard clap, if not outright bang, of door. This was a first. It left Victor Jr. hanging, too, as he stood beside me fresh from a quick shower in his white hotel robe. I went to shower, too, as I was splattered all over, and when I came out in my own robe (I'd ordered us three matching ones), he was already tidying up the rest of the place. He surprised me with how efficiently he was going about the work, even though Val and I did the nightly postdinner breakdown. The kid noticed everything, and I think we both wanted to make a present of the place to her, understanding that we should steer clear of her at least until morning.

This meant the living room sofa for me, and as it was still early

in the evening we decided to fire up a pay-per-view movie, Victor
Jr. choosing. No surprise that it was a comic-book superhero flick,
a genre I can take or leave except for the wall-shuddering explosions
and bursts of automatic gunfire that I was sure would disturb Val.
So I rigged headphones off a splitter and with the almond-milk chai
Victor Jr. requested we tucked in, for the first time, to our version
of a boys' night, not quite father-son, not quite mentor-apprentice,
not quite even comrades, but more like a pair of wandering dogs,
each lonesome enough to want to share a dugout and take warmth
in the other's fur. Even with the movie's thermonuclear blasts, Victor Jr. soon fell asleep and started drooling on my chest. I unclenched
his headphones and then mine and thought to carry him to his bed
but suddenly I felt twined all wrong inside, and my eyes teared up
with the realization that however close I was getting with Val and
Victor Jr., however much I might adore them and they me, the reign
of circumstance would eventually prevail, bringing ruin just as readily as it might succor and joy. For myself, I don't fret. I know now,
after my travels, that I can bear extreme hardship. I can be ground
down to nothingness. But I can't bear the idea of dear ones eating
sorrow. It just crushes me, to picture that grimace. I get that this
holds for everyone, and has and will forever. It's just that much more
a bummer because with me and the Vs there's no blood or family or
history tying us down, we can decide during our morning coffee if
we'll re-up, and if all human endeavors are fragile—as they seem to
be—you can't help but wonder if it would be best for all to go their
separate ways.

I awoke with Victor Jr. still clinging to my chest, our feet still
shod with slippers. Maybe I drooled on him, too. It was the kind of
sleep that feels extra lengthy and luxurious, nine hours for sure, no
dreams registered, just a cushion of absence, but the cable box indicated it was merely three in the morning. I carefully dislodged
myself from under the boy's mochi-like mass and shut down the

monitor and suddenly a sky thick with stars and a crescent moon was revealed, drawing me to open the sliding glass door and go sit on the low wooden deck inset in the rear of the U-shaped ranch, my slippers nested in the droopy, uncut grass. Coolish, damp, crickety late-spring night. It smelled better than I thought Stagno could ever smell, fresh and primordial, somehow almost marine, and I couldn't help but cast off my robe and lie down in the dewy strands. The wet chill jolted my back and ass and legs but I suppressed my shaking and soon enough the temperature equalized and I must have dozed off while staring at the delicate hook of the crescent moon, because when I opened my eyes Val was standing at the foot of the deck, looming above me like a fairy-tale ghost.

"What . . . are you doing?" she asked, my positioning and/or nakedness stunting her speech.

"Not sure, actually."

She cinched her own robe about her neck; it glowed blue with the moonlight. "Aren't you freezing?"

"Not really," I said. "But you know me."

"Yeah," she said, but with no added endearment. She normally would have cooed, *My Hot Pocket*, because I generate a lot of heat in the bed and am a ready foot warmer and spooner. She just muttered, "I guess I do."

"Want to check out what it's like down here?" I asked.

"Looks cold and wet."

"I'll be your carpet."

"You're not hairy enough," she said. "Or in the least cushy. You're useless as a rug."

"Then I'll spread out my arms and legs." Which I did. "I'll be your platform."

Val appraised me for an awkwardly long beat, long enough that I think we both imagined how we might appear to a neighbor. She motioned that I should bring my limbs back in. Then she straddled my body and lay atop me, aligned so that she was hardly touching the grass.

"I'm too heavy for you. You can't breathe."

"I can breathe." It was true, I could, though with some subtle gasping. I wouldn't care if I had to spend the rest of my life pressed like that. This was our style of physicality; Val and I don't merely hug when we hug, or when we get busy, instead we totally vise each other, we jam ourselves until we can read some gnash of cheekbone, of rib. It was something we took up with each other from the very first hookup, sharing some instinct that if we didn't stick tight some reverse momentum would prevail and send us tumbling wildly away from each other into the infinite sea of space.

"I'm frustrated with you," she said, her breath still medicinally traced with vodka. Her face hovered above mine, her hair a groovy, moonlit curtain.

"I know."

"What was going on? I mean, like what was that?"

"I was worried."

"Worried?" She propped herself up on her forearms. "That we met some new people? That I was trying to make a friend? That Victor Jr. was actually engaging another child in somewhat normal play?"

Of course I was pleased about those things—the only other time Victor Jr. had a playdate, with a neighbor boy whose family has since moved away, he decided it would be cool to entomb the poor kid's head in duct tape, thank god leaving slivers for the nostrils and mouth, and affixed letter magnets across his face and the back of his skull, spelling out **LICK PUSSY** and **EAT ASS** and showing off his work to the moms—but I was having trouble articulating why even such everyday things could be concerning, at least for people like us. Every couple, I don't care how close they are or how long they've been together, lives with some critical, unsaid notion hanging between them, something unresolved such as *You always loved your-self more than me* or *We're hopelessly, tragically mismatched* or, in Val's and my case, *We act like regular people but we're totally not.*

There it was, but I still couldn't say it to her, because I knew this was the last thing she wanted to hear.

So I murmured, "We ought to take it slow with our social life."

"I thought that's what we've been doing," Val said. "I mean, un-til you and Victor Jr. warped into hyperdrive. Really, T, what the fuck?"

"We thought we didn't like Keefer."

"And now you do?"

"He's okay. VeeJ I think is still dubious. We watched a movie together. He's sleeping on the couch."

"I saw. Since when are you two so synced?"

"Maybe we've always been."

"I guess you're going to gang up on me now," she sighed, though I could hear some happiness underpinning the exasperation. "Hey, what's that?"

"What?"

"You know what." She gave a tiny buck of her hips. "That."

"Oh."

Tiller the Barbarian. Okay, Tiller Junior.

"You're trying to change the subject."

"I'm not. There's a naked woman on me, is all." Naked under the fabric, as Val always sleeps in the raw. The stirred one had begun nudging through the now-vented robe.

"I'm still frustrated."

"You should be."

"I could be frustrated for a while."

"Okay."

"You've never experienced me like that. Victor Sr. did, way too much, which I'm so sorry for. I was fed up all the time."

"Because of his businesses?"

"None of that bothered me. It's that he never wanted to stay at home, despite how much I know he loved me and Victor Jr. That's partly why it's been so good with you. But we can't stay home all the time, right? We can't hide out forever, can we?"

I shook my head, though *can* and *should*—at least re her and Victor Jr.'s well-being—were very different things. For who knew who'd appear next on the doorstep, what their associations might be? I was still imagining Todd Brown every so often, his finger hairs poking through the air holes of his driving gloves, catching my breath with the sight of every big black SUV rolling down the street. So yeah, I wanted to hide out forever, full stop, to preserve the wonderful thing we had in a safe amber. But safety is a figment, and the second you achieve it your great wonderful thing becomes virtual and lifeless. You think you're still moving but you're not.

Right then, weirdly and not weirdly, I had the urge to tug on the belt of her robe but arrested my hand just before Val took hold of the sash herself and untied its bow. She sat up, anchoring her knees in the damp turf, partially tenting us with her robe, and I had an inkling then of what it must have been like on the Mongolian steppe, getting busy *en plein air* with the awesomely kick-ass woman who had just helped you scare away a saber-tooth tiger, interlocking flesh and earth to root the coordinates of the only axis that matters.

Maybe I'm getting mystical in my old young age, but it was like that, I swear.

The next day the three of us were blown out, utterly whomped. Victor Jr. slept in, and Val and I got up late ourselves, sipping blankly at our coffees, and we didn't speak of anything, not the circus with our maybe new friends, not the moonlit sex sonata (we had grass stains in odd places), not how the house smelled like an old pizza box splattered inside with a spoiled strawberry shake, instead ceding whatever residual energies to the lint-hued weather that had parked over the region. One of those I-never-quite-woke-up days, for sure, but also, it occurred to me, the climatic equivalent of what a long-term union can be like: this airless vortex, stalled over a vast, shallow inland sea. This was the impression I got from my folks, who, whether at the dining table or in the car or at the mall, seemed stuck in a waiting room, when something might happen or not. Then, after my mother stopped talking altogether to anyone, poor Clark was still locked in inertia mode but periodically glanced around to check if anything might have changed. Of course nothing had.

This is not to say that Val and I were dead to each other, but we were zombies whose fleshlust had been temporarily suspended. Zombiehood, like anything else, is best if you have a purpose. Otherwise it's immortality gone way, way wrong. For me and Val, schlumped at the kitchen table, the half-and-half curdling on the oily surface of our coffees, the dregs of the morning about to be eclipsed by a dilatory afternoon and a slog of evening fast unfurling in its wake, the day marked the first time we seemed completely out of rhythm, our few words blurty and unfinished, our gazes furtive, both of us grinding gears on what we wanted to do, which was the opposite of our typical yes pact, which had us watching, for example, *The Godfather: Part II* for the fourteenth time, or laying waste to a tub of buffalo wings and splits of prosecco, or getting a family rubdown at Massage Magic, all while empowering/enabling Victor Jr. to make/do/see whatever his whim was targeting.

So there we were, pulled up lame, when Victor Jr. emerged having dressed himself in a fresh set of clothes, baggy cargo shorts and a Buffalo Sabres T-shirt. He'd combed his hair and even brushed his teeth, judging from the nub of foam at the corner of his mouth. Anticipating his usual *I'm famished* harangue (he only prepared the dinners), Val and I instinctively pushed back in our chairs, my mind already rifling the fridge packed with leftovers from the past week's dinners, when the boy announced he wanted a "workout" and proposed that we go bowling.

"Bowling?" Val said. "Do you even know what that is?"

"I saw it on TV once," he said. "I'd like to try it. Liam said it's really fun. He goes to Rock-a-Bowl."

"And might Liam happen to be at Rock-a-Bowl today?" she asked.

"How should I know?" Victor Jr. replied. "I'm not *Jee-sus*."

Val and I had to twinkle at each other, realizing that the boy was doing his part to get our blood pumping. We all know kids can instantly register even the slightest diminishments, they're the most sensitive instruments, and if at certain moments you look through their eyes, you can call bullshit on just about everything.

"Bowling sounds good," I said. "Let's get dressed and go."

"I'm hungry, though!" Victor Jr. cried, now that part one was solved.

"We can have lunch there," I said. "I'm sure you can get a cheeseburger. It'll be cheap and bad, but we haven't had enough cheap and bad food lately."

"Will the fries and chicken tenders be bad, too?"

"I'd bet on it."

"Well, come on, then!" he said, tugging at his mother's wrist. "Get dressed!"

Before we could exhale we were toeing into our sport sandals, the garage door was rising, with Victor Jr. already buckling himself into his seat, when I realized that Val was hanging back in the doorway.

"Yo, sexy lady," I called, "are we doing this?"

Victor Jr. was madly drumming the inside of his window, and Val and I listened for a moment, I think both of us impressed by the strength of the safety glass.

Val said, "Hey, kiddo, why don't you two just go? I'm so tired, and still hungover. Plus, I hate bowling. Putting on those rental shoes is so gross."

"Just come and hang out."

"I'm going to sleep some more, then give this place another scrub-down."

"Sorry if we didn't do a better job."

"You boys did fine, considering," she said, and came up and pecked me on the cheek. "Have fun."

By this time Victor Jr. was leg-pressing the back of the driver's headrest with enough force that he bent it unnaturally forward. I got in and had to push it back. Val waved to us as we left, then pressed the garage door button. We waved from the street as the door rolled down to cover the sash of her robe, her knees, her bare feet.

And that's what I was thinking about when we pulled into the garage a couple hours later (this after three bumper-aided games and a full-on pinball session fueled by enough bowling alley food and soda to sicken a junkyard goat), how whenever you say goodbye to someone you should always think that this might be the very last time you see them, that this image will be your final keepsake. It would be pretty crushing, for sure, to go about your days like this, but on the far side of it, kind of exhilarating, too, in having in-grained all that sorrow and impermanence. Your capacity for grat-itude would go off the charts.

Needless to say, it's the getting there that's rough. And no more so than for a little kid, even one as atavistically self-centered as Victor Jr., who didn't notice for at least a half hour that his dear mother, my stalwart partner, was gone.

8.

I'LL RETURN TO VAL and our suddenly upturned life in Stagno soon enough, but first let me go back to the beginnings of my time abroad.

Pong got back to me a couple weeks after I visited his house, this after I had resigned myself to never hearing from him again. Did I feel jilted? Definitely. I took it pretty hard, moping around the house and doing an especially shitty job of dishwashing at the restaurant. I felt like my already wan existence was that much wanner, I was just melted tofu ice cream, which is sort of funny to say for a kid whose mom disappeared forever one day and for the most part handled it pretty well. Or maybe it's not funny at all. Maybe it makes perfect sense. When I got a text from Pong during my shift asking if I wanted to meet some of his local business partners, I took off my hazmat dishwasher apron and gloves and groaned to the manager that I was about to shit my pants because of a stomach bug and he told me to get the hell away from him. I shuffled out holding my ass but then biked as fast as I could on the overpass to the mall on the other side of Route 111, where Dunbarites shopped when they craved brands and bargains.

Pong and his partners were meeting at a mall steakhouse called the Chop Station. Clark took us once, on my seventeenth birthday, for a Men and Meat Night promotion that seemed like a good idea at the time. You know, for testosterone-loading and bonding and such. But my dad isn't at all the type, nor am I, and we sat there hardly able to hear each other over all the raucous grab-assing. Anyway I was pedaling there fast because I was eager and also because it was late on a weekday, and I figured that I'd just catch them for dessert and after-dinner drinks; this is suburbia, after all, where few souls over the age of thirty-five will dare lift a fork after eight p.m. The Chop Station purports to be a bespoke local gem but is actually a chain restaurant in disguise, an overspacious and overpolished dark-wood-paneled club-style room with Edison bulb lighting and carmine-colored banquettes and a ghoulish glassed-in refrigerated gallery of mold-encrusted sides of aged prime beef, this and every other detail focus-group engineered to make you feel you've arrived with buttery aplomb into a well-deserved prosperity, where even if you're not running up a corporate tab you can't deny yourself the Kobe double porterhouse.

When I told the hostess I was joining Mr. Pong Lou's group she flickered, both impressed and then puzzled, no doubt because of my grimy work T-shirt and jeans. It was good she couldn't see my slime-splattered sneakers. She had a look-alike underling escort me through the restaurant to the private dining room in back. The place was actually hopping, the booths filled to capacity with garbage-mouthed investment managers one-upping each other, and execs from BaderGarth scanning the room with their coaly shark eyes, and empty-nester couples slurring through a chardonnay buzz, and toned divorced cougars and aspirational yupsters entwining at the bar, and you had to wonder where all this angling and consumption would lead us.

As value-minded Clark nerdily says whenever seeing stuff like that, *Keeping up with the Dow Joneses!* Which is why at Men and Meat Night we Bardmons simultaneously ordered the cheapest thing on the menu, the $22 Chop Station burger, even though we both desperately wanted to murder a porterhouse with a huge serrated knife. I couldn't help but check out the seared NY strips and filet mignons and rib eyes on people's plates as I trailed the hostess, the aroma of burnt fat fuel-injecting several different glands as my eyes helplessly tocked to her metronomic pear-bottomed swish. This establishment knew what I wanted, and was doing its best to give it to me. I wondered if I could somehow order a steak without looking too cheeky or greedy in front of Pong's partners, so when the hostess opened the door I was happy to see a waiter placing a faux pizza paddle laden with fresh figs and salumi and hunks of cheese on the table, another handing out flutes of bubbly, while a third was very carefully decanting a magnum of red wine.

"You did not text," Pong said, ushering me toward the table. There were five or six other people standing by the appetizers at the far end, and I recognized Bags Patel among them.

"I didn't?" In my potty theatrics and eagerness to get there, I guess I'd not replied.

"I was afraid you returned to college."

"It wouldn't be until next month," I said, "but I'm supposed to go on a semester abroad, so I'm not going back anyway."

"Abroad? You never mentioned that. Where are you going?"

I stated the city where the program was located, and Pong nodded with approval, though of course what else would anyone politely do? Everybody knew the drill. You were a privileged kid going to a privileged place to engage in privileged activities like brushing dirt from pottery shards at a faux archaeological dig and touring the private art collection of a filthy rich alum and taking a sustainable food shopping class with a local chef with a bunch of walking, talking privileges like yourself . . .

"Our forecaddie extraordinaire!" Bags Patel cried. He offered his hand but when I went to shake it he cuffed me in a stout hug like I was his favorite long-lost valet. Then he clapped me on the shoulder. "What a blessing, to get to live in such a place! Do you know I've never been there? I'm fifty-five years on this beautiful fucking planet and the only spot I've been in Europe is the Frankfurt airport, while stopping over on trips to New Delhi to visit my mother."

"Bags, you work too much to go anywhere else," a man said in a vaguely British accent. He was a small-statured Asian fellow, if very lean and wiry, dressed in a sleek dark suit with an open-collared sky-blue dress shirt. His metallic bulb of a watch kept reflecting stabs of light into my eyes, like at the ophthalmologist's. "Plus, you're crazy cheap."

"All true, my friend, but no less tragic," Bags countered. "This is Lucky Choi, Tiller. He is a world-crushing gambler and investor. But no one needs to tell you not to fully trust anyone named Lucky. To befriend a Lucky means being doomed to never having good fortune yourself. Second, Lucky thinks because I am a well-credentialed professional of significant means I can and should do whatever I want. His fancy cosmopolitan background has obscured for him the reality that a brown man like me must stay ruthlessly vigilant. Prepared and focused. Existence for us in this present civilization is precarious. We can be plucked from any station, at any time, and be instantly dashed."

"At least they'll find you with a glass of vintage Krug in your cold dead clutch."

"I need constant fortification."

"As we all do," Pong added, gesturing to the server, who very quickly handed me a flute. "To being well-fortified."

We raised our glasses. I was introduced around to the other business partners, all male except for Dr. Raskin, Patel's colleague who played in the member-guest tourney, who pretty much was one of the guys. I was never keen to hang out with groups of dudes, of whatever age, as it always felt to me that when you get more than four or five together something really backward and maybe scary becomes possible. And then I was too shy or wigged out playing with girls, who without exception always seemed a hell of a lot smarter than I am, and effortlessly so.

Pong didn't act like "one of the guys," even though I was getting the idea that he was at the center of any association he joined or made. I could already see that he sort of hovered above the fray, at a slight but operative remove, like an ambassador on foreign soil he knew like home. Aside from Bags and Lucky and Deborah, the investment group was rounded out by an alarmingly dry-complexioned white dude named Perry Ault, and an actor-handsome, ultra-preppily dressed black guy named Marcus Fownes, who rocked plaid madras Bermuda shorts and slate-blue Italian loafers, sockless, and was a well-known orthodontist with a wildly popular practice in Dunbar Village. It seemed like three-fourths of Dunbar youth got sent to him for braces, the town's liberal white elites clamoring to set up their kids with this affable minority professional. I was one of the few untouched by orthodontia, and was resigned to my genetic mouthful, an unfetching hybrid tiling of Clark's northern European twisties ferally studded with prominent Mongolian incisors.

Lucky started with a report on the Chop Station—it turned out their investment group was the majority investor—and an upmarket Italian eatery in a Hunterdon County mall also in their portfolio, each member then following with an equally extensive report on the investment properties he/she was looking after for the group, running down the financials but also as necessary detailing issues of staffing, building codes, property taxes, et cetera. Pong gave his report on the construction progress of an organic tofu factory in some Amish village in Pennsylvania, and the second quarter's diminished cash flows of several executive car wash and detailing shops on Route 111, which were caused by rumors of immigration raids and the ensuing short-staffing.

"I got some guys from Palisades Park to fill in last week," Pong said. "But now they want to stay and I would like to make it possible. So I propose to run one of the shops twenty-four/seven for a week or two. There are many Uber and Lyft drivers now who don't have time for washes in the daytime. Also, this way there is less mixing between the Chinese and the Central Americans."

"They don't get along?" Bags asked.

"The opposite," Pong said. "They exchange their food on breaks. They teach one another new card and dice games. They show one another X-rated pictures on their phones. But nobody speaks any English and the mixed crews are not as efficient. So I need to split them up. Everybody okay experimenting with around-the-clock service?"

All instantly hear-heared. You could tell they completely trusted Pong, not just with the car washes but re their respective investments; Deborah wondered if Pong might know whom to call in a certain town's tax assessor's office; Lucky asked him if the local banker who had been favorably inclined to "work" with large sums of cash was still doing so; Marcus had Pong give his projections for commercial rents in neighboring downtowns. Pong might as well have been the unofficial mayor of Dunbar and its satellites, having manifold levers and pulleys for actualizing pretty much anything that might prove useful and profitable and efficient, and not just in the realm of commerce, both Deborah and Bags asking him for the best SAT cram school. Perry needed a recommendation for a family therapist, as his daughter, Lizzie, was having serious troubles with substance abuse. Lizzie also went to Dunbar High, a couple years behind me, and I remembered her as having unhealthfully freckled cheeks and forearms, as she and her dad spent much time sailing the bay near their Jersey Shore summer house.

"We checked Lizzie in last week to a rehab center. She's not going to start college this year."

Pong replied: "There will be plenty of time. Have you tried Dr. Leontoff, on Tilden Street? He was very helpful with our neighbor's son, who had many emotional issues, including manic depression."

"I will," Perry said. "She's a pill junkie, if he handles that."

"He's very experienced."

"What kind of pills?" Bags asked.

"Whatever she can get her hands on," Perry answered. "Valium, Ambien, some Adderall and Ritalin from her college friends. She started with leftover oxycodones I had around after my kidney stone attack. She was dipping into them every time she spent the weekend with me on the sailboat, where I guess I had some. I should have been suspicious when she never took up my offer of a Dark 'n' Stormy. What kid wouldn't want a nip of that?"

"Ah yes," Bags said. "Dark 'n' Stormy. A most unusual white people's beverage."

"I'll make you one if you come sailing again."

"You know I don't normally enjoy boating, but with you it's extremely pleasant."

Perry sighed. "Turns out she'd filch a pill and crush it up and snort it on deck while I fixed our dinner. Then another when I made breakfast. I only found out she was doing all this when my ex called from the emergency room after Lizzie collapsed at home. Nasty interaction from three different pills she'd taken."

Perry rubbed his face, splotchy and florid with inflammation, and free dived into his wine, the thirst of a beleaguered man. He was a mellow former burnout (plus a late-in-life father), part of a tiny, valiant hippie demographic in Dunbar that resisted the rest of the town's culture of high-toned achievement and commensurate self-satisfaction, a loosely knit gang of blue-blood misfits and academic radicals practicing rituals of tantric release and shrooming that drew my mother in for a time (resulting in a tempestuous hookup with another woman, Clark disclosed the day I left for college, weirdly), and that is pretty much extinct now.

"Maybe she ought to go on a trip," Marcus proposed. "Like to Bangladesh or Kazakhstan. Some wild and miserable and fascinating place. I mean as opposed to a pleasant, boring place, like here."

"I thought you loved Dunbar," Bags said.

"Of course I love it!" Marcus said. "It's just my speed. Freshly pressed and superficially progressive. Perfect for a secret black Republican."

"You're black?" Bags piped.

Deborah said, "And we know who you voted for."

"I vote for my wallet, doll face, which is the source of all power in this solar system. Everything else is wish and hope."

"That's all I'm hanging on to," Perry said. "She adores you, Pong. Ever since you got her those tickets to Lilith Fair when she was fifteen. She was so carefree and happy back then."

"She will be again," Pong said, with the pointed self-assurance of a heart surgeon. "I can also get some jamu for her, if you like."

"You mean that health drink we're thinking of investing in?"

Pong nodded. "Yes, but it would be custom formulated for Lizzie. Ideally the jamu maker would interview and assess the person in question, but I can describe her character and situation well enough."

"You think it can really help?"

"Why not?" Pong said brightly. "There are centuries of knowledge behind the practice. As I described last time we met, our natural tendency is one of homeostasis, and jamu, like other herbal remedies, aims to restore the balance in body or mind that has gone chronically out of balance, instead of treating only the symptoms. Working at BaderGarth, I know all about treating symptoms! That said, jamu has not been scientifically proven to cure people of their ailments. However, there are centuries of healthful results in the populations where it's used in Indonesia. Millions and millions of people. My own testing of samples and the concentrations of active components such as flavonoids shows very small concentrations in typical dosages. It would be the equivalent of eating a couple slivers of raw turmeric, for example, so pathological toxicity is highly unlikely. If nothing else, it's just natural, healthy juice. Yet you don't have to be a chemist to understand that whatever we ingest results in a response of the larger system, even if it is often immeasurable."

"Mine is measurable," Bags said, stuffing more cured meats into his mouth. He bared his gristly teeth at Deborah and she bared hers back. His tongue heaved out, long and dark and red. Her brow, shining, lifted.

"I for one believe in inputs and outputs," Marcus said. "That's why I will die peacefully in my sleep during my ninth or tenth decade, and Bags here will go out crazed and in diapers. If I were you, Commodore, I'd get Lizzie some. Pong knows what he knows, and we know that's pretty much everything. Sorry to get us back to business, but as this was on our agenda later anyway, we should decide about investing 25K each in Pong's elixirs."

Lucky said, "*Pong's Elixirs*. We could call it that. Regardless, I'll say right now that I'm all in for this. Come on, folks, what do you say?"

Marcus said he was in, and the others agreed, too, with Perry informing Pong that Lizzie was allergic to mangoes, in case that was an ingredient in any jamu he'd have formulated. Pong replied that he'd have the jamu maker address the allergy as well in the custom mixture.

"Gee, how about blending one for me, then?" Perry ventured. "Let's see. I have prostate issues, a frozen shoulder from my competitive tennis days, high blood pressure, and of course ED."

"Basically, old age," Deborah said. "We can all use a smoothie for that."

"This is our ultimate goal," Pong said, only half joking. "Who knows what we can come up with, once we apply modern supplements to the traditional formulations? Jamu is about enhanced longevity, after all."

"Then 'Pong's Elixirs' is the right brand name," Lucky offered. "Unless you have a different idea."

"I do," Pong told everyone. "Something similar, in fact. I was thinking we could call our line of drinks Elixirent."

"Come again?" Bags mumbled through the prosciutto in his mouth.

"Elixirent. From 'elixir' and 'excellent.'"

The table went quiet.

"Sounds like a prescription chewing gum," Marcus finally observed. "But I'm down with it, if everyone else is."

No one objected, and Marcus raised his glass, and the rest of us did, too, and that was that. While dinner was served the group discussed their other various investments, none of them, I realized, being the ordinary kind like stocks or annuities. They didn't invest in forms of money. They invested in what people used, or lived in, or enjoyed, and I wondered if this was because Pong was trained as a chemist but naturally seemed to understand best what people were like as well. Maybe bonds are bonds, both atomic and of the flesh.

Bags announced: "Before we get on to the heaviest drinking, may I report on Chutney Manor?"

"Please do," Perry told him. "By the way, a friend told me he went to a huge wedding there last month and that it was fabulous. Even with three hundred guests, he said the food and service were great."

"That was the Reddy-Bornstein nuptials. And the number was more like four hundred. I was a guest as well. It was what Pong and I would like to see more of for the wedding hall, to offer an experience more exciting and authentic. We brought in three different sets of musicians and dancers, with three different caterers, and had them in their own themed locales—rustic pastoral, night market, city clubbing. Very festive. Did your friend mention what happened with the groom?"

"No."

"He was injured, though just slightly. He was riding in on the steed we provided, when some devious child hurled some of those exploding rocks at the horse's hooves. What *are* those things? They were tiny sacks of paper that go pop when they strike a hard surface."

"They're called Snaps," I offered, no doubt being the only one present to have played with them, recently or ever. We'd rifle them point-blank at each other's foreheads, trying to get them to pop.

"Well, those bloody Snaps frightened the horse and he reared up and the groom nearly fell off, one foot catching in the stirrup. He righted himself but his ankle got turned in the process. He wasn't big on dancing anyway, so his limping didn't matter, at least to him."

"How profitable was it?" Lucky asked.

"Very! I'll tell you the place was abuzz, people congratulating the Reddys on the grandest wedding Central Jersey had ever seen. We booked two similar affairs immediately after. I just have to hold down catering costs with that ghee jockey Anand, who constantly bleats that I'm paupering him. Then he sneaks around the block and rolls silently away in his Tesla."

"I thought I saw Anand at the marina stepping aboard a fifty-two-foot Sea Ray," Perry said. "A stacked blonde was with him."

Bags narrowed his eyes, which shimmered with ice-hot envy. "I'd heard rumors of a big boat. And that was his new wife, who used to be his housekeeper. Very pretty Estonian woman, though I can't understand a word she says, save for 'Hel-lo.' You know what he said to me when they got engaged? 'I have tons of respect for her, because she so easily could have been a stripper instead of a house cleaner.'"

"Anand knows feminist integrity when he sees it," Marcus said.

Deborah said, "I understand his poor wife had to take the kids back to India."

"'Poor' is the word. She had little choice, as she was very traditional and could never make it here on her own," Bags explained. "She's living with her family in Chennai. Of course Anand didn't have to give her much of anything. I wouldn't be surprised if she ends up a wash lady in the house of some techie power couple. Eating only plain dosas, to make the school fees for the children. This while that fat fuck and his blonde wife have lobster risotto delivered dockside."

"I should have married and divorced a traditional woman." Marcus sighed. "I'd be downing more grand crus these days."

"I should have married and divorced a man with a career," Deborah grumbled. She knocked at her head. "Stupid, stupid, stupid."

Lucky and Bags groaned in commiseration, as did Perry; it turned out Pong was the sole never-divorced person in the group, everyone now chorally complaining about their net worth getting cut in half and how they had to economize, though they clearly still had plenty to throw at ventures like Chutney Manor.

"You never know," Pong said, trying to be game.

"You must be kidding us, man," Bags scolded him. "With that wonderful wife of yours? But then I must say I was in a similar situation, and look what happened to me. One sexy drug rep at a conference and I go crazy and soon I'm toast. But you're not susceptible, Pong, and never will be."

"We're all susceptible," Marcus countered, "otherwise we'd already be dead."

"Pong, of all people, might be different," Deborah said. "He's very yin, or is it yang? Whatever the cool side is."

"Textbook yin," Bags said. "But I'll say this. When you dig down deep enough, the yang is there. And it's voracious."

"I can only agree," Pong pronounced. "We are beasts before and after we are women and men. Shall we drink to that?"

Business was complete for the night, which from that point on was your classic red-meat-and-wine fest, fat cat paleo-style, the servers bearing in the charred ribs of the propped tomahawk steaks on a stretcher-sized platter, their processional like some pagan ceremony. Our napkins soon got splotched like Guernsey cows with Angus grease and bloody-black Shiraz, our teeth studded goofy with creamed-spinach flecks such that a grinning Perry looked like a couple of his teeth had been punched out. Someone brought a portable karaoke machine and with the two servers, Bags and Deborah sang a double duet of "You're the Reason Our Kids Are Ugly," followed by Lucky, who wailed a sentimentally hued Korean folk song. They tossed the mic to me but even though I constantly sang I only ever sang inside my head, and luckily I was reprieved when Perry took it and burpily started his rendition of "Good Morning Little School Girl," to which everybody bellowed, "I'm a little schoolboy, too!"

There was a pause in the singing when desserts arrived, cheesecake slices and parfait cups of tiramisu and rice pudding, Deborah feeding a droopy-eyed Bags with a spoon while mouthing *ahhhhh*. Marcus was musing on the differences between the snifters of cognac and Armagnac now arrayed before us, which, if I can remember his analogies, were like two beautiful sisters, one brainy and stirring and the other fleshy and lustful, or like a gorgeous sunrise and a gorgeous sunset, or like Rousseau and Voltaire. He could have gone on ad infinitum showing off his Dunbar University education, via both classes and his elite eating club. Frankly, it was more than a little painful listening to him hold forth, not because of his efflorescence but because it reminded me of how my mother would talk about her favorite books or music with a glass of white wine in her hand, like I wasn't really there, when I realized Pong was still out of the room on a call that had come in earlier. Just a plate of perfectly cubed watermelon arranged in a mini-ziggurat had been placed at his setting. No one else got this, just Pong. Lucky saw me examining the plate of cut fruit, and he asked me if I knew anything about Pong's background, his life before he'd come to America. He didn't know I'd first met him mere weeks earlier.

"Be certain to ask him about the watermelon," Lucky said. "As a new friend, you'll want to hear about those times."

The graphic on Pong's card suddenly flashed in my mind. When Pong came back in, tapping at his phone, he didn't even look at the plate of watermelon before him. At some point he simply plucked a cube from the stack with his fingers and put it in his mouth and chewed, his face showing no reaction, no gauging of whether it tasted good or bad or like nothing at all. He left the rest untouched.

When the evening finally ended, this well after all the other patrons and even most of the servers had left, Bags initiated a round of hugs as we stood outside the mall entrance. The parking lot was empty except for the group members' fancy cars, plus of course my rusty, shitty bike on the rack. I figured this might be the last I'd see of any of them, and I'd had my fill and fun, and for the first time in a long time I hugged with abandon, like we were comrades in arms and we'd been to hell and back, which made me well up with a glee and sadness, a good sickly feeling, even if Marcus nimbly sloughed me off after a couple clingy seconds.

"Hey, Tiller," Lucky said, tapping my shoulder as I unlocked my bike. "Pong and I were thinking. Would you like to tag along on our investment trip to Asia that's coming up? We feel you would be a good assistant. What do you think?"

"I don't have any money for a ticket," I obtusely said, eliciting a maybe regretful look from him. I should have asked particulars about where they were going and what for and all the usuals, but I'd already and instantly agreed to going wherever else they might be going, and like the dumb kid I was I just focused on all the ways I was bereft.

"We will take care of everything," Pong said. "Also, I have many, many miles. I can book you a seat no problem."

A week later I found myself packing a small overnight bag and texting Clark to say I was visiting some friends in DC, and he texted back from work with his usual *okey-dokey* followed by his usual blow-a-kiss emoji, which is just the one a deeply dorky dad would send to his deeply dorky son. I sent one right back. Trying to text the whole story about who Pong was, and how we met, and where I was going and why, was much too complicated, and ultimately not direly important to relate, so I didn't bother. I would be away a week at most, and then I'd be back in Dunbar for a while before finally heading off to my program abroad (which I kept forgetting about completely, like I had Alzheimer's or something), so we texted about getting some "quality time" in then. We were long practiced at assuring this, which worked for us. But we all know the truth: real "quality time" happens without you knowing it's happening, like when you've drifted far from shore but don't fret, having your mate or bud with you.

Anyway, on the long-haul flight—Pong, Lucky Choi, and I were destined for Shenzhen, via an overnight stopover in Honolulu—sometime after they served the champagne and warmed cashews in mini-ramekins to us in our business-class lie-flats, sometime after the bowls of bibimbap and the steamed buns with braised pork belly, sometime after the cheese plate and vintage port and espresso, with Lucky already eye masked and snoring in the row behind us, I remembered to ask Pong: So what's with the watermelon?

It was a good thing it was such a long flight, because Lucky was absolutely correct. It was one of several times Pong spoke to me about his past. A true friend of Pong's would want to hear about those days, and as a new (and I hoped genuine) friend, I did. As he began to explain those cubes of watermelon at the Chop Station, Pong started somewhere else, because everything starts somewhere else, and I got this weird feeling I should listen very carefully, so as not to forget.

9.

WATERMELON?

Well, I should begin with a portrait of Mao.

I say this, even if it's not exactly true. Everything would have changed anyway, eventually, because a person can't avoid certain conditions. He can't escape the weather, if he's depending on his own meager human power. He can't simply run or fly away. And if the weather is not just an isolated storm or dry spell, if it's the sustained onset of a prevailing climate, he must adapt, or else suffer the consequences of not adapting. He can blame others or the fate of circumstance, but if he can't improvise something to shield himself from the wind or the rain or the sun, there it will be, unavoidable, the truth of the elements.

As with every life, my life is the story of my mother and father.

They were junior professors of painting at the Central Academy of Fine Arts in Beijing, and we three lived in a two-room flat near the campus, in a dank concrete tenement where quite a few other Academy people resided. The year in question was 1966. My parents slept in the bedroom and I in one corner of the living room, where there was also a two-hob cooking burner and a washbasin where we cleaned both our dishes and our clothes. I was only five years old but quite aware for my age, and I could tell even then that we were a reasonably contented family, as my parents were busy teaching their classes and advising graduate students, as well as pursuing their own projects on alternating evenings at the studio they shared on campus. Alternating, because one of them stayed home after the woman who babysat me departed for the day. They'd come home within minutes of each other and together quickly prepare some fried noodles or a simple chicken or pork-bone soup to go along with steamed buns purchased from a street cart. There was hardly enough space but they rarely bickered as they nudged and stepped around each other, chattering away instead about some irritating colleague or an especially successful student painting. They worked very hard as teachers but they had a passion for their own work that I could tell even then was unflagging.

After we ate they always smoked a cigarette or two with their tea, and when they were done one of them bicycled back to campus to paint for a few hours, the other tutoring me in reading or composing characters or very simple mathematics. Never drawing or painting, though, which I was inexplicably secretive about and would do on my own during the day whenever my sitter, whom I called Auntie Red, fell asleep, which she did with a strange regularity. I thought then that all older people dozed off like this, but I see now that she was probably a narcoleptic, which may have been a reason she chewed betel leaves all day (which stained her teeth red), in an attempt to stave off the spells. Her people were from Burma, where the practice is popular. She made me promise not to tell my parents about her condition, and I never did.

Late in the evenings I'd be momentarily roused when my mother or father keyed into the flat, and I still associate the scent of the mineral spirits they used to clean their brushes with that almost painful torpor that feels like a great stone inside the chest, a stone so dense that it draws everything toward it. It is a scent that instantly gives me a feeling of well-being, and sadness as well.

My father was popular and highly lauded in the department, but my mother was the greater artist. My father freely acknowledged this was the case, as he was genuinely talented himself and knew his art. But my mother was unusually shy, and she also didn't crave recognition the way he and most other artists did, and they mutually decided that he would become the "success" at the Academy, so that they'd avoid appearing overly ambitious.

She was profoundly gifted, identified as such at the age of seven after her illiterate street-hawker parents found drawings of people and horses and dogs hidden under her cot, and assumed because of the virtuosity of the images that their daughter must have ripped the pages from a valuable art book at the school she'd just begun attending. They were so fearful that she'd be expelled if found doing it again that they decided to go immediately to the school and have her confess to her teacher and accept whatever punishment. At her classroom only the teacher was there, as the children were out doing calisthenics, and they presented him with the drawings, begging forgiveness and promising to lash her until she was bloodied. The teacher immediately recognized the drawings to be originals, though disbelieving they could be a young child's work. When my mother and the others returned from recess she saw the adults and the sheaf of her drawings in her teacher's hands and ran back outside. They caught up to her and the teacher asked if she'd made the drawings and if she could do another quick sketch, which she did for them without looking up, an exquisite drawing of three grown-ups bending intently over a little girl. She could work solely from what she composed in her mind. When the teacher showed them to an artist friend the man was overwhelmed, saying the drawings were reminiscent of early figurative sketches by Rembrandt, and within days she was transferred to an elite youth art academy.

My mother—her given name was Niu—was tutored in all the Eastern and Western styles and periods, working in pastels and watercolors and oils, and by the time she entered her secondary school years could draw and paint whatever was asked of her. This was in the early years after the Communists took command, when there was the expectation that all artists give over their talents to the revolution. But her instructors at the former National Beijing Art College—which was renamed the Central Academy—determined that her superior gifts should be devoted to classical Chinese painting. She was first among a small group of the most talented students— my father, Shang, was one of them—whom they designated as their successors, and who would master the techniques of the finest artistry of both the old culture and the West. Her instructors were not so much political as they were artistically fervent; they would encourage those of a more common facility to glorify the revolution, as no more than a sturdy competence was required for producing the often garish cartoons and portraits and murals then papering the city.

My mother embraced her teachers' plan for her, as she was happy to practice her art in any form. She was not constituted in the psychological manner of most artists, at least as we might like to think of them. She was not some self-obsessive misanthrope or renegade visionary. She was a person who simply made images for their own sake, discovering line by line, hue by hue, how it is to see and feel in this world. In this regard, as they say, she was an artist's artist. Her paintings and scrolls possessed all the texture and richly detailed motifs of the classical models—pastoral images of forested mountains, of nobles and their steeds, still lifes of birds amid spring blooms, panels of highly stylized tigers and cranes—but still somehow stood out from even the most prized historical examples. Even when the colors and shadings were muted or dark, there was a luminescence to her work, this singular energy that graced everything she made, as if she were channeling some transcendent power.

Yet she was the most modest of persons, someone who, as the saying goes, would not even boast that she breathed particularly well, a quality that in my father's regard made her that much rarer as a talent and person. He kept asking her to a tearoom at the end of studio hours, and after her many kind but clear demurrals he finally brought tea in, along with sweet bean buns and a small clay sculpture he'd made of himself bearing a tray of tea and buns and an even tinier self-sculpture. He posed before her with a placard hung around his neck that he'd painted with the title: THE THREE HEARTBROKEN SUITORS. She couldn't help but oblige him, and they shared his offerings that evening and the following evenings. By the time they were appointed apprentice instructors in 1960—they had quickly married after realizing she was pregnant—my parents were acknowledged as the Academy's golden pair, a strong match of gifted opposites.

My father was not like his bride. He was the charismatic third son (of six children) of a once-prominent Beijing textile merchant family, and grew up in an immense traditional house with numerous internal courtyards, the Western-style rooms layered with luxurious fabrics and decorative furnishings and rare Chinese artworks and porcelain. The household was in decline well before the Communists came to power, and quickly fell apart once they ascended, the market for their opulent wares diminished to almost nothing. My father and his siblings were separated and sent to live with various relatives, as their parents were hopelessly derelict in character, not to mention totally bankrupt. The grand house was sold to another merchant before it was expropriated soon after and made into a state school, where my father actually briefly attended classes. What that must have been like for him, to see his home stripped of all its color and character and overrun by brutish cadres scuffing the walls and spitting on the floors! Perhaps this clarified his aesthetic sensibilities, and made him dream even harder. For while he was ambitious and sociable and a natural leader, my father was a dreamer most of all. His mature paintings, stylistically influenced perhaps most by the Impressionists, were often depictions of urban people at leisure, scenes of huddled mah-jongg players, upper-class women practicing calligraphy, fleshy, jowled merchants eyeing a fully laden banquet, tableaus that might have easily been viewed as decadent and counterrevolutionary but that through his hand appeared effortlessly naturalistic, and somehow innocent, and thus faithful to what *should be*. They were undeniably lovely as well, this no matter who you were, and whether you experienced them as delightful or facile there was nothing you could do but keep looking at them, as you might a rare blood moon.

So it was my parents and their group of junior colleagues who would be at the helm of the Central Academy for the coming decades. They led by example, showing equal dedication to their students and their own work, which now received prominent placing in the halls of the major exhibitions. My father was assigned a key administrative role in faculty appointments for the department, and my mother in student admissions. Naturally there was some grousing by certain smaller-minded colleagues but really everyone could agree that besides their talent and devotion to their students they were plainly good people, which I knew, too, in my boy's heart. I think someone's child can understand best his or her essential character, no matter what we might purport in later years. We can see them back down to the seeds.

Which is why for me there is another layer of sorrow beneath the general sorrow of that time. We know being "good" is no shield against misfortune, no insurance against being crushed. But perhaps it's this very powerlessness that makes goodness all the more cherished, especially after it is gone.

It happened in a matter of weeks, in that summer of 1966. Had I been older, I might have better understood that the wider circumstances had already changed, that after years of economic and political struggles (from which we were mostly insulated at the Academy), the country was pitched toward some profound reckoning or shift, but no one could have foretold the great quaking that would unmoor everything.

Of course my parents and everyone else had heard about gangs of young Red Guards, some barely pubescent, radicalized by Mao and his circle, who had begun making sweeps throughout the cities exposing and overturning what Chen Boda coined as the Four Olds: old ideas, old culture, old customs, old habits. These were the markers of a sclerotic, exploitative past that was still infecting the people and preventing progress. I remember my father being vaguely sympathetic to this new campaign, as what choice did he have but to wonder aloud to my mother and one of the senior instructors who'd come over for tea about what exactly these Four Olds were, in practical form. Traditional clothes? Ancient literary scrolls? Old-time recipes? Even irreplaceable books of family genealogy, which they'd heard were being burnt in head-high stacks in a precinct of Beijing? Could the idea of one's lineage really be an "old"? No one could be sure, as everything was left to the whim of the Red Guards, cadre by cadre making spot determinations as they roamed the hutongs and avenues with their banners and megaphones, shouting revolutionary epithets.

"They've begun disrupting schools and universities, too," the senior instructor said. He was Old Zhou, and I can picture him well because of his bulbously round, close-shaven head, and the amoeba-shaped, plum-colored birthmark that splotched his right cheek, just below the corner of his eye, so that it made him, despite his general bright disposition, appear bereft and mournful. "It would be less unsettling if they were outsiders, but my friends say they're their own students, if often the less talented ones, who tend to head up the Guards. They rise from within, and then draw the rest to their mob."

"I can't believe this will happen at the Academy," my father said. "We're all artists here, teachers and students both. Our kind would rather not fret too much about the real world. We value line and contour and color. Light and dark. Beauty, in all its possible forms. This is what we care about, no, with all our blood and bones?"

"It's what we should care about," Old Zhou said, winking at me, before turning to my mother. "What are you thinking, Niu? When I see that sudden shading in your eyes, I know you're turning something over."

"Oh, I don't know," my mother said, her voice characteristically hovering just above a murmur. She tried to smile. "You shouldn't mind me."

"We do mind you," my father said. "Always."

She took one of the almond cookies that Old Zhou had brought over, though just held it. "I am being silly. But I think I am wary of the people who might care too much."

I didn't understand what she meant, but it was clear that my father and Old Zhou did, as they both ruefully nodded, rubbing their chins, Old Zhou's more stubbly than my father's. So I did the same, which made my mother laugh—I loved her laugh, a song that piped high and soft—and then the men laughed, too, and the remainder of the evening we shared the cookies, and listened to Old Zhou's amusing stories, including one about how his deceased wife used to model nude for him before they were married but not after because she knew those early paintings could never be equaled, both for the wild-eyed wonder of their maker and the tender shape of the model.

The next day I was stuck on a mental picture of Old Zhou's wife, wrinkly and unclothed but with my mother's pale, smooth breasts (the only ones I had ever seen), though with the stained teeth of Auntie Red, with whom I was walking through the street market near our building. As we did each day we were picking up a few groceries for my parents, with Auntie Red gossiping with certain merchants, when we heard some shouting at one of the stalls. It was at the merchant who sold newspapers and other sundries such as candies and tobacco (though like many of the sellers, he sold numerous other random items). A dozen or so Red Guards were gathered in front of the stall, and the owner, a man named Yu whom Auntie Red sometimes chatted with, was standing rigidly before their number, blocking the single aisle to bar them from going farther inside.

The Red Guards, young men and women wearing their brown PLA-issued uniforms and caps, were reinforced by a smattering of regular folk (several clearly indigent), who had just attached themselves to the gang. It would happen like that all around the city, these restive, spontaneously expanding swarms. This one was demanding that Yu let them inside to inspect the rest of his wares; the ground was already littered with torn newsprint, the remnants of a Japanese newspaper they had found and that Yu was now promising he would no longer carry. "Besides," he shouted, "there is nothing else, no other foreign newspapers or books, nothing counterrevolutionary, just sweets and nuts and cigarettes!"

The most vocal of the Guards, a petite young woman with high-set catlike eyes and a single thick, meticulously braided snake of hair, scoffed at him, saying the Red Guards would be the judge of what was counterrevolutionary or not. The mere fact that Yu carried this offending Japanese rag revealed his corrupted state. Her argument unsettled him, his face screwing up, and she took the moment to try to slip past him. Yu, shortish but thick of shoulder and neck, instinctively jutted out his hip as she maneuvered, causing the young woman to lose her balance and tip over in what was a supremely slow, almost elegant fall. She landed on one of the low display boxes on which Yu had laid out little packages of jellied candies and nutmeats, scattering them in a wild mess, and it seemed to me and Auntie Red—our hands were gripped tightly—that the entire market had tilted toward Yu's stall.

The cat-eyed girl wasn't hurt—her tumble was much too gentle—but after plucking her up her comrades now bulldozed through poor Yu, who could only step aside. We couldn't see what was happening within the stall, but soon enough the Guards were tossing cartons of certain brands of cigarettes onto a pile in the street, shouting that they were of Dutch and Taiwanese origin, although Yu contended they were fakes, which only incensed them more, another young Red Guard pointing this out as further proof of the proprietor's rapacious, capitalistic ways. Yu stayed silent, lowering his miserable head. We watched them burn the cigarettes in question, which were in truth not so many, along with several other items that didn't seem especially offending, like a toy guitar and a used set of roller skates, plus some local newspapers, though these only because the Guards required more fuel. The small pyre burnt hot and bright but briefly, and as the Red Guards decamped to search out other violations in the area, Yu, scratching his head, looked upon the smoky ashes with seeming relief, realizing perhaps that this particular cohort was as yet a bit green.

Auntie Red pulled us away from Yu's and I thought we were going back to the flat, but like many others around us she was helplessly drawn to the spectacle, and we became part of the crowd that trailed (and unintentionally emboldened) the Red Guards as they roved the neighborhood. We watched as they invaded other stalls and also some larger, long-established shops, calling out their owners and humiliating them in the street, in one case not for specific items but for occupying a prime site for generations and charging the highest prices. Did they believe this location was their birthright?

NO! the crowd answered for them.

Were they serving the people with their profiteering?

NO! they shouted even louder.

These joint interrogations pleased the throng. The Guards even accosted two elderly monks on their way to the temple, denouncing them for their useless, backward piety. I waited for someone to defend the poor monks, who stood there with their elbows tightly linked, but nobody did; people started jeering them instead, making fun of their dung-colored robes and their dirty bare feet. Someone demanded they do a dance, like a married couple, and when at last they began shuffling awkwardly I wanted to cry but I saw Auntie Red chuckling along with the rest and I started laughing, too, even though the monks' cowed, pleading eyes made me feel sick. Soon enough it seemed everyone was taunting them, shouting with hot glee, and I must have joined in as well, because when we got home my throat tickled when I tried to speak, my voice creaky and hoarse.

I didn't tell my parents what had happened when they returned from the day at the Academy, nor did Auntie Red mention anything. As always she laid out for them what she had purchased at the market before handing over the change and leaving. After supper I asked to go to bed. I was exhausted, all my weight seemingly settled in my arms and legs, and I must have fallen asleep immediately, though it couldn't have been for very long; when I woke they were putting away the dishes, and through the haze of my half sleep I heard them discussing the Red Guards, which confused me, as I was sure I hadn't seen either of them at the street market. But of course they were talking about a different cohort of Red Guards, at the Academy, spontaneously arisen from among their own students, who had that very afternoon staged an impromptu parade on the campus with bright flags and big-character banners they'd made, calling for enlistees.

I couldn't understand what they were discussing, only that my mother seemed more concerned than my father about what this new period would bring to the school, as he was the one trying to reassure her that all would be fine. Neither of them was politically minded, though he was clearly the more pragmatic one.

"This is a movement," he told her, "that the leadership believes will spur the country forward. Whether it does or not won't matter very much to us. We will have to let the youth exercise their passions, and go along as best as we can."

My mother agreed, and although they didn't discuss it further they must have been quite unsettled, because for the first time I could recall they both stayed home that evening, neither going to work at the studio.

The next day—or perhaps it was several days later—the air was heavy and exceedingly warm, a typical August afternoon in Beijing, which I remember because Old Zhou was complaining about it to my parents when we met him on campus. Normally it would have been a regular day, with Auntie Red looking after me, but the dean decreed that instead of classes there would be a special convocation devoted to the rededication to and promotion of the socialist revolution at the Academy. There were no details aside from a general meeting scheduled in the main hall at two p.m. My parents had gone to campus in the morning but returned to the apartment after seeing the notice, sending Auntie Red home early. It was an oddly quiet stretch of time as they awaited the appointed hour, the three of us sitting in front of the creaky table fan, my parents restlessly smoking, drinking tepid tea, while I looked through my picture books.

We came upon Old Zhou just inside the southern gate, where he was blotting his forehead and neck with a dampened handkerchief, his face flushed and shiny with sweat, his birthmark seemingly darker of pitch. He seemed even more uncomfortable because he was overweight; he was a fan of sweets and rich foods, which he had always favored but especially since his wife died, as he said the eating helped with his periodic bouts of missing her. I can see now that he was unusually open about his feelings and moods, which is perhaps why certain people like my parents immediately took to him, and why certain others found him a suspect personality, or even pitiable.

Why my parents had me go along with them that day is unclear. Perhaps it was simply that they didn't wish to pay Auntie Red for unnecessary babysitting; they were poor, as most everyone was back then, but they were also naturally resourceful artists, who besides having little extra money were inclined to make complete use of all available materials, foremost themselves. I wonder now, however, if the reason for my presence was more psychological than anything else: perhaps they wanted or needed to believe that the gathering would be nothing extraordinary, that whatever would transpire would be beyond me, or if not beyond me, then certainly not disturbing.

When we arrived at the entrance of the main hall the doors were all opened and flowing out was the sound of hundreds of elevated voices, which to my ears seemed trebled by the heat, and I remember actually pressing my palms against them as we made our way inside the building. It was full of Academy people, whom I could pick out from their simple civilian dress, but present were also many animated Red Guards both in uniform and not, some with caps but all with red-banded arms. It appeared that they were composed of several separate cadres that were now crowding the far end of the hall, each bearing a banner with a different slogan (*Red Rebels Unite! Mobilize the Proletariat! Build a New World!*), with many Academy students now standing within their ranks.

A gray-haired man in a suit and spectacles appeared at the lectern near them and waved his hands until the room was quiet. Old Zhou whispered to my father, "Look at our poor dean. It's like he just shit his pants." My father nodded, though somberly. The dean kept pushing up his eyeglasses before he finally mopped the perspiration from his nose and brow with a handkerchief. There was no microphone and he couldn't stop clearing his throat as he fitfully spoke.

"Fellow colleagues, administrators, and students . . . this morning . . . excuse me, this afternoon . . . I wish to open a special meeting of our community . . . As you know, there has been a call by our esteemed Chairman Mao to renew the great revolution and . . . and it is our pleasure here at the Academy to support this important campaign with this convocation in which . . . we have invited several speakers, who . . ."

He was about to continue when one of the Red Guards, a tall, very lean young man with a very angular, freshly shaven face, stepped right in front of the lectern and shouted, "It is not your 'pleasure' but a binding duty, old citizen, to support this revolution! We are the Red Guards, whom Chairman Mao himself has mobilized, and we are here to upturn the Old for the New!"

There was a surprisingly fierce roar of assent, at least from the Red Guards and the Academy students who stood with them, to what would have normally been taken as a deeply offensive tone from the young man. The dean reflexively stepped forward to confront him but against the bristling sway of the exercised cadres he shrank in midstride, receding as the young Red Guard went on in his rant: "We have not been *invited* here! We don't need any invitations except from our great Chairman Mao, who has deployed us as his thought weapons throughout the land to target recidivist traditions and institutions! We are here to root out decadent practices! We are here to denounce revisionist ideologies! We are here to upturn the old for the new! Snuff old lies to let live new truths!"

He led the newly charged assembly in this last exhortation, with seemingly everyone except my parents and Old Zhou and a few of the other faculty near us chanting the slogan. And although the hall was now much louder than when we arrived the din did not bother me. The blanketing heat was now strangely energizing, and gazing upon the troubled faces of my parents, I felt suddenly matured, as if I understood at that moment something they could not.

"Newest and brightest Red Guards!" the young man cried, pumping his fist. "Let us break the chains of the olds!"

It was then that a young woman and young man, both Academy students, emerged from the throng of the Red Guards. The woman, Meng Pei, was a favorite of my parents and Old Zhou. She was an exceptional watercolorist, and I remember her as full-cheeked and girlish, though at that moment she and the man were both marked by this very hard, bright look, as if they were about to mount a most arduous expedition.

Uniformed Red Guards appeared beside them bearing sledge-hammers, the sight of which drew a gasp from the assembly, who must have been afraid they were going to bludgeon someone like the dean, break his arms or legs. There were many reports of vicious beatings by the Red Guards, some resulting in deaths. A platoon of Guards pushed people back, clearing a large ring of space around one of the dozen statues that ran in two parallel rows down the central axis of the main hall. These were replicas of mostly famous Western works such as the *Venus de Milo* and *The Thinker* and Michelangelo's *David*, made of plaster but of a very high quality that made them seem genuinely precious, which were used by all the Academy students for light and shadow studies. You would see groups of them arrayed about the works throughout the day, sketching and drawing but sometimes simply sitting and leaning upon the pedestals as they socialized.

Now the statue—the *Discobolus*—appeared abandoned, small and alone. My parents and Old Zhou had pushed to the front, pulling me along. When I saw Meng Pei again she was holding one of the sledgehammers, the other student hefting his own. The Red Guard who had belittled the dean then repeated his slogans, and ordered Meng Pei and her classmate to "attack at the heart of decadent influences."

The classmate strode forward, lugging the heavy hammer, and with a lame windup swung laboriously at the sculpture, missing its head but snapping the downward arm of the athlete, exposing the underwire structure. There was an uneasy silence. He wound up again and this time hit more of his mark, the iron partly decapitating the statue. Only the lower lip and jaw remained. There was some cheering now, and he finished by smashing the discus and the arm and then the rest of the body, the pedestal and floor a mess of rubble and white dust.

Meng Pei then took her turn, moving with purpose toward the nearest sculpture. It was the *David*. She was much more adept with the hammer than the young man was, appearing as if she had used one before—perhaps she was once trained as an athlete—knowing to feel the weight of the head and lever it; she swung rhythmically and with an almost effortless chuck crushed the angelic face. She caved in the chest. Then she methodically and completely obliterated the rest of him, loins to legs to feet. I gazed up and saw my mother was covering her mouth, her eyes swollen with tears. My father and Old Zhou looked on grimly as their dear Meng Pei now gave the sledgehammer to another student, who was begging for his turn.

Eventually, every Western-style work in the hall was destroyed, though I didn't witness this, as my mother dragged me away after Meng Pei was done. When my father returned he began describing what happened after we left but my mother didn't want to know and disappeared into the bedroom. The next morning, they sent Auntie Red home again, though paying her, as my mother felt unwell and didn't want to go to school. It turned out that classes were suspended anyway, and then were canceled for several more days, which for my father were busy with gatherings of certain colleagues like Old Zhou, a couple meetings taking place in our tiny apartment late at night, people jammed so tightly into the front room that they had to fold in the legs of our small table and prop it in the hallway to free up space. They were hotly arguing and always angry-sounding, but my mother, who stayed with me in the bedroom, tried to explain that they were not angry with one another, a distinction I could not quite understand. She was welcomed in the discussions but she declined to take part; she wasn't working in her studio, either, and it seemed she always wanted to lie down between preparing food for us and simply read, or perhaps not read at all. I must say I loved it, the two of us lying in my parents' lumpy bed, the scent of her on the sheets, and I ate when she ate, read when she read, dozed when she dozed. She would let me take a puff or two of her cigarette. I think we began to realize how much we had missed each other in the normal course of our family's life, which must have made that most unsettled time even more trying for her.

When classes resumed several days later she and my father went back to teaching. Auntie Red stayed with me as always, but even I could sense that any return to normalcy would be short-lived. There seemed to be an altered pace to my parents' movements in the mornings, my father scrubbing his face especially vigorously at the kitchen basin, soap suds nested in his ears, and my mother conversely brushing her hair ever, ever so slowly, as if the strands might otherwise fall out or break. In the evening neither went to the studio, my father if he went anywhere heading over to yet another fraught gathering of terrified faculty. My mother simply stayed in with me, listening to his reports when he came home. But one afternoon my mother returned to the apartment unexpectedly and went straight into the bedroom, telling Auntie Red to take me for a walk, and from within

I could hear these throttled, lungful sobs the moment we shut the front door.

Auntie Red knew to pull me away and we loitered within the street market for a while and then found ourselves back near one of the gates of the campus, Auntie Red reading aloud all the new big-character banners that were strung from the ramparts of the building and atop the gates, these instructions urging the "bombarding" of all counterrevolutionary offices, the exposing of agents of corrupting values, of realigning the Academy along the needs of the proletariat, et cetera, et cetera, which she did not seem to understand much better than I did but was clearly stimulated by, at least from her expression, which was fierce of chin, if still somewhat puzzled. Did she clench her fist and murmur, "People are the power"? It may well be she did. Most all of what you will read now about that period will describe it as one of the darkest times in modern Chinese history, and it truly was that for people like my parents and other professors and intellectuals, but for the vast majority of the populace, the generally uneducated and penniless people like Auntie Red who had already endured a deadly decade of famine and privation, it was not a fraction as tragic. Their lives would trudge on. The new movement was nominally for their sake, and if it did not improve their lot at least it bolstered their belief that the struggle for them would never die. Which may be righteous cause enough.

When we got back, my father was already home, sitting with my mother at the kitchen table before cups of cooling tea. My father was smoking. Seeing him, Auntie Red mumbled something about being paid for the entire day and my father, who of course would not have shorted her, reached into his trouser pocket and brusquely slapped some coins on the table. I think everyone was startled, as my father was never the sort to lord himself over others; in fact, he was sociable, many would say, to a fault. Auntie Red let go my hand and slid the coins, one by one, into her tattered canvas purse. She patted me on the head and as she turned to leave grinned tightly and said to me, "We saw all the pretty banners at the school, didn't we?" That was the last time I saw her stained, crooked teeth.

My father took a long draw from his cigarette, exhaling with what seemed a great effort. When we arrived he was describing for my mother what had transpired after she fled the gallery where the student leaders—now full-fledged Red Guards—had curated a special exhibition of faculty artworks that they'd deemed "black works," paintings that bore counterrevolutionary motifs and themes. He would tell me later, when I was much older, what had happened. Traditional Chinese ink paintings were featured, those vertically oriented landscapes of steep hillsides and forested valleys, often marked by a romantic pavilion, placid animals, perhaps a tiny noble figure. These were works of several senior faculty, including Old Zhou, whose paintings had always been celebrated for their elegance and delicate brushstrokes, and who was my mother's dear mentor. When she saw what the students were displaying my mother couldn't bear it and left. A separate brigade of students, some of them armed with batons given to them by the Red Guards, eventually brought in Old Zhou and two other elderly professors, Wei and Fung, roughly handling them by their shirt collars. The Academy dean was present, too, though he could only look on helplessly.

Each of the professors was then pushed down to his knees, while one of the students read from a list of "charges" accusing them of promoting, through their paintings and teachings, the oppressive traditions of a diseased culture, and of having little or no zealotry for the plight of the workers, who were the lifeblood of the nation. The rant went on in expected fashion, and then more specifically denounced their most lauded works, belittling them most cruelly for their decadent aesthetic flourishes. Finally, the student cried, "You are enemies of the revolution, are you not?" To this Old Zhou and his colleagues nodded, as if they had agreed beforehand to accept all criticisms and charges without resistance. A different student then appeared with a small bucket and brush and messily wrote in bright red paint the character for *infiltrator* on one of the professors' works. Wei rose to stop the defacement but he was struck in the back with a baton, and then another student stepped forward with her uniform belt folded thickly in her hand and whipped him with it. Old Zhou and Fung cried out and they were whipped, too, the steel buckle gouging their defending hands and scalps until their faces were as smeared bloody as the swine heads at the street market.

Of course the onlookers, including my father, could do nothing to shield the poor professors. They were venerable men, until that very moment first-rank artists whose works might someday be national treasures, but against the surging of the Red Guards, who with stunning speed and conviction improvised a complete (if temporary) control wherever they went, they were no sturdier than anybody else, mere saplings in the path of an avalanche. It was a time, my father would tell me later, when one could feel very large and very small and when neither scale nor perspective held any meaning.

Quite something for an artist to say.

Old Zhou and Fung and Wei were stripped of their positions, as were several others of their generation at the Academy, the group of them collectively tried, convicted, and sentenced by the local prefecture court to ten years of reeducational labor. Some of them were sent north to mining areas, the rest to agricultural camps in the southwest provinces. Old Zhou labored at a farm digging irrigation ditches, barely sustained by the meager rations, and in a matter of weeks he collapsed of a heart attack and died, a shovel in his hands. Though likely accurate, this last detail is my father's. Years later I learned from someone who was there in the labor camp that Old Zhou had made these exquisite, if morbid, vignettes of his friends and colleagues from those days, which he'd unconsciously sketch on a piece of scrap paper and then immediately tear into tiny rough squares before throwing them away.

For a while the Red Guard elements at the school allowed my parents to go uncriticized. My mother should have surely drawn their fury, given her classically styled works and her close relationship with Old Zhou, but she quit teaching after what happened, clearing out her brushes and tools and paintings from the studio, which I helped her with, and then completely disappeared from public view. She and I were partners then, going to the market, keeping up the apartment, sometimes singing or reading together, though never drawing or painting or watercoloring. My father went the other way; he subscribed himself fully to the Red Guards, and as he was always universally liked by the students, his swift conversion to their cause (and his own artistic inclination for squarely bourgeois themes) was not overly scrutinized. Instead they chose to see him as someone who, like themselves, had been long subject to the influences of Old Zhou and his cohort and thus unwittingly corrupted, a narrative that my father, ever pragmatic, further ratified through his suddenly keen efforts in evangelizing the younger faculty and radically altering the curriculum. I remember him quietly rehearsing what he would say to a key gathering of militant students and colleagues, namely that the Academy was now at the vanguard of the revolution, and should redirect its collective talents to mobilize the populace and reform the nation into the ideal workers' society that Chairman Mao had always envisioned.

As far as I recall, once he resituated himself, he and my mother never spoke about Old Zhou, or argued about his new stance at the Academy, or even discussed the wider politics of it all. Again, they were not political people, just passionate artists who were up to that point genuinely devoted to their students. Now everything was upturned. I think they purposely engaged this new reality as naively as they could, this counterpart world in which my mother would take a sabbatical from painting and embrace full-time motherhood, and my father would preserve his family through the graces of his naturally sociable character. He would do this through his own work, too, for like everyone else at the Academy and the other art schools across the country, he was drafted into the campaign that would produce the thousands of drawings, cartoons, paintings, and murals meant to educate and inspire the populace; whether caricaturing enemies of the state as craven running dogs or vermin, or valorizing workers and the PLA in the promoted style, these larger-than-life canvases showed comrades gazing undaunted to the far horizon, their eyes burning with a revolutionary purity and zeal.

It could be said that for a short span of days in the autumn of 1966, my father was the most lauded artist at the Academy, and thus, arguably, in the whole of China. The warm, rich palette he used for his previous works, those glowing, color-saturated paintings of the hutongs and boudoirs and parlors of a fast-disappearing era, he now supercharged for the campaign, and especially when he rendered its most important subject, Mao Zedong. The officially prescribed style for painting the Chairman's face was *hong, guang, liang*—red, smooth, luminescent—which is the way we now and will perhaps forever picture the man, his iconic, full, ruddy cheeks radiating an unflagging vitality, and that my father surpassed in his work.

At first glance my father's Maos appeared much like the countless others, the Chairman at the fore of some heroic grouping of workers or Red Guard youth, the viewer's eye drawn in on an ascending line of his devoted acolytes right up to his raised, beckoning visage. Yet the more one looked at my father's versions, the more one could not help staring at them. After an informal showing of new revolutionary works by faculty and students, my father's paintings became the talk of the Academy, seemingly all the students lobbying to work under my father's tutelage. People from other art schools began visiting, as well as some of the local citizenry. The work was stunning, if not immediately or easily pleasing. A few would go away looking piqued, perhaps unsettled. But most stood before the paintings, their eyes wide, their mouths slack. Of course the paintings captured Mao's likeness with near-photographic accuracy, and by virtue of their grand scale could manifest the sudden lode of a chest pang, but they possessed as well a different order of illumination, as if Mao were not only the Sun, but a Sun that could be looked upon without harm, and was in fact ever fortifying. You felt an inflow of undeniable energy, a dizzying rushing out. After seeing my father's new work one of his colleagues confided to him, "You know I don't blame you for what has happened to our school. We all do what we must. But this is too much. I don't want to love Mao yet you make me love him."

Soon after, the dean tasked the faculty to mount a public exhibition to showcase the Academy's talents but of course make plain its institutional fervor for the movement, not to mention his own fealty to the Party. But then most everyone was trying his best to get along. "Art should be a sharp implement of the revolution," I heard my father advise a student (repeating one of the many slogans bannered about the school), and whether he believed an iota of that notion does not matter now. I know he simply wanted to preserve our place in the Academy. He wanted to secure the future. He wanted to protect us, in the only way he was able.

The exhibition was by design a large one, with art schools from as far as Shanghai sending their most exemplary faculty and student works to the Academy. Of course Academy paintings were given prime placement in the hall, with two of my father's paintings, a kinetic grouping of flag-waving Red Guards, plus his best portrait of Mao, an intensive reworking of the one his colleague had praised and bemoaned, centrally sited within those. He could have easily left the portrait as it was, but he spent three long nights in the studio retouching and repainting, undoubtedly concerned that he had not yet perfected that most important of important faces. I can imagine him in his customary stance before the large canvas, one arm cradling the other, the raised palm propping his chin. He'd push his round-framed spectacles higher on his nose and then shift his perspective, tilt his head to the side. What has he missed? What else can he do? The Chairman stared back at him and right through him, offering no answers.

Just before dawn on the day of the exhibition my father returned to curl up in my little bed in the front room, as I was slumbering with my mother. She let him sleep right up to his first midmorning studio class, rousing him with his favorite, a bowl of hot congee. But he wasn't hungry, and only took a few spoons before hustling out for the class and then the exhibition's opening day. He kissed my mother and then me, gently squeezing my ear, and then left. Again, my mother never criticized him; she never questioned his integrity, artistic or otherwise, choosing to see him instead, at least in his vocation, as another laborer among laborers, another set of hands among hands, all collecting stones for the rising mountain of the movement. "We are people and we are small but together can build greatness." This is what was said.

The exhibition was popular, attended by hundreds of art students and faculty from the participating academies, area schoolchildren and citizenry, random brigades of Red Guards, and of course local Party officials and various cultural committee members, everyone—whether they cared to be there or not—self-primed to walk through the maze of freshly erected display walls with their eyes and hearts wide open, their veins throbbing, thirsty for the surging color of revolution.

That day there was a clear hero of the show. There was no competition per se, it was simply an exhibition, but the massing pattern of the visitors told the story of which painting was the champion.

My father's Mao. It was an immense portrait, roughly two meters by three, with no side figures in the work, only a graphic of red and gold sunbeams radiating from the cottony halo around Mao's head, part of the extensive reworking my father had labored over the previous nights. This was not an unusual treatment, nor was his any different in how he had the Chairman dressed, in his drab olive uniform with plain brown buttons; it wasn't as though the work was formally special compared with the two or three dozen other portraits of Mao around the hall, some even larger than my father's, and executed in the typical motifs.

What it was, as that doleful colleague of my father's would one day describe to me, was the extraordinary, arresting magnetism of the revised portrait. The prior version had been amazing, it was the most flattering picture of the man you could ever conceive—this was a younger, less paternal Mao, his hair slightly longer and thickened by the subtlest lilt, his cheek fully bloomed with that unrelenting, generative vigor, Mao the visionary, Mao the searchlight and the beacon, Mao the means and the ends.

But what my father newly achieved in the Chairman, as his colleague related, was to bring out in the man an as yet unknown order of his appeal. There was nothing particularly conspicuous that made it so, nothing even the most experienced artist could point out as the critical detail or details, say, the execution of this facial feature or that, the orchestrating of hues, the cast of his gaze, et cetera. Not any patent technique. The mastery was underneath, derived from a felicitous twining of the artist's intent and improvisation, his ambition and fear, the mystery of his knowing and the certitude of his incomprehension, everything transmuted into a skin-tingling charge. It was not abstract. Many of the viewers grew agitated, nudging and nosing one another to get closer, to find a better angle. Children drifted forward to touch but were blocked by Red Guards, who quite early on had to be stationed before the painting. Old women called out with hoarse, pained voices, some of the younger ones crying. Men were stricken, too, if unconsciously trying to quell their fervor by crossing their arms, bouncing on their heels.

"I remember thinking," my father's colleague said to me, "that these people were quite something, to come out and perform like that. The exhibition wasn't really about the art, this was understood, but it wasn't supposed to be some sort of rally, either. Perhaps aside from the artists themselves, it was not expected that one show zeal. But then I thought about the other galleries around the hall. Nowhere else had I seen anything but mostly quiet regard, as in a museum, much less such passionate, almost inappropriate, demonstrations. So I pushed my way through the people to see your father's painting again, which I'd assumed was the same and hadn't yet come around to see. This was near the close of the day's session. There were several dignitaries gathered, including an upper-level cultural official who had been a classmate of mine at university, and for a time a painter himself, decently talented but something of a hack. Minister Ma. He had the face of a camel, wide full lips and drowsy eyes, which made you think he wasn't too bright. But he was sharp and extremely ambitious and surely wanted to acknowledge the exhibition's most popular work, maybe show off his knowledge and discernment for his colleagues. A spot was cleared for their group and they stood before your father's painting nodding approvingly, one of them lightly clapping his hands, when Ma's expression, I noticed, began to turn, his grin melting into a slack wonder as he viewed the work. Without being aware of it he plied his parted lips with the tips of his fingers, massaging them deeply, almost pleasurably, and it was then that I followed Ma's eyes back to your father's work.

"Naturally I was already viewing it, as it was right in front of me. Again, on first glance, it seemed unchanged. Because the reworking was technically subtle I wasn't truly seeing how different it now was, how radically altered. But as I went over it the portrait revealed itself more. I was awestruck, feeling as if I might be overcome, though still not certain exactly why. By this point, however, Minister Ma's chin was a rigid triangle, his brow knitted up tightly. He, too, had begun to register what your father had achieved, and I have to admit that he comprehended it before I did. He cuffed his fellow bureaucrats into a circle and spoke to them at length, periodically pointing back stiffly at the portrait of Chairman Mao, who peered out at all of us with the most imperturbable glow.

"It was fortunate your father was busy in another part of the hall. For no one should have to witness a work of his being taken down in the midst of an exhibition. There was a groan from the onlookers when Ma ordered it removed, and even stray remarks like 'Hey, what's going on?' and 'But that's our favorite!' though of course nobody owned up to them. After it was gone they moved on, and those others who hadn't yet viewed it couldn't have a care for what had been hanging in that blank stretch of wall.

"But I will tell you that your father's Mao was etched into Minister Ma's mind, as it was in my own. I can still see the portrait clearly. I said how your father had compelled me to revere Mao, to love him, when I had no wish to. It was sublime political art. But this rendition went beyond that. I am an open-minded man but even to me it was very unsettling. In your father's hand, as Ma indicated to his cohort, Mao was too beautiful. Too lovely. There was a hedonistic cast to the portrait. And he was right: it was not simply that his Mao made you love him. He made you want to *make love* to him. He made Mao, well, erotic. An object of carnal desire."

Soon thereafter, Red Guards located my father and escorted him from the exhibition hall. He had no idea what was going on, as no one told him what he had done wrong. He was marched to the local police station, where they put him in a holding cell with thieves and drunks, who must have been tasked with beating him, which they did. When my mother and I were finally allowed to see him two days later, he had two black eyes and a broken nose. A lower tooth had been knocked out. My mother could not stop crying, her sobs making her nearly choke. My father was crying, too, foul spittle streaming from his grotesquely swollen mouth. I was as upset as they were but I couldn't cry because I was frightened into a state of shock, seeing my father like that. All the while his cellmates mocked us.

The minister enlisted the other officials and had my father brought up on charges of sedition and, aptly or not, public indecency. A trial was held during which his previous works, those lavishly colorful paintings of Old Beijing and their bourgeois tableaux, were unearthed from storage and displayed in the courtroom as evidence of his long-corrupted, decadent character. The dean of the Academy, along with several of my father's faculty colleagues and students, testified to his moral degeneracy, which he did not dispute; though he never quite understood why he was being pilloried, as he had no intention of denigrating Chairman Mao, there was no benefit in refuting the charges, the only hope, via complete cooperation, being a more lenient sentence, which in my father's case was nine years' labor (instead of twelve) at a coal mining facility in Inner Mongolia. After the sentencing, he was paraded through the street market in an ox-cart with two university professors convicted of related crimes, shoppers heartily jeering at them and hurling pieces of steamed bun and rotten fruit. We were reunited eventually, but he was not at all the same. I'll tell you more later, but he was not my father when I saw him again. He was just another man.

All this happened with breathtaking swiftness, like a ferocious but short-lived summer storm. For we didn't know that my mother was already under investigation, and that within days she would be indicted and then jailed in the same police station where my father awaited trial, though in a small holding cell crowded with a dozen or so other women. Meanwhile I was taken in by a distant cousin of my mother's, a pleasant enough man whose wife forbade me to go outside, so their neighbors would never know I was there. My mother, along with many of the others, got terribly sick in the holding cell, contracting what must have been influenza. She was unwell to begin with, not sleeping much or really eating during the ordeals at the Academy and my father's trial. I knew instinctively that she was in peril. It happened that she was one of two women who developed pneumonia, or so my mother's cousin delicately tried to explain as he handed me off to a state foster-care worker. It wasn't until I was officially resettled with a new family, in an agricultural area in north-central China, that I fully understood that she was dead.

Now, finally, I can come to the point of what I've been telling you.

It is often difficult to live just one life. I was sent to a village somewhere south of Wuwei, in Gansu province; it wasn't actually a village, where I lived, more a series of small farms that formed a loosely knit commune that snaked in a narrow column up and down the valley. But what it most seemed like to me, as a boy of the city, was a grim infinity of arid plains and brown hills. This was even before Mao's "Up to the Mountains, Down to the Villages" program, when millions of urban, mostly privileged, youth were sent to the countryside to learn the lessons of rural work and life and shed their bourgeois tendencies. I was young enough that I had no such bent, although my foster brothers, both older and stronger than I, believed I still did, and for several years, until I grew big enough to defend myself, regularly pummeled any sophistication out of me.

Heng and Fu: merely thinking their names brings an acidity to my tongue. Imagine a pair of skinned rabbits, though standing erect and near man-sized, with ropy, muscled limbs and crew-cut hair, massaging their pectorals while grinning at you, and you'll know the fundamental scene of my youth. Picture them shirtless, because most of the days we were all shirtless (save my foster mother), for it was a desert valley and easily reached 40° C before dropping sometimes to 4° C at night, so that I'd even find myself wedging between

Heng and Fu for warmth, which they'd allow without thrashing me, for selfish reasons of course. They were not complete idiots. Coal was costly and we had to squirrel away every last stick of firewood for the winter, as there were hardly any trees, just scattered thickets of brush and thorns. But if I wasn't quick enough scooting away in the frigid morning one of them might try to jab his thumb in my ass, crowing like a rooster as he poked.

Otherwise I'd slip out and feed the chickens, pissing while they ate in the dawn and watching the steam rise and dissipate against the faraway backdrop of the leathery hills, the lingering moon, from crescent to full, floating above them. It was the sole beauty in that place. I'd start my other chores of collecting the eggs and drawing well water for my foster mother and after breakfast sweep out the chicken house before the sun made it too stinky. She and her husband were probably just a few years older than my folks but they seemed like grandparents to me, their faces so drawn and lined and deeply lacquered from the ferocious sunlight that they looked slow-smoked, barbecued. Unlike their sons they were mostly kindly people, slow in their movements and quick to chuckle through the gaps in their teeth and almost preternaturally resigned to anything that might happen, no doubt from living in a forsaken place, where there was little water and poor soil and constant winds that in winter sawed through you and in summer plugged every pore with a fine bitter dust. They were illiterate as well, which their sons, who managed a few years of school, took advantage of every chance they had, misrepresenting, among other things, the annual notices from the prefecture office indicating a scant increase in their stipend for housing and feeding me, the boys skimming most of the difference. I would have alerted my foster parents but was afraid Heng and Fu might actually dispose of me in some gully if I was no longer a source of monthly profit, my role as punching bag being only so valuable.

I was a worthy hand in the fields, at least once I grew strong enough. For aside from the two dozen or so chickens, which gave us eggs and then a treat of meat whenever one of them stopped laying or got mauled (there were foxes we had to keep at bay), the family farm produced watermelons, my foster father always saying to the wholesalers who seasonally trucked them away that they were the finest watermelons in all of China, and therefore the world. They must have heard that from him every harvest, and every harvest they surely shrugged him off, not wanting to pay him a yuan more. But he said it out of sheer pride, for it was likely true; his watermelons, smallish, about the size of soccer balls, were better than any I have ever had, the flesh practically crisp to the bite, gushing with the sweetest pure juice, the exact flavor of which we have been trying to capture for a special bubble tea at the frozen-yogurt shop, though as yet unsuccessfully. It was the extreme dryness and the heat that made the watermelons so great, but waiting around for them to mature in that climate was a punishment that you could not help but think was warranted, for there was very little to do once the fields were prepared and the planting was done. We'd maintain the irrigation channels for the infrequent rains but otherwise a watermelon plant is self-sufficient, it sends out its lair of vines and nests its fruit within spiky thickets of foliage that seem to turn greener and more vigorous the hotter the sun burns. Not vulnerable like grapes or tomatoes, a watermelon grows with a steadfast confidence.

Because of this, sloth was our primary mode. My foster parents tended the family vegetable garden that by high summer was meager and desiccated, and there was no school in session for us boys. There was no radio and no TV, and no programs even if we had had them. I got a few books from a kind teacher, which I read over and over again until I could stand them no more, tales about Mao's circle and their exploits and deeds, written and illustrated for children. So we hid from the harsh sunlight beneath personal lean-tos we fashioned from burlap sacks stitched together and extended like an awning off the chicken fencing and propped on walking sticks, each of us boys lying down on the bare dirt beside where the hens scratched about, though usually they crowded themselves within a wedge of shadow next to the coop, unmoving, unblinking. The adults drank a gritty, milky liquor one of their farmer friends made and then snoozed in the house, which was stifling but less so in the sunken well of the cooking area, where the ground was damper and cooler. When the sun finally set in the early evening we'd have a meal of beans and squash and boiled eggs and then we boys would set out to hunt for squirrels or rabbits that we rarely bagged, Heng and Fu being poor shots. I wasn't any better but the times they let me have a try I could bear waiting for the quarry to come into the clear before pulling the trigger, and had a slightly higher kill rate.

Naturally there were children on the neighboring farms but we saw them only at certain harvest times, when we could hitch rides on the trucks that moved produce up and down the valley. Once, we got dropped off quite far from home and had to hike back through fields and then the foothills on a trail that led past a farm worked by people we didn't know.

It was late afternoon and viciously hot and we were hoping the farmers would let us drink from their well, but as we approached the homestead we crouched behind a busted old cart when we saw a young woman bathing herself out back with a bucket and soap and washcloth. There were a few people still down in the fields and so she'd probably taken this opportunity to come back solo and bathe, standing contented in the sun, completely naked. Her complexion was dark from farming but otherwise she was as pale as the flesh of a pear, and to us boys—I was ten, my foster brothers twelve and thirteen—she was the perfected ripeness of the earth. She had a friendly face and was probably fifteen, though already womanly, her breasts shuddering as she scrubbed an underarm, the dark hair between her legs clumped sudsy and slick, and I think we only noticed that something was different about her when she reached over to scrub her other foot without switching hands. Amazing, that we hadn't realized it: one of her arms was badly shriveled and foreshortened, its hand also smaller, stiffened and clawlike.

I was startled by the malformation but it only made her more precious in my eyes, her beauty somehow magnified, rather than marred, by the stunted limb. One of my foster brothers must have guffawed and the girl, instantly covering herself, turned in our direction and caught sight of our figures huddled behind the junked cart; she screamed, which prompted the people in the field to start running toward the homestead. We ran then, too, Fu bolting first back up the foothill path, with me closely following. Heng, the eldest, tottered behind us, unable to avert his gaze from the poor, terrified girl and having some difficulty running, as his member was distending his sackcloth shorts.

That girl was the source of conversation for us boys for the rest of that growing season. We called her One Wing and my foster brothers wrestled over who would marry her, and I'm quite certain that it was this lovely image that lit their feral minds when they got the idea to molest a hen one afternoon, just getting badly scratched and pecked for their moronic trouble. They tried sex with rotten watermelons, too, poking a hole and humping until the whole thing split and disintegrated. I was steering clear of them then, slipping off to hiding places I had, a dry creek bed and a cave, rereading my handful of books, sometimes even backward. Meanwhile everything browned and withered under the unblinking sun as we waited for the watermelons to mature for market. We never went hungry but by late August our burnt-out garden was pretty much depleted and our well was near bottoming out and brackish and we resorted to harvesting some of the melons to get by, sustaining ourselves in that last lean stretch of weeks with watermelons and eggs, eggs and watermelons. It's not a combination you'd ever choose if you were deserted someplace and could have only two things to eat, but it turns out that they're a sustaining pair. The watermelon was our drink and our fruit and our sweet, plus our salt and sour, too, as my foster mother pickled the rinds as an accompaniment to the eggs, which we ate fried, scrambled, steamed in a custard, boiled hard and soft, and then, when we finally ran out of cooking fuel, that we gulped down raw. Even raw, for sake of variety, instead of from a cup or bowl, we'd either crack them straight into one another's mouths (I'd only let my foster mother or father do that for me) or else lop off the top and suck them in such a way that you drew out the whites before the creamy yolks. Heng and Fu would have a competition of eating them whole, popping them into their mouths as a snake might crush and drain them and then try to spit out the flattened shell casing in one piece. Try it; crushing an egg with just your tongue and hard palate is much more difficult than you'd think.

By the end, just before the middlemen came for the small mountains of melons we'd mounded in the yard, which meant my foster mother could go to Wuwei and buy bags of white rice and potatoes and fresh greens and meats and fleshy fruits like peaches, we'd feel like watermelons ourselves, our bellies and veins groaning with juice, our eyes shot through with pinkish lines, our breath candied. We were half starving but totally bloated. I remember having to pee hourly, relieving my pent-up bladder in forceful, hosing arcs, making muddy patches wherever I went. Heng and Fu naturally splattered everything in their path: the carts we used to collect melons, the sides of the barn, the long-suffering hens, each other, me. My foster mother would complain about the sharp stink, hollering at us to use the outhouse, but she understood how quickly the urge could well up, as I'd regularly catch sight of her squatted in the fields, her skirt billowing with blasts of hot breeze, my foster father shamelessly fountaining his weak, sporadic sprays mere steps beside her.

10.

A QUANTUM OF SWEETNESS.

Pretty boss, how Pong put that. He rarely failed to startle me with everything he knew or did, but it is the unexpected felicity of his expressions that still haunts me. I'll admit in this instance it's my underlying plain vanilla bigotry, for Pong employed the English language as well as any highly educated native, my diluted hapa self still too lame to bridge the divide between his funky accent and superior word-and-idea making. For what he meant was not just that a person should have a rightful share of whatever way you'd like to define sweetness, but also that the sweetness itself carries a special levy of contemplation of the infinitudes of sweetness that will go untasted, be forever unknown.

Sure, it's sad to consider the vast waste of it all. But there's hope, too, for the more you ponder all those fields groaning (metaphorically and not) with overripe, about-to-split #1 Gansu watermelons, the more you feel a duty to clang the triangle, gather folks round, and exhort them to do as I learned after being abroad: be greedy in your appreciations. Practice extravagant gratitude. Savor whatever your portion. This may sound like *carpe diem* but what I really mean is for the *dies* to *carpere te*, to have the moment, the person, the world, grab you right back in their full rankness and glory.

Still, I'm lucky that I'm vertical, and ambulatory, with a near-total-recall memory and a decent appetite and junk that still works. Maybe that's funny to hear from someone only twenty years old, but once I started hanging with Pong and his friends I began aging like a wheel of soft cheese, some process of ripening slowly churning inside of me while to everyone else I just sported a slightly crustier rind.

Am I the better for it? Hope so. More generous and wise? Maybe. Or just some gamier version of myself, this Tiller who's become even more of an acquired taste? Likely. Ultimately, though, you can't know what's really developed until someone or something cleaves you open.

Sometimes, of course, that cleaving is also a closing, like in the case of Pong's once supremely gifted artist father, who now just hoards cut-rate scallions and frozen tilapia, already brown-spotted mangoes and limp Thai basil, the papery skins of garlic cloves forever petaling from his apron. But maybe it's merciful that he's fogged in with the senility that those years in the labor camp brought on, this reeducation that the human animal must self-practice in order to persist.

But speaking of persistence, let me return to my dear Val.

You'll recall she had disappeared, or at least gotten scarce. Needless to say, not the ideal scenario for a boy like me. Think of how you feel at the very top of the roller coaster, just before the apex, when the pulley chain beneath you makes its last click and you're about to free-fall, for how my chest kind of floated, anchored to nothingness.

After spending a few minutes composing myself on the tiled floor in the corner of our bathroom, I came out and pretended everything was fine and normal. I had to assume Val had taken a walk because we only have the one car, but when an hour passed I started to wonder. And then desperately tried not to wonder. I told Victor Jr. to chill but he hardly heard me for the music he was listening to on his earbuds—maybe he was psychically bunkering, too—and I slipped out, at first walking, and then sprinting, straight up to the quarry. It was very bright and very quiet, the drilled white rock faces harshly reflecting the sunlight. Below, the quarry floor was obscured by weedy bushes and random chunks of stone. I called her name, the echo of it so clear and euphonious that I thought I had a twin, which only trebled my worry. *Val Val Val.* I called again and made myself feel even worse. A terrible image then crossed my mind and I hopped down the stairlike ledges, going lower and lower. Finally, I peered over, bracing for the sight of some limb jutting out from the brush or from between the stones. But there was nothing; just newspaper circulars and plastic bottles and plastic bags and broken plastic toys. The sight of litter was never so heartening. It was harder to climb back up and by the time I reached the top I was breathing so hard I had to sit on the metal divider to catch my breath, my body sweaty and ponderous. Though to tell the truth, ever since sending Todd Brown off with his slashed tire a couple months before, I'd been getting an awful sensation in my chest, like every sad, weird, scary thought I had was catching on something and gathering into a gnarly, choking mass. It's enough sometimes to make you want to be rooted out, wholly scoured of everything that makes you *you.*

I hurried back to the house, checked that Victor Jr. was still jacked in, then parked myself on the front stoop and waited like any loyal dog. But unlike a dog, who isn't burdened by a sense of time, who might wait out there forever if he doesn't get too cold or hungry, I immediately initiated a process of self-immolation, beginning by calling Val a thousand or so times on one of the flip phones we tossed every month as recommended by the feds, finally chucking it into the pachysandra that grew along the front property fence. I soon retrieved it, panicked that it might be buzzing. I felt too buzzy myself and so went around to the back deck and grabbed from our bedroom the mini-bong Val and I fired up nightly, hoping to chill myself out, when I heard the sliding door open. I lowered the pipe between my thighs but the first thing Victor Jr. said was, "I know what that is."

"I doubt it," I said uselessly. Though we never tried too hard to hide it, Val still didn't want him to know we smoked weed. It wasn't about its being a drug, as she regularly went on about the ravages of alcohol abuse (her folks had been heavy drinkers), but that she didn't want him thinking we would do anything even remotely illegal or against the rules. She'd chirp at me whenever I rolled through a stop sign, or crept even a notch over the speed limit, and she had always stated his actual age at all-you-can-eat restaurants, when a tiny fib would set him loose on the buffet for free. Of course it was because of their situation, now our situation, which she would eventually have to explain in full to him, meaning the traitorous trade Victor Sr. and his business partners had been involved in and how she was the one who snitched. Full disclosure. She was afraid of the boy growing up with the idea that illicit conduct was in his blood, and that this knowledge would make him think less of himself and lead him to do antisocial things. Not that pot smoking is antisocial, often exactly the opposite, but still.

"It's a peace pipe," Victor Jr. said, sitting down next to me. I figured I had to show him the bong now, which was shaped like a chemistry lab flask. He held it like a pro, though he tried to wrap his lips around the mouthpiece instead of tucking them inside the opening. My reflex was to show him the correct method but braked, picturing Val's aghast face. He swirled the water and sniffed it.

"It smells so bad! I want to try."

I shook my head. "Have to be old like me."

"You're not old!" he bellowed. And in his Movietone narrator voice: "Heck, you're just a goddamn kid!"

I couldn't argue and didn't try.

"I can smell the smoke sometimes. Then you and Mom get all quiet."

"That's how it works," I said. "Peace and quiet."

"But how come Mom makes those funny noises?"

"What funny noises?"

"*Uhh . . . uhh . . . uhh.* After the peace and quiet."

"That," I said, starting down a path that I knew was already leading nowhere, "is her relaxing."

"She sure loves relaxing." He looked like he wanted to ask a certain question but he didn't yet have the knowledge to understand what he didn't know. Or did he? "So where is she?" he muttered, something in him trying to make it sound like "she" was just another person among all the other persons on this planet.

"Shopping mall," I said, a seriously lame answer, as he knew we ordered everything online. I could feel his disappointment in the quality of my lie, which made it that much harder for him to pretend that nothing unusual was going on. I wanted to pretend the same so I clammed up, and we sat there for a long brain-dead stretch, but finally I couldn't help myself and torched a bowl right in front him, going especially deep and coughing one of those coughs where you're sure your eyeballs are going to pop and fall out. Victor Jr. saw his opening and tugged at the bong but I resisted, if only because I was sure Val would walk up right at that moment.

But she didn't, and I didn't budge, though to placate the boy I blew a stream of blue smoke into his face. He made a show of inhaling, clasping his hands behind his head while filling his lungs like it was dawn breaking over Mont Blanc. I realize this is the sort of idiotic shit frat boys do to their pets, but I wasn't looking for anything like laughs. I just wanted the chubster to be okay, to blunt the incipient edge, plus I definitely couldn't deal with the idea of his wondering whether his mother had abandoned him. Or worse. I'd been starting to think about his situation/being/fate a hell of a lot more than I'd expected, which I guess adds up to a genuine devotion, something I would say to Val when she finally showed: *Hey, lady, look what I had to do for your son, look at how infected with loving I am.*

Victor Jr. must have read my mind, because he snuggled against me, slinging my arm around his shoulder and resting his head against my chest. Whether he was stoned or not he was definitely not behaving like the usual Victor Jr., mewling weakly as he nosed deeper into my armpit. I pictured Clark witnessing this, me and my de facto son, and him thinking that I was both more breathtakingly messed up and sneakily capable than he had ever imagined. In fact, I had the urge to take a selfie of us and send it to him, but in the end that would have been most unfair, and kind of cruel besides, and I couldn't ever bear that.

VeeJ was now drooling a little, and let out a pirrup of a fart, and I wondered whether the weed was causing him to revert in a way I sometimes do, too. Don't I want to suckle at a lollipop or a cold longneck of beer? Don't I need Val to dab the corners of my mouth of Doritos dust with her pinkie, so I don't leave stains on the pillow-case? Don't I want to tent under the sheets beside her warm, smooth skin, infuse myself in her emanations, and just plain exist?

I do. I do. I do.

Somehow I found myself back in the car but now with Victor Jr., and we set out and looked for her. I probably shouldn't have been at the wheel after smoking, especially with our tyke writ large in shotgun, but he, too, seemed to want to try something, anything, rather than hanging around like tree moss. We slowly crossed town six or seven times on various vectors, my mind mapping points where she might have holed up, a coffee shop or department store, the potential routes in between, both of us doing recon inside the stores, then meeting back at the entrance. At this point Victor Jr. had grown strangely quiet and I thought I'd distract him with some drive-thru French fries but although he pushed the golden batons between his choppers like someone feeding logs into a wood chipper, he looked no happier when he was done, idly drilling (using the straw still in his mouth) at the remaining ice crud in his soda cup. Then, without warning, he began to sniffle. He wasn't much of a crier so I couldn't pretend that this wasn't out of the ordinary. I touched his shoulder and a fierce shock of static jolted us; he stared at me like I'd intended it, not angry but scared. And then he began to cry harder, and rather than try to soothe him I drove as fast as I could back home.

I hadn't even turned off the ignition when the poor kid leapt out and bolted into the house. When I entered he was dashing about as quickly as I'd ever seen him move, checking every room, peering into the closets, even insanely opening some drawers, in case she had shrunk herself to hide. I trailed him, trying to come up with something consoling, but by the time I caught up to him he was lying facedown at the foot of our bed, felled by grief into a catatonic sprawl. It was no joke. I know the coldness of the moment. You're suddenly in a tundra, the light so bright you can't see, the whole great swirl of everything you ever knew or did with her about to blow away like the smoke wisp from a match, gone so fast it never seemed lit.

I looked down at Victor Jr. as if from a dizzying height and flashed on the idea that maybe I should get scarce myself. Just walk out the door, you dope, and start running. This was my fear talking. But then in one swift clean-and-jerk I picked him up and craned him onto his mother's side of the bed. He was like a sack of tapioca, this marbly heavy jelly. He didn't open his eyes or make a sound, pretending to be dead. I played along. I straightened out his lifeless legs. I folded his arms in an X over his chest, traced a cross on his forehead, even smoothed down his eyelids, like I knew he knew I should. And then I pulled the bedsheet up over him, inch by slow inch, lightly veiling his face. He stayed corpse still, not even moving the sheet with his breath, which for a second really scared me. But I understood his psychic instinct in the face of this worst of all worlds: hibernate forever. He needed a proper send-off, so I started humming the opening bars of "Amazing Grace," really letting myself go, trilling and running, and I was actually working myself into a proper wretched feeling, which I sensed Victor Jr. appreciated, churning it up deep from my gut like an old-time preacher. And as my pipes warmed, and the air heaved, I couldn't help but wonder if my mother, out there someplace in the universe, might pause for a long second, tuning in the bars of a phantom song.

"What *the fuck* is going on?"

It was Val, sporting a three-alarm scowl, but it was Val nonetheless, which was joy enough. She looked okay, if tired, her hair matted on one side, like she'd fallen asleep at a desk.

"We're playing Dead Baby!" Victor Jr. shouted, popping up in the bed like a haunted-house ghoul. You'd think that he would have leapt right into her arms, but no, the boy mastered himself and fell back in the bed, covering up his face and lying stiff. We waited for him to budge. Val announced she wanted a hug. Nothing. She told the lad she'd missed him. Not a toe wiggle. She said goodbye, and finally he bleated an *O-kay, Moth-er* in a Liam-like voice, a notation that he was still angry with her and traumatized but in no way a basket case. Victor Jr. was nothing if not aptly named.

They hugged then, the boy clinging to her like a baby koala bear, his weight making her hunch over. He let go and ran out, hollering something about making a fresh-pasta lasagna for dinner. I tried to sidle up and sniff at her but she sent me off, saying she wanted to shower. I offered to join her but she gave me a look. My terror for what she might have done up at the quarry or, say, out on the inter-state, sashaying into the nighttime truck traffic, was now mixed up with this raging, self-nuking hell of thoughts about what she'd done all night, and where she'd bedded down, and although I was not the jealous type—I have never felt entitled to anybody's loyalty—it felt like a dull shiv was unstitching my lungs from the rest of me. I wanted to say something simultaneously self-pitying and mean but I was unable to form any words. So I went to the kitchen, where VeeJ was already getting busy, and he imperiously waved me off like any fo-cused chef de cuisine, and I loaded up one of his active-shooter-training games but soon got tired of exploding zombie brains and wandered out to the back deck, which was becoming my favorite place in the house aside from VeeJ's laden table and our flannel-sheeted bed. Here was my unkempt rented Eden, ringed by rusty cy-clone fencing that was a perfect trellis for the weeds, the neighboring ranch houses identically cloistered, and I thought that if something happened to me I should be buried in this anonymous ultra-ordinary place, because what other spot could be as suitable?

I thought this is what I ought to say to Val, when suddenly she sat down beside me on the steps. Of course I was mum.

"I'm sorry, sweetie," she said. She had put on a Stagno Y sweat-shirt and pajama bottoms, her hair still slicked wet from the shower and blotting her collar. "My phone died sometime yesterday but I should have borrowed someone else's."

"Where were you holed up?" I said, surprised to hear myself making it sound like some kind of welcome junket.

"Oh God," she said. "It was some dive bar near the hospital. It was empty most of the time except for me and a few semi-hobo types."

"I bet they were lining up to buy you drinks."

"Yeah but with what? One guy in a Robin Hood hat had to count out coins to pay for his beer. The bartender had to spot him a quarter."

"So what were you drinking?"

"Does it matter?"

"I just want to know. I want the picture."

"Ginger ales with lime."

"No bitters? That's how I do yours."

She nodded. "Definitely no bitters. It was a shot and beer place, with a pool table and one of those shuffleboard bowling machines."

"Did you eat anything last night?" For some reason it felt right to be solicitous, if only as a way of not getting to a subject I didn't want to get to, but unfortunately would.

"I wasn't hungry. And at the bar they only had a jar of those pickled sausages. So no."

"But you ended up hanging out anyway."

She glanced down at her hands. "I was about to leave. Then it got crammed with people in scrubs. I guess the evening shift had just ended at the hospital. Nurses mostly, and some paramedics, too. Did I ever mention my mom was a nurse?"

She hadn't, as we were only intermittently drilling down on our family stuff, but anybody could see where this was heading, the linkage to her mother, how she didn't want to stay but got caught up in a swell of feeling at the sight of those sea-green scrubs, the nostalgic scent they brought in with them of rubbing alcohol and latex gloves, the padded footfall of their orthotic shoes. And I was pretty much right; Val told me how one of the female nurses got to chatting with her, then introduced her to the gang, and they coaxed her into doing a Kamikaze shot with them, which is how they opened their postshift festivities. The Kamikaze led to a Buttery Nipple to an Irish Car Bomb, the whole thing quickly pivoting to several rounds of Jägers. Naturally things got fuzzy after that, Val confirmed. I should have gotten up then and checked on VeeJ in the kitchen, but I sat there tasting the souring spittle in my mouth. You'd think that after enduring certain unendurable moments on my recent travels, a little relationship trouble would be nothing but a blip of my aortic valve, the briefest extra flapping. But I tell you it was a swollen river, overrunning the banks.

For that's when Val, being the stand-up woman she is, told me about the rest of the night. After last call the nurse who'd introduced her around invited her to have a nightcap at her place nearby. Two male paramedics tagged along. Val didn't go into extensive details, and I didn't ask for any, but I could picture them no problem, two fit, stand-up dudes who were more community-inclined than Keefer and Tommy, one of them a swarthy guy with tatted, muscled forearms perfectly suited for chest compressions, the other a soft-spoken weekend dirt biker with longish blond hair. They were all pretty hammered but continued drinking some White Russians one of the guys fixed and during some drunken swaying dancing the nurse was bumping and grinding with the Chest Massager, as they had some history. By the time the song ended they had decamped to her bedroom, leaving Val and Dashing Dirt Bike to their slow juke.

"What was playing?" I asked.

"The song? I don't know. Maybe it was U2?"

I began humming the melody from "I Still Haven't Found What I'm Looking For."

She shook her head.

I hummed some moany measures of "With or Without You." A weary frown fogged her face, the bars obviously jogging something.

"We didn't dance for long," she said. "I was so tired. We sat on the couch and I think we both passed out for a while. When I woke up we were kissing."

I must have looked freaked because she said, "It wasn't like that. He wasn't a creep. It wasn't an assault." She took an unsteady breath. "Listen. I was bombed but I knew what was happening."

"What else happened?" I said, which in this case was the verbal equivalent of intentionally sticking your hand into a whirring fan.

"Kissing, mostly," she weakly answered. She was going to say something else but then stopped. Of course the *mostly* laid waste to me. I was instantly charred rubble. A too-well-lit porn trailer was already surging through my circuits, featuring a totally shaved Val, a mud-flecked naked dude in a motocross helmet, and an S&M restraint fashioned entirely from stethoscopes. I wanted to tear out my skewered yakitori heart but a tingle was simultaneously swarming my lower unit, the confusion and welling only deepening my agitation.

Val rubbed her cheeks and temples hard with her fists. She had started to tear up but braked herself into the sort of semi-crying that didn't seek consolation, like when you're a kid and accidentally injure yourself doing something you knew you shouldn't.

She said, "You want to hit me?"

"What?"

"You can hit me, if you want. You can do whatever. Victor Sr. did sometimes. It's okay."

"I don't want to hit you!" I cried, nauseated and then shocked by the idea of her husband doing that to her. Of her cowering. But if I was telling the truth, I almost did lash out, at least in that millisecond of heinous rage. I could have so easily done it. Slapped her face. Just once. It was because she said it that it became something real, though that's no excuse at all. The thought of having done it, and playing it back forever, I'd die every time, hating myself incrementally more, until I couldn't stand it any longer and ended up wanting to hit someone again.

"You want to split up with me?"

I shook my head.

"If you do I get it . . ."

I said no. No! No!

"I'm sorry, T. Oh God. I'm so sorry. What's wrong with me? I'm fucking miserable . . ."

We were hugging then, both of us wildly shaking, and trying to quell each other's shaking. The part of me that was aggrieved and righteous kept darkly counseling to draw this out, make her wallow in her misery, taste every drop of my bitterness, but what was more frightening than my own hurt was her gloom, which I could see now wasn't just a lingering system, some atmospheric disturbance, but something with firm contours, its own purposeful shape. I could practically feel its pulse while we embraced, beating away inside of her, and I understood how if you couldn't evict it you might get on to the idea of obliterating yourself, to be freed for good.

I said, "There's nothing wrong with you. Nothing we can't fix. You're great."

"I'm not great," she said, uncoiling from me. "I'm actually awful."

"Well, I hate Victor Sr. now."

"Please don't," she said. "He only did it a couple times. Okay, three. And never in front of Victor Jr. I probably did something to make him. I know I shouldn't say that but it's true. I could make him crazy. All day I've been thinking how it is that I've gotten here, with you. How lucky I am. Fuck!" Her mouth went crooked, her chin wrinkling, like she was about to undam a whitewater of tears. But Val's a tough chick. She reset, sighing deeply, the sigh of a thousand sorrows.

"Do you know how much I adore you? You're always good to me and Victor Jr., who adores you, too. You know that, right?"

"I guess so."

"He does. You get everything he needs for his cooking with that magic card of yours. You let him watch whatever movie he wants to watch. You taught him how to do fractions! You always say yes."

"Sounds like I'm a spoiler and enabler."

"Only if he took you for granted. I made him promise me he won't."

"What about you?"

"It's not like that." She spoke softly, soberly. "Sometimes, for no reason, I ruin things. I don't want to, but I do. Now you know. I haven't been hiding this from you. I've just been so calm and happy since we met, I thought it was finally gone."

I tried to kiss her but Val got up and stepped barefoot into the sorry grass, her just-showered soles getting soiled by the patches of dirt. This was her torturing herself, as she was fastidious about her feet, their soaking and buffing and lotioning, which she did at least every other night. Sometimes if we'd smoked I rubbed lotion into her heels, because she'd be relaxed and not too ticklish. It was then that I could glimpse her as a much older woman, reclining against the headboard with her eyes gently shut, her same-styled hair more salt than pepper, her cheekbones more pronounced, the skin of her throat slightly mottled and pebbly, and I'd get this quiet burst of happiness from the thought of all that rich time having passed through her, like a good radiation.

Of course it's never only good. I wanted to tell her if she was still heartbroken it wasn't because of anything she was or did. I know this as well as anybody. She was heartbroken because of the world, which will betray us without even meaning to.

I said, "Maybe we should make a change. Let's leave this house and this town. It certainly won't be hard to find a nicer place. We can live large, or at least larger. I have the card. Nothing's stopping us."

"The case officers won't like it," Val answered. "It'll just be more work for them. Plus Stagno, remember, is meant to be a kind of a punishment for me."

"They don't have to know," I said. "We can hide out from them, too. We can leave most of our stuff here and just go, like we're heading on an extended vacation."

"An extended vacation from my alias life?"

"Then think of it as a sabbatical, like professors take."

"Okay, T," Val said, brightening a little. "But what the fuck are we researching? What the fuck are we working on?"

I couldn't give a good answer, because what is anybody working on at the end of the day, the century, the epoch? A handful of extraordinary people come up with world-tilting ideas, but the rest of us, the 99.99 percent, we simply orbit.

So I told her, standing now, too. "VeeJ. He's got amazing talent, but also drive. What makes him tough to handle will also make him one of the greats. We'll throw everything we have at it."

"That's fine for me," Val said, taking my hand. "But you have your whole life ahead of you. I know you don't think it, but you're still so young. You have so much to go. Someone should be devoting herself to you, going step by step. Like me."

This last bit panged, and not because of the obvious chasm in my life. That will never be filled. What really got me was the idea of Val offering to be there, to ride along on my bumpy way. I fell into her then, and she let me, even pinning my face against her neck, and I couldn't help but assay her scent, try to parse whatever wasn't showered away, residual traces of secondhand cigarette smoke, the dried, boozy flop sweat, ambulance dude pheromones. But it was just Val, fleshy and soapy and damp. She squeezed a fistful of my hair. I slipped my hand down the back of her pajama bottoms, tracing her crack. She flared her end and kissed me, hard.

"Come on," she whispered, her voice huge in my ear. She tippy-toed so I could reach around and up. We were sucking face like the starved. It was awkward and then it wasn't, her one leg hooked about me. Our Stagno tango. The neighbors could easily watch us, or Victor Jr. could emerge any moment, but neither of us cared. Let them see our animal exertions. We're beasts of our own burdens, which never lighten.

11.

BUT I SHOULD GET BACK to the beginnings of my year abroad.

When we deplaned in Honolulu, I felt strangely remade. The nonstop from Newark had taken twelve hours, which in pauper class on a dreary US airline is tantamount to a harrowing, soul-snuffing bid in a medium-security penitentiary, though without even being fed, but with our Asian-based carrier's lie-flat seats and down-filled blankets and ever-topped-up drinks and snacks—it was my first time up front—the flight was a sort of buddies staycation, Pong and I eventually dozing off in our respective pods to some inane movie you wouldn't even pirate otherwise. I don't know what Pong dreamt of, if anything at all, but after listening to the woeful tale of his parents and his own harshly fostered youth, I dreamt I was one of those Gansu watermelons, rooted there in the crumbly, dusty earth beneath the roasting sun, my rind burning on the surface but my insides steadily filling, densifying, packing in so much juice that I could feel myself about to shear open, while dreading it and wishing it all at once. Someone might assert that I was fearful of my own potential, or transparently exhorting myself to develop some fucking psychic grit, and in neither case would I disagree. But the way things were different, after getting to know more about Pong, was that I felt less alone. I didn't mind being away from home and Dunbar, which was too complicated anyway. I didn't need to go back to my smugly non-elite college. I was simply keen to stick around Pong, and wait for whatever might develop.

That we were on Oahu seemed a crazy bonus. We walked through a section of the terminal open to the air and it was evident to my lungs to hoover all they could, they were instinctively greedy for the breeze that was not too wet and not too dry, and laced with what must have been plumeria, and calla lily, and wild ginger, and whatever else grew like weeds there even by the airport. It was a floral atmosphere that one of Pong's countless Chinese business partners actually canned and sold in smoggy Beijing and Shanghai, air supposedly drawn from the serene well of Diamond Head crater.

"You know what he called it?" Pong said to me at baggage claim, having noticed how I'd been lingering outside. "Diamond Head Morning Breath!"

We were still chuckling about that in the pickup area when a pearlescent-white crew-cab truck with spinner rims and a bed rack of surfboards flashed its brights and rolled up to us, followed by an electric-blue supercar, its roofline I swear no higher than my thigh. A sumo-wrestler-sized dude emerged from each vehicle, and they introduced themselves (they were brothers) and with their huge hands very carefully deposited our luggage in the truck bed while Pong and I climbed in the backseat of the cab. Lucky Choi curled himself behind the wheel of the sports car and without a word took off, squealing the extra-wide rear rubber. I'd figured we'd check in to a hotel and hook up later at Lucky's vacation home, where we were scheduled to meet with a jamu consultant Drum Kappagoda had set us up with, but in the middle of the ride one of the brothers, Lono, passed back beach towels, plus two pairs of board shorts and rash guards, each appropriately sized.

Pong said, "Lucky got word while we approached the airport that the swell coming in was too good to pass up. Plus, he'll only go at dusk so he can avoid tanning. He doesn't want to look like a peasant."

I peeped, "We're going *surfing* now?"

"You have surfed before?" Pong asked.

I told him no but that I'd done plenty of bodyboarding, this in the cold brown waves at the Jersey Shore.

"Well, you can hang out at the beach park."

"We-got-bo-dy-board-and-fins," Lono said, in a lilting local accent that was like a continuous single-note song: *da-da-da-da-da* . . .

"Very good, thank you," Pong said. Then to me: "Lucky has everything for the water, snorkel masks, paddleboards, outrigger canoes, plus more than fifty surfboards, by my count. He is something of a madman that way. But if you're too tired from the flight . . ."

I realized now that Lucky kind of scared me, much in the way an older cousin of mine, Drew, scared me. Drew was not a physically imposing kid or openly mean but he had a way of presenting things that made it clear the choice wasn't yours, like jumping off a rock ledge into a reservoir, which we did one summer when I was ten, only one of us having a fun time doing it.

"I'm game," I said, which was true enough. Lono then torched the end of a fat spleef and I passed it back to Pong, who took a most gentle toke, a measured dosing that seemed emblematic of his approach, trying everything while constantly assaying, monitoring, keeping things in balance.

"Too much bothers my throat," he said, aware of my observing him. "Plus, I don't want to be too relaxed, you know, out in the big waves."

I took a snarfing, choking hit, to calm myself, and I guess we must have gotten pretty chill, hotboxing in the crew cab as we inched along in the heavy traffic closer to Honolulu, then accelerating for a stretch as we passed peaky Diamond Head looming darkly on our right. It was just a few minutes before six p.m. but it seemed like night was coming on fast, the long, flat clouds turning from bloody orange to a bruised purple. When we reached the small seaside parking lot from where we would paddle out to the break, Lucky was there waiting for us in his lime-green rash guard and white board shorts.

"Haole boy gonna bodyboard," Lono told him.

"Great to hear!"

"Not full haole," Pong said, with a localized tang. "Korean, from mother side."

Lono glanced at me again, if still unimpressed. "Okay den, hapa."

I liked the sound of that word. Even though all my life people assumed I was just another average white boy, I now got a flash of surprise when reminded that I read that way. Maybe it was hanging out of late with Asians and South Asians, or getting tighter with Pong, or watching Lucky whitewash his face with handfuls of zinc oxide even at this late hour, which made me think of the opposite action, but whatever it was I felt drawn into some larger, broader flow, one that might rush me forth but not ruin me.

"Light's dying, brothers, let's go!" Lucky urged.

Pong and I changed behind the bushes while Lono and his brother, Derek, laid out our gear on the springy Bermuda grass. Derek, like Lono, had a planet-scaled body and was shaved of head, sporting these tiny gnarly ears that looked like the flappy fungi that sprout from trees. He dropped a nub of board wax in my palm. "Gotta love dat wave action, brah!" he cheered, and smiled like I was either his best bud or a complete fucking idiot. Then he and Lono curled themselves into the truck to sip beers while we had our water session, the bass box thumping out a jam of Hawaiian-style reggae.

Pong and Lucky launched themselves into the waters off Wailupe Circle and I followed, kicking forth on the bodyboard. The ocean was buoying and soft, like warm herbal tea, hardly any gradient from the skin, and within twenty yards I felt stable and centered atop the bodyboard and was moving efficiently through the water, using both my fins and my arms to keep up with Pong and Lucky, who were rhythmic and smooth as they glided through the calm water of the channel. The few other surfers out this late were now coming in, although about fifty yards off I could see someone dropping into a clean and well-formed shoulder-high wave. We paddled quickly toward the spot. After fighting through a set and duck diving three times we reached the swelling but glassy water beyond the break.

Pong said: "You don't have to catch anything. You can simply enjoy the nice water. Truly." He could see I was totally gassed from all the duck diving as I was gripping tightly on the board; it felt like a crust of lead had suddenly formed over my limbs. These guys were decades older than I was but when you lollygag as much as I do there's no magic reserve in youth. Lucky whistled to us, as we momentarily had our backs to the sea; a long, welling wall of water was approaching. The two of them immediately paddled laterally and I knew if I didn't kick hard toward it I might have to take it, too, or else go over the falls. The wave reached me and I floated up and over its smooth face and then watched it begin to crest in front of me, Lucky's head and then shoulders becoming visible as he got up and rode it, but it was a short one and he peeled off. Pong had duck dived and popped up about ten yards away from me.

"You know what you're doing!"

I nodded, though maybe more because my neck was stiffening from the prostrate position; I hadn't boarded much since middle school, though I'd go for any wave even if they were gnarly closeouts and was known as a hard little charger by the older local kids at the Jersey Shore, skeevy death-wishing shredders who by high school were snorting speed and trying to pimp out their girlfriends.

"But be careful," Pong said. "Do not allow yourself to go too far inside. A lot of reef there."

"Let's quit with the coffee talk!" Lucky shouted, as he skimmed back toward us. He led us to the lineup. We were all wearing the same highlighter-lime-green rash guard, which was critical in this dying light; soon enough it was the only way I could see them. The funny thing about watching skilled surfers is that they appear to tame the water, make the unruly waves into docile partners, and I was hollering with glee as I watched Pong get up on his longboard right in front of me, nearly catch the nose and wipe out, but then right himself and execute an elegant bottom turn that he followed by riding up on the shoulder and down the face before kicking out just as the wave collapsed behind him.

Lucky, using a much shorter board, carved some pretty radical turns against the backdrop of a shadowy horizon, the sun now setting but its lingering halo intense enough that their rash guards glowed, making it look like they were fireflies dancing over the water.

The sight of it got me motoring to catch a wave despite the fact that I could hardly see where I was going. I dropped in on one that was fatter and higher than any before, nearly head high if you were standing. I caught some air falling down the face but was able to carve a turn and zipped through the dimness, the wave rocketing me forward. I should have pulled out but kept going, skipping like a big flat stone out in front of the whitewater. Anyone with half a brain knows to be wary of an unfamiliar break, no less a reef break like this, where razor-edged crags of coral could be mere inches beneath the surface. I dropped off the board to stall myself and began the paddle back out, my arms already gone sodden and stiff, my lungs aching. When we'd first paddled out Pong had indicated the telltale "boiling" swirls on the surface that marked the danger, but now it was pretty much all simmering and I realized how reefy

it truly was. I'd had my head down trying to paddle harder and as
the jetting roar of an onrushing wave filled my ears I saw a wall and
thought, *Stupid boy, you're in the shit.*

"Shit."

Funny, how muted that voicing is. Unlike when you spill a few
drops of coffee on your shirt and you freak out like you got sprayed
with Ebola; now, when you're suddenly spinning head over knees in
lightless reef-studded waters, you burble, you murmur, you squeak
for your life.

I popped up in a vortex of foam, gulping air. Schooled by my
tumbles at the Jersey Shore, I had instinctively held my breath.
Somebody sharply whistled *Pheeeht!* but another, more ferocious
wall of water plowed me under again, the bodyboard ripped from
my hands. My right knee banged on coral and although it didn't
hurt right then I could tell from the spidery numbness that it had
been gouged. I curled up to shield my head but a second thought of
my poor knee and more jagged reef panicked me, making me buck
for air. I had to open up my mouth, take in my fill. I saw Clark,
opening the door to a couple grim-faced Dunbar cops. I saw my
mother, eternally unknowing. I was going to drown, or worse,
drown by half and for the rest of my days get fitted each morning
with a fresh colostomy bag and bib.

Then a flash caught my eyes: the neon green of a board shirt,
twisting and jerking mere yards below me in slightly deeper water.
Whoever it was, he was somehow stuck. I righted myself and bobbed
to the surface. The twilight was made brighter by a new rising moon
and I could see a green shirt paddling in the distance and I shouted,
"Over here!" but had to dip beneath an oncoming rush of whitewater. When I rose I took in three quick breaths, then the deepest
one I could, and dove.

I only had to go about five feet under, which was fortunate, as
the flow of the surf was working against me; without fins it would

have been impossible. Then I saw the figure move, his leash snagged by a bulbous column of reef. The surfboard was straining upward toward the surface. He'd undone the Velcro ankle strap but the rest of it had somehow wound around his calf, and now he could only weakly tug. I somehow found the cord. I braced myself against the prickly coral with my feet and pulled as hard as I could, twice, before it tore free. Then I kicked both of us up and corralled the surf-board, hugging him to it so that his head stayed just above the water.

It was Pong. My own breath sputtered. But before I knew it Lucky swooped in and pulled Pong across his board. I steadied it as he massaged Pong's back and chest and rolled him on his side, putting pressure on his belly. Pong soon bucked, coughed, then finally retched as if he were expelling a whole jellyfish, Lucky cradling him so he wouldn't get submerged in the wash. Pong managed a weak thumbs-up. We got him to lie belly down on the board and then positioned ourselves on either side to kick and paddle him in through the channel to shore.

Lono and Derek came for us fast when they saw their boss Lucky shouldering Pong. With my fins still on I was walking awkwardly behind them and dropped to the grass like everyone else, too exhausted to pull them off. I just sat there tasting the seawater dripping down from my hair as the others made sure Pong was all right, which he kept nodding that he was, at least between spats of nasty, gut-inverting hacks.

"Fuck!" Lucky finally said, wiping his face. "That was some superior surf, fellas, was it not?"

"Some of the biggest we've had here," Pong gamely added between coughs, his voice low and raspy. "Memorable, to say the least."

Lucky snorted. "You're a beast, Pong, to take that one on. It was huge and already breaking."

"I believed I could do it," he said.

"I'm really sorry," I said, knowing that he'd come for me. "You whistled to warn me. I shouldn't have gone so far inside."

"It happens," Pong said. "You could not see how big that wave was that hit you. I underestimated mine, too, thinking I could ride it to you. I know you would have done the same for me."

Lucky patted my shoulder. "Ballsy action, young blood."

Pong nodded, reaching out and fist-bumping me. "My wife and girls thank you." Then he added: "Okay, perhaps just my girls."

"Are you kidding? The whole world thanks you!" Lucky declared, roughly mussing my wet hair. "What would it be without Pong swimming its waters? We nearly had a tragedy but now look, we have celebration ahead of us. I propose a slight change to the agenda tonight. We require something extra after this session. But be honest, Pong, I'd understand if you wanted to go straight to bed right now."

"I will be myself again shortly," Pong replied, still regaining his breath.

After Lono and Derek loaded everything back into the truck, Pong and I climbed into the crew cab. We poured cups of the toasted-rice tea for each other from an insulated jug that Derek passed to us. Pong raised his paper cup to me and I raised mine. He looked better now, the blood risen back in his face. I wanted to say something suitably salty, to connect and not have to connect in the way men do, but I was just breathing in rhythm again myself, simply glad that he was fine, and that I was fine, moving myself into what felt like was going to be the best time of my life.

We trailed Lucky, as he led the way in his exotic wheels. I figured we were headed to his vacation house for a low-key evening but thought something was up when Lono called someone as he drove and muttered: "He goin' wit da full setup, tutu."

I asked Pong what Lucky actually did for a living, besides being a gambler. "He's an international inspector for the Food and Drug Administration," Pong huskily said, coughing. "He's actually based in China but isn't there all that much."

"He's a *government* worker?" I said, now looking at the chrome exhausts of his low-wedged supercar. We were stopped at a light on the Kalanianaole Highway, two smoking local chicks in a convertible next to him eyeing his oligarchian ride as he serenaded them with growly twelve-cylinder raves.

"Like myself, he supplements his regular job."

The light went green and Lucky shot away; Lono kept up for a short stretch until with breathtaking deceleration we pulled off the highway and turned up into the hills. The road was very steep and dark and winding and when it seemed to plateau it got bright again, lit by a gatehouse with not one but two guards and ornate wrought-iron gates on either side of it. We were waved through and then ascended again through a residential neighborhood of large houses and some outright mansions all lit up in their cake layers, then pulled into a walled property whose wooden gate slid open in perfect timing with our arrival, such that Lucky's car hardly slowed as it rolled into the compound and then under the already rising door of the garage, barely missing both.

Lono let us out in the courtyard, where Pong and I were beckoned from the doorway by a tiny elderly woman with close-cropped white hair. She was wearing a cherry-red muumuu with a pattern of white peonies and smiling so widely that I was unconsciously smiling back, my own cheeks pinching up hard into my eyes. Her sun-hardened face was a shiny chestnut brown, and grooved by lines of such acute definition that I wondered if they itched, or even hurt. They were kind of stunning, actually, these rivulets steadily etched by time.

"How you can stand my bastard son?" she said, taking Pong's hand between her pixie mitts. "You think he know how to welcome guests! But he have you walk in by yourself!"

"We don't love Lucky for his etiquette, Auntie," Pong said, now bear-hugging her, despite his wet rash guard and board shorts. She couldn't have cared less, cupping his face with both hands.

"I send Meelee for shopping Chinatown today, to make your favorite."

"Laksa noodles?"

"Sambal okra, too! Tell me you hungry, after long flight and surfing!"

"Yes, Auntie, I am," Pong uttered, like any boy come home again. He introduced me and she pinched my cheek hard, which was fine with me except she also goosed my ass with all five fingers as we walked inside the house. I figured it was an accident but her helper, Meelee, an equally old South Asian–looking woman who was even shorter and was unusually sour-faced, smirked. Pong was busy telling Auntie about his daughters and their activities so I couldn't consult.

Auntie now led us through the expansive and surprisingly modest one-level house that was clearly unaltered since the '70s, everything still hued in almond and avocado, with groovy glass lamps and felt/velveteen art abounding. Where we ended up in the illuminated backyard lanai was similarly decorated with funky outdoor furniture and lighting, but instead of a typical patio with table and chairs there was a pavilion, beneath which a raised row of three tiled plunge pools were set before a dense floral garden; each pool was around eight feet square and contiguous to the next, and on the tiled wall on one side was a bank of four handheld-shower stations with token privacy partitions and a plastic step stool on which to sit, as the shower heads were merely three feet high. Each shower station had a mirror and a fully stocked caddy of shower gels, shampoo and conditioner, shave cream and packaged single-use shavers, plus a long-handled scrub brush for the back.

"Okay, okay, *bule*," sourpatch Meelee said to me as she tugged on my rash guard. I resisted, as I didn't see how this fit in with the meeting we were to have with some master jamu maker from Kuala Lumpur.

Just then Lucky appeared and immediately dropped his board shorts and gave them to Meelee, as did Pong, both hanging totally loose while they pulled their rash guards off over their heads. They then squatted at their respective step stools, spraying themselves and beginning to lather up.

Auntie and Meelee stood there waiting for me, the others' swim stuff in their hands. Up to that point I'd been nude in front of women (aside from my mother) exactly twice, both times freshman year, both times in total darkness, both times failing to consummate (too drunk one time, putting the condom on the wrong way the other, which initiated a debate on whether I'd contaminated the outside with pre-cum seed, which started a deflationary action, which, despite mutual efforts, could not be reversed). I pretty much felt that way now, as the ladies stared at me, receded and receding. Auntie, who I was now gathering had pretty much seen it all, began unpeeling me of my rash guard, while Meelee began untying the belt laces of my board shorts. Before I could say *No, thanks*, they had me buck naked. A cool gust shooting down from the hills swirled about the lanai, and I would have shivered were it not for a surprise cupping of my sea-shriveled plums, now suddenly in the firm clutch of the clawlike but warm little hand of Meelee, her extended middle finger plied against my asterisk. My hands shot up in surrender, the rest of me too terrified to move. She rasped matter-of-factly to Auntie, "This baby *bule*, still he can grow."

Auntie sucked at her teeth, unconvinced.

Her helper just as quickly released me, and the two of them padded away with our swim stuff. Lucky was sniggering as I sat on the low stool, Pong shaking his head. Lucky tossed me a washcloth. He confessed to having Crab Claw punk me, which I had to laugh at, though part of me was unsettled by all the male bonding, being raised and educated in a well-to-do progressive enclave and demographic that championed egalitarian ideals like inclusion and justice but of course were built and sustained on exclusion and exploitation, real-world stuff that the vast majority of us privileged chauvinistic dudes didn't much think about, me included. On my travels I would soon be delivered into other situations, situations that I didn't want to partake in but somehow always did, because that's what we fellows do, wittingly and not, and to everyone's detriment. But that didn't mean I didn't also revel and enjoy, even as a voice in my head was now haranguing me that I ought to flee. Yet I didn't flee, even as most of me wanted to, which says plenty of sad things about who I am.

Anyway, at that point in the evening, bared and confused, I figured I might as well wash myself. I observed how Pong and Lucky were going about their ablutions, and particularly how at ease they were in that low-slung position. Was it an Asian thing? The honky part of me had this perhaps pathological need to stretch out, always take up more space. It was definitely awkward at first, as I wasn't used to sitting, say, while shampooing my hair, but soon enough I appreciated how you could relax, rest the elbows on the knees, really get in there between your toes, scrub hard at your soles, the dingy shallows of your ankles; the only trick was propping yourself up briefly to soap and rinse your crack. Maybe tall, long-legged people wouldn't like it, but maybe tall, long-legged people have chronically gross feet.

When we were thoroughly scrubbed and clean we soaked in the three plunge baths (it went cold, hot, boiling) and sat in mostly silence, the fuller appreciation of what had almost transpired now perhaps seeping in, Pong even letting himself drop below the surface of the hottest water, and maybe for a beat too long, in a kind of exorcism. Was he purging his brush with death? If anything, I thought, Pong would see it as a stout brush with life. To taste whatever sweetness, even if contained within it was a hard seed of fright, and wondering.

I unconsciously mimicked him, though I couldn't submerge myself for more than a half second, becoming afraid my eyeballs would get poached and pop out. Afterward we rinsed off and put on robes that Meelee laid out, Lucky leading us inside to a darkened room, where padded recliners awaited us.

"You've had a Chinese-style foot massage?" he asked me as we lay back in the loungers. I hadn't, and he assured me I'd enjoy it. Why wouldn't I? At this point the jet lag and frantic exertions in the surf and that last lava-hot tub soak had tranquilized me to a state of blankness, neither here nor there, neither white nor black, a chasmic void that wanted for nothing but could take in anything.

Suddenly I had the peculiar sensation of my feet getting bitch-slapped by the wings of angry seabirds; I opened my eyes and saw that people were kneeling before us, priming our feet with some kind of tonic. Getting the blood up, I guessed. There were three of them, two women and a man, all in their late fifties or sixties, all quite fit and dense of body, like pulling guards or wrestlers. My masseur, a guy with a blank, oxen expression, had especially wide, thick hands and broad shoulders and a badly stippled complexion, perhaps from a childhood bout of measles.

"There is nothing more restorative than expert reflexology," Lucky told me. "I've instructed them on what we'd like. Pong will get an emphasis on his foot's upper axis, to stimulate the action of the lungs and trachea. For the rest of us the focus will be on the alimentary areas, so we might fully partake of the food and drink to come."

This sounded great to me, even if I was getting a little overwhelmed by what I would learn was the full-on Korean baths setup, the in-house squad of Chinese foot massagers, the flash supercar, not to mention Lucky's very kindly but somewhat coarse mother and her immodestly probing helper. It was all sort of "kooky," as good ol' Clark might say, and definitely not adding up to anything I could recognize. Yet I wasn't here to *recognize*. Or to dance a familiar dance. It was good enough to be simply oystered in this warm plush robe, going slack and drooly with the liquor of well-being hormones now cascading through me. It was only when the masseur started in earnest that I suddenly roused.

Having never had one, I figured the foot massage would be pure pleasure after the initial plying of the tonic, a flowing harp-playing of the hands as they slathered on aromatic emollients, a gentle kneading of the myriad ligaments and bones and muscles, with multiple mini happy endings of smooth but firm toe pulls, pluck-pluck, pluck-pluck. Instead I found myself wishing for a piece of wood to bite on, like in the movies, when some poor fuck is about to get a field amputation. I didn't want to cry out and disturb the others, who lay as peacefully in their loungers as casketed heads of state. I, on the other hand, just kept wondering why this dude was so angry at me: he crushed my toes with his relentlessly forceful fingers; jammed my tarsals and metatarsals together like they were meant to be fused; ground at my arches with his granite knuckles; pinched and hyperextended my Achilles; and finally, repeatedly jabbed a sharp bamboo pointer into my soles in what felt like a Little Dipper pattern, until I was sure they were bleeding.

Qing zhushou was my reptile-brain moan, the words miraculously bubbling up from a spring semester of Mandarin 2 that I mostly skipped. Yet there were the words, like flavors I'd always known. Was I an idiot savant? A magical speaker of many tongues?

Or just a freak of language?

"*Qing zhushou, qing zhushou.*" Please stop.

The masseur paused, clearly surprised to hear this *bairen*'s plea. He murmured something to Lucky, then had to repeat himself before Lucky just waved him to shush.

"*Wan*," the masseur then said, with a last rough backslap of my foot. Finished.

I tried to communicate my thanks but was mute with relief that it was over. My jaw ached from the reflexive bracing, as did, incongruously, my left ass cheek. A tendon in my upper neck was playing tug-of-war with itself and short-circuiting a nerve behind my right eye, its vision now fogging. The funny thing was that my feet were feeling kind of good—maybe even superb. I twirled and flexed them. They'd felt like baggies of crushed tortilla chips but were now tensile and alive, tingling with a ninja readiness for whatever wall to be scaled, whatever span to be leapt. This steadily conducted up into the rest of me, and soon I could let myself marinate in the vibes of the spa music and the honey glow of the vintage incandescent bulbs and the papery hiss of the palm fronds brushing against one another in the breezy lanai. And why not? I'd done a solid out there; for Pong, of course, though for myself as well. To be honest, I was already mourning the prospect of someday not being with him. And maybe also, a little bit, I was losing my longtime handle on who I was, which for me was a good thing. When you're not remarkable in any way or shape, when you're short on special smarts or looks, wealth or talents, charisma or virtues, when you're not even plain vanilla ice cream but an experimental flavor that people will readily take a sample spoon of but never end up wanting, you don't wig out like most would when picturing oneself and coming up blank. You don't slog desperately through a long dark night of the soul. The nullity, actually, is a reprieve. But then maybe, chilling with new homies, you catch a glimmer that beckons like the lit frame of a shut door, making you wonder what's cooking on the other side.

This wasn't a totally random thought, as I was suddenly aware of a presence beyond the room. It was a smell, dense and extracted, a palpable presence charging the air like just before a lightning strike. It drew me out into the wide hallway that led to the large messy kitchen, where I could hear pulses of a blender. There, at the island counter piled high with a massing of roots and fruits and leaves, measuring various ingredients into commercial blenders, five of them in a row, was a tall and skinny guy with mousy hair done up in a man bun and a Vandyke going weedy on his chin. He was dressed like some sort of swami, his torso wrapped in a tangerine-colored muslin, a leather cord necklace with carved stone hoops of jade and garnet set loosely about his throat, his Pattaya Beach look finished off with suitably ratty cargo shorts and worn Adidas sport sandals like any burnt-out Westerner who'd long run out of money and exploitable friends. As I got closer I couldn't help but get buffeted by the sharp poke of his most unusual BO, this greasy, highly spiced stank that was like a takeout container of curried chicken that had been left in a gym bag of dirty socks in the sun and fermented for a week.

"Where you have been?" he asked me, his tone churlish. "Aunties say they send help but no help coming anytime."

"I'm just visiting . . ."

"Peel this things and this things, right?" he said, pointing to some nubby gingerlike roots and handing me a peeler. "Ready to go, right?"

He nodded and without my answering or assenting he went back to one of the many plastic pitchers and checked its level of green-gray, vomit-looking juice, decanting little shots from it into several other pitchers with a careful inexactitude, sort of like how a stoner in college would pack herbage into his bong bowl. By now I realized this odorous dude was the jamu master, and so I took one of the counter stools opposite him and got to peeling. The roots were a dark orange inside and stained my hands as I tried to peel them. As noted, we Bardmons aren't cooks and I fumbled the tool and nearly shaved my own fingertip as I went, then no doubt took too much of the woody flesh.

"Will it be too much a challenging, for more carefulness by you?" he snapped with unvarnished exasperation. "Do it your direction, not your other way!"

This was sound advice, although he had to show me twice how to do it, rather than how I was trying to whittle at it like it was a stick. I guess I wasn't concentrating, not because I didn't want to help, but because I was mostly wondering why this whitish dude spoke such mashed-up English. In fact, I was enjoying the trip and jaunt of his speech, how it rolled along like a shined-up jalopy, the bumpers and doors and hubcaps looking like they might fall off any second, the engine about to go kaboom, but the whole funny contraption of it staying put and clattering forth and conveying us down the road.

"I guess this is all jamu?" I asked, pointing at the blenders.

"Is and is not!" he cried. He lifted a pitcher off one of the blender bases and thrust it under my nose. Fumes of a fruity, jungly dankness rose up, momentarily dizzying me. "In the sensibility of origins it is jamu, yes. However do you understand the power of jamu even? Do you understand its full meanings?"

I told him I'd learned a little about it, being an assistant to one of Lucky's friends. He came around the counter and gripped me by my shoulders and zoomed his face uncomfortably close in to mine.

"You will receive wisdoms from me! Getty, everybody say he is number A1 jamu man. So why they are repeating this?"

When I shook my head he gave me some more of the jamu story, detailing like some cross between a nervous new college professor and an on-TV-only pitchman the cultural aspects of what Pong had briefly run down back at the Chop Station. While I peeled more turmeric root (the orange stuff) and grated some cinnamon bark and zested the rind of a limelike fruit, Getty tutored me in everything jamu, which was made mostly by women from secret, age-old recipes handed down from their mothers and grandmothers and so on, blends designed to alleviate pretty much every affliction. They could make you a jamu for acne, for lower back pain, for constipation, for insomnia, for fevers and colds, for rheumatism and diabetes, even for cancers of the organs and of the blood, and most ordinary Indonesians would take them periodically, some religiously, the local jamu monger acting as the neighborhood pharmacist/psychotherapist/healer. Getty had lived in Jakarta for two years, then three additional years on one of the countless islands of the vast archipelago, apprenticing with a jamu "sorceress" who taught him how to forage for stuff like nyamplung and secang leaves and a rare variety of galangal and the various curcuma, then mash and render and distill them into concoctions of the most ancient provenance. They were preparations, he held, from the "time before islands had names even, the time before the peoples were a peoples even."

"Special health drink, huh?" I said.

He practically spat at me. "Usual Western foolishness! Jamu for mind and body all in one! This is what you all must understand about jamu. Everybody believe jamu for body goodness. Yet this is not whole stuffing. Best jamu, top-class jamu, will be for your spirit. Then you will understand, yes, how everything will becoming different, because you will be having greatest human power. So what is this meaning? Getty will tell you."

I waited, holding my breath for multiple reasons.

"You can be living forever," he gasped. "Forever!"

He said *forever* like he meant it, poking his finger in my sternum and staring at me with the wild-eyed sparkle of a true believer. Up to that point I was fully subscribing to everything he said, because it was entertaining and colorful plus why the hell not, though this last emphasis made me wonder if he was more than slightly off. I never liked the idea of *forever*, my grade school therapist will extensively tell you why, maybe that's why Clark and I, together and separately, have been stuck in this super LP groove, as comfortable as it may be despite the history of our nuclear family. And maybe only a deep, crazy jarring will make us jump out.

Anyway, we had the blenders redlining when Pong and Lucky, berobed and beslippered, strolled in with an almost regal majesty, their expressions flushed and puffy with satiation. Getty immediately laid what must have been a funky bear hug on each of them, which they all seemed accepting of, though Lucky visibly winced. His mother and her helper came in, too, and they and Getty got into some friendly barking about the proportions of one of his mixtures, as evidently Meelee had some major-league jamu experience herself.

"Remember last year, Meelee, when he made me one for my lower back?" Pong said to her. "It hasn't hurt at all since."

"You have too much heated blood, honey," she said, pinching his earlobe. "Building up too much stress. I cool and shrink you with mint and ginger."

"Please don't shrink me!" Lucky pleaded. "I'm hung like a gerbil already."

"Honey, you have a very nice size," Meelee said, I thought, not nearly facetiously enough. In fact, a panic flashed through me that I'd been incorporated into a grouping that was way more decadent than I'd anticipated. Could I handle that? I wasn't sure, to be honest, but back then I was a fundamentally younger twenty-year-old than the twenty-year-old I am now, and still assumed I could take up whatever the world thrust forth.

"Getting back to my jamu, gentlepeoples," Getty broke in. "Can we be doing this now?"

We moved on to the business at hand, sampling the various jamu Getty had blended, obviously more for flavor and texture than for any restorative effects, so the partners could sign off on the final potions that their newly formed LLC would produce and bottle in an industrial park just outside Shenzhen and then sell all around

Asia, first in lower-end markets like KL and Bangkok, and eventually, they hoped, in tonier places such as Shanghai and Tokyo. Looking at the blenders of various puddle-colored juice, it all sounded a bit optimistic to me, but then these guys were confident, prosperous, globe-surfing entrepreneurs, and I was your basic know-nothing privileged American college kid, who, if you really think about all that's desperately wanting in this world, might well be the lowest of the low.

"In bright future these shall be famous too in the West," Getty proclaimed, pouring out sampler glasses for each of us.

What did they taste like? It's difficult to say. This was quite a leap from WTF Yo! I guess they tasted okay, in that they were, respectively, sweet enough, salty enough, bitter but like a bitter chocolate, with the last one weirdly meaty, as if from a vegetable full of hormones, not juice. But it was how they felt in the mouth that struck me as literally sensational; think of the chilly burn from an intense breath mint, or the good dull ache in the gums after a dental cleaning, or the tingling vibrato when the girl you're kissing suddenly sucks in the tip of your tongue and the rest of you would instantly fold yourself forever into that glistening space, and maybe then you'd get an idea of what Getty's jamu were, not just flavors but this insistent presence in the mouth, like you'd become the host of a thing with its own undeniable life. Yeah, I know, they were the first jamu I'd ever had but you had to believe that Getty was a legit jamu master.

"Very nice," Lucky said, licking his lips. "I think these formulations are perfect. If I remember correctly, this last one is meant for sexual vigor, right?"

"Biggest help for that, yes," Getty replied. "But you are being too strict. You are businessman I know but when you let our jamu go into America let it be jamu, not medicine. Please remember, gentlemens. My jamu is not regular jamu. You must know my jamu as the beginning of a good way, not the ending of a problem. Do not believe in the idea of healings. There are no healings, because there are no wounds."

"I think we know what you mean," Lucky assured him. "Holistic integrity and all that. But we have to go to market, too, right? We can't educate the world in an instant. It'll take one bottle at a time, for the people who feel they need to be whole. And what do you think, young blood? Will younger people buy into this?"

Everybody turned to me, awaiting my answer. What popped up was a picture of Clark at the kitchen table each morning, a mixed herd of meds scattered next to his coffee mug: one pill for his hypertension, another for the rashes he got from the hypertension pills, another for the insomnia from the rash pills, for which he then needed an entire pot of coffee in the morning and a couple more pots at the office, for which he periodically needed reflux pills, which messed up his appetite, which made him anxious and definitely raised his blood pressure, and so on and so forth, none of which seemed to appear until after my mother checked out one blustery spring day and never checked back in.

"We could get into jamu," I said. "Though maybe if it were marketed as a natural energy drink it would be more successful. You know, like an all-organic Red Bull."

"Very good idea," Pong said.

"I like it," Lucky said. "A Rockstar-boosted Jamba Juice."

Pong said, "Tiller has a most discriminating palate. He can help formulate a youth-targeted cuvée."

"Definitely, and please, something sweeter. These are all too bitter for anyone under thirty," Lucky said.

Getty groaned. "Please, gentlemens, my jamu is not to be as American soft drinks!"

"That's enough, blender man," Lucky said sharply. Getty sniffed but said nothing. Suddenly I could see Lucky's family resemblance to his mother, the shared subtle flare at the corner of the eyes, this almost ancient Egyptian edging that cast a cold and sober gaze. "We have a capable new associate at our disposal who also happens to be representative of our potentially largest demographic, younger whites. I know Tiller is not all haole, but he knows what I'm saying."

"He certainly does," Pong said. "He's one of us now."

"My *soon dubu* brother," Lucky muttered. "But you get my meaning, right, boy? You can lend us a perspective we don't have."

I nodded, for I was the most Caucasian person present, Getty having long transformed himself into a race of one. He now regarded me hotly, marking me for some ornate and awful fate. Yet it felt funny to be singled out, even positively; the few times it had happened to me it was definitely the other way around, by people who knew me and wanted to make a lame joke, like asking me how they should hold their chopsticks, or which Hello Kitty character was my favorite. I wasn't at all bothered. I never had much racial or ethnic pride, but of course that's my haole part talking, which doesn't require much girding or encouragement, already having most of life valeted. But now I'd already forgotten how I appeared to the world. And I liked it. I felt sharper, stronger, my feet now actually tingling with both litheness and rootedness, the diluted part of me maybe now coming together, concentrating, if not yet bloomed in a brighter, bolder color.

It was then that a funny thing happened. My foot masseur appeared in the kitchen and began cursing at me. He was calling me, I'm pretty sure, a cheapskate and a sissy and a pasty ghost-white fool. I realized now he might have been shorted when I fled the massage, and I tried to communicate that I had some *money* wherever my pants were (we were still all in our spa robes), but it came out like I was saying I wanted more *lettuce*, which he took for taunting and which prompted him to unleash a string of even harsher insults about my manliness, several that I knew from my Mandarin 2 audio-lab partner, J. J. Fung, whose dad lived and toiled alone in toxic Harbin while he and his sisters and mom condo'd in high style in breezy Palos Verdes, California. Lucky snorted in delight at the sudden spectacle, while Pong couldn't help but grin at my sorry Mandarin, though in my defense it's a language that's rife with punning, for even native speakers need to be wary of saying something unintentionally awkward or insulting.

Frankly I didn't know whether I should deflect, or defend myself, or else start shooting back, when Lucky's mom stepped in, guns blazing. She and the masseur instantly got into it, spewing this crazy gravy of Mandarin and Korean and English, the masseur not ceding a millimeter to her; it was their version of one of those "Fuck You," "No, *fuck* YOU!" fests, when any hierarchy is suspended and it's just a mano-a-mano rumble, this raw clawing that red-striped the surfaces but scratched a deeper itch, too, their real beef not ultimately with each other but perhaps with unjust economic schema. I'd witnessed a similar partnering during my dishwashing stint back in Dunbar between a longtime waitress named Molly and the owner, Phil, who were by all accounts doing the nasty on the side. They screamed at each other with their faces so close you thought their teeth would clack. Anyway, the masseur and Lucky's mom were still slashing at each other because of me, so I stood with my hands pressed together and began apologizing to him as plainly as I could, but all he kept hollering to everybody was, "I want to earn my money! I want to earn my money!"

"So shut up and work, you useless eunuch!" Lucky's mother countered, in a truly excellent Mandarin.

"I will, like you wish you still could, bitter old slut!"

"Even when she's dead she'll be twice the man you are," loyal Meelee hissed.

"You ancient whores are pathetic."

Lucky's mom didn't blink. "So show us your skill, why don't you?"

"Right here?"

"Where else, you homely dolt!"

"If that's what you fancy, you dried-up abalone."

"We'll see what we both are. Now earn your pay."

She lifted her skirt. A wearer of undergarments, I must report, she was not. The masseur took to his knees, having to bend lower still because Lucky's mom was so short.

The man's head disappeared. A stop-time iced the room.

Lucky looked at me and sighed. "This is how it is, young blood, to be raised by an ever-enterprising woman. You learn that life, it gets done."

12.

ONG AND I didn't stay much longer at Lucky's, or on lovely Oahu, and our travels would not revert back eastward to the cashmere clutches of Dunbar but sling us farther across the Pacific, where we would open up the veins of Pong's various enterprises, Elixirent included. We would scale them up, as they say. But of course there are things you have seen that you wish you hadn't, because no matter what you do, they will never be erased. We're engineered with an ever-ready PTSD, maybe because surviving usually means suffering. But after a while, if it's not totally crushing, you can't help but be the tiniest bit thankful for certain shocking lingerings, especially in the leaner, emptier moments, which can always be filled by their undying glow. No warmth, but at least some light.

What I am thinking of now is how messy our relationships are. Consider, for instance, the encounter between Lucky's mom and the masseur, which you could easily take as the same old song of the standing and the kneeling, of the lord and the serf, of the lash and the back, which anybody knows is the number-one show of the ages. But you had to notice, too, how if at first Auntie was suitably rough on the masseur as he swabbed belowdecks, soon enough she was grabbing his ear and tugging in time with the subtle bucks of her hips, while he in turn was cupping the backs of his madam's knees. They found their common measure until a single baritone *uhhhh* sonically thumped forth from her chest, and Lucky wearily observed, "Mother, your promptness is a lesson and a blessing."

Well said, Mr. Choi. Their mother-son familiarity was by some very particular perspective thoroughly heartwarming, for there's no way you could say Lucky and his mom weren't close. But it's all in a range, isn't it? I was quite young when my mother finally skedaddled, but that's when you're perhaps closest, mentally and physically, plus I was also just old enough to glean the gradual dissolution of the life of our home, that she was her own tortured, difficult entity and not just a mom bot, that she was already elsewhere. There are numerous moments I could relate to demonstrate these notions, but given what we witnessed, I should call up one morning when I stayed home with the flu.

This when I was in the second grade and she was oddly frantic about my condition. I'd woken up having not eaten for most of two days and still had an elevated temperature and I remember her getting annoyed at me for not wanting the cream of wheat she'd prepared from the pouch. She'd boiled some eggs, too, and then even blended a blueberry shake, but I guess I had no appetite. I just crouched there in the window bench of the kitchen-nook table, watching my snot drip onto my weak and fever-palsied little hands. She got fed up and roughly sat down and half cradled me, to coax me into sipping the purple smoothie.

"Please drink, Tiller, will you please?" she said, like I'd die if I didn't. Of course there was zero danger of that, but my mother seemed sure I might, and I must have realized even at that young age that it wasn't me she was obsessing on, because I stopped trying to take a sip.

"For fuck's sake, drink it!" She pushed the glass against my mouth, banging my front teeth. I cried out but she didn't give in, and I had to swallow. It tasted like mud, and when I recoiled she gritted her teeth and cuffed my head in her arm and with the other pushed aside the flap of her thin terry-cloth robe, to expose her breast. It was smallish but full and glowed with a first-morning-light paleness. Her areola was the color of a walnut shell and either by my craning or her pushing it filled my mouth. I closed my eyes. I sucked for I don't know how long. Nothing came of course, just the rising button of her nipple, faintly salty, and I remember now how I was straining to breathe because of my stuffed nose but I didn't care; I knew she wouldn't let me die, and at some point I was back in my bed to sleep the rest of the afternoon and night.

We didn't talk about it the next day, or the next, and very soon she was gone, and there was definitely nothing to say then.

What do you say?

What?

Nothing, I guess, though maybe you start on something else entirely, hoping it won't ever arc back. Was that why I was so keen and open to going along with Pong? Because I knew I'd end up back home in Dunbar eventually and thus wanted the fullest, most distracting delay? Very possibly. Regardless, I apologize if this seems like one of those sojourning *gweilo* stories, in which some willful Western dude ventures abroad and learns the local ways and uses them to gain the trust of the natives and in turn show them how it's really done, say, dispatching a malign princeling while saving a beautiful serf girl in the process. You know, "Fish in strange water ultimately enhances the water" sort of tale. Well, I'm here to say that's not how it will go down. My presence did not fundamentally change anything, anywhere, for better or worse. All I did was unhesitatingly follow my mentor Pong, as any loyal assistant should, doing whatever he asked of me to promote the flow of his commerce.

Commerce of course was the blends of jamu that Getty helped

formulate. Pong and Co. had other investments in this part of the world but Elixirent, as we were now officially branding it, was the primary venture. Toting a few cases of one-shot samples Lucky's mother arranged to have bottled the next day in Honolulu's China-town, Pong and I flew to Shenzhen to visit his production people and market the jamu to potential vendors, with Lucky heading to KL to sign up distributors there before all of us would rendezvous back in "Shen," as they called it. All in all, Pong outlined on the plane, we'd be away from Dunbar a bit longer than he'd anticipated, more like a full week, this because of an invitation from Drum Kap-pagoda for us to stay at his hilltop estate outside of the city, which Pong hoped would work with my schedule.

Needless to say, it was no problem. I texted Clark to tell him that I was leaving DC but had decided to go early to my Euro program to start work before the term as an assistant for an engineering pro-fessor, changing the ticket already in my name for later in the month, which was definitely not in any plan we had. Of course, it was our MO not to discuss much of anything except for the bare happy min-imum, and he likely had a rough handle on when I was originally leaving and where I was going. He did text back a couple hours later to say thanks for the update without giving me any shit about the sudden change, which is again the long-standing Bardmon policy of mutually assured psychic ease. I hated to fib, but it was only because I love him and never want him to worry. We both understood it wasn't critical what I did this year—it was going to be a "program" in the narrowest sense of the word—and any getting out of our re-spective and shared usuals was good reason enough.

Clark did ask if I'd brought along my clothes for the semester and I told him I had a rolly bag full, plus a down jacket, which I figured would be plenty for when the weather turned. Mostly just Speedos for Ibiza, I joked.

Use plenty sunscreen, he texted back. **But wait, engineering??? Did you just get a whole lot smarter? What's next, string theory?:):):):)**

To which I replied, **Frayed knot!!!:(:(:(,** briefly explaining that I was helping the professor with coding, which my dad didn't question, figuring all of us youth automatically knew how. Again, I didn't enjoy lying. He worried enough about not having been a hands-on dad, whether the buddy-buddy or helicopter or drill sergeant kind, fathers he could never be. Clark is a classic back-office guy, most comfortable with verifying and processing what's already been executed, and made miserable by the prospect, so to speak, of having to PowerPoint some grand vision from the head of a conference table. He'd much rather sit and receive than stand and deliver. It's the way he is, and, I guess, the way I am, too. So I told him I'd be back at Christmas and he good-naturedly replied, **I'll transfer some more € to your ale and frites account,** and **Will talk turkey,** which meant I should give him a call on Thanksgiving (aside from the periodic email check-ins). I know he loves me unconditionally, likely to a fault, but I don't care what any family counselor or therapist might say about the importance of being present for your loved ones, of staying front and center, because for us it's indeed the thought that counts, for that's all we can manage.

What might Clark have thought if he knew I was texting him from downtown Shenzhen? Probably what I did, which was *Whoa.* I'd been to NYC a few dozen times, Chicago twice, LA and Houston once each, but standing there on the jammed broad sidewalk of one of the many jammed broad avenues that were all eight lanes of cars and buses and motorbikes and pushcarts and mini- and macro-trucks busting through a city so dense and vertical and vastly sprawling that even I knew this was a megalopolis of a different order. I would soon see that it was a city made up of the units of whole other cities, the shore city plus the hillside city plus the city on the delta that forty years before sprouted from a backwater fishing village built on bamboo stilts. The bottomless municipal-parts bin included prewar hutongs veined by hip-width alleyways and multidecked megamalls with stadium food courts, skyways and bridges, corporate parks and skyscrapers, light-assembly buildings and warehouses, and block after block after block of laundry-festooned tenements and sparkling glass office towers and balconied high-rises and shoehorned Florida-type condos and ersatz Tuscan villas out on the ring roads where the more prosperous of the twelve-plus million lived. "Shen" was still growing because it was still hungry, unslaked by the resources and space and people it had already taken up, this beast of a civilization, where everyone was angling, striving, the jungly weather of this season just another thing to be withstood and mastered.

This place was the future before the future and likely after it, too.

It sure was hot like the future, a steaming 35° C with maxed-out humidity, though I seemed to be the only one of the thousands of people around us who was suffering, even though I wore only a tank T-shirt and cargo shorts and sport sandals I'd just bought off a street seller, tossing my nasty, ratty collegiate huaraches. Pong certainly wasn't wilting, strolling coolly and vented in his linen shirt and crisp trousers, knockoff designer shades shielding his eyes from the high-beam white haze that hung over the city. He'd bought me a matching pair, and with my darkish hair and similar build I toyed with the idea that on the quickest glance we could be taken for cousins, I the aimless, mucky younger one who without the draw of a strong wake would curl constantly into eddies of blunder.

Apparently this is among the numerous psychological character-istics of orphans—technically I'm not one, but a shrink I got sent to when I was nine years old and having myriad difficulties at school said I was essentially marooned as an emotional being—that they have trouble with decision-making and are always veering off course, the flip side being that they latch on easily to relative strangers. I admit I've tended to latch on too quickly, with women most often— well, duh—but the truth is that I'm ever ready to hang with any decently friendly dude, too, any brother who would pass the time with me either not talking about everything or droning on about squat. Pong of course did neither, as he was always purposeful and instructive and illuminating, and not unwilling to tell the unhappy family details of his life. He hadn't asked about my unhappy family details, not because he didn't care but because he seemed to sense how bereft I actually was, the particulars hardly mattering anymore.

Our body clocks were haywire from the jet lag and we had some time to kill before our first business appointments so after dropping off our bags at the hotel Pong decided we'd have some fun and took us to a well-known commercial district of the city, Huaqiangbei. This is where you can buy in parts or whole every electronic gadget ever invented, with entire indoor malls lined with shelves and bins and rooms full of switches, motherboards, soldering irons, memory chips, smartphone screens, LED lights, vitals-tracking wearables, a million million tiny screws and pins and batteries, not to mention larger consumer items like digital cameras and drones and Bluetooth speakers and what Pong purchased for us to use for the next few hours, which were two hoverboards with flashing neon wheel rims, his black-light purple and mine lemon yellow. The story is that the hoverboard was invented right there in Huaqiangbei, and while Palo Alto and Cupertino will always have a hallowed perch in the annals of tech history, this locale, like the contraption itself, will always be more fun and dangerous. Both of us needed a few test drives to get comfortable, though with his surfing and yoga experience Pong rode with balance and speed. I had more difficulty, falling on my ass a couple times after jerky accelerations and then nearly grinding my face when one wheel hopped a steamed *bao* someone had accidentally dropped on the mall floor. Nobody seemed to mind that we were buzzing through the building as we checked out the shops (imagine a big Macy's store but cleaned out and then over-loaded with a thousand different sellers right next to one another, their wares displayed in plastic bins and even cut-out boxes), Pong buying little gifts for his girls like phone cases and selfie sticks and me buying a fake Apple watch for Clark, who had professed admi-ration for one he saw a colleague wearing, though he would never splurge on it himself. This knockoff could only take calls from his phone and track the number of his steps for the day, but then tech-wise he couldn't handle much else anyway. Pong casually but dog-gedly negotiated the price down with the grumpy seller from the RMB equivalent of $30 to $20, and with part of the savings I treated us to styro snack bowls of volcanically spicy cold noodles that we slurped while wheeling at speed through the crowded lunchtime side-walks of Huaqiang Road.

Pong's mobile rang and he answered. We were in front of a long series of outdoor stalls in a tree-shaded flea market area, and while he took the call Pong handed me an unusually heavy dark-matte-gray metal credit card without any branding or numbering and mo-tioned for me to shop, mouthing, *Get something!* as he adjusted his remote earpiece. I tried to ask, *Who for?* but was swept up in a phalanx of boisterous and possibly drunken older tourists (they all wore Korean flag lapel pins) led by a young woman waving a stick topped by a blue pennant. The men were all bowlegged and the women sported the same tight curly perm and they all seemed to be bickering but with a kind of lusty enjoyment, all of them jawing and guffawing while fanning themselves with whatever they had in hand. They were certainly eager as they descended upon the stalls of lug-gage, goofy hats, and slippers, drapery and clothing fabrics, fans, kitchen tools, dried seafood, beauty creams, power tools, live and fake plants, eyewear, plus an unusually rich assortment of items for activities associated with camping and crafting and the decorative cutting of fruit. What drew my eye, along with a couple Korean grannies, was an immense and universally complete display of colored markers and pens in front of a writing-implements and stationery stall, which you really couldn't help test-driving on the demo sketch pad already scrawled with squiggles and signatures and doodly drawings of anime characters and animals.

I've always had a decent hand (something I get from Clark, who was the campus newspaper cartoonist when he was in college) and for some bizarre reason I'd rather not interrogate I found myself outlining a fluttery-eyelashed unicorn in day-glo pink, its horn tipped by a star, which elicited claps from the two ladies, one of whom tore the sheet from the sketch pad and firmly tapped it, signaling that I should do another. It was purely amateurish work but at least it was marked with some personality and flair I don't have in walking-around life.

So I peered at the Korean ladies for a moment and then, in a royal blue marker that matched their tour group's pennant, I drew a pair of smiling penguins wearing oversized visors (as the ladies were) and giving the thumbs-up sign. They tittered and hopped as no penguins could, which attracted more of their compadres over to us.

Before I knew it I was working as fast as I could, employing appealing animals like lions and pandas and dolphins but then moving on (when I needed to capture certain facial or bodily attributes) to giraffes and bison, camels and alligators. You'd think somebody would get irritated at my caricaturing but it turned out people enjoyed these even more, poking fun and laughing harder at one another the sharper my marker got.

I lost track of time but I must have been standing at the display for a decent while, the queue stretching almost three stalls and including some uniformed police officers and a grimy backpacking

Caucasian couple, when I noticed that Pong was observing the proceedings. I figured we had to go and filled in the finishing strokes on a ravenous wild boar (the one grandpa had these crazy prominent canines), and his vigilant meerkatlike buddy (very close-set eyes), but Pong signaled that I should keep at it, which I did for another handful of groups until the proprietor came over and quite rudely gestured that I cease, a reasonable request given that nobody was buying anything and we were blockading potential customers.

The Koreans groaned but then without a beat dispersed and went back to their browsing and shopping, some of the men clapping me on the back and one of the penguin ladies handing me a small stack of RMB. I declined but she forcefully pressed the bills into my palm and cried, "For eat and drink!" maybe assuming I was some scrounging and desperate backpacker.

"You should accept," Pong told me, and so I did. He smiled at the woman and she and her friend smiled at him and they gave me double thumbs-up before they rejoined their tour mates. "Nice ladies. You in fact have some talent," he said charitably, both of us knowing *some* was the operative word. He had the world-class artist parents, after all, and I, well, I have secretly high standards.

"Okay," he said, stepping back to pose on his hoverboard. "Now for my spirit animal."

I chuckled and tried to wave him off, not to mention that the proprietor had already plucked the marker from me, but to my surprise Pong now laid into him, berating him, I gathered, about being a better businessman, plus saying something about purchasing his wares. The proprietor rasped defiantly and they got into an exchange that I couldn't understand but it ended up with the guy stuffing the marker back into my hand before trudging to his stool behind the counter, where he'd been eating his lunch with his teenaged daughter.

I didn't quite know where to begin with Pong; aside from his surreal head of hair I'd say he was normal in his appearance, if anyone can be normal. He had typical Asian eyes, and a somewhat prominent, if near bridgeless, nose, and the shape of his face was an elongated square rounded of its corners except of course where it wedged down toward his chin, which was marked by the barest cleft. It was a friendly face, a composed, confident face, though more than that, I'd say *unperturbed*, rooted in the calm before the calm, and this made me flash on a fact from the chronology of Pong's unfortunate childhood, and I began to draw the brow and snout of an ox.

Why that? Back in freshman year I'd given an oral report in Mandarin 1 about the Chinese zodiac, totally juvenile stuff, but like an idiot savant I somehow got imprinted with the birth years and associated animals and instantly knew that 1961—he'd noted being five years old in '66—was the Year of the Ox, with those born under its sign supposedly hardworking, inspiring of trust, and rich with unadvertised talents. A quiet leader. Pong could see my work and grinned when the image began to form, no doubt connecting the dots.

My Pong Ox was stolid and steady, coal-eyed and unflared of nostril, no yoked beast of burden but an animal surveying his rightful range, this musk ox with a woolly coat and a characteristically middle-parted crown that curled down and then up into sharp horns, the base almost matching Pong's helmetlike coif. Another caricaturist would have certainly made hay with his hair, drawn up a veritable petrified forest of a do, but I focused on his stance as he deftly hoverboard-surfed a fro-yo wave full of electronics flotsam.

"Very good, Tiller," he said, carefully tearing the sheet from the table and folding it up to put in his laptop case. "If you don't mind. I think my wife and daughters will enjoy this image of me, as they often say I'm bullheaded and spend too much time on business. If I'm correct about your age, you must be a Rat."

I was indeed, the first sign in the cycle of the Chinese zodiac.

Naturally not the most beloved of the zodiac animals, at least I was supposed to be alert, clever, inquisitive, and ever flexible to changing conditions, though I knew the one attribute that made any sense was the last; if nothing else, I'm as adaptable as they come.

"I thought so," Pong said. "You must know, too, that the Rat and Ox make good business partners. This may or may not be fated for all, but I can see it is the case for us. I feel I can count on you whatever may arise. Do you think this is right?"

I definitely wasn't sure whether it was but I nodded anyway, because what else could I possibly do? I had no idea what the world wanted from me, or how I might please it, but it seemed clear that the best chance I had to glean anything of my destiny would be as a ready adjunct to the man, literally rolling with him wherever he might point us.

Before we could leave, the proprietor approached and reminded Pong about his assurance of making a substantial purchase. Pong was game and told him to show us the best products he had, and the man had his daughter fetch a portable Plexiglas display case of knives of various sizes, all culinary types except for one, a small toylike folding knife. They looked brand-new even if the display case was scratched and dinged and poked in the corners with holes through which it had once been bolted to a wall.

She unlocked the front panel and let Pong handle them.

"Do you appreciate knives, Tiller?" Pong asked, taking out the small folding knife with its hammered steel handle. "Because these are very fine ones."

"I guess I do," I said, though recalling only the Swiss Army knife I had when I was a kid. I used its awl more than anything, poking squared-off holes on the underside of our oak dining room table. I'd fill the cavities with BBs of wet paper or my own snot, which is gross enough, but the creepier thing is that I was crouching under tables with regularity.

Pong handed me the blade, its edge sharpened to what paradoxically seemed a near disappearance, and emitting a pure cold glow.

"Certain Japanese knives, like this one, are the best in the world. The origins of their production, you can guess, come from the making of swords for samurai, knowledge that has been passed down for more than seven hundred years. This is actually from one of the top makers, and is a good example. Knives are made of various grades of stainless and carbon steel, ranging from softer varieties to hard. The ones for the masses are on the soft end and are more easily dulled and sharpened, and made from one or two kinds of metal. They are machine-produced. But a knife like this is entirely made by hand, and from only the hardest blue carbon steel. In the forge it is hammered into shape by many thousand experienced strikes, and once fashioned and honed, is sharper than a razor."

Pong tore off a sheet of the sketch-pad paper, which he held by its corner. He then wielded the blade, working the sheet of paper with these swift and delicate strokes, feathering downward and upward, just as if he were standing with a watercolor brush in a field of sunflowers in Provence, all these curvy ribbons lazily corkscrewing to the floor. And I tell you, the sound of it! It wasn't like any cutting you'd ever heard, not even the satisfying *schhhwipp* you get from that scary paper chopper they somehow still allow in elementary schools. The sound was low in volume but of a peerless clarity, as if a nanosized plane were cleaving a paper-domed sky.

"Your turn," Pong said to me. I thought he would hand me what was left of the paper, this narrow dangling strip, but he transferred the blade to my hand. He held up the remaining paper.

"Do it."

I shook my head.

Pong said, "You cannot injure me, Tiller. Your mind and body won't allow it."

"No fucking way," I squealed.

"You already saved me once," he said, with a casual levity that in fact scared me. "Whatever else happens now is an afterthought."

"I can't do it," I replied, feeling a bead of sweat trickle down my ass crack.

"Go straight across," Pong advised. "From the bottom up. You can make three cuts at least."

My arm tingled with a palsy.

"Don't focus on the paper. Slice the air."

Something in his voice both intimidated and steeled me. I gave a stiff, awkward try, the wind from my lame pass pushing aside the paper before the blade could quite catch it.

"No, no, think of an orchestra conductor," Pong said, demonstrating a neat one-two with an invisible baton. "He is marking out a quick little march. I mean it. Try."

I could see he did. So I set my feet. I pictured myself in white tie and tails, with messy composer tresses stuck to my sweaty brow. I took a lighter hold of the blade, more in the fingers than the palm, and half closed my eyes and flicked.

What remained in his fingers was the stub of a movie ticket, a taxi-meter receipt. And Pong was dead right; the edge was so fine that I'd felt only the merest graze of the paper. Here was a righteous tool, it, along with the magical ATM card, the only things I still have left from my year abroad. I clutched it merrily, shaking, belly laughing, as was the girl, as was Pong.

13.

AFTER MY IMPROMPTU MALL PERFORMANCES, Pong and I made calls to various potential vendors who owned retail outlets all over China. We briefly stopped at the hotel to change (dress shirts, summer-weight blazers, pressed trousers—similar but not matching, mine procured in the men's shop of the hotel lobby) and grab our rolly bag of jamu samples packed in dry ice, a car and driver hired for the day to shuttle us around the city.

It wasn't just the two of us, for in the sedan was a woman in a smartly tailored white business suit who greeted us with firm hand-shakes and addressed me warmly as *Teerer*, and I realized that it was the lady on the phone call Pong had taken in the car that first night in Dunbar. Her name was Lily Zhang. She was probably around forty but looked twenty-five at most, sort of like how Pong was midfifties but might still easily pass for being much younger. Lily was wonderful to look at, with shimmering dark shoulder-length hair and a creamy smooth complexion and prominent but rounded cheekbones that gave her the look of being well-fed, even if the rest of her was very petite and trim. She had an achingly wide, fullish mouth that I would have normally tried not to stare at but once again I was instantly drawn to the texture of her voice, which was on the high side of the scale but had this superfine texture, this wet-paint glossiness that you wanted to reach out and touch.

She and Pong sat in the back of the sedan conversing unintelligibly fast as she tapped at various screens on her tablet, while I was in shotgun watching the traffic steadily coagulate around us, our driver texting while driving while playing, of all things, a monster truck driving game, at least in between the pinging messages. Pong and Lily didn't seem to care even when there was a reprieve in the traffic and he sped us along with his blinking and vibrating smartphone pinned against the steering wheel as he broke for daylight between the other vehicles to get us to our first appointment on time. I cinched my seat belt and closed my eyes and listened to the cheery burble of Pong and Lily's conversation, which was vigorous and focused but also marked by some warm repartee and easy joking that in turn made me wonder about the levels that he and Minori conversed at, their not sharing a native tongue. Minori spoke enough Mandarin and Pong enough Japanese, for sure, and of course they spoke English grammatically and fluently, but everyone gets that it's not just about knowing the words. Then again, my folks had only the one language so what does any of it matter?

When we got to the office building Lily stayed in the car, as she needed a lift back to their production facility for her own meeting. I was sad that it might be the last I'd literally hear of her, and Pong must have sensed this and he mentioned that we would be seeing her later in the evening, when we were meeting with Drum Kappagoda. As they drove off Lily gave us that cutesy double hand wave certain Asian women seem to favor, at least on TV, and we cutesy waved back.

"I told you about our troubles with third-party compounds so we started building our own facility earlier this year. Lily is the general manager of the project and I have come to trust her judgment completely. She's done a great job, starting from just a temporary scouting position a few years ago. I believe you can learn a lot from her. But she doesn't speak much English. You should practice your Mandarin. How much did you understand in the car?"

"Not a lot. Something about a palace?"

Pong laughed. "Wrong tone! But almost close! You may need some brushing up."

More, I knew, like a wholesale retrofit; "almost close" was an apt description of my foreign language acquisition skills, Mandarin being the latest and definitely last in a series of NSA dalliances with Spanish, then French, the briefest *Liebelei* with German (on account of a sultry young Swiss teacher on an exchange visit to Dunbar High), my level of proficiency in each being characteristically American in that I can reliably decipher a news headline and request change and order food and booze, though somehow I always understand more than I expect. In Mandarin, as you may be aware, there are four different tones plus neutral, so it's four or five times harder to learn, even for those of us who focus on the sounds of things. But if I could only understand a quarter of what they were talking about it was okay because I trusted Pong would tell me what I needed to know when I needed to know it, plus I loved just hearing them sing its lovely slushy, swervy song.

We called on our potential business partners for the balance of the day, with me trailing Pong with the bag of our samples. He was just as comfortable here as he was shuttling between his shops back in Dunbar Village, or riding a swell off the south shore of Oahu, or addressing his golf ball on the very first fairway he'd ever strolled, moving with unhurried purpose like this was his very own planet, which should be the case with us all. It is ours, right? I realize now that this was one of the reasons people took so readily to him, that wherever he was or whatever he was doing you got the idea that he was meant to be there, that this was *his* gig, though without bluster or cockiness or entitlement. Most of us can't accept that the gig is *ours,* so we lurk around, we tug and scratch at ourselves as if in borrowed skins, and never fully belong to the moments that can steadily add up to nothing a lot quicker than you think.

We took our time with each visit; while I very carefully poured out the various jamu in teensy fine Japanese porcelain cups set on a teensy turned-wood tray, Pong gave the pitch. Not that I know what Chinese businesspeople are like, or what exactly he said, but I could tell from his rhythm and tone and posture that he was bringing everything to bear, his many flowing and integrated identities, speaking as this diasporic Chinese and new-epoch American, the PhD chemist and the globalist entrepreneur, this one-man enterprise whose every activity seemed cast to be potentially profitable but who gave you faith that he didn't value solely money. He was all the above but above all he was his utterly expert, supremely reasonable Pongness, odd of coiffure but otherwise sleekly and elegantly togged, a person who registered absolutely everything while never forfeiting a second.

Pong explained the provenance and composition of the potions and their particular applications for health and well-being, any initial hesitance morphing into the surprise enchantment that snuck up on anyone who dealt with him. The way he had the pharmacy heiress leaning in to listen to the details of his evidently exotic story of the tiny island archipelago where Getty learned his craft from the jamu witch got me thinking how Pong was a sort of jamu himself, a human tonic to dissolve our habits of inattention and complacency. The organic-food-stores couple, obviously more analytically inclined, heard his professorial description of the particular amalgam of roots and herbs in our sample bottles, while the convenience-store magnate, a self-made guy who belched and talked rough and was by far the most skeptical, got Pong's no-nonsense take on his customer base of overworked, harried, sleep-deprived wage slaves who could use rejuvenating boosts that were actually healthful, unlike the typical energy drinks. He tailored these pitches for sure but what I admired was that they weren't in the least fake or over-flogged. Pong offered them the angles they needed and wanted to make a free and confident decision that you could see became ulti-mately theirs and theirs alone.

Pong, I realized, made himself their partner, not the other way around.

All three signed up for nearly twice the orders that Pong and the crew had projected for them, in sum still a relatively modest level but a clear indication of the upside potential of Elixirent. As we waited outside the office tower for our car to come around Pong complimented me on my spotless drop-by-drop decanting—those teacups would be perfect shot glasses for Stuart Little—as well as my calm demeanor.

"I hope you don't think you have to remain silent," Pong added. "They all know enough English, even Mr. Jiu"—the convenience stores guy—"whose kids attend boarding schools in New England."

"I should have figured," I said, surely familiar with how many Chinese nationals there were in the States, even at my tiny in-the-boonies college. Their families were much more globally adept and literate than most of the other folks in Dunbar, who are certain they live at the very center of the world, and who have no idea that the center has already shifted. "Not sure what I could have added, though."

"Nonsense. You are not a servant. You are not a robot. You are my associate, and a qualified one. I know you learned everything I did from Getty about jamu and our product. So you should not be afraid to offer your perspectives."

I nodded, glad for his confidence, if still drawing a blank on what I might have contributed.

"For the moment, we will sell jamu for specific conditions, like lack of energy, sexual dysfunction, poor digestion, and so on. But as Getty insisted, there is always an underlying circumstance, which is as much rooted in the mind as it is in the body. We must understand this, too. I can foresee the development of a system of personalized jamu, like from a cart on a dirt street but on a mass scale. Perhaps through some kind of home-based technology, an apparatus with AI that could employ instant blood panels and biometrics and other tests to diagnose the physical. The ultimate scenario would be to unlock a more lasting well-being by composing a unique, customized formula for each person for a certain duration, a month or week or even that very day. People don't simply want to live longer. They want to feel like when they were young like you, without reminders of the mortal limits of their bodies. If something like our jamu could help them do that, to allow them to live fully without having to be aware of living, that would be wonderful."

"Is that really possible?"

"Why not?" Pong said, now flagging our driver. "Don't you feel limitless? Don't you feel wonderful?"

I thought about what Pong was proposing, about how people wanted to feel like twenty-year-olds, which naturally I never thought about but I guess made sense. Except for when we nearly drowned together back at Oahu, and the foot torture/massage, and maybe the time in eighth grade when Missy Cantor agreed to give me a Halloween-night hand job but only while wearing her red pleather gloves, I'd not been bothered too much by bodily anguish, but the ways in which my mind felt stricken and infirm and hopeless, this (depending on how you look at it) from my miserably happy or happily miserable childhood, were pretty much innumerable. "By the way," Pong said, "did you check your blazer pocket?"

I dug inside and found a slip of a cardboard box. I opened the end and out slid the Japanese folding knife. After our frightening circus act at the mall we'd quickly left and I hadn't noticed that Pong had bought it.

"There is little need for carrying something like a small knife, living in a place like Dunbar. But I believe it can be a welcome tool in a variety of situations."

"I bet," I said, totally on board in principle, though no scenarios were popping into my head, for I was just another desultory, harmless kid from the slightly less nice side of a nice suburban American town, and thus could have no clue as to the knife's diverse utility.

"At the very least, keep it as a memento of the trip. And our friendship."

So I did, still do.

Our driver dropped us off at our dinner. I had the last of our jamu samples but Pong told me not to expect Drum Kappagoda to want to try them. He might but might not, even if he made a large order.

"We will let him guide our actions."

I wasn't at all anxious, given that we'd been warmed up with all our selling already, but when we entered the restaurant in a precinct of the city that somehow hadn't yet been razed and modernized, a nervy colonic murmur conducted up through me. It was not the place that was unsettling—no doubt the tidy, modest establishment was unusually set up, with high-backed stools set around a central semicircular table-height bar that took up most of the single low-ceilinged room—but instead what made me pause was the small huddle of men awaiting us, who, even in my extremely limited experience, appeared to be the incarnation of mayhem; they were, I would have to say, thugs, which might have been uncharitable of me but I had no choice, in that they looked abraded and angular and seriously hard-used, like tools long tossed and banged around in the toolbox, their frames menacingly bulked up with prison-yard muscles and fatty après-crime meals, their necks and forearms tatted with designs of flames and measles-looking red dots and scripty

Chinese characters. One guy, shaved bald and wearing dark aviators, had a spiderweb inked over his entire face and scalp, the
spooled end of it knotting into a thickly corded noose that wound
around his neck. It was menacing, painful-looking handiwork that
made me long for the pharmacy heiress in her boiled-wool Fendi suit
and pearls. I glanced to Pong in the hope that he was pivoting us
out to the street but he was already shaking hands with an older
man, who was not tattooed at all, at least as far as was evident.

"Let me make an introduction of my associate," Pong said. "Mr.
Kappagoda, this is Tiller Bardmon."

"Welcome, young man," Kappagoda said, taking my dampish
hand. His, on the contrary, was as cool and dry as a winter-morning
newspaper on our Dunbar doorstep, his grip firm but slightly trem-
ulous. He had these wide-set and somewhat sleepy eyes, which in a
weird way made him look a little like Jackie O, if Jackie O had had
a salt-and-pepper crew cut and was an older man of multi-Asian
heritage. He took the chair at the center of the semicircular counter
and had Pong and me flanking him, and although the bunch of us
were in pretty close quarters I felt a bit forsaken, especially with
stony-jawed, tattooed Spideyface on my other side breathing audibly
through his mouth. I naturally wondered why a successful international businessman like Kappagoda would need such a badass crew.
It was clearly *his* crew, from the way they didn't hesitate or quite
meet his eyes when he motioned them to sit; they were all like that,
whether they were smoking or drinking or both, they were doing it
with a certain desolate reckoning, weighing some play they'd made
or would make as if they were at the final table of the World Series
of Poker. Drum Kappagoda, being the boss man, was the most desolate of all, maybe because he'd done a lifetime of reckoning.

"You have experienced *robata*?" he asked with an avuncular lilt.
Pong nodded but I had no idea what Drum was talking about so

I shook my head, afraid that I had misunderstood Pong's quick description in the car that this was a restaurant for grilled food, *robata* sounding somehow penal and exotic.

"What good timing then for your visit to Shenzhen!" Drum brightly said. He was clearly eager for us, almost nerdily so. "I should tell you, there are many robatayaki restaurants in Japan, of course, but even there, very few are worthwhile. There is a famous one in Tokyo with pictures of celebrities on the walls but that place is utterly useless. This robata is the only one in the city, and is run by a Kyoto native, but it is not often open. Tonight it happens to be."

I couldn't help but steal second glances at him. There was something about him that I was trying to figure out, and I realized after checking out his frame and his gait and even the timbre of his voice that it was in fact his face that was the issue. It wasn't that it was odd-looking or good-looking or somehow remarkable in its Jackie O features. It was his complexion that took me aback, for even in the murky lighting, it was remarkably pale, aggressively pale, although different from Lucky's pallor, which came from being untouched by the sun. With Drum the paleness was not just the hue of his derma but more a kind of emanation, this heatless internal glowing, like the light from an LED bulb.

Drum explained, "Robata, if you do not know, Tiller, is vegetables and meat and seafood that is grilled over coals, simply and with minimal seasoning. For this reason, the freshness of the ingredients is obviously important. But at this robata, freshness is not just about exquisite flavor—say, that a piece of squash or eggplant is the finest example of squash or eggplant you can ever taste. Which I hope for you it will be. But taste is not only something pleasurable. I like to believe it's a sign of an essential vitality. It's a portal to a more lasting and virtuous energy that is everywhere in our world as well as in us. I gather my men here whenever possible so we can partake of this vigor."

Drum raised his small glass of tea and Pong and I raised our pilsners and Drum's shadow crew did the same and we drank and gaveled down our glasses on the counter. We repeated this, in a formal rhythm, four or five times before our first courses were ready, waiters bringing double-sized bottles of beer for each man. You could already smell the initial round of vegetables slightly charring, earthy scallion bulbs and sweet carrot and slightly funky cabbage. Drum directed the chefs to serve Pong and me first. It was an unusual process of eating, as the chefs were too far back from us diners to simply hand us the dishes. So they used what looked like long pizza paddles, placing a small dish of food on the extra-small head and then extending it across the wide counter to each man. We got the first round, which I ate probably too quickly, as I was suddenly feeling starved. Then came a dozen more veggies, a single bite of each, then the rest of the bites, including an ocean's range of goodies such as baby octopus and head-on shrimp and the collar of a small freshwater fish, crunchy and fatty at once, which was followed by mini-skewers of every last part of a chicken, including the butt and gizzard; snout and foot and belly of pork; tongues of veal and lamb and duck; and then some cubes of beef that I barely needed to chew and could practically let melt in my mouth.

I would have thought that I wasn't the ideal taster for such plainly prepared food, being that I was self-raised on lab-engineered freezer fodder like Extreme Nacho Jalapeño Poppers and pizza-flavored chicken wings and pigs in honey-biscuit blankets, but there was something so simple and pure in each mouthful that I was sure the hatchet-faced chefs had secretly brushed some Kush shatter on every one, for how the flavors bloomed on my tongue in super-high definition. A hint of woodsmoke laced every bite, and yet deeper down I felt I was not so much eating as I was the receptor of special messages from the world, each speaking of its originating ground, its air, its water, its geological or animal *whatness*. It was not a question of liking or not liking the flavors, of the pleasure or displeasure of taste. Instead, I realized that perhaps these were the containers of the "vigor" Drum was talking about, the essential live material of the realm, most simply rendered.

Pong was enjoying the meal, too, but he was mostly focused on Drum, refilling his tea and insisting he select first from the paddles and even pulling out the stool for him when Drum returned from the bathroom. To my eye the kindly attention had little to do with selling. Nor was it the fawning of a junior. If anything, his guiding touch on the shoulder as Drum sat back down, or the steady, careful pouring from the teakettle, felt like the solicitous hand of a son, one that simply said, *I'm here*. I don't think I've ever handled Clark in such a filial way. Sure, we might do the shoulder-first man-hug at departures and arrivals but otherwise didn't physically engage. Funny thing was that I also couldn't imagine Pong doing likewise to his own father, who, despite all that he'd endured and lost back in the Cultural Revolution, still had to cook in a separate room.

And then it finally came to me, doofus that I am, regarding the off-color cast of Drum Kappagoda's visage: the man was not physically well.

"Tell me, Pong," Drum said, between sips from his tea. The cup ever so slightly oscillated in his hand. "In Scottsdale you briefly mentioned the yoga practice you do with your wife. Are you quite expert?"

Pong replied, "Not at all. I just follow along. I enjoy it but she is the advanced one. I'm a happy intermediate."

"I ask because as you know I'm quite avid. In fact, I'm hosting a special conference for my top yoga teachers from our worldwide studios. It'll be held at my villa here in Shenzhen."

"Boss is true top yoga master," Spideyface said, surprising me with his English.

"Ji-Ji's loyalty is admirable but in this case overdone. I'm not a gifted person. I am simply a very hard worker. I don't give up. But I'm also innately impatient, which is my great flaw as a yoga practitioner. Can you imagine, trying to unlock the secrets of yoga while in a great rush?"

"Perhaps as long as you are not too breathless . . ."

Drum chuckled at Pong's lame joke. "I suspect you could do poses without breathing. You have a look of great flexibility. I am not naturally flexible, it turns out. But I toiled and pushed myself and somehow I reached quite a high level. My teacher was genuinely amazed, and said I was ready to begin training as an instructor if I wanted. But as with all endeavors, it's not simply more effort or exertion that leads to mastery."

"One has to open that door another way," Pong said.

"Indeed," Drum concurred, now turning to me. "What do you think, Tiller? How should we open that door?"

Both men casually awaited my answer, which was daunting enough. What made it worse was that Pong looked completely unconcerned about what I might say, as if he either had every confidence in me or already knew I was doomed, which basically iced me some more. I took an awkwardly deep gulp of beer. I had zero opinions of course but at this point in my travels with Pong I was already relying on imagining what his moves might be—WWPD was my mental bumper sticker—and so murmured: "See that the door isn't there?"

"*Waaah!*" Drum bellowed, clapping me on the back. "It's a matter of possibility, isn't it? Rethinking every question. The door is not there, and never was!"

I nodded, just smart enough not to utter another word.

"Where did you find this one?" Drum asked.

"Tiller's a local hometown boy," Pong said with pride.

"I must visit your hometown, then."

"Not necessary," Pong said, now giving me a wink. "Tiller is a unique resource. You will see more of this. Maybe renewable, too!"

Pong laughed, and Drum laughed, and so did I and Spideyface, with the idle merriment of men bonding via vittles and drink. Drum nodded at me approvingly, I thought, or at least like I wasn't some less than fresh morsel he had to endure.

We stayed for another couple hours, the chefs pacing us nibble by nibble. In the end it still wasn't a lot of food, and I felt more filled up with the lager that was oiling the gears of Drum's crew. It was getting more boisterous in the room with their throaty strum, a rolling murmur that further warmed the smoky air, and without realizing it I found myself jawing away at a level that would have made my long-suffering Mandarin 2 instructor glee-weep her undies. I was breezily asking Spideyface what brand of local beer he favored, and opining to his muscly associate on the best hoverboard deals in Huaqiangbei, and show-and-telling the nifty mechanism of the mini-switchblade Pong had given me, which Spideyface then took up and with it instantly whittled a chopstick into a lethally sharp spike that he used to impale some Wagyu cubes.

We traded depth charges of *shochu* shots in beer, moving on to smoking their menthol cigarettes, and I got even more expansive, blowharding on the high quality of Asian airports and how to chat up American college girls and the strength of certain varieties of weed, the guys as delighted as if they'd come upon a talking dog, tickled by my fluency that I heard as standard but was likely as cockeyed as Getty's guerrilla English. Emboldened, I asked them what they did for their boss and after a pause to appraise me Spideyface ran down some of their current projects like running MMORPG treasure-mining operations in southern China and trading cryptocurrency in Korea and managing hostess bars and pachinko parlors and lottery kiosks in Japan, his open mention of this quasi-legit side of Drum's numerous enterprises demonstrating, I supposed, his boss's trust of Pong and, by extension, me.

Meanwhile Drum and Pong discussed introducing Elixirent

through his yoga studios, targeting flavor blends for certain regions (salty and sour for South Asians, a sweeter blend for northern Asians), strategies for varying packaging and pricing, et cetera, although my ears pricked up when I heard Pong mention a bottling they referred to as "HG." It was clear that Drum had a special interest in this, as he had now turned to face Pong straight on.

"So when do you expect my formulation to be ready?" Drum asked. I thought, sure, why not mix up a custom drink for their prime partner (I was picturing HIGH GRADE written in marker on a stoppered bottle), a potion targeting his particular wants, ills, bodily and otherwise.

"As soon as possible," Pong said. "We are still awaiting several key components. I expect they will arrive by next week. Once they do I am confident it will be ready within a month."

"Oh," Drum said, suddenly deflated. "I thought our friend Mr. Choi spoke about it being no more than a week or two. He seemed quite sure about this. Is he mistaken?"

"Lucky is an optimistic man," Pong answered, taking in a breath. I remembered what Bags Patel had said back at the Chop Station, about having a friend thusly named.

"I cannot promise, but we will try our best."

"I know you will." Drum took hold of Pong's wrist on the counter, gently shaking it. "Thank you."

"We must thank *you*," Pong brightly answered, bringing me into the conversation. "We are fortunate for this opportunity to work together. Tiller is as excited as I am. Isn't that right?"

"*Wuyi!*" I blurted, instantly boosted that Pong was so naturally drawing me in on this sidebar. Drum noted this, too, his eyes momentarily widening, but then he said "*Wuyi!*" back, and we drank in unison, beers for us and for Drum his lukewarm tea. When Drum excused himself to use the toilet I asked Pong what exactly Drum's formulation was.

"The specifics are not important," Pong said, indicating to the server that he should refill our beer glasses. "Most critical is that the players get to know one another. Everything, especially business, works best when partnerships are strong. No doubt this was the case with your fellow dishwashers, yes?"

It sure was, our mean machine in the steam, though pinging bright in my head was that I was now, according to Pong, one of the players in the play. So let us play!

Soon after that we hit the steamy midnight alleys of what was left of old Shenzhen. Pong insisted on paying the robatayaki bill, saying he knew Drum would be taking care of the rest of the evening, which would no doubt be a big ticket. Drum let him. I didn't know what anything cost though I figured it couldn't be too pricey, given that it was simply cut-up raw food grilled over wood, but when I saw Pong handing over a mighty stack of cash to the waiter I asked him while walking out and he said about $300 per man, including beer and tea, which made me marvel not only about the perceived value of said food but what that suggested was still ahead of us.

"Where are we going now?" I asked Pong, as we ambled like gangbangers beside Spideyface and his guys. Drum had gone another route, to pick up someone.

"To sing," Pong stated plainly, as if there was nothing else we could possibly do.

14.

THROUGH MY WHOLE SHORT LIFE, I sang all the time but never out loud. Maybe you're like this, too. You're not even a shower star, or an expressway belter, the diva who's always rocking her personal La Scala.

My mother was a singer. I'd hear her when she washed her hair in the evenings, her voice warbling down the hall from her bedroom like an antique radio. Throughout the day she played her cherished vinyl, stacking them five at a time on the post of the automatic holder, each LP dropping down with a cushy *phhlott* after the previous one finished, with me flipping the stack when done so we could listen to the B sides. At the start of the day she didn't sing along, but just hummed like she was warming up, or grooved in place while she fixed us an egg salad sandwich or folded the laundry. But at night she would let them out, the ballads, the gospel and folk songs, the R&B and the country, and if my parents' bedroom door was already closed I'd take a picture book with me into the hallway and press my side against the wall, the water in the pipes slurring backup. I could feel her key before I heard it, the melodies reaching down my spine and warming my vertebrae.

I never sang with her except to myself, silently, in the empty arena of my chest, and I've done it like that ever since. So when Pong and

I and Drum and his crew reconvened at a place called Karaoke Garbo (inside it was literally plastered with film stills of the sleepy-eyed star), I began strategizing on how I could defer to others and skip turns singing, maybe via well-timed trips to the bathroom or pretending (or not pretending) to pass out.

Once, freshman year, I got caravanned to a dorm room sing-along where they had a karaoke machine and after an hour of listening to the defacement and mutilation of too many fine songs I felt literally nauseated (partly because of the Jell-O shots and the butterscotch fudge laced with hash oil) and had to run out. Only this one guy could sing; he was a nice enough kid who was more than a little doofy-looking because of a serious underbite, and to whom nobody paid much attention, but when he unleashed the chorus of "You've Lost That Lovin' Feelin'" I thought the pair of mean-girl blondies everybody including the other girls hated but wanted desperately to screw were going to tug the kid back to their room and rock his world, for how they leapt up from the couch. Man, the kid had some pipes. The meanies went wiggy for his blues-a-billy rendition of "Sweet Child o' Mine," clawing wildly at his "Feel the Bern" T-shirt. They creamed their skinny jeans when he slow-rode the velvet rails through Pearl Jam's "Last Kiss." The girls unfortunately ruined his final song, "Don't Stop Believin'," getting all pitchy and screamy beside him. The kid didn't care, of course, being psyched that he was cheek to cheek with the hotties play-fellating his mic in front of everybody, but a few days later at the dining hall salad bar I saw how his expectant expression instantly shattered when they didn't even recognize him.

Lesson: Keep on singing, bromeo.

Anyway, I felt like we were spelunking as we were led by a host down and up and sideways through the fire-hazard maze of Karaoke Garbo, which was off a side street of a side street, and by the time we reached our room I had no idea whether we were above or below sea level, which didn't matter except that I was still scheming how I'd slip away when the time came. It's not just fear and embarrassment about singing in front of others. It's like this: I can't bear to butcher what should only be beautiful, I can't handle defiling what ought to be sublime. With poetry and painting and baking bread, I once overhead my mother say to my father (who was at that point attempting to make baguettes), one ought to refrain if you're merely okay. Not so gently brutal, she was. And IMHO, song belongs in that category, too; like anything sacred, it's more fragile than you know. Whether my mother could have been a professional singer is debatable but at the very least she had perfect pitch and a grooving sense of rhythm and a tone to her voice like long-laundered flannel, and nobody could ever say it was anything but a blessing to listen to her.

Our room at Garbo was long and narrow, fitted along the walls with a sectional sofa and low table commensurately proportioned and laden with platters of sliced tropical fruit and strips of dried squid and sushi, along with bottles of Korean-brand Scotch whiskey, whatever that was. Garbo was owned by a Korean-Chinese woman who had a couple other nightclubs, and I realized this was who Drum's guys were, in whole or part ethnically Korean, a rough caste probably emigrated from northern China, and I could hear tidbits of their natal language as they spoke with the Garbo staff. Drum wasn't there yet but Spideyface directed us to our places on the plush three-sided banquette that lined the walls of the long rectangular room, Pong and I next to each other at the far corner, with a seat left for Drum at the head, a few of his crew taking their places along the length as they arrived.

When Drum entered we all rose, in deference to him of course but also to acknowledge the person with him, a young woman dressed in a clingy fire-engine-red velour tracksuit with white striping down the legs and arms. She was his daughter, Constance, who, I'd later learn, was his only child, and was a few years older than I was; his much younger wife had died of a stroke shortly after giving birth. Constance was slightly taller than Drum, five-ten at least in her thickly soled cross-trainers, and she had a wonderfully sturdy, athletic build that pushed out from the form-fitting tracksuit.

Like Drum, Constance sat erectly, her forearms posed on the table as if for negotiation; like Drum, her neck was regally straight and extended; like Drum, the quietly engulfing intake of her gaze regarded me to a state of unsettlement, though hers through large square black-framed eyeglasses. She was a big gorgeous nerdy-looking brute of a gal, with a full head of wavy shoulder-length black hair that was probably what Drum's would look like, if his weren't crew-cut short. She had a very shapely and full bosom but it was the sight of her hands that drew my attention. Her hands were largish and sinewy and even sturdier-looking than his, as the skin of her father's hands was papery and mottled with age spots. We'd only bowed to each other so hadn't shaken, but I could almost feel the hard tendons of her grip jamming my knuckles together.

Constance, I thought in Getty speech, *she is strong.*

While the other accompanying members of Drum's crew came in and the staff set up mic stands, the Garbo owner came in and greeted us. Drum called her Madam. She was a beautiful older woman, with darkly shadowed eyes and long silver-painted nails, and she wore a designer skirt suit, and demurely shook hands with Constance and Pong and Spideyface and the rest of us but gave Drum a big woolly American-style hug and kiss on the cheek that made me wonder if they'd once had their moment in the sun. With mischievous eyes the two of them conversed in a thick congee of English and Mandarin about their physical states, each heaping flattery on the other's good form but denigrating his/her own, and then she gave us a quick toast of welcome with the glasses of bubbly her staff had poured for us, Drum actually taking a sip of his after clinking her flute.

Next to come in were a line of young women in cocktail dresses and full-on red-carpet hair and makeup, each carrying a tiny dangly purse. There were eight in all, one for each of us, including Constance, and from my severely limited suburban American perspective they were legitimate knockouts, professional-model quality; they certainly stood there like real models, jauntily posed on their spike heels without a hint of effort or awkwardness as they simultaneously acknowledged and ignored us.

I quietly asked Pong, "Are they, you know . . ."

"Oh, it's not that way. They're simply hostesses. Their job is to converse and drink and sing with us. That might sound very old-fashioned to you, and even backward, but it's all quite innocent. Naturally, if you liked one of them, and she liked you, a dinner could be arranged. As with any other date, what happens after that is a mutual decision. However, it could involve a more substantial investment. Gifts, if not money." Pong's brow lifted. "Why, Tiller, are you interested?"

"No way," I said, simultaneously charged up and shrunken by the prospect of going out with any of these stunning young women. In the ruthless teen scene of Dunbar it was nearly impossible to date outside a very narrow lateral band of looks and social skills/cachet, which for me meant meeting up with symmetrically attractive girls (meaning, mirroring me, not totally funny-looking), who were of course totally complex and thoughtful human beings. Not that these hostesses weren't complex and thoughtful, just that as usual I was instantly taken hostage by their superior physical beauty, which I know I shouldn't be but I am.

"I prefer more down-to-earth looks as well," Pong said, somehow sensing my timorousness. "But I don't mean to criticize. Most probably are not quite succeeding yet in acting or modeling and so are here, where they can earn good money while they keep their dreams alive. They are doing what they need to, and that is honorable enough."

Madam now took the prerogative of pairing us, each hostess taking a seat beside her designated guest. I was assigned the one who spoke English best, which I was thankful for, as I could hardly think otherwise. She was without doubt the most lovely human specimen I will ever be in such proximity to, one seemingly cast in pure white chocolate. We got along right away, as she was eager to use her English. Her Garbo alias was Prada; her real name she wouldn't disclose, but the handle she went by when she lived briefly in the United States during her middle school years, somewhere near Harrisburg, Pennsylvania, was Maureen, after Maureen O'Hara, the old-time actress, whom her grandmother admired. That is what she wanted me to call her.

How cool, I thought. *A goddess named Maureen.*

"In my whole life I was most happy there," she said, pouring out two shots of the faux Scotch. "It's small town that's so quiet, with many beautiful trees. People are so nice, so friendly. Okay, some boys not so nice. Bad boys everyplace, right? China full of them! Beijing terrible. Shanghai terrible. Guangzhou worst. Shenzhen okay. But I think not you, right?"

Maureen winked, and I winked, and we drank to that, because for sure some of us are not so nice, even when we try to be, which I know is no excuse. Anyway, she plated us some cut pineapple and mochi and we talked all about Shenzhen air quality (better than most Chinese megacities), her favorite American foods (mac 'n' cheese, California roll), career aspirations (starting a floral design business). Was I falling in love with her a little? Sure. In truth, I fall a little in love with most any woman who is halfway kind to me, due to my maternally devoid upbringing, I'm sure. It can happen at a coffee shop counter, at the public library, while getting my hair cut. All I was hoping for was that sometime before the evening ended Maureen might let me snuggle up to her exquisite confectionary goodness and have some of that goodness melt a little on me.

The others were settling into their pairings with varying levels of enthusiasm, certainly none seeming as eager as I; it was standard operating procedure for them, even given the top-shelf hostesses, but nonetheless I noted how to the man Spideyface and his guys were exceedingly polite and solicitous, with none of the rudeness or crass behavior you might expect from semi-gangsters but are more likely to get from finance and corporate types, who are the real gangsters in this world.

Pong seemed comfortable chatting with his hostess and, I noticed, kept plenty of air space between them, like she was any schoolmate of his daughters. He even cut up the bigger cantaloupe chunks into smaller pieces for her, and so I did the same for Maureen, who fed me first before popping a piece into her own mouth. Drum was insisting on pouring the liquor for Madam, while a now-bifocaled Spideyface was paging through the karaoke song-list binder with his young lady, who made suggestions as they went. The only person who looked uneasy was Constance, who sat beside her own hostess quietly observing the proceedings. She glanced over at me every so often, and when our eyes met she looked away. Yes, it was strange that she was here with her dad but family life is a complicated venture and I was a nobody who knew squat and at that point I was as open to whatever was cued up as I'd ever been, or might be again.

There was a knock at the door and three young men appeared at the head of the room and bowed deeply. In unison they leapt and shouted an exhortation that sounded to me a lot like *Fuck yeah!* The lights went out, everything going black, and for a second I wondered if this was an ambush by a rival crew; I instinctively grabbed at Maureen, who said, "Hey!" But then maybe the loudest house music I'd ever heard started thumping the space and the three guys literally lit up, these rails of light glowing along the lines of their limbs and heads so that all you could see were these neon stick figures. They started juking to the beat, shifting in this rigid dance like they made up the inner mechanisms of a clock tower, and just at the moment I began to lose interest they switched into a different routine, and then another, churning locomotive wheels and then a ratcheting pipe organ and then actual cheer-squad backflips and floor dives, strobe lights popping off and piña-colada-scented fake smoke gushing from hidden spouts in the ceiling. It was weirdly retro and kind of tacky but sneaky awesome, too, and whether the hand clapping was part of the audio or just us I couldn't tell, primed as we were. But then we heard, in the pure darkness, a woman's lovely voice hum the opening bars of a song I'd heard long ago, maybe from my mother's turntable; delicate woodwinds arose to back the voice, and then a dimmed spot illuminated Madam, who stood before the mic where the performers were, the spot glowing brighter and brighter on, I now realized, her Garbo-like face, pearlescent and perfectly smooth, as she slowly, tenderly, sang:

Last dance . . .

Spideyface, seated beside me, hollered in a guttural English: "Sing it, diva lady!" And boy, did she, serenading us with that slow-burn opening, milking it and us, and when she sang those lines about being *so bad* I hooted before I could quell myself.

The speakers busted with the full musical accompaniment and a second beam lit a rotating disco globe and we were all up and shimmying to that unmistakable beat, and the whole room sang the famous refrain with her, though just that, for none of us wanted to obscure the rest of the performance, which was as sultry and vivacious as any Donna Summer ever gave, and sneakily sexier, coming from a gorgeous sixty-plus-year-old in pearls and glossy hair. We hit her with a standing O led by Drum and Spideyface and Pong, too, who was grinning superwide and nodding rhythmically like a bobblehead, and I found myself bleating, Maureen hooking her arm around my waist and hoisting her shot glass as we and everyone else toasted our siren queen.

The lights went up and Madam bowed and hugged Drum and bid us much gratitude and enjoyment for the rest of our evening, and then left to greet patrons in the other rooms.

"She sings only for special occasion," Maureen told me. "Like for Mr. Drum."

After that, Drum's posse took their turns, the hostesses either backing up the guys if they asked, or else singing separately. Every song was accompanied by a video (not related, just gauzy scenes of young Asian couples strolling hand in hand in parks or on long piers) and a scroll of lyrics on the big flat screen. There were varying levels of singing talent and polish but actually everybody could carry the two or three tunes they probably always sang, complete with characteristic tics all singers have, the dramatic pauses, and gestures of hand and head, and eyes squeezing tight as they reached for certain high notes.

A great moment was when one of the crew kept lunging forward à la Elvis on certain verses, really getting down and dirty, but then groaned and pulled up lame on the last lunge, grasping at his hammy. His mates had to help him to the banquette. It wasn't a serious pull, luckily, and everybody had a good laugh about it. The songs were varied, too, with a few that Pong had to fill me in on, including a fizzy Hong Kong pop tune from the '90s, and a somber Korean folk ballad that made Spideyface tear up. But then, to my surprise, Drum cued up a rock 'n' roll classic that I heard a lot when the cool kids wanted to go retro: "Hotel California." I got kind of sick of the song, just the way you would with pink champagne on ice if you had it too often, but hearing that long twelve-string guitar opener made me picture my parents sitting in the living room with big goblets of white wine and not talking but not too unhappy, just marinating in the hi-fi. Everybody got real quiet now, too, anticipating those three drumbeats, as Drum started to sing. His singing voice was a bit scratchy, like Don Henley's, though lower, and rougher, which I liked immediately and maybe even better than the original, his voice portending the quiet horror to come. We were mouthing it with him, not needing the scroll, as every sentient being in the known universe somehow knows every last one of the words.

When we got to the title lyric, we couldn't help practically roaring it, Drum holding out the mic to us so that the reverb shook the room with an ear-knifing whang of feedback. Since most of the selections were American pop and rock, I could hum along with most every number, hoot and clap at the right moments, mouth the choruses and bop in rhythm at my seat, which is to say simultaneously semiparticipate and go camo like I have most every day of my brief but oddly endless-feeling existence. Now things were moving much faster, and I wasn't so conscious of completely enjoying myself, which I was. How could I not, being there at the snug end of the table, coddled by Maureen and her dense, great-smelling cascade of hair while we snacked on mini-mochi and slices of mango, appreciating the care and respect each person had for his or her own songs, yes, but more the gathering, with no puffed-up irony or apology like with most people back home, who are so conscious of being judged. Maybe I never ran in the right pack, or maybe it's just me, but the brother/sisterhood vibe in the room and elsewhere in recent weeks was something I never experienced back in Dunbar or summer camp or college, or even in the rare instances when our still-intact nuclear family got together with uncles and aunts and cousins, the adults drinking lots of wine and talking loudly past one another, except for my mother, who'd wander in and plunk down with us kids mute and stomach-tubed on the Cartoon Network. And although I didn't perfectly fit in this latest of Pong's pan-Asian lineups there was also nothing to say I couldn't someday belong, for as his loyal protégé and new friend, I felt I was being rekeyed, my notches bearing a freshened edge, brighter and more defined, ready for serendipitous use.

Aren't we all master keys, if we truly want to be?

It was Pong's turn coming up, and for a moment I wondered if he might defer, as he looked perfectly content to lounge in the banquette with his hostess, head bopping and laughing and taking judicious sips from his glass, not to mention that I couldn't quite imagine him singing. But then this was not his problem but mine. If I had simply bumped into him on a Dunbar street, I couldn't have imagined him being all the other ways he was. I would have assumed he was like any other latecomer Asian immigrant, focused and industrious and leaving nothing to chance. A worker-bee bench chemist at a mega-pharma, but only that. Eyes on the prize, even if it wasn't clear what the prize really was. I couldn't have seen him as the multitargeting entrepreneur with ventures as varied in scale and kind as a fro-yo shop and car washes and an Indian wedding hall, and personal interests like yoga and surfing. I couldn't have placed him at the center of so many orbiting bodies, how each of us was drawn and held by the force of his peerless competence, the diverse skills and discerning aptitudes and effortless generosity that made him seem like he was the wealthiest person in the world.

Just then the door opened and a club employee ushered in a new guest; it was Lily Zhang, looking fresh and vigorous even this late into the evening. Pong popped up and introduced her to everyone with a round of quick handshakes and bows and she took a seat with him and his hostess. Pong poured her a drink and his hostess made up a little plate of snacks for her and although I couldn't hear them over the singing of one of Drum's guys, I could see they were whispering exuberantly about his performance, which veered at times off-key but was impressively self-assured, even cocky. People were getting real comfortable. At Spideyface's prompting, everyone did a "love shot" with their partner, intertwining arms while we drank, with Pong and Lily doing an acrobatic three-way with their hostess. Even Constance did one with hers, if dutifully. It was all good clean fun, goofier than anything else, though I admit I took the opportunity to lean in as close to Maureen as I could and breathe her in like she was a freshly baked Toll House cookie.

Spideyface finally mewled, "Mr. Lou!" and without a beat Pong patted his hair and walked to the front of the room. He consulted with the karaoke valet, who tapped in the codes to the songs he wanted, and waited, head bent in anticipation, for the flat screen to flare and the chest-high speakers to bellow.

Was Pong a good singer? Definitely, yes. Anybody with ears would have to agree. His tenor voice was precise and resonant, a radiating tone that inscribed a line in your chest like a marble rolled across a wooden table. He sang a sentimental Chinese song first, lovey and sweet, and then, to my surprise, "A Song for You," by Donny Hathaway, which I knew from my mother's LP library, made up of stuff from her own youth. He did it in a bluesy way, keeping in time and hitting most all the notes, and he moved about with the confidence of a cabaret pro, lifting his free hand with the soaring of a melody and casually pointing to us folks to punctuate a lyric. It was all a bit cheesy, which in fact made it great. Most notable, though, was how he embodied completely what he was singing, his face expressing the yearning or loving as if he'd not only written the song himself but also had lived out its dream, its hope, its lamentable tale. Then he waved to Lily to join him and they sang "Don't Go Breaking My Heart" with a jaunty in-sync pep that made me realize they'd done the number together before. I flashed on Minori in their yoga room, and wondered if she ever traveled with him, or how aware she was of his activities on business trips. Pong asked

Lily to do another with him but she said she wanted to hear one more solo from him and sat back with their hostess. For his last number, the valet had cued up "When I Was a Boy," from the second iteration of ELO, the opening bars of which made me picture the band's classic album covers on our shelves with those rainbow-lit disc starships.

Pong opened the song in a more textured tone, which was perfectly suited to the wistful lyrics. I already knew the song but now rooted deeper into the lyrics for the way Pong sang them, those phrases about doing what you dream of doing and nothing else, which seemed especially descriptive of Pong himself. After all he was Pong the Irrepressible, Pong the Buoyant, who in his own way was ever prevailing, ever rising. Coming from him, or at least what I knew of him, the longing and nostalgia of that melody felt especially poignant. The whole room went silent, no one singing along or cheering as they did with the other numbers, all of us simply happy to listen to him tell the story of the song. Drum was clearly moved, absently rubbing his chin, and he must have noticed me mouthing the words, because he made a motion that I go to Pong, quietly insisting, "He's your boss."

Of course Pong didn't need any help, but I knew what Drum meant, that I should simply stand up there with the man, get myself on his stage, and for fuck's sake maybe learn something, if not about karaoke. He was right; I was the only guest who hadn't yet performed (well, aside from Constance, who made it clear by her unstinting muteness that she was exclusively an observer), and although nobody cared a lick what I did, I began feeling that I was letting Pong down. He was my big brother, my mentor, my spirit guide to this and every other demimonde we might find ourselves in, and I realized I was crying, if only on the inside, because for the first time since we'd met I was mourning a time when he didn't exist.

Maureen must have picked up some whiff of my obliteration and she kissed me on the cheek, her peck tender but chaste, instantly evaporating. I let her take me by the hand to the front of the room, where the valet handed her a cordless mic. We gripped it between us as Pong began the last verse about being young and having no money, his eyes widening with our accompaniment that was really all Maureen, whose unusually powerful voice was the little sister to Dolly Parton's. Spideyface shouted something and she quickly bowed and stilettoed it back to the banquette, leaving me there as solo backup while Pong finished the song. Drum and his boys and the ladies gave him bravos, including Madam, who'd slipped back into the room. Even Constance was clapping in her seat.

"That was amazeballs," I said to him, while the valet put on background tunes.

"Thank you, I think!"

"My mother loved the ELO, and when this song came out a few years ago I played it all the time. You sing it as well as Jeff Lynne!"

"I heard you, too, even though you were singing very softly. You should have told me, Tiller. You have a very fine voice."

I shook my head, explained how I never sang aloud, couldn't hold a tune, et cetera, et cetera, and then hadn't even heard myself just now. But he simply twirled his finger at the valet, who restarted the music of "When I Was a Boy."

"We will sing it once more, this time with equal strength. Agreed?"

"I can't," I said, trying to push the mic back onto the valet, who wasn't sure if he should take it. "I don't know how."

"*You do know how,*" Pong said in a low tone, a new force to his Mandarinized accent somehow dispersing the flock of panic thwapping around my chest. "Let me give you advice. Yes?"

"Okay."

"Do you know *The Sound of Music?*"

I nodded, because of course I did, watching hours of Christmas-season TV, but also because my mother often crooned the soundtrack, for some reason, whenever she cleaned the house.

"Then think of the 'Do-Re-Mi' song in your head. You know, those lines that simply play the scale. Remember 'When-you-know-the-notes-to-sing, you-can-sing-most-an-y-thing.'"

Pong sang it, and so I heard Julie Andrews sing it, and soon I was hearing my mother, too; I could practically smell the ammonia and the lemon oil and the bleachy-minty scrubbing bubbles, and then I was singing it myself, even if weirdly I wasn't hearing a thing, as if some internal frequency was canceling me out.

"Bravo. In pure B-flat, and with perfect pitch," Pong said. "You have it in you, I knew. Now we will begin. Let yourself go free. Everybody is waiting."

I looked back at the long table and it was true, everyone was poised for our gig, cradling their lowball glasses and cigarettes, lozenging the cubed fruit in their mouths. Maureen, small-town-America trained, was flicking a butane lighter held high. Pong cuffed me and we stood shoulder to shoulder. I was only psyched to be his Kato, his Tonto, his ready satellite, but when the music to "When I Was a Boy" started again, I had to shut my eyes. I held the mic tightly. I drew a last, long breath.

Pong hit those first wistful lines, and I quickly joined in his key, but then he shifted and began harmonizing, which was fine, although now at an alarmingly lowered volume; I could hardly register the clean beam of his sound. I tried to drift downward, too, realign our duet, but by the time we got to the second stanza and I peeked again, Pong had stepped back off to the side. Was he even holding a mic? I shut my eyes tightly, sending myself into an inner space. I couldn't bear looking out toward the others and instead conjured up the songlines of Pong, and of Jeff Lynne, and then those of my mother, of how she might have testified, all their strains girding me as I let my voice roam with the gospel of a reckless and unbounded liberty.

The music ended and I nearly fell over in the wake of its vortex. A rueful quiet. But then hoots and howls rose up from Spideyface and his guys. Madam, who had slipped back in during my song, was applauding in the way the Queen of England might if she went too heavy on the Benadryl, these proper, if manic, bursts. Lily was beaming. With both hands Maureen was covering her heavenly beautiful mouth. Meanwhile Drum and Pong were eyeing each other across the room, neither quite sure of what had just happened. I wasn't sure, either, only feeling the sweat leaking down my spine, though it was in the cast of Constance's face that I understood that whatever had cracked open might not be easily closed up. She strode athletically forward and addressed me matter-of-factly: "What's your name again?"

I told her.

"All right, Tiller," she pressed me, maybe equal parts eager and mad, the way a kid is when she's afraid she might not get what she was counting on getting. "Again, please. Another song."

"I'd rather not."

"But I'd like you to keep going." She looked to her father, as if that would be enough to compel me.

"Please, miss, I wasn't going to—"

"Come on now, will you? I prefer your singing voice, I think, a billion times more to your talk."

Pong had caught my eye and he glanced across the room, directing me to Drum, who was pitched forward in his seat at the same expectant angle as Constance was leaning toward me.

"Here are the songs," she murmured, opening the ring binder the valet had handed her. "This is the page of my father's favorites, the ones he requests most."

Pong had already started back for his seat, which indicated clearly enough that I was locked and loaded. I scanned Drum's page but more in the hope of some reprieve than to figure out which songs to choose; I actually knew most of his selections, pop and rock and R&B classics from the '60s and '70s, many represented in my mother's vast LP collection, which took up the floor-to-ceiling shelving in our family room, the array so groaning and heavy that we never got around to removing them.

"I'll choose," Constance said, taking the folder from me. She dictated a string of song codes to the valet. "If you don't know the song, follow the words on screen."

Music began and I had to avert my gaze to the disco globe— Drum and his gang and Pong and Lily and Madam and the ladies appeared to me as an array of thousands—and I thought darkly, feeling the dense little baton of metal in my trouser pocket, the razor-sharp folding knife that I could now slash myself with and get taken to the hospital.

But the first song was one I knew, Van Morrison's "Caravan," lucky again because everybody could chime in on that part, you know, *La la la la, la-la-la*, which helped embolden me, and I didn't try to sing it through the nasal passages like the great man but from the belly instead, like a choirboy who's finally singing what he adores, and by the end I was gliding, soaring, drafting on my own contrails, and was hardly conscious that I went right into "Without You," which I knew via a tattered, ancient Harry Nilsson album, extra soft-pedaling it until the chorus jumped up an octave and I belted the reprise, about not being able to live without her. Then I tapped on Blood, Sweat & Tears' "I Can't Quit Her," with all that accompanying brass, and although it's not a natural karaoke tune I sang it with a shade of rough reckoning as I looked straight at Constance, who was looking straight at me. I have to say when this happens it hardly matters who the parties are, because when a real song arises between you there's not just a connection but in fact a sudden breach in the world, an opening that lets you touch a mystery. Sometimes, during a song she really loved, my mother would hold me by the shoulders and in her crazy way spear me with a lyric, right between the eyes, instantly wilting my tyke's frame and leaving my heart like a burst water balloon, torn and spent.

I'm not sure how many songs I sang after that, or what else was happening around me, everything running together from the flood of an instinctive fear with cascades of glee and this raging rush of a liberation. I was in the zone, upright but hardly conscious. I was flying at full speed through the fog of my former self. But who was I now? The one thing that homed me was the sight of Pong, who was back in the banquette with Lily, the two of them, I noticed, nestled shoulder to shoulder, swaying to my song. Aha. *It is difficult to live just one life.* All the while Constance was slowly blinking at me through her oversized spectacles, not budging from her spot that was so scarily close to me that she probably felt the heat of my breath.

"One more," she said, the sharp corners of her tone now blunted soft. "Will you sing one more?"

I nodded at her selection and she gestured to the valet. It was "Tiny Dancer," the one tune my dad would try to sing along with if it came on the radio, and would ply my mother with in his gentle, dopey, dorky way. He believed she was, until that bright blue afternoon when she wasn't, his blue-jean baby, his LA lady, seamstress for our band, and so I channeled good Clark, who, although he had no voice at all, had plenty of unrequited generosity, and recklessly laid it all over Constance with the few breaths left in my aching lungs.

15.

AFTER MY LAST SONG AT GARBO, and the progressive rounds of congratulatory shots with Spideyface and crew, after the many bows and hearty backslapping *Good night*s outside in the street, Drum made us promise to visit him at his compound in the hills northwest of the city. He'd practically hugged me, awed by my display, which he couldn't know was a capacity I didn't know of myself. It made me think that all of us fragile, flailing beings might somehow be secretly awesome at *something* and effortlessly connect with the sublime like a true and destined Natural. To thank him I piped a hero high C, and a tinny middle G clanked out instead, curdling the moment, but Pong stepped in to say my voice was undoubtedly tapped and that we should all retire, it being close to five in the morning. Drum mentioned again the upcoming conference for his best yoga instructors, and it was agreed that it was a perfect opportunity for us to introduce our line of jamu, as well as recruit them to be brand ambassadors to their colleagues and students. We were scheduled for a last two-day blitz roadshow to Korea and Japan before heading back home to Dunbar, but Pong promised we would make a brief visit after our next day's meeting in nearby Macau with some mainland investors, which I was happy to hear.

I liked Drum, was drawn to him as Pong had anticipated, even if there was something scarily murky about him, a dark pool of water that could be two inches deep, or two stories. But in my heart of hearts I didn't think so; maybe Drum was an unyielding semilegal businessman who required tough guys like Spideyface and crew to keep things and people in line, but there had been only genuinely joyful eating and drinking and singing, he had been only kindly and warmhearted in his exhortations and praise, and I felt sad for him that he had been a bit faded out by whatever serious illness was ailing him, his original color maybe never coming back.

I mention this because even though I wasn't old enough to understand, I instinctively knew my mother wasn't perfectly well herself. She didn't get infirm the way some people can be when they're not particularly happy, like battling chronic headaches or backaches, or suffering digestive problems, or being so drained of energy that she had to retreat to bed for a few hours. If anything my mother was fit and healthy, and usually on the move, either meeting a friend in town for a coffee or doing the grocery shopping or cleaning the bathrooms or running to the college's stadium and doing the steps of the entire visitors' section, up and down and up and down, which I watched her do whenever she took me after pickup from preschool. You could say that she was maybe too much on the move, roping a bit manically from this to that while Clark grew moss at his back office or in his favorite recliner in the family room, where he read biographies or watched cable news. Even when she was playing her records she'd pull down a couple dozen and spread them out on the floor in a messy but kind of cool collage and then restack them in the order they went on the record changer, six at a time, which she'd resleeve after playing and shelve back in their appropriate alphabetical slots, humming to the next tunes while going about her chores and to-dos.

Because we mostly avoid such things I've never talked seriously with Clark about what exactly her deal was, but I think we both know how in her own subtle way she grasped everything too tightly, without pause, until the minute and hour and day she couldn't anymore and had to let go. I remember once when Clark had an especially severe attack of vertigo and had to stay in bed for nearly a week with an eyeshade on—he'll still get one every so often, when he's feeling particularly tired or stressed—and she had to explain to me what it was.

"Everybody has a natural sense of balance and your daddy's has temporarily gone haywire. He doesn't know what's up or down or sideways. That's why he can't stand up."

I asked if it would happen to me next.

"I doubt it," she said. "You're just a little boy."

"Will it happen to you?"

She didn't answer immediately but then emptily smiled and shook her head, which heartened me because I was afraid she'd end up next to him and I'd be on my own, but picturing that absent expression now I know she was fighting off a different kind of vertigo, this disturbance rooted far deeper than in the inner ear. It was subtle, how she managed. She was much like any other young mother, but I can see now, if not understanding it then, how those constant movements and activities were her way of dealing with the shadows that were creeping up on her.

One time, when I was in kindergarten, we got together with a playgroup of other mom-and-kid pairs at a neighbor's house, the moms in the kitchen having rosé and potato chips, we kids in the backyard collecting dirt and branches and rocks for some undoubtedly critical project. The backyard was fenced and abutted the heavily wooded three-hundred-acre campus of a world-famous scientific institute—all sorts of painfully nerdy-looking people, mostly younger men with bad haircuts and spectacles, could be seen strolling through the neighborhood with their heads down or with slightly skewed grins of genius—but you could get through the fence via a swinging door and the resident kid suggested we look for our treasure farther afield and off we trooped, along a path and then down other branching ones and then ventured off trail to find some deer clearing and then bushwhacked to another and another until we realized we were lost, which made us panic and get more lost. It was high summertime so it wasn't getting dark anytime soon but the woods were jungly with weed trees and brambly with blackberry bushes and we could hardly move and kind of stalled in a group panic. Suddenly the weather changed and it got overcast and cooler and we could hear thunder rolling in and we started to get eaten by mosquitoes and it began to rain hard and at some point somebody started crying and so the rest of us started crying, too. I don't know how long it was but it seemed forever that we were like that, just standing there and whimpering, the sky starting to flash with lightning. Luckily we heard one of the moms calling her kid's name in the distance—two of them had come out in a search party—and we shouted and wailed even harder. It turned out we were pretty far away from the house, and had been AWOL a full hour, and I could tell from the poor lady's face that she was genuinely sick with worry, and about to get teary herself.

When we got back inside the house each of us hurtled ourselves face-first into our mothers' bellies, getting comforted and assured as you might think, the moms half giddy and casting off the surplus energy with lots of gentle scolding and joking. But what felt funny to me was how serious my mother was. Of course she was relieved that we'd been found and was hugging me hard, maybe as tightly as she could, but unlike the other moms she wasn't fixed on her child, she wasn't locked on me, for when I craned up she was staring off into the rainy woods, her face pale. When she glanced down at me she warmed, smiling broadly. Mussed my hair. But that look. I'd seen it enough before, when I caught her in repose between all her activities and chores. I couldn't know it then, but it was the look of dread, like she was seeing an infinitely unfurling emptiness.

You could say I'm just backfilling here, that I'm viewing this with a tidying retrospective lens. Probably so. I do think that if she was growing more and more intent on leaving us, it wasn't for the typical reasons. Okay, Clark couldn't have been the most exciting husband, and I wasn't the most inspiring child, and for sure our family life was as routine and undistinguished as any other, but her disappearing wasn't the result of some dire early midlife crisis where she acted out and drank too much and began dressing like a goth teen and slept with some slick PTA dad before realizing she had better get off this track for good. There was the one notable night when they went to a neighbor's psychedelics party and she and others ended up naked in the hot tub after Clark left for home early and she very publicly fooled around with another neighborhood woman whom she never talked to again, but that was a one-off happening they could compart away and live with, even if Clark visibly grimaced whenever the words "hot tub" were uttered, whether in conversation or on some TV commercial. What they couldn't master was my mother's mental state. As noted, Clark and I rarely talked about her—he might bring her up for no reason once a year—but he did once ask me when I was going through a rough time making any friends in a new elementary school whether I ever had a feeling of "blankness," especially when trying to connect with other kids. This was a half year or so after she left us. I didn't know what he was talking about and he described it more and I guess I finally understood and said I didn't, because I didn't. In fact, my heart was always quivering and leaping and swollen with bloody wanting at the time, which evidently came off to my classmates as creepy and pathetic, and one of the popular boys dubbed me Clingy, instantly dooming me to be shed by all at every instance.

My mother, according to Clark, had the opposite problem; thus the notion of "blankness." In the middle of one night, he told me a couple years ago, she woke him in a panic and said she had a dream she was eating a slice of a Divincenzo's fresh clam pizza, her very favorite, and it was like nothing to her, just a mouthful of gummi-ness and heat. *I couldn't taste anything,* she cried to him. *But even worse I couldn't even imagine what it tasted like!* I guess she thought she was losing the ability to feel emotions, even as she desperately wanted to feel them. Of course Clark flippantly told her she was crazy, which probably wasn't the ideal word, and she went back to sleep and never again brought it up with him. As noted, I was too little to add up what was going on with her, I was just your average massively self-involved boy, and if I noticed anything it was like that time I was almost lost in the woods and she embraced me too tightly, as if in doing so she could provoke the appropriate emotional re-sponse. She'd often push too hard, get us into situations that would be fun and scary, like briefly accelerating to one hundred miles per hour on an empty stretch of narrow Route 111, where the speed limit was forty-five. We'd both be breathless and shaking and I'd beg her to do it again but she'd have gone completely cold and would slow way down and practically crawl us home.

Was this what made her freak and cut herself out of our life? Maybe she really did have a kind of dementia at the tender age of thirty-three and like those much older folks had started to grow numb and disassociate from loved ones. Or maybe it was a creeping, sinister insanity she could see was closing in on her but could do nothing about. Whatever it was, I have to think she suffered. She must have thought she was a horrible wife, and a horrible mother, basically a horrible person not to love the people she wanted to love, and was steadily gnawed away by the guilt of it, such that she had to free herself of the feeling and disappear, a final selfish act that was mostly out of her hands.

It's out of our hands.

You'd think by now I'd be wary of seeing that same depleted look in Drum, knowing how people who are unwell can disappoint you, or worse. But as the song goes, I was young, dumb, and broke, at least emotionally, and simply psyched by being invited along. Besides, Drum seemed to like me, and clearly admired my singing, and he made sure to say he had a full-on professional karaoke setup in his villa that we could use when we visited. Then there was Constance, of course, who was still totally mysterious to me, although my body did involuntarily thrum whenever I looked at her, an unexpected pistoning that was not (quite) sexual, at least not just yet. It was the sort of magnetism that might draw a person to the buffed sloping hood of a classic car, or to the trunk of a massive lone oak, or even to a slab of slow-rusting steel left at a job site.

"Nice to meet," Constance had said as we were exiting Garbo, her tone as unswerving as her gaze.

I shook her hand and she practically crushed mine, holding me for a long and agonizing second, before departing with her father in their chauffeured sedan.

In the taxi to the hotel, Pong said, "You made an enormous impression tonight, Tiller. Drum was amazed, as I was. You didn't say you could sing so well."

I didn't say, because I didn't know, which seemed too weird and embarrassing to admit.

"Tiller's no conceited boy," Lily said, her Mandarin slurred with drink and sleepiness. It was nearly dawn. She was in the rear seat with Pong, shoulder to shoulder, her head tipped back as she spoke. "He's a good boy, yes?"

"*Hao haizi,*" Pong echoed, and I could see her nod, smile a little, and then doze off.

Her place was out of the way relative to our hotel so it took a long time to drop her. By the time we arrived she was dead asleep

255

and when Pong roused her she was so gluey with torpor that she could hardly step out of the car. She'd drunk a lot of whiskey pretty quickly without eating much at all, then did shots with Drum's guys the rest of the night. We both helped her to her feet and walked her to the entrance and Pong had me wait back in the taxi while he took her up to her apartment. From the rear seat I saw a window light up about four stories high. I must have fallen asleep for a while because when Pong returned the fare on the meter seemed to have increased by a few factors, plus the driver sighed irritably as he checked his watch. He gruffly asked where to next but Pong ignored him.

"Beg your pardon," he said to me. He must have been tired but didn't look it—Pong was one of those people who always seem freshly popped from the tennis-ball can—and checked his phone, texting something quick. He got a text and emojied back and I glanced up and saw the apartment window light go out. Pong said the name of our hotel to the driver, who protest-squealed the tires as we accelerated away.

"Lily wanted you to come up and sing some more," he said, chuckling. "I told her you needed to save your voice for the next time with Drum."

"I would have if you wanted."

"I'm certain of that," Pong said. "But we all need rest now. When Lily drinks, she cannot help but drink too much. Always too much. Yet you can be sure, tomorrow she will be at the facility before anybody else, ready to go. She will call a car to take us to Shekou and have emailed our ferry tickets for Macau."

"She never married?"

"She was once," Pong said, with a grim sigh. "She has a daughter, actually. The father is from a prominent Hong Kong family. He invests the family fortune from London. From the time of the divorce, when the girl was very young, she has lived with him. It's different in certain Asian families. I believe now she's in a boarding school in Switzerland."

"Does she ever see her?"

"I don't believe so, no."

I couldn't help but wonder if my mother also sometimes drank too much, or worked too hard, or pushed herself some other way, because there was nothing else to do.

"Anyway," Pong said, now putting his head back and closing his eyes, "Lily may be with us from time to time. You like her okay, yes?"

"I do," I said, because I did like her, and I realized, too, that maybe she and I had something in common, for having been left on our own by a deliberate kind of circumstance. And if that's why someone like Pong gathered us up, and why we were so eagerly gathered, it made sense enough to me.

The next afternoon we rode the turbojet ferry across the South China Sea to meet up with Lucky in Macau. He was bringing a couple potential Elixirent vendors down from Xi'an and Beijing for a few days of wining and dining and of course gambling, which is why most people visit the place. For tax reasons a certain percentage of the LLC partnership needed to be Chinese, and Lucky, through his job as a China-based FDA inspector, had made the introduction. Again it seemed it was one of those part-time full-time jobs, maybe like the tenured professors had at my cozy expensive college, the sort of career that allows plenty of freestyling that folks most unlike them—e.g., Pong and Lucky—would make financially advantageous. Lucky of course liked Macau, so Macau it would be.

Macau is a seaside Asian Las Vegas, the grand casinos and shopping promenades all done up in a rococo vernacular for the Chinese nouveau riche extreme, and come dusk the sheer blaring wattage of the lights fitted onto the cupolas and flying buttresses and penthouse aeries of the multitowered hotels and vaulting sky towers seemingly boosts the already balmy night air another few degrees, such that you're just that much thirstier for the games and buffets and shows and the many other licit and illicit activities on tap. What was most interesting about it touristically for me was the historical Portuguese and Chinese architecture, which dated from the time when Macau was a colony, and not just the ornate sixteenth- and seventeenth-century churches and mausoleums and fortresses and temples but also the simpler harbor-style dwellings and customs houses painted in bright colors.

Lucky had booked a line of ocean-view rooms in one of the top luxury hotels and I figured mine would be a basic compartment in some internal annex reserved for the traveling helpers and nannies, but he got me the same huge suite as everyone else's, seventy-five square meters of gilded furniture and high-thread-count sheets and plunge tubs for both your face and your ass, and every kind and shape of mirror everywhere, which made me not want to walk around naked. Apparently Lucky was one of those VVIPs, gambling-wise, so he got us comped, including freshly replenished fruit and champagne baskets each day, reservations at prime restaurants and nightclubs, a tee time at the top golf course, with luxe Sprinter van chauffeur service in between those points and the hotel. The expectation was that our group would be high rollers if not outright whales, with Lucky leading the way. Lucky was of course no billionaire—he was probably not even the richest of Pong's investment group—but he would wager like one after a big haul at the poker table, using his winnings to play nonskill games like craps and roulette. It was an unusual thing for a poker player, especially such a good one like Lucky, to want to subject himself to the stacked odds of the table games, but Lucky said he got a special high from beating the fate of the numbers, which was like beating the world. Pong told me he nearly busted a small casino in neighboring Cotai, winning nearly three million USD in the course of a few White-Russian-and-cigar-fueled days/nights at roulette, though he lost most of it the following month in a high rollers' superyacht cruise to Thailand sponsored by the same casino. When he played he said he got a feeling he called *ondol*, saying his Korean feet got so hot that he had to take off his loafers and socks and gamble barefoot.

After check-in I expected we'd first have a formal meeting with the mainland businessmen in one of the hotel's conference rooms and transition from there to a gentlemanly round of vittles and drinks, but no, Lucky Choi was our host and as our host he treated our potential partners like comrades we'd been marched with to Bataan, splattered with one another's sweat and piss and blood and now, having persevered, we could at last rest and recreate together with full-throated abandon. There was a pair of brothers from Beijing and one very skinny guy from Xi'an, scrubby, salt-of-the-earth fortysomething men who'd accumulated some serious bank via serial ventures like this one, and I think even they were somewhat surprised when first thing after they settled into their rooms Lucky gave each of them a heavy black-velvet pouch of slot machine tokens (I received a smaller pouch), and directed us straight to the main gaming parlor. Pong didn't gamble but sat our guests at reserved seats at the bigger-payoff machines and ordered drinks while telling them colorful historical facts about the famed trade that once routed through Macau, the flows of fancy silks from Japan and silver and gold wares from Lisbon and spices and teas from Malacca and Goa. He did this in his distinctively game, engaging brand of Poindexterhood, charming them with how genuinely fascinated he was by his subject, all while intermixing the cultural and commercial details and insights with cheery commiseration about the slots action, though without any toadying. Not being as fluent, I did my job of rounding out the cohort by cranking on the levers and drinking the sweet tropical drinks. Lucky gulped down his signature White Russians as he harangued and nudged and entreated his machine.

"Come on, you conniving little strumpet!"

"If you're going to fuck me at least me tell me you love me!"

"That's it, that's it, whirl just like that!"

The rest of us took his cue, and even knowing it was prior arrangement with the house, a rigged program I found myself uttering Lucky-like things, sweet-talking and trash-talking the inscrutable goblin carny of the flashing, dinging box with dark glee and umbrage. Each of us won a token payout, perhaps by house design. No surprise that Lucky won a fairly big one, if not on a scale that registered for him, and he gave a good chunk of his winnings to our guests and generously tipped the waitstaff with the rest.

The next thirty-six hours were something of a blur, though not in the fear-and-loathing or lost-weekend kind of way. Maybe Asian guys are different, or maybe they're not, but these particular Asian guys didn't seem hell-bent on destroying every last brain and liver cell through a dark night of the soul's journey to a good time. Yes, there was plenty of overeating and drinking; yes, there was nearly continuous gaming; and yes, there were a couple potentially hazardous moments that were somehow skirted. All very typical, you'd say, which would be accurate, but because Pong was setting the agenda along with Lucky (or in fact the hotel's VIP fixer/concierge assigned to Lucky, a creepy young Armani-suited fellow with a blinking blue earpiece), we enjoyed a wider universe of delights. In the daytime hours we toured a local maritime history museum, and took a Sri Lankan cooking class, and banged the gong at an old Chinese temple, and even visited the world's largest aquarium, on the neighboring island of Hengqin, where we actually donned wet suits and scuba dived in the massive main tank in full view of the aquarium-goers.

The guys from Xi'an and Beijing had never scuba dived, nor had I, but that didn't seem to matter to anyone during the fifteen-minute tutorial as we squeezed into our wet suits in the employee locker room. The casual pointers about how to breathe and not breathe and equalize the pressure in our ear passages, et cetera, seemed sufficient to us at the time although the Xi'an guy, Lo, was still pretty hungover from the coup de grâce nightcap of VSOP brandy and Cuban cigars Lucky plied him with in the wee hours of the first night, and by that juncture in our day's activities was dragging a bit, if still excited to plunge into the eleven-million-gallon tank, which is basically the size of a four-bedroom Dunbar Colonial, that was teeming with large oceangoing fish like rays and tuna and grouper.

The thing about scuba is that it looks so fun and easy on the cable shows, you imagine flippering through the blue perfection with a majesty that will reconnect you to a primordial yearning for the serene gill-based existence we once enjoyed and maybe should never have evolved out of, when the truth is that the first time you strap on the mask and stick the regulator in your mouth you feel like you've been transformed into a badly designed personal submarine that features poor visibility and a gag so you can't scream. Claustrophobia sets in. You breathe too fast, maybe because the rest of you naturally understands that you don't belong underwater. The pressure builds unexpectedly quickly as you descend, your eyes pushed from the side and behind, and it's now that you need to remember how the aquarium diver said to swallow hard to equalize, which doesn't work, so you have to pinch your nose instead and blow it out your ears like on a plane but in doing so nearly dislodge your mask. The other aquarium visitors assumed we were a crack crew of marine biologists conducting specialized research; they were pointing and waving at us, the children banging at the glass, and you had this idiotically valiant idea that you shouldn't disappoint or scare the kiddies by freaking out and pulling off your mask and surfacing, which is what poor Lo did when a man-sized hammerhead shark curled past and brushed his flippers with its dorsal fin. I would have ripped my mask off and split, too, had I not spotted a hollow in the coral reef and motored there as fast as Hooper does in *Jaws*.

Lo from Xi'an got a heinous earache from rising too fast, and one of the brothers from Beijing had to barf because of a sudden attack of nausea, but otherwise we were whole; I had bunkered in my niche of coral, sheepishly waving back and forth to a darling little girl in a blue-and-white polka-dot dress who perhaps thought I was a strange kind of sea life, until Pong found me and eventually coaxed me out and up to the surface. After years of an unsupervised childhood watching Shark Week on cable, I was as rooted as a big old barnacle-crusted mussel, and it took Pong practically shoving his hand in the hammerhead's mouth to show me what a domesticated pup it was. Otherwise I would have simply crouched there until my air tank ran out.

"It may surprise you," Pong said to me afterward in the aquarium café, where we were warming up with green tea and lattes, "but I have a sea-related phobia as well."

"Really? You always seem so comfortable in the water," I said, flashing back on when he was stuck under the waves, when he worked to free himself with such matter-of-fact curiosity, like he wasn't afraid at all.

"It is true. I am very comfortable. I have a recurring dream, however, of being stranded on a remote island, with nothing but ocean for thousands of miles around and no fresh water to drink."

"No food, either?"

"I don't know. It doesn't seem to be important. What I'm focused on in the dream is how to get fresh water. I keep staring at the skies, looking for rain clouds. But they are hopelessly clear."

"Are you dying of thirst?" I said, thinking about Pong's foster childhood in arid north-central China, waiting on the watermelons to ripen.

"Not yet. But I will be. It is all I can think about. I know the time is coming."

It would be easy to interpret this as the successful striver's fear of privation, which is how I automatically read it, Pong fearing the day when he had nothing. Sometimes dreams can be totally transparent. I wondered if I had emphasized the wrong thing about Pong's dream, which maybe wasn't only about "thirst," or about "thirst" at all, but about being alone, an isolated speck afloat on the giant sea. For when I thought about Pong and his Pongness it was always in the context of him and his multiple teams, first at Bags' golf club and at his shops in Dunbar and with the diverse population I encountered at his massive ever-telescoping house, and then every other meeting we'd had, from the Chop Station to Lucky's mom's place to now, whether among family members or employees or business colleagues or friends, and I realized the man was never actually solo for any significant stretch of time. I wondered if Pong was aware of this about himself, this unconscious habit of constant association. It was always eventful and entertaining hanging with his various crews, but what might it say about a person who never allows himself to be alone?

I knew what alone was like. I was by myself plenty in our house. I got used to it but there were days when I would do funny things to compensate. We had three toilets in the house and I'd pee in each one and not flush, just so it would feel like there was somebody else around when I went to pee again. (We are "If it's yellow let it mellow" people.) Clark never said anything about the piss in his masterbath toilet but probably because he often had to sprint to catch the train in the morning and sometimes neglected to flush anyway. Another thing I'd do was drop bread in the toaster even if I didn't want any, then run to another part of the house and wait for the smell of it to drift over. I'd play music of course, via a stack of LPs on the turntable, but here, too, it was stuff that I didn't particularly like, which would give me a flare of irritation that I could use for feeding a grudge against a phantom family member. Well before I learned how to drive I would even start the car out on the driveway and let it idle, the sound of the motor like somebody was waiting for me to come out, but one time I forgot to turn it off and it ran until it stalled, which totally perplexed Clark on the weekend when he wanted to go to the hardware store and found the needle on E. All of this is kind of pathetic, I know, because I'd end up having to eat or throw away that toast, and flush those stinky toilets, and resleeve each of the LPs, which only made it all the clearer how alone I was, and how I didn't want to be. Who really does? Because if you imagine yourself truly alone, islanded off from everybody else, you end up facing, whether you want to or not, a lot of gnarly, unsettling questions. After school I'd sit at the kitchen table and stare at the sugar-and-butter sandwich and glass of milk I'd prepared for myself and completely zone out to the electric buzz of the wall clock until my butt cheeks started to tingle with numbness, when I'd snap back to the moment and shiver at the pasty still life of my existence. And even an obtuse kid like me had to wonder, *What do you want and why do you want it? What are you doing here? Why do you even care?*

The only reason I could consistently come up with was *So that Clark won't worry.* But I thought if my dad were suddenly out of the picture, there truly were no answers. No angles, no anchors. Just me, breathing. That's all I amounted to, the scant in-and-out. Pong, on the other hand, had countless people and things tugging at him, girding him, enriching him, serving to root him wherever he went so that he was never in effect an interloper. And as was the case with our potential new business partners from Beijing and Xi'an, he was perpetually adding to the thicket of connections that made up his own world within the world.

There *was* a moment in the wee hours of our Macau day-to-night-to-day that gave me some pause. This was after the various cultural touring and activities, after the aquarium, after the many extended and brief rounds of gaming between and during said activities, after Lily unexpectedly appeared and met us in the lobby of the hotel looking somewhat aged by the late night back in Shenzhen, after the feast of Singapore-style salt-and-pepper crabs piled so high we could hardly see one another, after the nightclubbing and the steady drinking and the fourth and fifth meals of sidewalk koftas and fried noodles, when Lucky had us taxi to a club named Evergreen Shores, the bulbed signage in Space Age script flashing in emerald and gold and making you think we were checking into some retro lakeside motel in Wisconsin or Maine. I knew something was up when Pong, with Lily beside him, said, "Listen, Lucky, do you think this is perhaps not the night?" to which Lucky replied, "Then what night is it?"

The Beijing brothers tittered and Lo from Xi'an wickedly bleated and for once Pong didn't have a ready answer, so we all went in. I was still clueless about what was on tap as we were greeted and ushered into what could have been the gaudy home theater of a gaudy mansion, complete with a couple rows of green velvet auditorium-style seats arcing about a junior-sized stage curtained in shimmery fabric that looked like golden fish scales. We took up the first row, me sitting between Pong and Lily and the others. Some waiters hastily served us beer and liquor and a White Russian for Lucky like we'd arrived there just in time for a performance, but instead of the lights dimming they got brighter, some Chinese rap music busting out of hidden speakers, and I was about to ask Pong what kind of show this was, when I noticed that he'd placed his hand on Lily's. They weren't being furtive, their hands perched on the padded armrest between the seats, and although they weren't looking at each other I could tell from the way his hand had landed on hers that they were lovers.

I flashed on Minori, naturally, immediately picturing her back home alone in her yoga togs, sipping coffee in their huge kitchen, but it was I who got a sock to the gut. Pong hadn't exactly lied to me—he'd said Lily was going to be around a lot—but it still felt like the time in seventh grade when Katy Riordan started dancing with the loutish (lone Asian) jock Connor Ching, when she was my supposed date for the spring dance, later sucking face with him under the gym bleachers with such a perfect cinematic stance that I was sure they had been planning it all along. I was insanely jealous of Connor and deeply wounded by Katy, who I thought was too much of a brainiac to fall for Connor's muscle-bound diffidence and smug rich-boy Abercrombie look. That I was panged by Lily and Pong's intimate clutch also struck me as kind of gay, as if I was in love with Pong or something, but then damn, I did love the man. I did! And why shouldn't I? He'd intrigued me from the start, delighting me with his many resources and interests, towing me along in the mostly smooth wake of his sundry and ever-unfolding commerce, and I guess I thought that my being his number-one apprentice, his charged-up-and-ready protégé, meant that I was also *his* primary focus. I thought I was being seduced because Pong was seducing me, when in fact he was simply being his natural generous self, drawing in all.

The truth is, I was just being myself as well, if I didn't yet fully know it and everyone else did; no surprise that I'm someone who craves being swept up, a baby chick scampering randomly, sidling up to whatever beauty or charisma or warmth comes my way and then not easily letting go.

A seducible boy is what I am.

I caught Pong's eye and he must have seen a certain bleakness in my gaze and with an almost wistful pause he extended his free hand to me.

"Later," he said, tapping lightly at my wrist, "we will talk."

"That's okay," I replied. I was curious to hear him out, but in fact I didn't need any reasons or justifications for what he and Lily were up to. Or how it fit or didn't fit into everything else. I did feel badly for Minori, but as with all couples (probably it was the same with Clark and my mother), everyone knew from early on what they were probably signing on for. Maybe Minori and her buff yoga teacher were having a special friendship, too. Regardless, it was Pong's life and he was a grown-up and I thought that if I was going to be a grown-up someday, too, I should just renew my wild gratitude for being allowed to occupy a tiny patch of it. I was going to say all this to Pong humbly and stoically when the curtains opened to a man in a powder-red tuxedo with black lapels standing before a line of young women in high heels and wearing black bikinis so stringy that they hardly covered anything at all, unlike the Garbo ladies.

I got a bad feeling that was only sharpened by a round of hoots from Lucky and our guests, but there was nowhere to flee. I expected the man, who with his drowsy, puffy face and wry smile and wavy, unkempt salt-and-pepper hair looked like an Asian Dean Martin, was going to sing or at least emcee whatever the women were going to do, but he simply went down the line and mime-introduced each one with a different juvenile flourish of his hands like he was presenting prizes on a game show, flagrantly shaping his gestures to some aspect of their physiques that he took as notable, such as a full chest or long legs, and then offering bug eyes or a lappy, hanging tongue. He was also pretty inebriated, or was acting like he was, and soon enough I began to think that he was actually making fun of us, sneakily aping our rank male desires. Pong and Lily, on the other hand, weren't much reacting to the glaring illumination of all that exposed flesh, and murmured to each other as though they were at some nighttime café.

The young women were Asian except for a blonde white one who looked Siberian or Russian and a darker-skinned woman on the end. Like the others she was not smiling, if not obviously unhappy, but even through a heavy buzz you could see that she'd switched to endurance mode, her expression that of someone who knew she'd have to walk through a hard rain without an umbrella. And that's when I knew what kind of place this was.

Lucky now said to me, "You probably wondered why this establishment is called Evergreen Shores. It's because they rotate the girls so they're forever young, even younger than you, Tiller, though from the looks of you I think maybe you're cougar bait. But to us middle-aged fucks Evergreen Shores is the fountain of youth."

Lucky roused the one less conscious brother, as well as Lo from Xi'an, and they all stepped wobbling onto the stage. Lucky proceeded to counsel the men in selecting their dates, which wasn't as easy as you'd think, for it was quickly apparent that both brothers wanted the blonde, each taking hold of one of her hands, and now Lo wanted her, too, as he was busting a stiff and awkward twerking move for her, though to me it looked more like he was shivering while pinching a loaf out in the elements.

"Will you please get off your asses and join your brothers?" Lucky now berated me and Pong, having hopped off the low stage. Finishing his milky cocktail, he was splotched lobster red in the face and neck. He raised the glass and the drink was immediately replaced with a fresh one by a young male waiter. Lucky momentarily cuffed him. "You know you can have a shiny new sword, Lily, if you're tired of an old dull one. They're available here, too. I am treating everybody tonight!"

Lily waved her hand without looking up.

"Whatever," Lucky grumbled, letting the kid go. "Comrade Pong! What say you? Will you march with us?"

"I'll be fine tonight, thank you."

"You're fine a lot, aren't you?" Lucky cried. "Okay, no problem and fuck you, too. Go scoot back to the hotel. Don't bother to put on a show for us. We're big boys, okay? But c'mon, Til-do! Don't be a pussy."

I didn't mind his harsh challenge but was taken aback by the flintiness of his tone toward Pong, because even if he was drunk and the kind of manic he got at the roulette table, I hadn't yet heard a whisper of complaint toward Pong from anyone. We were all endeavoring together, killing brain cells together, promoting business together, Evergreen Shores or not. I started to rise from my seat but Pong and Lily got up first.

"Please stay if you like," Pong said. "We should all do what we want to do."

"Fuck that!" Lucky hissed at me. "What kind of business associate are you? What kind of comrade? Are you a brother or are you a traitor?"

I wanted to decamp, stick by my mentor, but I felt my preternaturally threadbare resolve flayed to nothing. I'm an addictive joiner, for better or worse, and can't abide not joining. Plus, to be perfectly honest, the sight of all the bared flesh was stimulating an autonomic reaction in me, my chest aching, even if my fright glands were working overtime.

Pong just nodded, his eyes only kind and generous, and bid me good night as Lucky pulled me into the harsh lights of the stage. When I looked back Pong and Lily were gone, and I couldn't help but think about how this moment played out in old movies, in which some terrified teen or greenhorn serviceman is thrust by his bullying friends into the woeful lair of some broken-down prostitute, who for some reason decides to discharge the hapless kid from sure humiliation and sends him back out with a newfound appreciation for the wretchedness of men, a wretchedness that for the moment was finding expression now in Lucky and Dean Martin managing the Beijing brothers in their contest to be with the Siberian Snow Queen, positioning themselves between the men and her. She clearly understood the power of her whiteness, crossing her arms and shaking her head at whatever the brothers were proposing, until Lucky finally whipped out a thick roll of RMB and she icily indicated she'd go with both. Lo from Xi'an suddenly teetered and was down on one knee while holding on to the leg of one of the young women, who was trying to slough him off. He was ushered back to the theater seats, where he promptly passed out.

Lucky was waiting for my choice, but was going to be disappointed, because I somehow grew enough spine to indicate I'd just sit with Lo and wait. I wished Pong and Lily were still there, so they could witness my attack of integrity.

"No fucking way," Lucky said. "You have to choose."

I shook my head.

"Now!"

His thunderous shout frightened all of us, including the line of young women, who scooched away from him. But Lucky wouldn't have it, pulling forth a couple women from the line and dragging them over to me. They resisted him and suddenly bouncers appeared and got between him and them, with Dean Martin trying to calm everyone down, when the darker-skinned woman stepped forward and grabbed my hand and said, "I'll go with him."

"You?" Lucky said, releasing the girls. He then looked at me. "Okay?"

I didn't answer and so the girl firmly grabbed my hand and pulled me to a set of rooms off a corridor behind the stage. I was already awash with guilt and self-loathing for acceding, even if it clearly seemed she wanted the business. I figured we could simply chat and pass the time and everybody including Lucky would be satisfied. We said our names—hers was Nenita—and she told me she was from the Philippines and that she was going back once she had enough money.

"So here we are, Til-ler," she said in her pretty, singsong way.

When she opened the door I expected the room to be swathed in the same evergreen velvet wallpaper and silken throw pillows heavy on the tasseling and those creepy Tiffany lamps, perhaps a faux hearth flickering in the corner, but instead it was functional and bare, like a dorm room on move-in day, with low-wattage LED ceiling lighting and a grayish linoleum floor and whitewashed walls, and a platform bed with only a fitted sheet and two pillows set in the middle of the windowless space. There was a closet-sized bathroom with a sink and toilet. It was quite chilly, over-air-conditioned. The one other piece of furniture was a rolling rack with some wire hangers, no doubt for the john's clothes, and to this Nenita pointed.

She sat on the bed and told me to strip. I told her I didn't want to, which made her brighten, but she asked if I would take off my clothes anyway, in case one of the bosses knocked on the door. I got the weird feeling that we were being monitored.

"Please, Til-ler, it will be a big help. Plus, I have seen all kinds. I am like a doctor, that way."

She was saying this in earnest so I got down to my underwear but then decided to leave them on, my junk feeling especially meager, like what you'd find in the back of the refrigerator drawer, a branch of deflated grapes, a shriveled baby carrot.

We perched on the edge of the bed, making small talk but keeping it vague, not to hide anything but because it was beside the point. She was from outside Manila and I was from outside New York and she wanted to go to nursing school and I wanted to go into business (though not saying how I already sort of was), and she said business was hard, which shut me up. We chatted about Macau and what an unusual place it was, though we didn't get into the details of why. We didn't mention family or other more personal details aside from the fact that she was half Indian, half Filipina, and I definitely didn't broach how she ended up at Evergreen Shores. You could tell she was smart, self-possessed, and confident, and she reminded me of a brilliant and vivacious girl in Dunbar named Sally Mutthuraju, whom I secretly crushed on for the whole of ninth-grade Model UN, but then I thought about what Sally would say if she could see me now here with Nenita, and how many countless ways I was being a terrible person, which only made me shrink and dwindle some more. It was also freezing from the strong air-conditioning, my arms folded and tucked, but despite how exposed she was Nenita didn't seem bothered by the temperature. I must have been shivering because she gave me a brief, light hug, which actually made me colder, her skin smooth and plush but as cool as putty. Nenita reached into the drawer and pulled out two hard candies, and we popped them and sucked while we talked.

"Your friends are much older than you. That one acts like a boy, like most who come here. Not you. And the one who left with the pretty lady. Who is he? He seems like a nice man. Is he your relative?"

I wondered if I'd heard her right, because even though I'm part hapa I couldn't see how anyone would ever think that Pong and I were from the same bloodline, given our very different body types, facial features, way of ambulation. Hair. I suppose we could be second or third cousins, once or twice removed, some part of my mother also descending long ago from folks in Manchuria, where Pong's people originated and somehow intermingled, with the ever-spinning slot wheels of fate aligning to forge our friendship and open up all the sights and doings associated with that.

"Yes, we are," I said, subscribing to the sudden reality of it, tenuous as it might be.

"I thought so," she said, placing her hand on my thigh. "You are a nice man, too, Til-ler."

"Thank you, Nenita."

"I know you are. You know why? Because you let me choose you.

Your friend was surprised, because he knows I am not chosen very often, because of my skin. But people who pick me are usually good people."

"I hope so."

"I think I am a nice person. I like to help people. That's why I want to be a nurse someday. I want to help old people, mostly, but maybe young children, too. Do you like to help people?"

"Yes," I said, if immediately realizing that I never actually did, being always somehow on the receiving end.

"Do you want to help me?"

"Yes," I said, now worrying.

"I made a mistake," she said. "I should not be here tonight."

"What happened?" I asked her. "Were you supposed to be some-place else?"

"No, it's not that," she said, taking my hand and interweaving our fingers, which to me is always the most sensual thing you can do with a person, whether you're lovers or not. "I should have told the boss I couldn't work. I'm in that way. You know."

"You're pregnant?"

"My goodness, no, Til-ler!" She laughed. "You know."

"No . . ."

"I'm bleeding."

"Oh . . ." I must have sounded disappointed, even though I wasn't—merely amazed by my obtuseness—because she proceeded to apologize, explaining how she should have alerted the manage-ment but wanted to satisfy her punch-in quota for the month and took the chance of not being selected, which happened a lot.

"I'm so sorry, but if you don't mind, would you say you had a good time? I'll get in trouble otherwise."

"Sure."

"Maybe you actually wanted to do it with me. You must feel cheated."

"I don't, honest," I said, which was true, and to prove it I squeezed her fingers. "I'm just cold, is all."

"I will warm you up," she said, and starting vigorously rubbing my shoulders and neck, then had me lie down on my belly and did the same on my back. She turned me over and was thankfully much gentler on my chest and belly, using lube from the drawer built in on the side of the platform bed as massage oil, plus a good wad of spit.

"Just like you saw," Nenita said, straddling me while she moved her hands in slow circles around my nipples, "Fredericka is the favorite one. The rest of the girls are in the middle, and I'm the least popular."

"I don't know why."

"Oh, Til-ler, you're so polite. Why, do you like me?"

"Yes."

"Why?"

"I don't know. Your belly button?"

"That's funny," she said, looking down and touching it. Her black hair fell to my sternum, tickling it.

"Yes," I said. "Yours is pretty perfect. It makes me realize how important belly buttons are, for people to have. I mean aesthetically."

"You're a strange one," Nenita said. "Tell me more."

"Looking at you, I realize how weird it would be if we didn't have them. We would all look unfinished and awful. Not yet formed. I thank God for your navel."

"You do?"

"I guess so, yes."

She paused for a second, a funny look on her face.

"You want to kiss it?"

I must have nodded. She shifted forward and craned her torso over my face, grazing my chin and nose with her small, firm breast, and hovered her belly hole above my mouth. Up close it was even more ideal than I thought, a supple suede crater with just the right pitch of collapse all around, save on the southeast end, where the descent was slightly flatter, a ready pathway for the tongue. I kissed there, chastely, and she lowered herself against me, snuffing my face for a longish moment.

"That's very nice, Til-ler," she said, moving back down and straddling me again. She squirmed most imperceptibly. "I see it was very nice for you, too."

For sure, as there was suddenly a lot of action going on down there. Or at least a lot of a little. In concert, maybe from habit, Nenita's lower region began a subtle ratcheting, north south, north south.

"Would you like another candy?"

"No," I said, a new craving, to my shame, gaining on me. "That's okay."

"There was an old priest in our neighborhood in Manila who gave us candies."

"Oh yeah?" I said, trying to tune in what she was talking about through the growing static between our parts.

"Do you know the ones that are popular in the Philippines? They are mostly peanuts and chocolate."

"Snickers?" was my idiot American answer, my mind emptying of most everything else, save the north south, north south of our lower regions.

"No, it's not that! It's called Choc-Nut. They are little tiny bricks of pressed chocolate and ground-up peanuts. Some coconut, too. When you unwrap each one you have to be careful because they're very dry and crumbly. They fall apart when you try to eat them, so you must eat them fast."

She was moving a little quicker now, too, maybe from a memory of running for the sweets?

"He was Father Duhamelo," she said, not really looking at me anymore but to someplace tangent from the crown of my head and very far away.

"Uh-huh," I said, imagining a portly old friar in a dark caramel cassock and sandals, his hands full of Choc-Nuts that I couldn't quite picture but because of my burgeoning state was seeing as more like chocolate-covered nutmeats; fat, arcing cashews; brainlike walnuts; me crouching down into a vat of warmed chocolaty sauce . . .

"He told us children in the parish that if we loved and served God only good things would come to us." She was moving faster, and pressing against me harder as there was more of me to press against, and along with the north south, north south there was some new travel from east to west and east, and then back again, such that I couldn't help but see a boy squirrel chasing a girl squirrel around and up and down a thick tree trunk . . .

"'That's why I'm giving you a candy,' Father Duhamelo said to us. 'It's in honor of His Greatness. You're His sweet gifts, all of you.'"

Her hips were pistoning, and mine were, too, and when she grabbed me with sudden force by the throat I figured it was because she needed an anchor, a stay, rather than thinking it would pleasure me, which it somehow did, as I spackled the inside of my undies in an eye-jittering, aneurysmic shudder. Nenita, however, just coolly raised herself up, still astraddle on her knees, bolt straight and high as she peered down at me.

"You liked that, huh?" she muttered.

"I did," I gasped, summoning just enough breath to form the words.

"May I do something?"

I nodded, the endorphins flooding me with a boundless and liberating generosity.

"Getting to know you, I think you won't mind."

"Whatever you want."

"It's something I've always wanted to do."

I nodded again, and she reached between her legs, pushing aside the ridiculously narrow strip of fabric. I thought, *Man, she's going to enjoy a little me time*; but after she curled a couple fingers inside herself her fingertips came out veneered by a thick fresh gloss of blood. For a second I thought she was going to taste them. Instead she slowly dabbed a double line on my forehead, my cheek, on my quivering chin. I couldn't move. It was an awesome scent, alive and dead all at once, like I was standing on the shore of a roiling iron sea.

16.

EXCUSE THE INAPPROPRIATE and weird segue, but back (or in fact forward) in Stagno, Val and I very much wanted to get along.

A few weeks had passed since the AWOL incident and we were trying our best to find the right new rhythm. It was an ungainly period at first, purgatorially wan like a late Sunday afternoon, when you're simultaneously spent from the weekend and anxious for the coming week, not sure whether to take a nap or a jog, drink a coffee or a beer, if you should meditate or copulate, if that last one is an option. For us it always was, though we hadn't been getting busy as much of late, which seemed mostly fine despite the fact that we were, according to science, each in our libidinous primes. Right after her Meet Your Local Medical Professionals night (of which no further details were disclosed, nor did I want them to be) we went at it like new lovers, using whatever chance we had, such as VeeJ taking a homeschool test or stirring a batch of cookie dough in the mixer, to slip into the bathroom or the garage and do something lovely and filthy to each other, all the better if only one of us got to climax, or even neither, so that there was no discrete beginning or end to the want and we were acting out the middle of the story, over and over and over, every notation becoming the pleasure, continually accruing an unending sentence. After a while, though, it was too much to sustain; at night, in our bed, there'd be wrestling, frantic cuffing, fingers in the mouth, but just as likely we would ply ourselves against the other, be both structure and cover, and meld into a hard sleep.

Sleep that we needed, as we'd transitioned from being the neighborhood's halfway house for the taste-starved to the not-so-secret underground pop-up of Stagno proper. This certainly wasn't the plan, though I think Val and I were looking for a different all-consuming activity that would distract us from the ache of our fleshness. So we worked in the kitchen every day but Monday (VeeJ learned that this was the typical off day for chefs), going straight from noon right up to VeeJ's 9:30 p.m.–sharp bedtime. How did this happen? Regulars like Martha (and Sleeves), and Rafe and his half brother, Hardtime, and the HVAC contractor and the rest of our hungry neighbors, not to mention Courtney and Keefer and Liam, who were actually becoming something like friends, internalized our cooking schedule and began to appear randomly a few minutes before six o'clock; although we never invited anybody, we had a feeling people would show and prepared more food, and so people started to figure that we'd probably have enough, and then word spread to their friends and to the development on the other side of the interstate, and then to people in the neighborhoods closer to town. Folks we'd never met rang our doorbell and sheepishly wondered if ours was the house with the boy chef who was "field-testing" recipes—I always asked who their connection was—and if they looked innocuous and/or zealous and desperate enough and we had seats at the table, I let them in. No reference, no entry. A few days later they'd come back with a name and maybe a story, once even a plea, a note the poor bastard had written out and read aloud about his volunteer work with a literacy program and crime victims' advocacy group, I guess to prove that he was a genuinely decent human being. I didn't realize that's what I appeared to be wanting, which I consciously wasn't, but in fact was. He was lucky that night, as we had an open seat, and VeeJ made his jerk-style chicken thighs, which blew the dude's taste buds straight to Port Antonio and back, obliterated and sated. He hugged me for several beats too long before he left. If I happened to be giving a hand to VeeJ in the kitchen, or setting places at the table, Val had to answer the door, which I didn't prefer, as she was much too liberal with her selections. She greeted any stranger with the same exuberance she'd had for Courtney that first time, ushering all inside our home with a warmth that was radiant and winning but seemed a bit too buoyed and even manic, at least to me. Since staying out all night she was a bit dizzying in her energy, always on the move whether inside or out, ready at a snap to go pick up some last-minute ingredients or supplies, constantly tidying and organizing and cleaning around the house and even the yard while faintly humming some Katy Perry anthem. She didn't even like Katy Perry (like I do), which worried me more.

Eventually friends and relatives of those strangers starting showing up, as exampled by the volunteering guy's hipster sister and her boyfriend, visiting from one of the Portlands, who showed up with a four-pack of craft brew and said they'd heard our place was the best eatery in the county, which was not saying much, but after they bussed their plates of the codfish ceviche and *ají de gallina* and green rice, licked cat-clean, to the kitchen sink, the boyfriend congratulated VeeJ and slapped two twenties into his chubby paw, saying, "That was some righteous grubbage, little genius man." Val protested and tried to intervene but VeeJ had already sprinted off to hide the cash somewhere in the house. They returned the next night with a bottle of red wine, as VeeJ told them he was planning a classic hangar steak au poivre vert with garlicky hash browns, a very popular dinner that ended up being seven covers not including us, everyone crammed around the table sharing their BYOs.

After that, "20 Whet," as people began to call it (our house number on Whetstone Street), pretty much blew up. Word got around, and fast. Before long, peering out between the front window curtains, you could see folks starting to queue at 5:45 p.m., then 5:00 p.m., even 4:30 p.m. on weekend nights, to make sure they got a shot at what legend might someday note were Victor Jr.'s early masterworks. Naturally, we were spending *a lot* more on raw materials, kitchen equipment, plates, and cutlery, but Pong's magic card never failed. I didn't feel guilty about it, for it felt okay to use it for what had become a high-end child enrichment program for VeeJ. Val gave up refusing people's contributions that were, with the exception of Rafe's wicked flower, now always cash, oftentimes a few hard-earned bucks (this was Stagno after all), periodically a wad (a bombastic drug company sales rep dropped a crisp C-note on us), everyone insisting they were donating to Victor Jr.'s college fund, which Val and I had never imagined would be necessary but were now thinking, *Why not?* The boy was surely self-ripening his pair; it's not easy commanding the stove for your loved ones, much less for hungry strangers anticipating something special, while not giving in to the heat and splatter and ever-threatening entropy to stay focused and patient and disciplined.

And growing wiser, too. "Life, friends, is a people business," Victor Jr. pronounced with a stained tea towel slung over his cushy shoulder, this after we'd fist-bumped Rafe and Hardtime and group hugged good night with Mrs. Parnthong, who was visiting 20 Whet for the first time. Val and I assumed he was parroting some philosophizing chef in a video he'd watched, but the dappled glints in his eyes made you wonder if another dimension had opened to him, that he was realizing—as a lot of grown-ups never do—that what was fundamentally good for you was staying busy, making something new every day, and having kind social contact. We realized something had changed in us when a drenching summer weather system settled on the area, bringing lightning and winds and heavy rains and even some hail, which was fine except nobody showed up at the door for a couple days. We figured we'd just cook for ourselves. But our trio played without balance, we kept barging into one another's parts, our timing off, VeeJ even getting a nasty steam burn. When the storm passed the doorbell rang again, and we got our hop back, going full throttle.

That stretch was our finest run. We gave ourselves over to the work and its unrelenting rhythms. The hours seemed like mere minutes, sending us to bed with our jaws slack, limbs numb, until we were boosted by the work again the next day. And the output deepened, though in a surprising way; maybe the single greatest thing I've ever tasted was a classic plain omelet in the French method (using no spatula, just shakes of the pan) that Victor Jr. made after going through a couple egg cartons of tries, this fluffy, buttery masterpiece that was like gliding tongue-first into a cloud. We weren't conscious of it, but after weeks of crafting increasingly involved dishes requiring special techniques and equipment, rarefied flavorings, everrefined sauces, laboratory timing, the boy somehow picked up on our cravings for the more rustic and elemental; he started to make downhome stuff like fried smelts, katsu chicken. Linguine with clams. He purposely kept to two ingredients, maybe three max. Comfort food, sure, but stunningly pure versions that our visitors, initially perplexed by, madly hoovered up.

A new family MO clicked into place. We stopped streaming shows and movies. We were smoking a smidge less mota, listening to EDM and lounge and Baroque chamber music to lullaby ourselves to sleep. Victor Jr. lost his taste for gaming and started reading the glossy cooking magazines we subscribed to, printing out pictures of favorite dishes and pasting the wall above his bed with them. All the while we were building up a sizable stash of cash, nobody counting it but rather just letting it fill a freezer bag, and then another, that we kept under the kitchen sink. We were too busy to think about what our efforts were adding up to, or where they were leading to. We weren't killing time so much as making it irrelevant, which is perhaps the freest state of mind, when you can truly riff and roam.

I'd still interview anybody who hadn't shown up before, entering personal info into a spreadsheet on a tablet to keep track of the who and the when and the how of their link to 20 Whet. Practically, though, aside from superficially soothing my psyche, my data gathering was useless, because if a bad person appeared he wouldn't do so by waiting in a line with wine and food dweebs chitchatting about which riesling (Mosel or Wachau) would pair best with VeeJ's tea-smoked squab. He—or they—would make a different approach, look to catch Val when she was out in the yard or on an errand at the big-box store, and so I always tried to be with her when she left the house, and then subtly kept us on the property as much as possible.

One thing did rub me raw: several out-of-town visitors said they got on to us via NeighborLady.com, which is basically a neighborhood community bulletin board for selling and bartering stuff, benefit potlucks, lost and found items, housecleaning and babysitting services, missing pet alerts, reports of suspicious activity and petty crimes, et cetera, et cetera, basically everything people might share with real neighbors. I visited the site and I tried to log in with Val's video-streaming user ID and passwords, and bang, there she was, with her full real name and even a picture, and although her Neighbor Lady profile was obviously not publicly accessible, her posts about garbage pickup times and traffic snarls in the new intersection downtown and the sorry produce at the supermarkets were tagged with her email and in one case the name of our street, not recommended if she were just a regular Joelle, not to mention someone under witness protection.

Luckily, though, these folks posting about 20 Whet were just nice-enough foodies on the prowl, the kind who can't do anything or go anywhere without a full round of social media due diligence. I logged on and found their thread, with many posts about the prodigy chef, but then our first names were mentioned and a few posted pics of the dishes as well as a good number that showed us in the background or standing in the kitchen. On our nightly chalkboard menu I had clearly written No Photography, but taking a picture of a plate of food is by now an involuntary human response and I might as well have demanded No Burping. The shots of me didn't matter, arguably not even those of VeeJ, who naturally featured in a number of especially darling snaps perched on the raised plank I rigged in front of the stove, sporting his red bandanna and his size-six orange Crocs and wielding tongs, but the incidental photos of Val in the background, looking sweaty if still her delicious fetching brunette self, those definitely alarmed. For there was Val, if Val was the woman you were seeking.

I didn't say a word about this to her. I just reminded our guests about the policy, or at least implored them to stick to money shots of the proteins. As noted, Val was in an energetic way, much like the Val I'd first met, game and cheery in the mornings as she went about stowing the cleaned pots and pans and dishes from the night before and getting VeeJ's mise en place organized for later, and after we finished the light breakfast and the pot of strong coffee I'd made she broke out the workbooks and storybooks and art supplies and we did our best, doing deep efficient dives into the three Rs and then savoring the electives like you're supposed to when homeschooling. We were learning serious stuff about geology, probability, human anatomy; VeeJ even agreed to a daily fifteen-minute jog on the treadmill, having read about some star young chef who dropped dead from a coronary. Truth is, we had a renewed attitude, plain and simple. We believed we were at a point that was surely okay, likely good, maybe even great.

Of course I couldn't stop scrutinizing Val. Positives did abound; she didn't seem interested in going up to the quarry. She wasn't furtively handling the knives. She spoke of tasks to be done tomorrow, next week, the coming season. But sometimes you can't know. Sometimes there's nothing, not a crumb, and all you have is a smooth reflective surface. So you look for some break in the light. Any dull glint. One afternoon I was collecting herbs VeeJ needed from the small garden plot we'd put in when I heard a sound from the garage. On the side of the garage there was a half-windowed door, and I angled myself just enough to glimpse Val standing with her back to me before the old wooden workbench in the corner, the overhead fluorescent shop light turned on. Neither of us was handy and only went back there to look for a tool—the landlord or whoever lived here before us had left mason jars full of nails and screws and bolts, plus various types of pliers and wire strippers and screwdrivers that were hung on a pegboard—and I was about to offer her help when she lightly tap-tapped at something with a small hammer. She tap-tapped again. I thought she was done but then she gave a last firm strike. She hung the hammer up and tugged the cord of the light and went in the house, empty-handed.

That evening, while she was reading with VeeJ, I snuck into the garage. I turned on the shop light. There was no project, just the workbench and the tool-festooned pegboard, nothing seemingly different. But when I examined the time-hardened surface of the top, I could see faint rings from the small hammer, and on closer inspection I realized that very fine nails had been driven into the wood, their numerous tiny nailheads flush to the surface and randomly spread, like some kind of pox. Normally you'd casually wonder aloud about such a thing, or make that dumb joke about being intimidated by working with hammers (because they nail it every time), or just say, *Hey, babe, like WTF?* but I couldn't quite bring it up that night, or the next day. I kept picturing her slipping out to the workbench, selecting one or two nails, efficiently driving them in. Done. What was so wrong with that? Other people go fluff the sofa pillows. Puff a cigar. Hammering a nail straight and clean, that can satisfy. And yet. I don't know when she started but she kept at it, new nailheads appearing almost daily, and I figured as long as she wasn't hurting herself or anyone else, both the workbench and I could take it.

I remained vigilant, though maybe too much so. A pair of recent diners did spook me. They said they were in IT sales and marketing, though to me they looked too old for the part; these two middle-aged white guys were dressed a bit too casual-Friday, one of them lanky and pale and the other heavyset and with that reddened complexion chronic drinkers can get, his nose and cheeks angry with burst capillaries. They introduced themselves as "Len and Pete," the sound of which rubbed me funny. Maybe it was the price tag still on the belt loop of Pete's trousers (he was the thin one), maybe it was the way Len gripped the bottle of wine he'd brought (down at his side like it was a billy club, rather than upright like a candle), maybe it was how they sat themselves in the center of our community table, rather than waiting to be seated, but I began to berate myself for inviting them in.

"So what's the tab for dinner?" Pete asked, scanning the chalkboard menu.

"Do you have those big wineglasses?" Len immediately followed up. "And what's the corkage fee?"

Nada, nope, and zero, I replied. They looked dubious, not quite believing me on any of the counts. I felt prickly but there were other new diners and I gave everybody the usual spiel that we weren't running a restaurant, that we simply enjoyed hosting people who shared our enthusiasm for our boy's talents, and that this was an evolving experiment intended solely to be educational and fun. Len and Pete stared at me the way passengers look at flight attendants going over safety and emergency instructions, which is to say they were hearing nothing. Mostly they were looking around, noting the other diners and, I could tell, definitely appraising me. But unlike others who weren't familiar with our living arrangement and saw my relative youth as odd, if not sketchy, they didn't ask if Victor Jr. was my baby brother, or if I was a neighbor lending a hand, or whether Val was my cousin or aunt, which made me wonder what "Len and Pete" were in fact up to.

Two other pairs showed up, both regulars, and the table was complete. The regulars were immediately chatty and compared notes on what VeeJ had prepared on prior visits but Len and Pete interacted civilly at best, nudging their chairs back a bit from the others. They must have known the seating arrangements from the online posts yet still seemed put off by the intimate spacing. Pete's face stiffened to a cold slice of pizza, and Len not so subtly man-spread himself, causing the woman next to him to sit at a slight angle to the table. He had poured himself an up-to-the-brim glass of wine—no doubt indicating his distaste for our small wineglasses—and was already on to the subject of how ungentrified and quaint the area was, complimenting his fellow diners, whom he assumed were locals, for choosing to live in such a "genuine" place.

"Driving around here is like traveling back in time. When do you ever see shoe repair shops anymore? Or a working bus station? I bet there's a classic VFW post, here, too. Am I right?"

He was right of course, probably because he had already driven past the one on Fudder Boulevard that looks like a small, decrepit airplane hangar and is cave dark inside save for the ancient lit signs for Crud and Crud Light, which is all they have on tap. I know because VeeJ needed to pee badly when we were out one afternoon and we stopped there, the few hunched-over souls present already snoozing, including the barkeep. It is what it is, and it worked for most people, but waxing about it and the other "authentic" Stagno establishments was Len's enthusiastically shitty way of throwing shade at these hometown folks, who had long accepted Stagno to be a charmless forlorn quarry of a dump and would flee it in a nano-second if they could. It was partly why they waited in a line for food they might not even like, such as the kimchee juice–pickled oyster shooters VeeJ sent out as an amuse-bouche, their half-throated *whoa*s and *interesting*s and *hmmm*s pleasure enough.

Pete conversed only with the other men, swerving the talk toward the subject of income taxes and government regulations, which he clearly believed should be abolished along with every constitutional amendment save the second, whereas Len paid a little too much attention to the women, in particular a cool biker gal with a tiny Jesus-on-the-cross nose ring who clearly wasn't into him, and not just because she was a lesbian, both she and her woman friend twice refusing offers of his wine. Pete joylessly sipped at his and kept me busy, requesting a side dish for the leftover salmon skin he couldn't abide staying on his main dinner plate, plus constant refills of spar-kling water and a different dessert spoon because the tiniest speck of something had dried onto the first one, while eyeing me pushing into the kitchen through the swinging door we'd installed that was fitted with a porthole as I thought maybe to get confirmed recon of Val. Listening to Pete's harsh brand of conservatism and Len's grotty compliments of the ladies made me think they were taking extra pains to be assholes rather than lowlifes looking to do ill, and when Val asked if I needed a hand I told her it was a mellow night and to keep sous-chefing for VeeJ.

I have to say the other diners were champs and clearly tried to make the best of the evening, but by the end they looked like they'd had to clean toilets all night. While Len and Pete lingered over their dessert the others brought up their dishes and glasses and deposited their donations to the college fund into the coffee can on the counter (we'd given up trying to discourage contributions) and gave warm kudos to VeeJ and Val before heading out. Through the porthole Val noticed the two men still sitting at the table.

"What's with them?" she said.

"Just some right-wing jerks," I blithely answered, not wanting to say any more. Victor Jr. was already out back on the deck, decompressing with a customary bubble-gum cigarette and a can of diet root beer. But when I saw Len and Pete angling toward the kitchen I firmly said, "Closing time," and spread my arms, ushering them out.

"So what's the suggested donation?" Pete said, taking out his wallet. He glanced back toward the kitchen. "We don't accept handouts."

"Well, tonight you're welfare kings," I said, nudging away his money. He and Len shared an icy glance. At this point we were on the short paved path in front of the house where it met the driveway. One of the couples waved from their car in the street, then drove off. Magda, the biker, and her friend, Jade, had strapped on their helmets and were mounting a matte gunmetal Ninja in the driveway.

"That was rocking, brother!" Magda said to me, now astride the driver's seat. She started the bike and Jade hiked up to sit on the tail. "We'll be back soon!"

"Sooner, please," I called to her, over the rumbling pistons.

"You play house nice," Pete said to me, with a suddenly grimy, goonish voice. "These tough gals here could use a frau like you."

"Frau this," Magda mouthed, flipping Pete a multiringed bird. Jade also popped him a two-hander.

Len walked up and grabbed the short handlebars and shook them, causing Jade to have to hop off the back.

"Shit!" she shouted, regaining her footing.

"What is wrong with you?" Magda hollered. She killed the engine and dismounted and got up in Len's grill, still wearing her helmet. She was nearly a foot shorter, so she hopped on her toes to shout in his face. "You are such fucking assholes!"

"I love you, though," Len moaned, leaning right over her. "Maybe you could love me."

She sneered. "Not if you were the last dyke in paradise."

Len laughed and bumped her with his chest, and Jade leapt between them and bumped him back, and by now Pete had stepped in to hold off Magda, who was trying to kick at Len, and although I should have been thinking foremost of Val, of quickly concluding this evening by locking our doors and planning our next moves before they returned, I became temporarily blinkered; maybe I'm a chauvinist, for had they all been dudes I'd have just let it be, but seeing these two excellent women in their frayed Daisy Dukes and bulbous helmets getting pushed around and taunted made my heart harden and swell, and not with loving. Suddenly I was charging at lanky Pete, breaking his grip on Magda. Len pushed me and I grappled with him but lost my footing and we toppled onto the lawn. He was bigger but somehow I got atop him and I remembered how in a certain black hole of misery at Drum's I didn't give up or out or in, even with Pete now stomping me with his loafer, if somewhat lamely. I locked my elbow around Len's neck, and when he started to buck and shake I wrapped him even tighter. I could feel the life force leaving him. Draining away. Would I really have done it? Shortened his stay on this earth? You think you could never do such a thing but with every rap of shoe heel on my shoulder and neck and skull I vised him more, because with all the possibilities of what could literally occur to Val, from both within and without, maybe I was okay with exiting early, too.

For what's scarier than a loved one caught in the shade of a dark design?

I guess, in this instance, a boy with a knife.

"Back up, vile cur," Victor Jr. said, his red bandanna still pig-tailed into angry upknots. Pete stopped kicking me, and I let go of Len, who gasped for breath. But even he was locked on VeeJ, who looked feral and badass with the temporary tattoos we'd let him apply on his pudgy forearms (like his hero cable-TV chefs), not to mention the very adult-sized bone-chopping cleaver he wielded, the flat, wide blade flashing orange in the dusk.

"What the hell is with you people?" Pete shouted, the fright con-torting his face. He was glaring at all of us, including a bewildered Val, who had just come outside, drawn by all the commotion. "Are you all fucking crazy?"

At this point I realized that perhaps we were.

"You stay right there!" he cried, pointing shakily at VeeJ. He helped up Len, who was clutching his throat, and they scooted to their car with a panic that made clear the horrible mistake I'd made. I felt awful, but their douchehood was confirmed when Len rasped, "Fucking shit food!" as Pete drove them off.

This did offend, even if it was totally untrue. You should never bad-mouth a kid's passion or hope, no matter what. There is really no more precious a thing.

17.

I T'S NOT SURPRISING, I'm sure, that I'm now someone who can't help but associate a place with its scent.

Maybe I always did but unconsciously. Even a buttoned-down locale like Dunbar has one, which, like a pat of cold butter, usually has no odor at all, except on those days when armies of landscapers lay siege to the village and leave the air swampy with just-mown grass and the spice of two-stroke-engine exhaust. My college stank of the dusty molder that wafts up after pulling open old oak desk drawers, plus dried beer and unwashed fleece; Oahu, as already noted, was fanned with a breeze filtered, league over league, by galaxial stretches of open blue ocean. The streets of Shenzhen of wet asphalt and barely contained underground rivers of sewage; Macau of overheated casino lights and spilled White Russians and Nenita and, well, you know what. You remember all that forever.

The Kappagoda property, situated in a valley somewhere between Shenzhen and Dongguan, was different again; as Pong and I and Lucky were driven up in a blacked-out Range Rover that Drum sent to meet us portside at Shekou, where the Macau ferry had us disembark, I cracked the window once we were past the pockets of densely populated settlements and then massive golf resorts that

seemed completely empty, and took in the air. The smell was familiar at first, the land forested with a mix of the usual deciduous and
conifer trees like in the countryside north of Dunbar, or the Adiron-
dacks, or West Virginia, but then dotted with stands of ficus and
magnolia and bamboo and also, I would learn, by bodhi trees and
black plums, shade trees the Buddha himself perhaps reposed beneath to contemplate the circularities of existence. It was sweeter
still with blooms of canna lilies and poinsettias and frangipani that
dotted the road winding in ascent beside the streams, random mas-
ticating animals peering at us as we rumbled past.

Where we were heading was high in the spiky hills, and I could
tell we were getting close when the road suddenly smoothed out to
the compacted, oiled gravel of Drum's private driveway. We climbed
and switchbacked and climbed some more, the atmosphere turning
fresher and more herbaceous, and finally rolled in beneath the
building, which was set on large concrete pillars rooted in the sloped
ground. It was hard to believe this was a private house—picture a
long, low, flat A-frame structure with a sundeck running the whole
length, the sort of building that belonged on an Alpine ski slope,
with smaller A-framed wings extending on either side.

"This was going to be a hotel when Drum bought it from the
developer after the Asian financial crisis," Lucky told us from
the front passenger seat. "He got it for practically nothing."

"He was going to run a *hotel*?" I asked.

"He was considering it," Lucky said, "but then thought better.
Who wants to take care of other people's needs all day and night?
Not that Drum would have been the innkeeper! Anyway, he decided
to make it his country retreat. All thirty-five rooms. This does mean
we won't be bunking up!"

Lucky reached back and tried to muss my hair. He had been
tickled by what he'd finally extracted from me about my experience
at Evergreen Shores, and was already calling me War Paint. Not that

I finally minded being the unlikely canvas for Nenita's unhappy memories. What I learned was this: whenever we can, we ought to exorcise demons for one another. Pong, of course, had merely shaken his head.

A swarm of staff unloaded the luggage from our vehicles—many more people than were necessary (two carried a bag easily handled by one)—and I couldn't help but notice that among them was a man who was clearly not a local; he was dressed like the others in a black cotton unisex shift, but he was differently scaled and shaped of body, as you might expect a Westerner to be. He was also exceedingly pale, and seemed paler still because of the black ball-bearing nose piercing he was sporting, its gauge large enough that it seemed that side of his nose hung down slightly. He was balding on top but the rest of his hair was long and stringy and dried-out looking, like packaged seaweed, and I realized that he was a dead ringer for Getty, the loquacious and odorous jamu master back at Lucky's mom's house. I instinctively tried to elicit the man's gaze but the attention of the staff was locked on the task at hand, and he ignored me completely. It was only as they were leaving with our bags that he glanced back at me icily, as if I'd done him some wrong.

I was about to say something to Pong when Constance appeared in the dimness, greeting and politely bowing to us but touching me on the arm. She led us up a wide set of stairs past a service floor and then a level where our bags were diverted before reaching the main hall of the building, which was indeed ski lodge–like, a single large expanse that was completely open to the valley we had driven up and the lime-colored hills on the far side. Above us was an exposed-beam ceiling that spanned what seemed like half a football field of teakwood flooring. It was a rustic, semifinished place but tidy and exceedingly clean, redolent of lemon oil and wood wax. The floors and paneled walls shined brightly, and what little furniture there was for the immense space—a few sofas, a half-dozen armchairs, low coffee tables, and standing lamps—was small and functional. What stood out to me was that there was no barrier separating us and the void, no railing or stem wall, the wood floor becoming a deck beyond the track of the opened sliding glass doors and extending out into the air. The drop-off was probably thirty feet to the dense growth below.

"Of course there was a railing here originally," Drum said, approaching us from behind. He shook our hands and we all looked out at the fetching vista as he ushered us nearly to the edge. Constance had casually plopped herself down on the end of the floating platform, her legs girlishly scissoring. She gestured for me to sit with her, but I declined. I don't like heights, or more to the point, I like the thrill of them but can't help getting locked on the idea of stepping off and dropping.

"This was meant to be a social space but since my interest in yoga it has been ideal as a studio, if a grand one. Once we began practicing here the railing more obviously marred the view. I had it removed and replaced with frameless glass but even that was not invisible. So we took that down as well. An architect drew up plans for an elaborate safety netting below but we haven't gotten around to constructing it."

Pong offered, "Perhaps simply knowing the netting was there would diminish the effect."

"That was my thinking, my friend," Drum said. "There should be nothing between us and this world, yes?"

Lucky piped, "Unless the world is stacked against you."

"How can someone as exuberantly game as you, Mr. Choi, be so pessimistically angled?"

"Fifty-one percent winning," he said moodily, "means forty-nine percent losing. The wear and tear of watching the little white ball bounce here and there. Check my eyes. See the profound psychic toll?"

Lucky let everyone peer closely, and we all had a laugh at his faux misery. But I wondered if the putting on was put on, noticing his smooth face crinkle just so as he chuckled along with us. On the slow, winding car ride from Shekou he had been badly hungover, ground down by the diverse excesses of the evening, but perhaps, I thought, to a core layer, which wasn't of the swashbuckling bon vivant bro, but rather, as with the rest of us, the stuff of a more ordinary person, someone with unaddressed deficits.

"How thorough he slumbers," he'd whispered Shakespeareanly at Pong, whose shut eyes jittered with some kindly dream as he deeply dozed in the third-row seat of the minivan. "Like the world turns for him."

"I guess it didn't begin that way with his folks," I said, feeling I ought to be Pong's ready second.

"We all had tough starts, War Paint," Lucky countered, breathing low. He eyed Pong for a long beat. "At least his are all behind him."

I didn't say more, pretending to fall asleep myself. As noted, I was instinctively cowed by Lucky and would always choose not to be alone with him, even if I mostly enjoyed his presence in our groupings. Clearly he was rankled that Pong had invited Lily, which altered what he had planned for the evening. Business had gone accordingly on our previous night together, the Beijing brothers and Lo from Xi'an pleased enough with the deal terms and the whirlwind carnival of a visit that they'd wired their initial investment deposit to the group's LLC account before getting on their respective flights home. But the vibe today was not quite the same. Lily had gone back to Shenzhen, and there was an aridity between Pong and Lucky. For Lucky, I was starting to see, was one of those people who was perfectly fine as long as things went how he'd envisioned them going, and got unmoored if the story suddenly veered off on its own, the untold story of his unusual mother and upbringing maybe the primary tremor. Was this how he dealt with the vicissitudes of gambling, subscribing to a longer-arcing tale to gird himself, a finale he could keep focusing on whenever his wager on red or black rolled onto green? I didn't know how Chinese guys and Korean guys differed, and then how these two, Pong and Lucky, with their particular backgrounds and trajectories, aligned and didn't, but if I had to say one thing it would be that while both men's tolerance for risk-taking was high, Pong would have mentally assayed all the hidden angles, the critical metrics, the prevailing trends, and then wholly accepted the inexact sum of it, in order to make the big bet. And if I was realizing anything long-standing between them it was that Lucky was stung by the idea that Pong in fact had never truly gambled.

Drum now said, "Why don't we have some tea and go over the details of the investment structure. I know you have other interests in the venture but you may find my terms to be more favorable."

"Do we have to right now?" Constance said. "It's so very dull."

"Why don't you show young Tiller around the property?" Drum suggested. "Then we can all gather for a refreshing drink before dinner. The yoga instructors are already here, but I believe they're on a group hike. You might be able to catch them."

"I'll give him a tour of the building," she answered, extending her hand to me so that I would pull her up. I was terrified of letting her slip, the consequences being catastrophic, so I grabbed her forearm very tightly with both hands, as well as dipping my shoulder into her armpit, to hoist her. She was satisfyingly solid yet pliant, like a heavy ball at the gym.

"Don't tire him too much, dear," Drum said.

"He'll be fine," Constance said, and before I could say anything she hooked her elbow in mine and took us in the opposite direction of Drum and Pong and Lucky, who were heading to Drum's office at one end of the building. She wouldn't let me unlatch as we crossed the carrier deck of the main hall, the way a little girl at the amusement park might manacle her sitter and home them directly at the cotton candy cart, although I was no sitter and she was no little girl; this was my first really close, long look at her in full daylight, and Constance was even sturdier than I recalled. She was an inch or so taller than I was, her dense, dry hand now gripping mine with what seemed a tiny fraction of its potential strength. She wore a see-through white muslin blouse with a clingy white V-top tank underneath, her muscled legs and broad, firm bottom encased in stretchy white yoga pants, her flared hips set off by a little white-leather fanny pack. Her feet, shod in white patent-leather Birkenstocks, were the color of walnut shells, her prominent toenails painted an icy wintergreen.

"I stay over here," she said, as if to emphasize how distant we already were from the men, who looked as small as action figures as they ascended a stair, presumably to her father's office. We went up the twinned stair on this side, to a turret suite of sorts, which looked over the forested valley. Her bedroom was spacious but modestly furnished with a couple wedge-shaped Thai floor pillows and a wide-framed opium bed and a wardrobe, plus a desk and chair and a couple of those rotating Western-style attorney's bookshelves, each full of classic-literature paperbacks you read starting in seventh grade, like *Robinson Crusoe* and *The Jungle* and the stories of Edgar Allan Poe. The adjoining bathroom was similarly basic, a basin and toilet and a round stone tub that was intentionally styled to be rough-hewn and primitive. All the rooms were similar, she told me, and sometimes fully occupied.

"My dad has been into gathering people of *demonstrated gifts*," Constance said, rolling her eyes. "We used to travel all the time but not really anymore so he brings people to us, depending on what he gets interested in. We've had jazz musicians and techies and climate scientists."

I found her diction and accent familiar, if not her manner, which, oddly, sounded to me like prosperous American high school, Northeast Corridor strain. It turned out I was right; she'd spent a couple years at a boarding school in Connecticut.

"Lately, it's been all about wellness for him. Wellness, wellness. So we've had nutritionists, psychologists, spiritual leaders. Now the yoga people. Just no doctors. My dad doesn't like doctors."

"Why not?"

"He says most of them think their patients know nothing, and that they don't listen, and that many of them actually hate what they do. He also blames them for what happened to my mother."

"What happened to her?"

This was when she told me how her mother died of a stroke right after birthing her.

Now I was super sorry, and mumbled unintelligibly, but she said, "Gotcha."

"Oh, thank goodness."

"Actually, I was telling the truth. I just can't help watching people's reactions. Yours was like 'I will disappear now, thank you very much.'"

I laughed, a little scared but curious. "So you never knew her."

"Duh, like yeah. I'm over that. Question. Do you have a mother?"

"No," I blurted, rocked by her question. Most people would assume a kid my age had a viable maternal unit and blandly ask where she lived or what she did for a job, and if they got some vagueness would get the drift that she was out of the picture because of divorce or something worse. Constance, however, wasn't interested in additional data or clues.

"You're like me, then. You know how it is having only a dad."

"How's that?" I asked.

"Being spoiled and kind of lonesome."

I nodded, agreeing, at least in regard to us relatively lucky ones whose dad scratcher ticket didn't come up beater or molester or emotional sadist. I know it's crazy, and the nauseating height of privilege to say it, but sometimes I fantasized that Clark got mean-ass drunk and kicked at my door because I disrespected him some-how and I'd have to pretzel him in a submission hold until he tapped out and then lay into him with a teary trenchant martyr's speech about the huge dried turd his life had become. But of course Clark was and is only gentle and mellow, at this point a light beer sipper if anything, and just rolled his knuckles against my bedroom door before asking to come in and kiss me good night, withholding com-mentary on the skunk smoke and the Marauding MILFs page I min-imized and thought was muted and paused but that wasn't muting and pausing, moans abounding.

Constance, who hadn't yet let me go, squeezed my hand extra tight, and I thought she was going to reel me in and plant a wet one on my mouth. I wasn't sure if I wanted her to kiss me, for although she was my kind of biggish sexy she was kind of biggish scary, too, her eyes funhouse widened by the extra-thick lenses of her spectacles.

"I'm glad you're here," she said, her incredibly prominent eye-lashes shuttering slowly, *phlut*, like a butterfly warming in the sun after a sudden spring rain. "I wish we weren't hosting the yoga peo-ple. I'm not into that, are you?"

I told her about trying that one yoga class in college, leaving out the details of how it seemed like the greatest excuse ever to stare point-blank at some chick's lululemoned crack, but with my two-way hangover from a vodka-and-Red-Bull pong session at my frat, plus the oniony stank from a very hairy bro in the cramped and overheated room, I fled the gym just in time to upchuck into a pile of dirty snow, fouling any pleasurable associations.

"I'm not flexible at all, see?" She finally let me go to try to touch her glittery toenails and could only reach just past her knees. "What about you?"

I bent and surprised us both by easily laying my palms flat on the floor, even with my legs straight.

"You're *funny*," Constance said, her brow crinkling with intrigue. "You sing like a pop star plus are super limber. Question. What else can you do?"

I shrugged. I truly had no clue. These latent capacities were starting to freak me a little, even if I was happy for the many new doors they were opening. But a dark delight refracted out from Constance's huge pupils.

"I guess we'll find out," she said. "We better show you around, in case my father asks."

So we toured the balance of the lodge's rooms, and I mean all the rest, thirty-three, to be exact. I figured we'd see a representative room and move on, but Constance took us inside the next room, and the next, and so on, until we exhausted that side of the building-length corridor, and then made our way back on the other side, pushing in each door and walking into the room and nodding at the bed and night table and perusing the bathroom and maybe the closet, before exiting and going on to the next. I thought then that she might be one of those special people who appear to be normal except for a single janky line in their coding that turns out to be critical if you want to live in society. Was this why Constance was still tooling around with her dad, despite her being young, attractive, and fabulously rich?

We were heading to inspect the next floor of guest rooms but I asked if we could perhaps see the rest of the lodge, like the basement or kitchen, assuming there was one, which somehow broke the chain of a compulsion and rebooted her. I was afraid of having offended— the one bad thing I could do was somehow scuttle our potential partnership with Drum—and so I made sure to be in no hurry as we inspected the garage level again, and then the rumbling genera- tor room, the storage closets of carpentering and landscaping tools, of linens and towels, of individual soaps and lotions and shampoos, of toilet paper and cleaning products, and then we went up one floor to the service level, where the vast kitchen was. It was a fetching mess, naturally lit like a pastoral painting, the space exposed to the valley on one side like the main hall was, the opposite wall lined with pantry lockers built into the abutting hill. Here again it was a modest and basic setup, bulky older industrial-style sinks and refrig- erators banked along the walls between steel worktables and a half- dozen hacked-down butcher blocks arrayed in the middle, the room charged with the intense mixed scent of various aromatics like gin- ger and garlic and tropical herbs and then also a sweetly bilious death funk that came from a basket full of spiky durians. A few aproned men and women both young and old were involved in var- ious prep tasks of peeling and chopping, one lady plucking chick- ens, another old guy gutting fat carplike fish, others steaming and rendering other small animals over a line of freestanding cast-iron cooking hobs attached by hoses to rusty propane tanks. They didn't look like trained chefs or professionals, just tough-skinned regular folk who might well know from experience how to skin a hare, which one man was actually doing, and which seemed funny, because al- though we were in the middle of a forest the forest was still sur- rounded on all sides by the booming, teeming urban-factory civilization of the Pearl River Delta, which had been booming and teeming for nearly forty years and thus, you'd think, would be short on such peo- ple. Maybe Drum had brought them in from some poorer, rougher place. There was enough space for a whole army of kitchen workers to come in if necessary, and it was easy to imagine them all silently doing their tasks amid great piles of feathers and root vegetables and leafy stalks and viscera.

"Look, look, is my Miss Connie!"

"Chilies!"

A scrawny man, barely five feet tall, had emerged from one of the pantry lockers and was now hugging Constance full-bore, his lined, dried crab apple of a face pressing into her bosom. From his swaggering gait I guessed he was the kitchen master. He wore loose drawstring pants and an Atlético de Madrid insignia T-shirt, which you could see because he wasn't wearing an apron like the others. He held out his hand, revealing a pile of tiny candies shaped and colored exactly like tropical fruits.

"*Luk chup!*" Constance cried, taking a papaya.

"You coming yesterday I know!" he barked, pushing another onto her. She chose a blood orange. "But how come you not visit?"

"I was sleeping all day."

"You not love Chilies anymore!"

"You're crazy."

"Crazy for you!" He stopped smiling when he looked at me. "Ya, who this *farang*?"

"It's Tiller!" she cried, as if he should already know. "He's doing a deal with my father!"

"Well, I'm not really . . ."

"Big shot, yah?" Chilies said, scanning me but clearly registering nothing favorable yet. He pushed the candies on me. "You try."

"I'm fine," I said, noting the grime in his palm lines.

"You try!"

Constance said, "You don't want Chilies getting mad at you . . ."

I chose the banana, which didn't taste like banana (maybe it was a plantain), more kind of grainy and sugary, and then, I thought, tainted briny by his palm sweat. I wanted to spit it out but had no opportunity. It was obvious she and Chilies went way back; he began immediately and openly complaining about preparing for yet another one of her father's conferences.

"One thing when I cook for Miss Connie and boss, other thing for bad strange people."

"They're not bad," Constance said. "Just totally boring."

"Farang always complaining about food," he said, glancing at me. "No can eat salt, no can eat sweet, no can eat fat, so afraid of everything! You afraid, too, farang?"

"I can eat anything," I said petulantly.

Chilies took us around the various vats and bins, inspecting the piles of carcasses for how cleanly they'd been stripped, as well the vegetable shreddings, pausing here and there to berate someone. Constance would later tell me that he was ethnically Chinese but grew up in Thailand, and had been hired as the caretaker and personal cook by Drum just after he bought the retreat, when she was a toddler. For most of the intervening years he'd been the sole employee, but as time went by and Drum began hosting larger and larger gatherings, the staff steadily expanded. Chilies—his specialty was Thai cuisine—naturally stayed in charge of the kitchen.

"You stay longer to get more amazing taste," he said to me. "My secret curry."

I told him we were heading back on our business road show in a couple days.

He sneered. "Your choice! But smell make you crazy! Cannot stop eating! But watch out. Make your smooth farang skin look like this!" He shoved his face up into mine, close enough that I could read the inner gouges of his wrinkles, painful-looking rivulets that couldn't have been grooved solely by the dulled linoleum cutter of time.

"Oh, Chilies, you be nice to him."

"You sure, Miss Connie?"

"I think so."

He slow-motion knuckled me hard in the chest. "Whoa, farang! Maybe Miss Connie like you!"

I kept to the other side of Constance for the rest of the kitchen tour. My wishbone still pinged with a dot of soreness as she led us around the other floor of rooms above, where our crew was staying. Again Constance showed me room by room, Pong's and Lucky's included (their bags had been delivered, their clothes hangered and folded for them in the wardrobes). When we got to my digs, which were actually directly below hers, my things had also been hung and folded, my comb and floss set on a hand towel beside the basin, my toothbrush standing ready in a bamboo-wood cup. It was all perfectly attentive and hospitable, if a bit creepy, and I couldn't help but see it as an extension of Constance's peculiar brand of thoroughness. Was this a legacy from her deceased mother? Or from some part of Drum that was not yet in evidence? Or just Constance being Constance, who like any other person was home-brewing a madness, just far less secretly?

"Would you like to change?" she said, poking through the neat short stacks of my T-shirts and shorts. "By this time of day it gets really sticky."

She slipped off her gauzy cotton shift and the little fanny pack around her waist and tossed them on the bed, revealing the magnificence of her dense chockablock physique. I was suddenly sheepish and had to look away. I didn't know what was up in this realm but something was definitely off, as it was unprecedented for me to be in such regular close quarters with attractive women, though poor Nenita had no choice in the matter.

Constance was standing before me now in this wrapping of white leggings and the low-cut white top, a fine shine on her cleavage from weeps of perspiration, the clay-colored atolls of her areolas pressed extra wide, her nipples resilient and pokey, the jut of her lower belly a welcoming ledge for the chin, and I was reminded in a flash of Biddie Dortmund, a lovely bruiser of a girl a couple years above me at Dunbar High, who was the star of the girls' ice hockey team and was All-ECAC in college and last I heard was practicing with the Olympic squad. We weren't friends but shared a semi-intimate moment, just once, when I was drinking from the water fountain outside the girls' locker room and a few b-ballers came flying out the swinging door and I caught sight of Biddie strolling across the frame behind them, totally nude except for a towel turbaned on her head (why she was in that front part of their locker room I have no idea, as the boys' locker room was its mirror image and the showers were appropriately tucked in the far recesses), and with the water dribbling down my chin we locked eyes and a tiny crease of a grin brooked her oddly petite face and the door swung closed and she was gone. Sometime after that I went to a game and watched how powerfully she skated and how the ends of her dirty-blond locks tasseling out from her helmet got quilled sharp and dark by sweat, and I found myself roaring when she scored the last goal of a hat trick and to this day when I need a sexy sparking image it's the heavy tent of her garnet-and-gold number 99 jersey that I click on, mentally sous-viding myself beneath all those layers of padding in what had to be a wicked-hot steam.

Constance could have been Biddie's body double. Or Biddie was Constance's, though either way I felt a twang, naturally lower down at first but then all over, these warm, fat, jellied strands of goodness extending from my spine and enrobing me. Constance told me to sit on the bed and although I thought I was still standing I was already flat on my back, peering at the ceiling, the intense daylight from the other window shutter that she was now sliding open making me squint. I was reaching for her but she was out of range, and I realized I wasn't reaching at all, that my arms were quietly tingling by my side, my legs becoming logs of luncheon meat. My mind seemed to be working just fine except that I had no will, no agency, everything she was saying and doing a thoroughly acceptable proposition.

Some part of my brain was waving frantically at me, trying to goad a flight response, but nothing in me was being marshaled.

"Let me help you, Tiller. Okay?" She had already picked out a pair of my board shorts and a Weezer T-shirt from the wardrobe. "We have to get you out of these city clothes first."

"Sure."

She started with my shoes and socks, unbuckling my belt and tugging it out from the loops like she was priming a lawn mower. She placed the belt on the tea table next to my socks, both flattened and laid out in parallel. I must have said something about being thirsty because she brought me the bamboo cup full of water and let me drink deeply from it. I finished it and she brought me another and I downed it. I could have swallowed the whole of the Xi River. The yeasty sweetness of the candies Chilies had given us was lingering on my tongue, and it occurred to me, without any alarm whatsoever, that the *luk chup* must be the thing. That Constance was moving about and controlling her own limbs didn't quite compute, and I wondered as much aloud, to which she busted a belly laugh.

"Chilies is always right!"

"He is?"

"Without fail," she said, with an almost motherly awe and pride. In his voice she barked, *"Yah! Farang choose same every time! Banana and pineapple. Pineapple and banana. Like every farang, who only want pad Thai!"*

I laughed with her, and said, "But there wasn't a pineapple."

"Pineapple no easy to make!" she said, laughing again. "It's true, you know. I've watched him since I was little. They're difficult because of the skin and spiky top. He doesn't do them every time."

"What if I chose something else?"

"But you wouldn't have!"

"Why not?"

"Come on, Tiller! You're a farang!"

This made a certain sense to me, and not just because of the spiked *luk chup*, which Constance now confirmed was laced with a local version of burundanga, that infamous South American Devil's Breath, which allowed normal sensation and feeling, at least in the derma, while totally zombifying the rest of you. I should have been freaking with the idea of being roofied, but if anything I was snagged on what she'd said, about my being a farang. I didn't want to be a farang, some just-deplaned honky. Not anymore. Despite my ruddied bloodline, to her and Chilies and most all of the world I was a farang, a Triple-Crème G (gweilo, gaijin, gringo), and at this point pinned inside a box and observed, the tables finally turned so that I was now the specimen for study.

Constance propped me up with her strong arms and unbuttoned my dress shirt. She was cooing at me the whole time. Then she laid me back and while bracing herself on the bed with her knee craned me up by the thighs with one ferociously able arm, freeing my hips, just as you'd do when diapering a baby.

"Better?" she said, having slipped off my trousers and then my briefs. The mountain air was a downy tongue of chamois on my skin.

"Yes," I said, now watching Constance beginning to scan me, methodically, patch by patch.

"You're very pale."

"I guess I'm a farang's farang."

This elicited a gleeful snort from her. She sat next to me, her weight on the mattress making me tilt toward her. I could feel the smooth, hard sheath of her leggings against my kidney. Tiller le Deuxième was tilted over, too, as yet agnostically eyeing the scene.

"I don't want you to leave right away. I want you to stay. Do you want to stay here for a while?"

"I do." This must have been true, as Chilies' sinister candy was also a powerful truth serum. I did want to stay, more or less. Or at least not go back. It's not just that I craved the new locales, and the many new fun people, and simply had nothing better to do (my typical pathetic reason); it was all of that, sure, but this was my year abroad, and the program brochures had gaseously promised that if I challenged my assumptions and altered my perspectives and immersed myself in a diversity of ideas and peoples and cultures, the experience would last a lifetime, which nobody really believed; but now with Constance coolly looming like an iceberg, her wonky bespectacled gaze appraising my fully bared nativity, I wanted to give myself over. Become a simple clay. As Pong said in the story of his father's life, like *dirt on the heel of a shoe*. I wanted to disappear, though disappear not from life but into it.

Constance air-traced a lazy question mark down and across my belly, then scooched down with her forearms on the mattress while kneeling on the floor, hunching over my groin the way we'd watch my neighbor Benny Lipscher's pet agama lizard, Cheeto, after Benny dropped a live cricket into its terrarium. We'd wait and wait and wait and the second we lost focus, *whammo*, Cheeto would be staring at us with his glum wrinkly mug, a twiggy pair of legs antennaed from his mouth.

Now Constance simply blew. No, not that. She actually exhaled, though with purpose, directing a stream of her breath like a mini oscillating fan all along and around my sweaty, hairy Bardmons. I should apologize for perpetuating more rank mythologies about Asian women and their erotic practices, (and especially to Professor Aquino-Mars), but I swear that's what she did, airing me out, as it were, until my wurst was risen from its stew of slumber.

"We shouldn't let my father find out we did this," she said, moving her face toward mine. "He doesn't like to think about me being with men. It's totally silly, because he knows I've had plenty of boyfriends, but still. He won't like it, no matter how much he admires your singing. And I want him to like you."

"You do?" Besides being drugged ingenuous and compliant, I guess I'd been rendered hopeful, too.

She kissed my cheek in reply, not vigorously but with a warm and clinging tenderness. Who is this person? I took a deep breath, wondering if this was how a bride about to consummate an arranged marriage might feel, all mixed up with wanting everything and wanting nothing.

"We have to look at you now," Constance told me, somewhat coldly. I was confused, because it seemed she had been looking at me the whole time. She stepped to the desk and unzipped the little fanny pack, pulling out a black cylinder that looked like a large butane lighter.

She screwed some loose piece onto one end of the cylinder. When she clicked it I realized it was a lit scope, the kind an ear-nose-throat specialist would use. And this is what she did, starting with my ear canals but also the whorls of my ears, my scalp, the nape of my neck, zeroing in on every bump and mole and skin tag. She flashed my pupils, peeled back my lids to check out the whites of my eyeballs and their red meat surrounds, and switched out the head of the scope for one that would better explore my nasal passages.

"It's funny," she said, her one eye and mouth shut crookedly, "how you have so few nose hairs, compared to most."

"Most?"

"One guy had none. Not a single hair. I think he had a genetic defect. Another had so much hair I was sure he could breathe only through his mouth. We did a test and I was right." She winked. "Question. Is your sense of smell really good or really bad?"

"I believe really good."

"That's what I thought. Please open your mouth. A little wider."

She looked at my teeth, my tongue, my upper palate. I followed her orders as closely as if she were Dr. Minerva Oh, our family GP, who had been friendly with my mother (they were in the same book club). Dr. Oh would never mention her, but during an appointment some years later she took me by the shoulders as I sat on the exam table and nearly touching foreheads with me said, "It's all right if you get really furious sometimes, Tiller. You should just *scream*." She herself practically vibrated with livid energy.

The truth was I never felt like screaming, more like something else, something I could sustain, a note you could reach and hold and pierce the air with for a long, long time.

Anyway, Dr. Oh was of course the first person other than me (and I guess my folks) to handle my privates, this while checking for a hernia, and when I got old enough I'd pretend not to hear her ask me to cough so that she'd hold them a half second longer. The clutch of her latex-gloved hand was what I imagined the velvety cradle of a lemur's might be like, which I was sure was the opposite of what the rock-wall-climbing grapple of Constance's mitts would be. At the moment Constance was peering through the little square glass viewer of the scope, its probe spelunking my sinusal recesses, and I thought I could feel a tickle at the very bottom of my brain. But I didn't lurch.

"You're such a relaxed guy, Tiller! You're doing beautifully." A kind of funny thing for her to say, given that they'd dosed me with the high-potency *luk chup*, but in my condition I warmly bathed in the compliment.

"Thank you." A moist, floral-laden afternoon breeze flowed in through the fully opened windows, and I couldn't tell if I was naked anymore or not, at least in feeling. If Chilies ever marketed the candy as a pharma drug it should be called Copacetic.

I said, "I want to do beautifully. Will I remember this?"

"Question. Would you like to remember?"

"I think so. Yes."

"Then you will remember. And you'll be happy."

"Okay, thank you."

She set aside the scope and began actually touching me, the wide pads of her fingers wonderfully cushy. These grand hands were not laboring hands. She clearly wasn't intending to be sensual with her explorations, topographing me for no other reason than her compulsion to note, but with her going so slowly and methodically it was pretty hot all the same. She began from my brow and temples and cheeks and then worked her way down, orienteering herself patch by patch of skin. She smell tested me, too, poking her nose into my sternum, then beneath both of my arms, turning me over onto my stomach and sniffing the very top of my likely gunky crack, the backs of my knees, the gritty ridges of my Achilles tendons, all of which would have normally made me shrink with shame. Instead, and precisely because of her forensic indifference, I got engorged with a flush of what I have to say was a pure and unstinting desire for openness. If I could've moved my arms and legs they would've been cast wide in welcome.

My pelvis must have been arching up awkwardly, because Constance flipped me onto my back. Tiller II was at this point feeling like he could raise the big tent, go ICBM, but Constance didn't much notice; she had unthreaded the viewer of her scope and was taking out a travel-sized tube of something from the fanny pack. When she flipped open the top a loogie of clear jelly plopped onto the desk.

"Whoops!" She scooped it up with her thick fingers, their fat tips glistening. "Shouldn't waste this!"

Wise before my brain was, my butthole reflexively puckered. But the rest of me wasn't as adamant. Maybe it was Constance's suddenly saintly and yogic expression. Maybe it was the *luk chup* talking. Or maybe it was a brand-new me, this newly coalesced self who had truly gone further and deeper than he could ever imagine. Constance squeezed out more of the goop on her palm and in a surprise move gripped my unit, which looked dishearteningly petite in her largish hand. She worked me gently, the slick new rime at first bathtub hot and then spring-melt cold and though my little friend was staying as hard as titanium he also went kind of numb and I thought, *Wait, I have it all wrong, what we've got here is a woman of experience, who knows how someone like me can pop off too quickly.* She let go and I figured she was going to peel off her top and leggings so we could get cranking but instead she fitted a new apparatus onto the body of the scope, a longish filament that when she clicked brightly luminesced on its end, like the lures of those nightmarish fish that dwell at extreme and lightless depths.

"Question. Have you ever been sounded?"

"You mean recorded?" I said, puffing up a bit higher in my prostrate stance with the idea that my voice was studio worthy.

"Oh," she muttered, with a little bit of dismay. But she brightened. "Okay then! Not to worry." She toyed with the threadlike filament, letting the scope rest on my lower belly.

"There'll be some initial discomfort. But it'll be amazing, you'll see."

I had no idea what she was talking about but her enthusiasm kept me buoyed above any swamping alarm. When she retook hold of My Thing I figured we were on our way; she was peering at it with the fervor and absorption of a high priest, of an impassioned artisan. It cyclopsed her back. She pinpointed the light, going closer and closer. Closer still . . .

Wait.

Wait.

What?

And where she went was a place I didn't know could ever be reached.

18.

QUESTION: What happens to you when you've gone way too far?

Not just off trail, not even bushwhacking, but venturing into a region where it turns out that the usual physics don't much apply. Where there's no heading forward or backward. Where time neither speeds nor slows but instead dissipates altogether like slabs of dry ice at a spoiled rich kid's birthday party, by the end the emptied wooden sushi boats marooned on nothing but scant wisps of steam.

To look back at myself during my stay at Drum Kappagoda's lodge is to slough off every notion of whatever had made me *me*. I would look in my bathroom mirror and see my face but it was the face of a default person, as distinctive as a honeydew in a bin of honeydews. I lost the ability to recognize myself. Drum—and by extension, Constance—had a clear view of what a person fundamentally was, and took no heed of such things as where that person was born, or who raised them, or which artistic or religious or cultural traditions they were exposed to, those normally crucial factors that too many of us spend our whole lives trying either to escape or rationalize. To Drum, we were all—including himself—basic material that could be enhanced, which explained his keen interest in yoga, and in our Elixirent venture, and in what he and Pong spoke of back at the robatayaki, his customized blend, something that I would eventually become privy to, for both better and worse.

I was feeling pretty corporeal, to put it mildly, after what happened with Constance. There are countless unusual human practices, which, seen from the outside, can seem highly irregular or extreme, even downright cracked, but to the adherent they are simply what ought to be done. Sounding, as a practice, included. I was still blinded, as it were, by the harsh light of her inquiry, and like any novitiate didn't really know what to think. I should have been angry, I should have been ashamed, I should have been bewildered, but I wasn't yet sure if what happened had happened. All I knew was when I regained full consciousness, my room was brighter than it should be for the late afternoon hour that I figured it was and that I was clothed in the board shorts and T-shirt Constance had originally proposed. She herself was gone, as were any signs of her devil apparatus. I tried to sit up but my limbs were damp clay, sodden with trauma, and I had to lie there and watch the sun not go down but come up, and realized it was dawn. Had I truly gone to a nether land for more than twelve hours? Or was I still in a nether land now?

It was possible, because, although I was alone, a pair of exceedingly small birds perched on the sill of the wide-open window, their plumage iridescently pink and violet. Their exceedingly narrow, arced beaks were almost as long as their bodies and with these they love-sworded each other, gently sawing back and forth like violinists testing their bows, and the tiny music they produced was inaudible to me except inside the now-plumbed groove of my loin pipe, which began to ring but not euphoniously. I wanted to weep, too, bellow for my shame, for my trashed innocence, for my pure fright at the unholy procedure I'd endured. But a funny thing happened. Those two micro-birds, which I guessed were a variety of hummingbird from the way their wings buzzed rather than flapped, lifted off and were now flitting around the room, perhaps lured by the potted orchid beside the bed. They were hovering just above me in an orbital waltz and I could feel the dual fan of their levitation raising goose bumps on my arms, my neck. I got tingly with a weird flush, maybe like birthing mothers or people in horrible accidents can get. My hearing sharpened, my nipples bloomed. And I remembered how Constance had fluttered above me, too, the needle eye of her probe sparkly and unblinking, and promised that I would never in my life feel anything like this again.

She was right and she was wrong. Right, because it was pretty much the greatest ever scratch for the greatest ever itch. I was sure I wanted to die, but then pivoted to wanting that feeling more. Wrong, because when she struck the dry well bottom—far, far past where I believed anybody could be fathomed—I'd found myself again in the breech, like when Pong and I found trouble in the surf at Oahu, this sensation of being in the barrel, caught on all sides with the narrowest tunnel of escape, then boomeranged free.

Well, mostly. Yes, Constance was compelled to examine me in literally excruciating detail; yes, she truly did have to see *everything*, but the truth of the matter was that I was beginning to see myself more clearly, too, as someone who couldn't help but invite the wider ecstasies and agonies. For I couldn't help but now shiver with the most unlikely of unlikely longings.

Hey, Constance, where are you?

Was I an S&M guy without even knowing it? I'd never had such inclinations. In fact, I cringed at the idea, mostly because I could only see some pasty blindfolded dude in a leather thong hog-tied with a ball gag stitched over his mouth, his lard ass reddened to a medium rare. Still, was this my destiny, if in some even more eye-watering version? Or maybe I'm not into pain equals pleasure, but just where it might take me, this realm of being where I'm indispensable, a key cog in the machine of someone's shadowy dreams. Better to belong in a darkness than not anywhere at all.

This is not to say I wasn't completely fracked. For the next hour or so I flickered in and out; when in, alternating between pitiful sniffling and a hyperactive giddiness; when out, dreaming that I was the drilling tool, my fevered skull the blunt tip of the bit driving down through layers of the earth, through all that unyielding rock and heat and lightlessness, and then turning to come up again, back to air. Gradually my motor skills came back online, and I managed to clean up my act in the tub, sprinkling my bedraggled bits with lukewarm water as delicately as I would a just-birthed joey. There, there, little blind one-eyed one. Don't cry. Someday you'll grow up and take on the world. At some point during my self-nursings I got myself dressed again, and there was a tapping at the door.

I wasn't going to answer, terrified that my aberrant wish for Constance had come true. But when I cracked the door, it was Pong. In my state of psychic alarm and distress I would have hugged him, but in his hands was a tray he'd had the kitchen prepare: cut fruit, sweet buns, a pot of coffee.

"I assumed you'd be starving by now."

I let him in and I placed the tray on the small desk by the window, Pong sitting in the chair and I leaning from the bed. I was indeed famished and somewhat rudely started stuffing my mouth with a custard-filled bun as Pong poured us coffees.

"Are you okay?" he asked, examining me. "Just before dinner I saw Constance. She said she thought you had taken a nap. I came by and knocked on your door. But you must have been deeply asleep."

"I guess so," I said, wanting to tell Pong everything that had gone down—well, not everything—but then I remembered what Constance said about her father's dim view of her consorts, so I kept mum.

"If you feel ill we can have a doctor see you," Pong said.

"No need!" I replied, panicked at the prospect of any further examination. Though I did wonder if the local clinic had a urologist on call. "I'm better now. Not used to so much traveling, I think. I'm sorry if I missed something important last night."

"It was a good evening," Pong said. He sounded game and affable as always, but I detected a subtle tightness in his jaw. "Drum gave an inspiring speech to his yoga instructors about the possibilities of the human form. Lucky made his usual call to arms. I briefly presented Elixirent but did not have a chance to speak in more detail to the instructors after dinner, as they retired early, having just arrived. It would have been better if you had been there."

"I'm really sorry . . ."

"No problem," he said. "I would have woken you if it had been critical. There is ample opportunity for you to present more details of our product and the business plan."

"Me?"

Pong nodded. "Drum and I feel you can address his visitors best. They are mostly Western millennials and Gen Zs like you, which he and I are obviously not."

"But I don't know anything."

"Please don't say that," Pong said, almost irritably. He poured me more coffee. "You can talk about our product. Better yet, *sing* the part. You got all the facts you need from Getty, yes? So you can speak to how our Elixirent line can serve as boosters of a more lasting well-being, one that is a bridging of the ancient and the modern, of the earth and the body. How you are all at the vanguard of a new way of healthfulness."

I couldn't help but notice that Pong's accent was more *shur*-ry and *wur*-bly than usual, the cadence of his talk a bit accelerated, and I flickered on the idea that he was singing a song to me, too. But what for? He had to know by now that I was all-in, my entire stack pushed forward, and that I'd do whatever a most loyal valet-cum-assistant-cum-sidekick would, namely run through a wall or leap over a chasm or light my own hair on fire, in order to help the squad. He had to know that despite certain shocks—which weren't that awful the more I thought about them—I was embracing the wide span of experience he was opening to me. He had to know that I loved him like a best friend, a big brother, people I always longed for.

"I'll try," I said. "But I don't know if I'll succeed."

"Who knows that, ever?" he countered. "Do you believe I do? Or Drum?"

"I guess so, yes."

"Tiller!" he sighed. "You think Drum has all he has because he was certain he someday would? You know he was born not far from here, on a western tributary of the Xi. Unlike my family, his was completely uneducated. Subsistence-level boat people. Nothing much could affect them, not even Mao! They were likely to live forever along the mud banks. No doubt he had a fierce idea, or some wild hope, but it was nothing like a conviction."

"Maybe I don't have a fierce idea. Or a fierce anything."

Pong said, "Growing up in a place like Dunbar, that may have been true. But I know you have a profound craving. I saw it first at Bags' golf club, the way you caddied for us. Not to mention the way you ate. Not the quantity of course, but how. It was the same with your singing at Garbo. There's a certain desperation in you, Tiller, a kind of hunger. What do you think it is?"

"I don't know," I said, which was the truth. The easy answer, of course, was that I was minus a mother. For let's be honest, who is entirely well, lacking one? I mean throughout your life, so that you can proceed steadily, confidently, and without certain inevitable collapses? At the same time, it wasn't the whole of the void. It can sure seem to be, when you venture into that cave; you wave your penlight at the cool, damp vastness and the familiar dreadful contours appear, but in fact it's the lobby of a much colder, vaster theater of wondering. So you click off quickly.

"Sometimes I'm scared."

"We all are," Pong stated, his firm utterance fully waking me. It's my own brand of self-centeredness, but I'd almost misplaced the fact that he had lost his mother, too, at an early age, and that his father was not quite his father, after serving his sentence. "So we often do things impulsively. Or not at all, when we very much should. I'm guilty of this as much as anyone."

"But you're so successful."

Pong half grinned. "It would appear so but I will tell you, Tiller, that my success is a happenstance like any other. This is not to say I haven't worked on and thought about my ventures as much as I could. I certainly have. I'm happy for my family. Like any immigrant, I'm very proud of what we have. The busy life we have built. But it's an outcome among many numerous outcomes. Like candies in a jar. You might not know this yet, but so easily, so effortlessly, the world can pick you a different one, and at any time."

Maybe something in my face blanched, because Pong said, "I don't mean to alarm you, Tiller. I certainly don't mean to be disheartening! You can be scared but in the end I'm confident you'll make do with whatever comes. I feel we're similar in this regard. We can withstand more than we think. We endure, and keep moving on."

I was beginning to fear that Constance had disclosed the full nature of our encounter, or that there was surveillance in place and that her father had informed Pong that I should pack my things. "But I don't want to go," I murmured.

"Who is making you?" Pong said. "Certainly not Drum. In fact, he was telling me how he would appreciate it if you stayed on for a while. You know he has a professional-level karaoke room here. His associates come periodically from the city but he asked me if you would stay for a little longer and socialize, and of course sing with him. You can also do more networking with his yoga people while they're here for the conference, as I know Lucky will be heading out."

"Sure," I said, but then realized what he was not yet saying. I felt my body lift up, abdicating all physical properties, instinctively detaching itself from a moment it wanted no part of.

"You're leaving?" I whispered.

He nodded. "A car will take me to the airport."

"But where are you going?"

"Back to Dunbar."

"Then I'll come, too!"

Pong chuckled, showing his imperfect teeth. He touched my forearm, to assure me. "It's up to you, Tiller, but I don't see why you should not stay on. I will be back early next week. I have rescheduled our last meetings in Busan and Osaka for then."

He looked out at the valley. "Listen. I wish to mention something. Minori has asked me to come home. It will not be a surprise to you that she and I need to have a discussion. You have only met her once, but it's not fair for you to have to think about our situation. Or about what she might be dealing with. I don't believe in that kind of friendship. I regret putting you in an awkward position."

"It's not so awkward," I said.

"Yes, it is," he replied, his head lowered. "In any case, I apologize."

He extended his hand, which honestly was kind of awkward, but when we shook I could feel the depth of his caring. Even if he did accept the chance of many varying outcomes, that the world could offer you, say, a most surprising *luk chup*, he didn't seem to have become fatalistic, or given up on anything. Plus, the man was thoroughly kind. Every tendon of me was wanting to stick with him, both for my own longtime reasons and because, really, who the hell did I imagine I was without him, but he clapped me on the shoulder and said, "I'm grateful you'll be our representative here. Forgive me once more, but I already told Drum you would." He winked then, and I clicked my mug weakly against his. We stayed there by the window, watching the dawn mists begin to thin out. It was quiet, save the back-and-forth chirrups of some perky birds. I asked him when he had to depart.

"Actually, I believe the car is already here. But it can wait a few more minutes. You know, I never inquired about your father. You mentioned where he works but you must think me very rude, as I haven't asked to hear more about him."

"That's okay," I said, accustomed to people asking and well practiced in my own quick snuffing of the subject. So I said, as I always say, "He doesn't mind if I take off time from college, or whether I have a fancy summer internship or just wash dishes. He gives me a lot of freedom."

"Sounds like a good fellow," Pong said, but I found myself wishing Clark and I were mutually vital in the way that could hurt to the core, if something awful were to happen. Maybe we needed such a happening. Or, more like, another one. I hate to think it, but maybe the majority of otherwise loving people do.

Pong, ever aware, didn't push for more material on Clark. I'm sure he sensed it on me from the beginning, my willingness to glom on from that first day at WTF Yo!, but now he could see how I'd so easily break off from my Dunbar and college lives to become his ready satellite. Still, he must have sensed my disquiet that he was departing, because even though he checked his watch, and was clearly pressed for time, he poured himself another coffee. Even took a bite of one of the crème buns.

"You know, Minori and I worked together in a restaurant? Well, not together."

"You washed dishes?"

"I wish I had been dishwashing!" Pong said, chuckling at both the idea and my self-reference. He clearly liked that I worked as a dishwasher, as he thought it was a good life lesson, to have to clean up after others. "I was kitchen help, but not in the kitchen. Minori was a waitress, but I didn't meet her until well after I started. It was a Chinese restaurant in Leonia."

"One of those fancy banquet places?"

"No, a typical place, small, with the same menu as every other Chinese restaurant. But this one had a very large basement, and I worked there with a couple others, for the first two years I was in the country. It was not a pleasant place, very dim and smelling of mold and always very cool, which was only welcome in the summertime. In the winter we wore coats and hats."

I asked what he did down there.

"We peeled, and peeled. Onions. Garlic and ginger. Sometimes shrimp. Whatever they sent down on the lift from the sidewalk. For twelve, even fourteen hours, we sat on stools and peeled the skins, the shells. We would start the day with huge piles of ingredients. They would take up a lot of the space."

"I thought it was a small restaurant."

"It was. But the owner also owned four other Chinese restaurants in the area just like it, plus one of those large buffet-style places, plus a Mexican restaurant he took over when they couldn't pay the lease, and so we were the ones who prepared the raw foodstuffs for all of them. Do you know how frustrating it is to peel an onion without cutting it first? We couldn't cut them, because the chefs would do that in the way they needed. So we peeled each one, without gloves, the skins sometimes coming off easily, sometimes with great difficulty. They can get very sticky. If you cook you know the skins are not always definitive. The papery part sometimes transitions to become onion, and the owner, a horrible man, would come down with one in his hand and yell at us about taking off a perfectly good layer. He'd demand to look at our pile of peels. This would be an outer half layer of one onion, out of perhaps a hundred onions. Same with the garlic, at least until they could buy prepeeled ones in bulk. However, if he got a good deal on whole garlic, we would have to peel crates of the bulbs. It was the worst with the shrimp, frozen blocks of them that we cut out of boxes, heads on, which we had to quick-defrost with hot water so we could shell and devein them. Then blocks of squid, whose mouths and ink we also had to remove. It was always a big mess. We hosed and mopped the concrete floor after the shift but it had a bad smell anyway, no doubt because of all the cracks in the floor. It never went away."

"But you started working upstairs."

"Yes, you could say that. But I was not a waiter. The owner didn't like me because I was from Beijing and he took pleasure in seeing someone educated toil like a peasant. I was on a tourist visa, and I planned to make some money to prove I had sufficient resources and apply for a student visa. I was a good kitchen worker. It was his wife who promoted me. I began helping her with the accounting. Her husband was extremely unpleasant but Ling was a good person. She was gentle and kind, very soft-spoken. She had a large birthmark that spanned her left eye and cheek and I often thought that was why she married someone like him, because no one else would have her. Asians can be extremely discriminatory about things like that, which are not even genetic! One day she saw me studying for the graduate school exam in chemistry and asked if I would help her go back through their books, as they were being audited. Naturally they were evading taxes but not in a systematic way, and I had to create almost an entirely new set of books, going back several years. I found a surplus store that had old unsold notebooks, and wrote with different pens and pencils. The job took nearly three months. It was almost constant work, but it was much better than working in the basement. The husband still refused to pay me more than what I was earning as kitchen help, which was less than half of minimum wage."

"What was that, like five bucks an hour?"

"It was three twenty-five when I started! Which was not bad back then. We helpers made seventy-five cents an hour. The husband wouldn't pay us more, he said, because he was also providing us very cheap housing, which was true. He owned rental houses where many of his waiters and dishwashers and cooks lived. There were seven men in our room, which was originally a bedroom that could reasonably fit at most three people. With the bad smells and snoring and overcrowding, it was barely tolerable. But you know what, I was able to save money. If I needed to save more, or if there was an unexpected expense, like getting a tooth filled, I would eat fried onions and rice for a few days. I wasn't special. We all did such things. And once I started helping with the books, Ling secretly gave me extra cash on the side. She knew I was saving them a lot of money, if not their whole livelihood. She was very frugal but smart about it, unlike her husband, who cut corners no matter what, and instructed the cooks to do the same. Sometimes an ingredient would be clearly spoiled but he had us prepare it anyway, and it was no surprise when customers got sick. The restaurants were always being cited and fined by the health inspectors, and business was steadily declining. In fact, so much so that they had to close down a couple of the restaurants and let go some workers. Our bunk room went from seven men to four. We were worried enough that I think we all worked harder, and I even started to wait tables whenever there was overflow."

"That's when you met Minori."

"Not quite. It would be another six months before she started working as a waitress at the main restaurant in Leonia, after giving up her pianist's career. She realized she hated it, and always had. She hated giving piano lessons even more. She wanted to start over from nothing, and was living across the street. Even so, she wouldn't have been able to get the job until after Ling's husband died, as he was very traditional and allowed only male waiters. His death was unexpected. He wasn't that old, in his fifties, but one evening he was robbed while closing up. He must have fought them off because his cash bag was on him and still full when they found him but he had a heart attack right after on the street, just as the police were coming. After that Ling depended on me much more, and I helped her with the various restaurants. They had a grown son my age but he was mentally disabled and she couldn't take care of both him and the business by herself, especially as her husband had to run the restaurants day to day. This is where I learned how to manage and run eateries. Naturally I did all I could right away to improve the business. We cleaned the restaurants from top to bottom. I changed kitchen practices, fired the bad cooks and hired new ones, and made inexpensive but necessary improvements to the dining areas. People appreciate quality and will pay for it. They also like something distinctive, so I told the new chefs to make more dishes from whatever province they were from, more regional-style food that I made sure to describe in supplements to the menus. They were very popular additions, and soon we had to add more and more items. Business greatly improved at every restaurant, including the Mexican one, where I had the same things done, and we even reopened one of the restaurants that had closed."

I hoped aloud that he finally got a raise.

Pong's face brightened. "Yes. Ling was very happy with the success we were having and gave me a large bonus, twenty-five hundred dollars. As I said, I was thinking about graduate school at the time and while I hoped for a fellowship I knew I would need money for better clothes and books and a proper place to live, so I was very grateful for it, even though we both knew my involvement and work had been more valuable than that."

"Plus, she got to look after her son," I said.

"For sure. She loved him, certainly. He was good-natured, and thus quite lovable. He was not able to take care of himself, and never would. He was an adult and had physical issues so it wasn't easy for her to clothe or bathe or even feed him. He also suffered from a congenital heart defect so he was always weak, pale, and sweating. The doctors estimated he would live only to his early thirties, which seemed to me optimistic. I saw him regularly because I would stop in at their house in Alpine with the day's receipts and cash, and sometimes I would have to help Ling maneuver him from the bathroom to his bed. One night it was especially difficult, as he had contracted the flu, which made his breathing very labored. Ling was scared and asked if I would stay the night and alternate with her so we could monitor him. The next day she showed me a bedroom and private bath in the basement, saying I could live there for free, in exchange for helping out sometimes with her son."

"A lot better than the rooming house."

"About ten thousand times better!" Pong said. "Actually their house was the model for my house in Dunbar Station. It was even larger, if mostly empty of things. Neither Ling nor her husband had any aesthetic sensibility; they worked all the time and took care of their son on their own, so they didn't care about furnishing it. They'd had contract health workers but some stole from her or would not be very helpful and she didn't trust them. At least it was clean and spacious. Still, I had no interest in living there. I wanted my own place. I was still hoping to go to graduate school someday, but first I wanted to stop working full-time at the restaurants and start a business. Perhaps, too, begin dating. Certainly pursue life on my own. When I told Ling I wanted to work less she countered by offering me a sizable salary if I would continue managing the restaurants, as well as live with them and lend a hand with her son. It was quite a raise. I had all my aspirations but in fact I had no prospects whatsoever. Yet I was afraid of getting trapped in Ling and her son's existence. Tell me, Tiller, what would you have done? Would you have stayed longer at the rooming house, building your savings little by little? Or would you have accepted the offer of lodging and a good salary but had your life joined with theirs?"

I think he knew what I would have done, which didn't hinge on anything like career or financial prospects. Aside from my not liking having to be alone, my lucky deal as a kid of (relative) privilege was knowing that as long as I didn't totally fuck up I'd end up at a decent college and fall into a decent job and maybe meet a woman way more special than I deserved and join the ranks of the daily showered while we all waited around for something compelling to happen. So, yes, I told Pong I would have signed on to live at Ling's, though not specifying that it would have been for nothing else than the regular shuffle of footfalls on the ceiling, familiar voices reverberating down the stairs.

"That's what I chose," Pong said. "With the many businesses I'm involved in, you may consider me to be a natural entrepreneur, that I was always inclined to take risks. But in truth it's not my nature."

He stared down into his coffee, curling his hands around his mug, and for the first time since we'd met, including when he related the events of his childhood, I thought he was being dredged by a sharp plow of sorrow, his face roiled and murky.

"You can't know this, but it has been a difficult few years. Fortunately, business has been acceptable. At home it is another story. My daughters are completely uninterested in talking to me, and although it may not be obvious, my father is getting more and more senile. Minori emailed me yesterday, saying he'd again stored his dirty laundry in the refrigerator. This has been a sore subject for us. I have been spending less time on the road, as our marriage counselor suggested, but it's not brought me and Minori closer. The reality is that we get along better when we've been apart. I can better focus on being useful to everyone I care about, taking care of needs, responsibilities, duties that are all worthwhile. Even appreciated. And yet there's a severe imbalance, because you wonder who this very necessary person is, in the lull between the doing. In the wondering, you begin to search. Eventually, you stray. Again, I don't mean to burden you with this. You're an unusually open and I think patient young man."

I'd never thought of myself as "open and patient." But then what else was I long practiced in throughout my brief inertial life but always waiting to feel people out?

So I said: "I know you have many colleagues, but if there's anything I can do . . ."

Pong said, "Staying on here is a big help to me, as Lucky has some work meetings in Shanghai. His day job! Plus, I know this about you. You're a natural listener. So we'll talk more about everything when I return. My business partners are a fine bunch but bringing up private troubles like Perry did when he mentioned his daughter's substance abuse is rare. We pursue many activities together and make good jokes, which is always fun. But there are times I feel at a loss. I believe this happens to a lot of men my age. One is quite settled in every regard, but you look around your circles and wonder if you've made any truly close friends. There may be a hundred somber people at my funeral but outside of family, would I rather have two or three people there who could speak genuinely and unreservedly about who I was? I think so, yes. Or even better, just one."

We sipped in silence, with me somewhat astounded by the idea that Pong didn't have any close friends. It seemed to me that he had dozens, and I'd only think of him as alone later on, after other significant events had transpired. Still, I liked the idea of the final measure of a person being what one person would say while holding nothing back, but then also thought that it was chancy, to rely on a lone witness to tell the story of your life. Would they tell the whole truth? Or the truth you wanted? Maybe Pong understood that this was as good an outcome as anyone could ask for.

I knew that if I had to speak about him, I would, and with everything I had.

Pong checked his watch and it was time so we picked up his bag from his room and went down and outside to the lower level where we'd first arrived. It was only us and a security guard and the driver of the black car, no Drum or Constance or even Lucky to bon voyage him, which seemed kind of funny to me. Of course it was still very early, everyone likely asleep. We shook hands and Pong got into the dark-windowed sedan and without pause it pulled away, and I stood there, strangely frozen, like the time the neighbors left me at sleepaway camp when I was eight. My father had to go to the city for a rare meeting and the kindly older neighbor couple took me, and when they finally drove off, the backs of their heads getting smaller and smaller until they were too far to see, my insides were still sprinting after them.

19.

AND THEN, WITH PONG GONE, everything slightly soured.

The dim underskirts of the building from where his car departed seemed suddenly a crypt, dank and unfresh. A chill scrabbled up my spine. It was like watching an otherwise engrossing low-budget film when the sound quality abruptly changes because of a last-minute dub-in and the spell is irreparably broken. You're in just another cruddy arty theater, your sneakers sticking to the floor. I thought I heard the screeches of bats but it was just the security guard sucking at something caught in his teeth. He leered at me with one cheek unnaturally skewed, his incisors and molars a cloudy urine color, and gestured to a flask tucked inside his security guard vest. I scampered off, finding my way back to my room through the dead-quiet lodge, and quickly shut and locked the door. I slumped against the bed and scolded myself for not insisting on leaving, too. I realized I didn't actually know any of these people, and in turn was unsettled by the egregiously intimate data they already had on me. Dunbar was an old lumpy pillow but I would have plunged my face into its musty nest if I could have been teleported back. I was wondering if it was too late to get a taxi and catch Pong at the terminal and plead for a ticket, when there was a soft knocking at the door.

I didn't move, scared that it might be the security guard on break from his shift, now thirsting for fresh company. After a barely audible "*Wei ni,*" I could hear the person move away. I crept to the door, cracking it open. There was a woven basket with a rolled mat and a pair of clingy men's yoga shorts and T-shirt inside, the handle taped with a notecard handwritten in thick marker: *Come try yoga!* I figured it had to be Constance's handwriting, the script much more girlish and exuberant than she actually was, and this, plus its cheery bougie welcome, somewhat calmed me.

I changed into the outfit and was heading out the door, when a figure emerged from the dimness of the hallway. It was the porter, the one who looked like Getty. I was about to say hello when he shushed me, mouthing, *Follow me.* Evidently he wanted me to follow at a distance, for he quickly trotted ahead and disappeared down a stairwell. I barely spotted him turning down the far end of a lower-level corridor, a run that seemed to head straight into the dirt and rock of the hillside, for how damp the air suddenly became. He pulled open a heavy wooden door to a very short length of hall, the industrial track lighting silvery and weak.

"Come on in," he instructed.

There were two doorless rooms on one side of the hall, his one of them. The other was unoccupied. Needless to say, there were no windows, just a couple of the same light fixtures on a track extending from the hallway. The plaster walls were unadorned and empty except for a thick L-shaped metal bar that swung out and was festooned with a few hangered shirts and shorts and a lone pair of trousers. He sat hunched on a low stool and motioned me in to sit across from him on his unmade twin bed, ripples of wrinkled sheeting spilling out from beneath the bunched-up blanket. I didn't want to sit, but he insisted and I perched gingerly on the blanket part. Behind him I could see a bathroom set between the rooms, a porcelain sink and handheld showerhead that stuck straight out of the tiled wall, no stall around it. There was no toilet, and no door.

"I'm Pruitt," he said. "I already know your name. Now you can tell me, Tiller. What's your subject? Tell me what you'll tutor her in and I'll tell you what we've done."

"Tutor?"

"Sociology? Art history? Econ? But you can't be econ, because she would never agree to study that."

"I'm just here for the health drink."

"I know that part!" He hissed under his breath. "Oh, I get it, because I'm just a staffer and do honest labor I can't be informed? I don't have agency? Don't tell me you're one of those people with rigid social ideas, because if so, this isn't going to work! It just won't!"

I was unmoored enough by Pruitt's fervor that for a moment I lost track of the idea that he could be Getty's fraternal, if not identical, twin; they had the same rangy frame, the same subtle hunch of the shoulders of someone who had grown too tall too fast during puberty, the same haughty profile right out of a seventeenth-century portrait of a pasty-faced noble in a wig. His speech was of course totally different, as was his manner, which unlike Getty's was consummately American, humanities grad school species, though both had that breezily prickly know-it-all style, though in the expat subvariant, the lost-soul Westerner trudging to a reckoning in $130 Tevas. The thing that made me almost sure they were related, however, was Pruitt's BO, which, to my nose, had a matching microbiome that gassed a powerful buffer to anyone getting too close.

"Do you have a brother named Getty?" I couldn't help but ask, but Pruitt stared at me as if I were a human non sequitur, not even bothering with an acknowledgment. Suddenly I wondered if he might actually be a figment, a misshapen invention of my now possibly and permanently *luk chup*–plaqued synapses. Was he a projection of my own deepest career fears of having only the historical luck of English-language skills as a viable currency? Or was Pruitt a piece of real-life crazy? The thing about crazy folk is that either they're truly crazy or they know something nobody else knows, or can even detect.

"Listen, I know the big boss has been wanting to bring in somebody for her. I get that, I do. We all have our time in the sun, and then it's dusk. We're not all meant to be the one forever. Just tell me what you're here to teach. I want to help. It's literature, am I right?" He was staring at me so deeply, so earnestly, that I didn't have the heart to say anything. His eyes went bright, almost moist. "I was her first English instructor, you know. Not just ESL! We started there but I didn't limit her. We tackled the great books, to set the foundation, Plato to Proust. It wasn't easy! There were times I may have overreached. She wasn't a natural critic, between you and me. She had absolutely no feel for it!"

By now Pruitt was glowing, and I didn't have the heart to say anything to dampen his mad spirit. He was clearly harmless, and maybe, also, broken to the root. I murmured some bromide about perseverance that I'd heard in a life-skills workshop during freshman preorientation and Pruitt lurched forward and gave me a hearty hug, clapping my shoulder blades a bit too harshly.

"You know where this leaves us, don't you?" he said, holding me at arm's length. "You know what I'm talking about, don't you? Don't you?"

"I think so?"

"Sure you do!" he cried. Up this close he wasn't as tall, just very skinny and restive, like he burnt his calories too fast. "I was just like you, truly. I thought teaching in some exotic place would be the coolest thing a young man could do. No, you don't have to tell me any more, brother, I already know it! You're on an adventure nonpareil. A purposeful wandering. I've wandered, too, and so witnessed and learned. I know how the sunrise refracts through the saline mists of Kyushu. I know the sound of hand-tossed Shandong noodles being slapped against a metal worktable. I know the scrape of an exhausted hairdresser's fingernails in Penang when she's giving a scalp massage. I can draw you the bus and train lines to striver suburbs like Ilsan and Beigao and Denenchofu. I know the different sewer odors in those places and all the others as intimately as I do my own gas! The sulfurous, the noxious, the fruit-rot sweet. Man, oh man! I envy you, Siddhartha. I envy your virgin stance. Your thrown-open arms."

He flung his arms wide and I flinched, thinking he wanted to bear-hug again, but Pruitt was merely being demonstrative.

"As I said, it hasn't all been fresh tofu, my friend. Ready yourself. She will be your first but not your last. I've had to assign a couple libraries' worth of compositions. I've waded through lightless thickets of second and third drafts. I've explained the concept of the enthymeme a *thousand thousand thousand* times. Do you realize I still only see color in highlighter tones? That I dream of billboards scrolling my name in Hangul? That I can sleep using any kind of pillow, from down to burlap to a block of wood? Hey, by the way, what do you think of my crib?"

I gave a thumbs-up, thinking that there was no answer that actually mattered.

"It's small and dark but that's what privacy comes with, along with some genuine asceticism, which we should have more of in our lives. I was like you, before I made my way out here, happy and fat with countless humane and progressive ideas. Gorged like everybody else. And why not? My life was like one of those huge blueberry muffins I used to get on my way to work each morning. It's loaded with trans fats and chemicals and syrups and maybe a few rehydrated blueberries, and it rocks you with how easy and tasty it is. It goes *down,* is what it does, and lasts right up to the moment of the next one. You know what I mean?"

"It stays with you?"

"You got it, my friend! The cycle self-perpetuates. You can go on like that ad infinitum. And here's a secret. They'll tell you it's not sustaining, but it is. Chances are you won't stroke out. You won't get diabetes and have to get a few toes clipped off. You'll just keep on, you'll persist, okay, maybe add a bonus layer of blubber, but that keeps you that much more bumpered and warm. You're getting my drift?"

Amazingly, I sort of was, understanding not Pruitt so much as Pruitt himself, for he reminded me of certain benign feckless kids I grew up with, whose deep-rooted privilege lent them enough gumption (and bank) to jetpack around the world trailing after some underdeveloped thesis about the essential righteousness of the world as reflected in their hearts and vice versa. Most found it, at least as reported via their social media pages, most often via iPhone shots of tropical and mountainous dawns and sunsets that always seem to grace them, because people of such means are particularly able to find what they need to find, surprise surprise.

Pruitt dabbed beads of sweat from his temple. It was chilly but he had really worked himself up.

"Needless to say, it has been a long time, muffinwise. So to speak! I was promised no easy path here and I got none, even after the teaching ended. But don't get me wrong. I'm grateful for the work I have. It doesn't drain you in the same way as teaching. It's physically taxing but you're not center stage, on the kick line. At some point you cease being able to get ready for your close-up. I can see you don't yet know what I mean! But you coming here has reminded me of what I was like at the beginning."

"When was that?" I asked.

"Almost fifteen years ago!"

"I mean with the Kappagodas."

"Like I said! I taught ESL for five or six years before that, all around the Rim. After my college graduation ceremony, I caught a cheap charter flight via Anchorage and then Seoul. I haven't been back since! Seems like yesterday, really . . ."

I was struck mute. I could only think about a scene in a sci-fi movie when part of the spaceship crew goes down to a planet that's in a different relativity and returns in what to them is a matter of a couple hours but for the lone crew member back on the ship it's like *ten years*. The man has gone gray, and obviously gotten a little warped by the isolation. But the part even harder to believe was how they all got right back to business, which of course they had to for the plot, but the more realistic thing would have been for the poor dude on the ship to have instantly disintegrated with surging emotions on seeing his crewmates again, or else gone postal.

I did think that Pruitt's living in this dank suite of rooms for what was nearly the span of my own lifetime could account for his brand of bent. Yet I could see how he was probably as randomly garrulous from the very first crack of the workbook of his first ESL gig, delighting and bewildering his students, and pretty much looking the same as now except maybe he had more hair and his skin was darker, for not yet having the SPF 1000 of this cavey dwelling. Would I be any different if I were in his flip-flops after all this time? I'd like to think so, but then again, we keep hoping we're each a custom-alchemized metal, even though all the evidence says otherwise.

"You haven't missed home?" I had to ask him, suddenly impaled by the prospect of not seeing Clark for a couple decades. Would he be the sprouted-ear-hair kind of old man? The great liver-spotted one? The after-dinner nodder-offer?

Pruitt snorted darkly. "By home, you mean our country? The way it is now? Ha ha. If you're talking family, I check in once every few years. I can't get into it now but my parents were workaholic, alcoholic socialites who were kind and gracious to everyone except each other and their children. My three siblings are just alcoholics. None of them has kids. They fly back and forth between their hobby businesses in Sun Valley and Santa Fe and Montauk to make sure the people running them aren't stealing too much. They love their dogs and their maids most of all and immediately replace them whenever they die or get deported. So do I miss my old world, my young comrade? Would you miss where I was?"

"I guess not."

"Don't guess!" He hopped before me into a half crouch, hands up and ready, like an offensive-line coach demonstrating a pass-protect stance. "Know! This is what I always said to my students, and to Miss Constance, too. Know what you know, and stand by it. Don't be shy! Don't be fearful! Not everything is an irregular verb!"

"I knowed."

Pruitt cackled, appreciating my grammar joke. "You and I would have been an amazing team. Want to see the rest of the pad?"

I nodded, figuring I was missing another whole part of this wing, but we stepped the one and a half steps into the aforementioned bathroom and I got the grand tour. It was a pit. Pruitt was middle-aged but clearly hadn't evolved a minute past college-dorm-level cleanliness, this not-privy rimed with soap scum and a feathery dusting of pubes and permanently infused with the smell of ass. The toilet flushed but it was the in-ground kind you squatted over, which is why I hadn't seen it. In an attack of tidiness, he picked up a tooth-brush half bald of bristles from the rusted bottom of the sink basin and balanced it on the rounded edge, there being no shelf, no mir-ror, and no cabinet, nothing to hold a comb or pills or deodorant. A fog-colored face towel was hung by its corner loop near the shower-head; an exfoliating cloth wound around one of the faucet handles. Stuck near the drain on the tiled floor was a dirty lozenge of soap.

"I've been lucky, because the rest of the live-in staff have communal bathrooms," he said, leading us into the adjacent bedroom. "There was another farang years back, an Aussie named Wilbur, but he didn't stay on. He chugged *baijiu* like it was beer, which even an Aussie can't do for long. Makes you *feng*."

Pruitt switched on the lights. The space was pretty much identical to his, right down to the swing-arm clothes rod and the camp-style cot, minus the clothes and the bed linens. The middle of the mattress was stained with a large darkish blot.

"Locals won't live down in a place like this, even with all the space and privacy! They're the sweetest sort of people but very particular. Like the Swiss, except nice. Now that you're here, well, I'll just say it's a special feeling to be with a compadre again. I guess the solo run of Pruitt Stanyan Rooks III is over! So be it!"

Pruitt's digital watch *bleep-bleep*ed.

"Gardening time!" he said, and we went back to the other room, where he changed into a rough cotton shirt. He was practically buzzing with the notion of having a new Western friend but I couldn't bring myself to tell him my tenure here would be brief.

I followed him up a flight and he opened a fire door onto an outdoor landing. In the near distance I could see a small troop of workers in a clearing, wielding hedge clippers and machetes, gathered no doubt for some bushwhacking and landscaping.

"We'll meet up later," Pruitt said, "and go over bunk rules. Expectations, operational responsibilities, such and such. You know what they say! We can work together or work apart. It's up to us!"

He gave me no chance to respond, hustling down the external stair. When he reached his fellow workers one of them casually tossed a machete to him, which Pruitt snagged by the handle with surprising aplomb. He hefted it and then turned back in my direction, waving it like a pirate gone ashore might to his mates back on the galleon, to signal the easy plundering ahead. Then he and a few others with their broad blue-steel blades marched back down the path and disappeared into the trees.

I FOUND MY WAY UP to the main hall after that, thinking that I'd just have to avoid him for the next few days, which, between my own duties with the yoga folks and the question of giving over my earthly flesh to Constance again, seemed doable. The latter idea had been crabbing sideways and back across the empty linoleum floor of my brain—skittle, skittle, skittle. I could only watch it angling closer, closer. I felt the tickle, the panic, but what was I doing to resist? *Niente.*

In the main hall there were a dozen or so ridiculously limber bodies, as well as a surprisingly fit Drum and the wiry surfer Lucky (though no Constance in sight), all of whom shifted and moved in unison. Drum waved to me to join in, and I rolled out my mat, thinking that all of us in our matching unisex yoga togs could background a scene in a James Bond or Bruce Lee movie, with me as the interloper embedded in the ranks. Had I entered the Dragon? We did three sets of breathing exercises and sun salutations and deep standing bends and more than a few high planks and cobras and downward dogs. To the yoga teachers this wasn't even the lightest stretch, merely something (as the session leader noted) to aid the purging of nasty travel hormones, but to me it was a legit strain, my pecs quaking through the chaturangas, my ordinarily limber back jangling like a sleeve of ice in my reverse warrior, the only thing feeling half decent being my jimmied Johnson, merely somewhat sore if still confused and mournfully tranquil after the not-quite-coital trauma.

I even keeled over once, drawing upside-down looks from the others through the A-frames of their crotches. It's harder to tell what people are like when they're all dressed the same but indeed they were mostly white and Western and young, craft-brewer beards on the guys and judicious neck ink and ear banding on the gals, the sort of hipster badging that bougies like me are fated to sport in early adulthood before reverting forever to ordinariness both inside and out. I'm being unfair because it was obvious these folks were legit pros; once the session began, the vibe of the room shifted, for although they were moving together each seemed to flip a switch and hermetically bubble and get down to business, every pose and transition and pose stilled and smooth and powerful.

We finished on our backs, eyes closed, inhaling and exhaling purposefully. The session leader, named Shaundra, a surprisingly very heavyset pale white woman with laughing, friendly eyes and a pageboy haircut, spoke in a resonating bell of a voice about the value of stillness, saying how "stillness opens our hearts to a love and acceptance that cannot be sought but instead accrues to us, one breath at a time." I liked that idea, and followed Shaundra's line, surrendering to the flowing. I swear I could feel calm waters trickling into every last niche of my still-aggrieved body. She kept talking about ice melting, then pooling wide, and soon my body fell away and remaining were simply the waters themselves, and then these, too, receded, and there we all were, Shaundra said, present solely as a kind of knowing, a knowing that had nothing left to know.

"That's when we are free."

I opened my eyes, kind of wigged out by the total erasure, and realized I was among the last few who were still lying down. Drum and Lucky and the rest had silently arisen and rolled up their mats and migrated in their bare feet across the grand expanse of the floor to where a juice bar and lengthy brunch table had been set up, not to mention our bottlings of Elixirent.

I introduced myself to Shaundra while I was refilling her glass.

She thanked me and said, "Hey, you, I want to know how you

got so successful so young! Selling your health drinks to a mogul like Mr. Kappagoda! You know he flew all of us here, from all over the world, and in business class? My seat went totally flat! How old are you, anyway? Did you even go to college?"

"Just two years." I was going to add "so far" but the idea of trudging the crusted icy pathways of the Diseased Oaks Quad again made me want to shrivel up and die.

"Community college is the best. That's what I did, where I grew up in Wisconsin. I had great professors. How about at yours?"

"They were good." I didn't elaborate, mostly because I couldn't remember any of them except for you-know-who. "Anyway, I'm just an assistant. He's the investor." I gestured toward Lucky, who was busy mingling.

Shaundra said, "Where did the other man go? The one with the funny hair and kind face. He was very informative last night about the health drinks."

I told her Pong would be back in a few days but that this was a last-minute detour, and that we were heading out when he returned to other appointments around Asia.

"Well, I like your health drink, and I bet my students will, too. Makes me feel super light on my feet."

I wanted to tell her she couldn't be lighter, but I thought she might take it the wrong way. I know I keep noting her size but it's because (a) she was an outlier, the few yoga teachers I'd come across being what I thought of as ideally built, not overmuscly or bulgy, not too lean or too thick, the sort of body that looks to have been crafted by the most felicitous amount of effort and not a drop of sweat more, that didn't look as if it might be painful while at rest like certain Olympian physiques do, plus (b) she carried her weight so casually, so effortlessly, like it wasn't even there, whether she was downward dogging or not. She almost levitated, actually, barely seeming to touch the floor. And it was a good load of weight—surely two-hundred-plus pounds on a five-foot-five frame—her chest and legs and arms these glorious freshly proofed pillows of sourdough that you could see yourself happily imprinting knuckles deep.

"I bet you're wondering what I'm doing here, as I'm sure some of these people are," Shaundra said, tipping her glass in the direction of her peers. Her voice was somewhat sharper than when she was guiding our breath all through the chakras. "It's subtle, but body shaming is more prevalent than you'd think. You'd be surprised but there's discrimination in our field. Not with Mr. Kappagoda, though. He visited my studio last year and saw my work and he asked me to lead these sessions. That's really awesome of him, don't you think?"

"He's a pretty soulful dude," I said, recalling how he had shut his eyes and rocked while his crew sang their numbers at Garbo, hooking himself into their riffs.

"I had real trouble getting jobs in the beginning, even when they knew I'd bring former students over to the new studio. How awful, right, when yoga is all about acceptance? In the regular world I get it. If I walked into the first class, would you think I was the teacher? Come on, you can be honest. I mean it."

I was not honest and overvigorously nodded.

Shaundra noogied me and asked me to sit with her at the long table. We were at one end, with Drum heading the opposite end, Lucky anchoring the middle. The conferencees mostly didn't know one another and it took a bit of settling in before everybody got comfortable and started freely sharing about their practices and the irritating aspects of managing a small business, and then soon enough dishing about their irritating students, and their irritating boyfriends and girlfriends and partners and the irritating rest. It turns out yoga people are like other people; once you get past the typically easygoing outer crust and bore into the layers of actual human variety and can clearly glimpse manifestations of the anxious and the smug, the profane and the pious, the messy and the meticulous, and yes, as Shaundra was referencing, all the hard and soft bigotries in matters big and small come apparent. The other thing I noticed was that these folks seemed slightly on edge, for soon they would have to strut their stuff before the group and in all seriousness compare and contrast themselves. After all, this was not merely a gathering, for word was out that there would be special recognition for the most distinguished practitioner.

"You mean a prize," a guy named Alexandre clarified. He was from Quebec City and had wavy Jesus hair that was stiff and perfect.

"I prefer not to think about that," a woman across from us said. Her name was Lizzy or Lissy, it was hard to decipher, maybe because of her chipmunky front teeth, or because she was from Barcelona. "We're here to work together, aren't we? Support and help one another to grow in our knowledge and abilities? I for one refuse to see this as a competition."

"I heard cash," said Devin, a hatchet-faced black dude with crazy sparkling blue-green eyes, like he could be some kind of future-seeing superhero. "That and being his personal yogi."

"Well, I heard he might give a regional ownership stake," another woman chimed in. "You know how much that could be worth?"

"Whatever it may be," Alexandre said in his gelid leftover poutine of an accent, "Kappagoda has brought us here at great expense. We are a much smaller contingent this year, a very select group. He clearly said he wants to understand what is possible. To witness something extraordina-ry."

"So what's your beef with that?" Shaundra said.

"No *beef* at all," he sniffed back, not bothering to look at her as he spoke. "I am merely pointing out the seriousness of this conference and his very high expectations. I am prepared for those. Are you?"

"We all are," Shaundra replied, leaning and flagrantly hoisting her belly roll over the edge of the table. "And no less than you."

"I am certain."

The exchange put an awkward pause on the moment, people prodding at the tropical fruit salad on their plates. I knew that Shaundra was actually fucking with Le Québécois, as she'd nudged my foot with hers just before she shoved her doublestuff at him, a squarely badass move. Our elbows accidentally smooched, too, hers as cushy as a red foam-rubber ball, and my chest tremored with fondness. This was happening to me a lot of late, maybe it was my trailing in the wake of what had happened to me in my guest room, and the sudden absence of Pong, but I felt instantly game for Shaundra, smitten with the bare phenomenon of her, appreciating someone thoroughly being herself—well, as long as that self wasn't a major asshole—which makes you delight in the world a little more. At our most ideal we are windows onto the wider realm. This of course included the maybe cracked pane of Ms. Constance Kappagoda, OCD body cavity spelunktrix, who I realized was lingering by the opening to the far stairwell leading up to her suite, having clinically observed us through her big black-framed spectacles for who knows how long.

I reflexively shivered, but then waved, half thrilled by the sight of her, but she had already stepped back and was gone. I thought about pursuing her but Drum stood clinking a glass and the table immediately quieted. He welcomed us to what he called the "Inn," which he very humbly hoped would be comfortable enough for us, to which we all assented with much murmuring. He talked about something called the eight limbs, and the five kleshas, including the dvesha, or aversion to pain, which was a notion particularly appealing to me, as my lower half was starting to ring with an unpleasant oscillation.

"In a moment you'll hear more details about these drinks, which will soon be shipped to your respective studios. My business partners and I would be grateful if you would speak to your students about trying them. Thank you in advance for that. I do wish to say how pleased I am that you have all come here. We have a stated purpose in gathering, but the truth is, we hope to connect to something that is lasting and eternal, isn't that right? In the past, pursuits like art and music and literature elevated us, they let us connect with the mysterious and the great. We know times have changed. Fewer and fewer people appreciate such things anymore, and value instead immediate access to the widest range of goods and services. By definition these are nondurables. They have little, if any, lasting worth. As you know, I have been very fortunate in this regard. This mountain house, my many businesses and investments. Someday there will be no evidence that they ever existed. They will have added up to nothing. This is no profound realization. So why have we bothered to gather you especially gifted practitioners here? Yes, there will be rewards. You will all, in one way or another, be well compensated. I'm sorry to be so crass and 'nondurable' but I thought I should let that be known. So let me end with this. We are here to celebrate our forms, even as they are borrowed and temporary. What we may discover through your efforts is an idea about the possibilities of our mortal capacities, and in turn the larger capacities of this life. Such true knowledge, my dear practitioners, will not easily perish. It can indeed last forever."

Everybody heartily clapped for Drum, as much for the surprisingly humble warmth of his manner as for the hopeful wisdom of his words. The man was humane. It didn't hurt that he made clear how these nongrasping yoga folks would also benefit in worldly ways—they enjoyed eating and clothing and sheltering themselves like everyone else, and didn't mind a periodic taste of the finer things, too. Brunch was promptly served, and it was definitively finer for sure, the staff bringing out a flotilla of dishes that I'd certainly never had in Dunbar or my woodsy small college town, including morsels of deep-fried rabbit drowning in chili peppers, and ribbons of beef tendon in a sweet, spicy sauce, and handmade noodles with pork and pickled cabbage, sautéed bitter melon, and gooey little tenders of braised eggplant, all of which I sent sailing down the stream of my gullet.

I only detail these because as much as I reveled in the superb grub, I got even more delight from watching Shaundra tackle the family-style platters rotating before us. You might think I noticed because people will unfairly pay attention to how large people eat, but I swear it was just that Shaundra was a special eater, plain and simple. She wasn't outright hoggish like I was; rather, she served herself with an almost royal propriety, each serving spoon or forkful delicately ladled or tipped out into her bowl or plate as if the food might instantly have disintegrated if she had been any less careful. For each dish she took a moment to survey its colorful stack and breathed in its vapors before initiating a metronomic action of hand to mouth that was wonderful to watch, this fluid levering that was as smoothly motored as any perpetual motion rig. It was beautifully mathematical and also kind of spiritual how she depleted it all, which was a kind of yoga itself, the noodles and meats and salads exquisitely integrating into this unflappably ravenous woman who was by far their best fate; if you were destined to be consumed, you'd hope to be consumed like this.

Chilies came up from behind me and Shaundra and chirped, "Ya, how like my food?" Everybody roared back with raves, and though it was alarming to have him draped over me, I figured like any chef he craved kudos from his visitors, even if we were a clueless Gang Farang whose opinion he couldn't have welled up enough spit for if he'd had to. "You not get taste like this again!" he said, which was probably true. It also gave him the opportunity to breathe practically down my neck with his tarry cardamom breath (he chewed the pods in lieu of brushing) and hotly whisper to me, "Look like Titty my boy now."

Chilies beamed his blackish teeth, and I beamed back, figuring he was talking about my gluttonous assault on his food, but he pincered the back of my neck with his sharp fingernails, and went looking for more compliments at the other end of the long table. I was unnerved but Lucky now caught my attention; he was motioning for a sidebar. Rubbing my neck, I huddled with him by the drinks table.

"So Pong gave you the rundown?"

"About Minori?"

"Minori?" he said, his perennially smooth face screwing up. "He didn't tell you what you have to do?"

"Maybe he did," I said, if fuzzy on the details. Actually, totally confused. I wondered if Chilies had somehow just roofied me again.

"Look, Tiller," he said severely, "this isn't some high school civics trip. It's not a fucking joke. We have a lot on the line here. I'm not just talking about what these yoga people might hand sell for us at their studios. That's fine at six bucks a bottle, but that's not how we're going to make bank. They have to sell it for sure, but it's more that we have to show accelerating growth. You know why? It's Drum's relationship with the director of a beverage conglomerate that we're ultimately targeting. Can I tell you how much it paid for some new flavored green tea brand recently? The equivalent of thirty million dollars. That was for the Japan market only! Our drinks will be all-Asia, in the EU, and then, we hope, the coastal United States. You have any idea what that could mean?"

I shook my head.

"A liquidity event. Life-changing. We'll make sure you get a serious taste, too, if you do your part. So don't fuck it up."

I weakly said, "Maybe Pong told me to talk about us youth and health?"

"Whatever," Lucky snapped, leaning closer. I thought I could smell the medicinal-sweet rime of *baijiu* backing the hot pepper on his breath. If he hadn't been drinking that morning, he'd drunk a lot the night before. "Pong keeps saying how you have boundless capabilities, and I'm starting to believe it. So just set them in the believing mood. You can do that, right?"

"Now?"

"There's no better time. I'm heading out later today for Shanghai."

"Your FDA job?"

"Unfortunately, yes. Anyway, Pong assured me you'd handle it. So let's open the show."

When I sat back down next to Shaundra, a dessert of egg-custard tarts was being served, and despite the suddenly cavey feeling in my belly after talking with Lucky, she and I made those pies instantly scarce, flaky pastry shards littering the tablecloth before us. Of course I felt even more nauseated when Lucky belled his water glass with a spoon and announced that I would be saying a few words. Everyone turned my way as I slowly got to my feet. Alexandre leered at me past the vaulting bridge of his nose. Shaundra cheekily winked, ready to be even more impressed. And Drum, well, he was sitting kingly and prosperous at the far end with an air of quiet confidence, no doubt anticipating something along the lines of what went down at Garbo. Yet I knew I was in trouble. I'd been there before, like at Eric Goldfluss's bar mitzvah, when I was oddly one of two kids who were asked to speak about our friendship (Eric and I were acquaintances at best, neither of us having close friends, which is how I was even invited), and I totally freaked out and rambled on weirdly about liking to watch his little sister dive at the town pool. In such situations, time suspends as you steadily self-destruct, your mind sharpening only in identifying what you don't know and can't recall, which in this moment should have included the basics of the Elixirent business model/plan, plus the volumes I'd heard from grungy Getty. All this was lost somewhere behind an impenetrable fog of stage fright and perhaps a reinfection from the diabolical *luk chup*, and I actually began to hum, the isolated animal in me desperate to fill with any sound what had become a black hole of silence.

Lucky's face had blanched even whiter than it usually was. I couldn't bear to look at Drum. It was then that Shaundra cuffed my wrist and said, "Hey, kiddo," in her sharp midwestern American twang, and somehow woke me, Getty's mishmashed trustafarian island patois suddenly gibbering in my head. I began calling forth those strange words he'd uttered in a pedantic fit to me, the semi-scientific names of the roots and leaves and fruits and barks that made up our concoctions. So I said, *"Zingiber oronaticum,"* and liked how it sounded, and then piped out, in the key of G, *"Kaemferi galanga,"* and then moved on to the rheumy Portuguese stylings of *"Tiospora rumpii* Boerl" and *"Gijeyzahyza glabra,"* before swinging back with classical form to *"Foeniculum vulgare* Mill," and then the local bad boy *"Jataninum sunbac* Ait," and chanted my inexplicable favorite, *"Physalic angulata* Him." I rattled on, holding forth for I don't know how long, whether mumbling or singing I couldn't tell, channeling both Getty and my ninth-grade science teacher Mr. Arcidiacono, a self-labeled anarchist who made us pen the classification of the kingdom Plantae on each forearm and reputedly grew his own turbohybridized buds, until the crawl on the pulsing screen of my mind finally ran out.

I knew something was off when I saw Shaundra's expression frame-frozen between confusion and pity. She was openmouthed, perhaps deeply frightened. The rest of the table was spooked mute, as you'd probably be, too, if confronted by some kid speaking in

tongues. The Barcelona woman was painfully smiling, her prominent buckers pinching her lower lip; Alexandre was tilting away
from me as though I stank as bad as Getty; and right across from
me Lucky sat granite still, his arms forming a rigid triangle on the
table with a fist pressed into his opposite hand, looking like a sensei
mulling the expulsion of a student from the dojo. Shaundra gently
tugged on my forearm and I took my seat, though I wanted to keep
going lower and crouch beneath the table and maybe tunnel my way
out through the flooring. If Drum were merciful he would have
already signaled a minion to whisk me off in a shuttle down mountain and valley and straight through to the dazzling terminal at
SZX, where I deserved to get sardined onto a miserable commercial
American long-haul flight manned by miserable American flight attendants back to miserable EWR, that mausoleum for the still-
breathing.

But now Drum stood up, raising a glass of bright green jamu.
"*Calophylum inaphyllu*," he said. "*Caesalpinia sappan* Hinn. *Ci-
trae aurantifalia* Sivingle." He enunciated clearly and deliberately,
as if announcing persons about to receive diplomas. I was awed, as
he must have either met Getty or at some point studied the lab sheets
Pong had brought with us.

He said, "Nature is broad. Nature is inexhaustible. Nature, evidently, enjoys odd designations." This drew some chuckles. "It may
seem improbable, but these and the other flora my young friend and
I mention are in fact a fraction of the botanicals and other essences
his associates have already researched. So why don't you join me in
thanking Tiller for offering this dramatically succinct review of its
diversity."

He paused for effect before breaking into a wide grin, he and
everyone else starting to applaud, not for me but for his gracious
intervention. Shaundra and Devin were gamely *skoal*ing and *salud*-
ing me, while Lucky, I was relieved to see, was looking on more

charitably, and described for the instructors how our facilities in Shenzhen and Kuala Lumpur had the strictest production standards, that the in-house labs at each tested constantly for pesticides and heavy metals, that we had independent inspectors visiting farms un-announced to certify EU-standard organic practices, all of which was genuinely impressive but was frankly news to me. Then again, what hadn't been news to me in the little or big picture of my life? What hadn't been a casually profound surprise, starting from that point in my happy unhappy childhood, when my existential stance as the informed rather than the informer was forged?

"Let's all rest and recompose ourselves today," Drum pronounced, "for tomorrow will be the start of two days of wonder." This was intended to calm the yogis, I'm sure, but it seemed instead to give them a start, all of them nodding tautly to themselves as the brunch broke up. Even Shaundra rose from her chair abruptly. She and the others were staying on the top level, and as everyone was heading off she said, "I'm glad you'll get to see my full-on yoga."

"Me, too. And it's only fair," I said. "You got to see my full-on stupid."

"It wasn't stupid at all!" she cried. "A little creepy, if anything. I wanted to give you a big hug, but then you kind of got a rhythm going."

"Yeah, like a lunatic in a park."

"You want that hug now?"

I leaned toward her and was about to let myself get enveloped in all that wondrous firm mochi flesh, when I heard, "We have to go now."

It was Constance, togged in her signature white Lycra, looming like a wraith between us. She took hold of my elbow and I felt in-stantly twiggy in her meaty grip, a balsa-wood glider that was easily snapped.

"Oh, sure, Ms. Kappagoda," Shaundra said, her shoulders softening in deference, though she broke out in a deliciously easeful smile and hugged me anyway, to Constance's annoyance. Shaundra would not be deterred. She said, "You might not be aware of it, Tiller, but there's a lot of the sublime flowing around you. Keep inviting it. Quoting the great swami Sivananda, 'This world is your body. This world is a great school. This world is your silent teacher.'"

I loved hearing her say that, and as unsilently as she did. I loved, too, the idea of learning from the world, this world that was also only you. Was this the secret circularity? That it belonged to you as much as it did to anyone? Yes and yes. The most pressing question, I suppose, which occurred to me while I was getting tugged away by Constance, was whether you belonged first to somebody else.

20.

LEN AND PETE turned out to be among the last covers of our home-dining project. After the scrum on the lawn, once the dauntless biker gals roared off and Val pried the cleaver from Victor Jr.'s fierce clutch—the adrenaline still spiking in his system—the three of us went back inside and wordlessly buttoned up, hand-washing and drying the wineglasses, scouring the burner grates and hobs, clearing the counters of the various spices and oils and vinegars, and when I turned off the kitchen light I think we all knew that our good run was done. The single nod to ceremony was that Val and I joined Victor Jr. out on the steps of the back porch, each taking one of his bubble-gum cigarettes and blowing white puffs of confectioners' sugar, before chewing together in silence. The night sky was stenciled by long batons of clouds streaming past a delicate perfect crescent moon, and I couldn't help but think how you could only guess whether things were waxing or waning in this existence, and that the best we could ever do was commemorate any beauty. Val was staring up at the moon, too, I hoped channeling the same thought, or at least warmed by its gleam, when Victor Jr. stood up and sighed, deeply. He took the pip of gum from his mouth and flicked it into the grass. His lips pursed, in a way I'd not seen from him before, half closing his sleepy eyes, and he breathed, "Thank you."

Val and I did a double take, not sure what was happening.

"Thank you, for everything," he said, looking straight at us. Then he announced he was going to bed, and kissed us both on the cheek. It seemed like we should rub his Buddha belly right then, for good luck and further enlightenment, but he skipped inside.

"Did that just happen?" Val asked me, after a lengthy moment's pause.

"I think so."

She shook her head.

And that was that, his utterance of a simple string of words making the weeks of toiling together even more worthwhile than they already were. It made me damn proud of him, but even more than that, I felt a renewed pride for our kind, because if our once beastly VeeJ could evolve to see beyond himself and appreciate the broader context, maybe we weren't doomed.

There was a wind-down period, of course; 20 Whet was still an active topic on NeighborLady.com, and for the next couple weeks or so, uninformed or hopeful diners would ring our bell. We still had a fridge jammed full of perishable ingredients, so we cooked oversized portions for our own dinners and had plenty left to hand takeaway bags to the folks who as yet didn't know but had traveled far; but after we got through that inventory folks had to go away glum and empty-handed. To make it clear that the shutdown was permanent we started going out to eat again, doing a tour of pretty much every establishment in the greater Stagno area. I tell you we ate everything, deep-dish pizza and mushu pork, enchiladas and butter chicken, cheeseburgers and dragon rolls, and if it all settled out to be in a narrow band of extreme mediocrity, none of us minded. I guess we knew what it took for food to get on a plate, and even at the big chains, where the workers mostly pressed buttons and waited for a ping, we stuffed our gizzards with respect, if not delight. The one place we vowed never to return to was the golf and tennis club in a fifty-five-and-plus gated community in the abutting town that advertised its "six-star dining," where they insisted on putting lumps of lukewarm crabmeat on the gritty pucks of filet steak, which for us resulted in an almost instant case of the scoots. I never drove that fast, ever.

Otherwise it seemed we were always kind of ravenous, maybe because we were suddenly lonelier, too, and sometimes Courtney and Liam and even Keefer would tag along. One night we went with them to the bowling alley, taking up two lanes (both with deployed kiddie bumpers) and ordering everything deep-fried off the menu and multiple pitchers of soda and beer that led to nothing but a grand old time and only one dangerous moment, when Victor Jr. tried to throw his ball as hard as he could and catapulted it up into the low drop ceiling, pushing up one ceiling tile and snapping another as it fell back to the earth and just missed braining Liam, who was watching his own ball steadily turtle down the next lane. We gasped, and then Courtney kind of guffawed, thrilled by her fright, and we all ended up hollering and hooting until the manager came over, justifiably pissed. No matter, because I had him take me to their ATM, where the magic card again provideth; I paid for the damage and all our bowling and food but also tipped him lavishly for his inconvenience and trouble, an amount that would have momentarily softened a big-city club-bouncer's brow but froze this fellow into mulling the fat wad in his hand even after I started walking back to our lanes, as if it couldn't possibly be his. I don't know what prompted me to do such a thing. As noted, I was always conservative with the card except for the cuisine-related expenses—not because I feared it would run out but for the shame of profligacy, which I surely get from Clark. But I loved the feeling that swooshed through me, which I supposed was like being a lottery winner (and not just your typical "self-made" filthy rich guy), someone who understood the craziness of chance that underlies everything in what ought to be a bountiful world for all, and after that I became an extravagant Uncle Santa. I started with Liam, taking him on a mall shopping spree at a smart kids' toy shop, where they have kits for home science experiments and building your own drone; Courtney and Keefer were along, too, so they received, respectively, furry house boots and duck-hunting waders; and this bouncy little girl, who was getting fitted for off-brand soccer cleats, got upgraded to the Golden Boot model in both silver-black and yellow-green, as she was having trouble deciding. Her very tired-looking mom hugged me. Soon enough waiters and waitresses were hugging me, too, the Gas & Go cashier pressing a fist bump to me through the bulletproof safety glass, the Stagno Library head librarian slipping me a special-ops lending card that let you keep books and DVDs a whole extra week, this after I made a sizable donation while returning our overdues.

As regards Val and Victor Jr., I would have happily spoiled them silly but Val squashed that idea flat when I offered to buy her a luxury watch from the lone jeweler in town and she said, "I had a sugar daddy and it brought me only misery." I didn't even ask VeeJ what he wanted. He was content to hang out with us, and play with Liam every so often, for he was also in a different place, a kind of blue period in which he seemed to be taking full measure of his journey from sociopathic baby hellion to wunderkind food engineer. He went around the house with a tablet fully loaded with cooking magazines under his arm, "To keep current," he said, though with the way he was sighing and brooding and restlessly drifting from one part of the house to another, I began to wonder if he'd ever tie on an apron again; the little dude had toiled in the magnificent heart of the crucible and now that he was in the wake of that heat, the knowledge of what it would take to achieve the same level seemingly weighed heavy on him.

sprints around the neighborhood, the sort of running that an older dude should avoid for risk of a heart attack but was a satisfying stressor for my elastic twenty-year-old arteries, blowing them out with redlining pressure. The runs didn't take very long, though by the end I still tried to go faster, thoughts about marauding home invaders pushing me like a tailwind; I imagined someone getting wise to our daily schedule and maybe posing as a courier delivering a package just as I was farthest from our lair. I'd already instructed Val and Victor Jr. to always arm the security system and never answer the door while I was away and of course not to leave. I tested them once and VeeJ immediately opened the front door without even asking who it was and the alarm didn't blare and so for a few days I switched to doing my intervals up and back on long Whetstone Drive in order to keep number twenty in sight, which seemed fine until I started thinking I was a crazy person. So I borrowed a basketball from Rafe and started playing at an old hoop and backboard one of the neighbors up the street had rolled into the front of their yard likely decades before so their kids and their friends could play out in the street and had since left to rust and fade in the weather. Back in Dunbar this would constitute a serious neighborhood blight, but here in Stagno it represented the tonier end of lawn paraphernalia, and the owner, a widower in a wheelchair, liked to watch from inside his living room. He gave a thumbs-up whenever I brought along Victor Jr., whom I was keen on introducing to an actual sport now that he was cooling on gaming. The hoop was at the far end of Whetstone as it turned up toward the quarry, and I could just glimpse the roof of our place during our dribbling and shooting and passing drills. I was already in the practice of pressing a tiny swatch of masking tape on the gap of the garage door whenever we left to see whether Val was driving off, although if I found she had I don't know what I would have said, if anything at all. We were in that liminal place between being certain she was wholly one as well—yet another surprising and wondrous expression of his fast-maturing being—and gave me his, pouring out another. He pulled up a video on how to dribble behind the back, and I went out to the living room. I analyzed Val's movements, noting if there was any change to the sawing push and pull of her left-handed technique as she patiently went about our space, nudging the chairs, rooting in the corners. Her expression was neutral . . . or maybe too neutral. Was her hand micro-quaking? Was she terrified by what she might have done? She wasn't singing along to whatever she was listening to, had no bop to her feet. I kept picturing her at the wheel, having started the car, maybe holding her breath for as long as she could and then drawing that first sweet carbon-laced inhalation, steady and deep.

"Don't do that again!" I shouted, barely hearing myself.

She kept on with the vacuuming, lifting the head to suck a cobweb from the ceiling light fixture.

"Please don't!"

She must have sensed something and turned in my direction, switching off the vacuum. She freed one ear from the headphones. "Ooh, that sure looks so nice."

I froze, laid low by her simple vitality. What a thing it is, to be alive. The subtle pulsing of her cheek. I offered the glass of iced lemonade.

She took a big sip, and then another, and I shook my head when she offered it back and I watched her drink the rest down, her smooth, pale throat lovely and long. Her thirst was excessive. She handed me the glass, secured the cup of the headphones back over her ear, and switched on the vacuum.

I tried to keep the car keys with me after that. Val would wonder where they'd gone if she had to go out, say, to get her hair done, rummaging through the kitchen drawer, and I'd pretend I'd just gone on my own errand, or better, contrive a new one, and thus tag along. I purchased my toiletries this way, one travel-sized toothpaste and lotion at a time. I suppose she might have grown suspicious but instead she casually assented, pleased for the driver. Of course in that case Victor Jr. had to come, too, for even if he might have rated a Michelin star he was still a mere child, and so every occasion became a family occasion, natural reminders to her of how good things were, I figured, her boy now self-possessed and self-pacified with his multiple reading platforms, with nary an urge to stomp the back of my driver's seat, or besiege her with pleas for a junky snack. He was still hungry, for sure, though hungry for things that weren't simply fodder for the pleasure of destruction.

"I think we should have him start writing more," I said, this for the sake of his intellectual betterment as well as to keep Val focusing on the next thing, and the next. Victor was in the backseat listening to a podcast about wild-yeast starters. "I saw him scribbling something the other day and I snuck a look. It was a description of the time he made his first soufflés."

"Really? That didn't go too well," Val remembered, as she'd helped him, though each came out and promptly collapsed.

"But it was about the failure, his anger, and then his realizing that it was failure teaching him. He may actually be a memoirist."

"Now, *that* would be a fitting, if unexpected, outcome." Val sighed, peeking back at VeeJ. "What we're capable of . . ."

I had plenty to recount in that regard, none of which I would ever tell Val, especially of the more negative variety, and *I ain't talkin' Keats* (quoting the ever-sassy Professor Aquino-Mars). Of course I had to wonder if Val was signaling me by how she phrased that, semaphoring about another imaginary vision she was darkly screening. When we got to the hair salon I suggested she go for the mani-pedi as well while VeeJ and I browsed the used records and comics shop next door. She liked the idea but only if VeeJ and I got them, too. Was there a yearning in her eyes? A wish we'd stay close? Soon enough the three of us had spacers between our toes, Val ending up with a creamy raspberry color on her nails, me going with a matte clear coat, and VeeJ somehow deciding on a licorice black over the alarmed susurrations from the Eastern European immigrant lady attending him. She had been dubious from the start (a child, a boy?) and now checked with me and Val about the color, but we both gestured that it was fine. VeeJ ended up looking like some zombie spawn and while I paid the bill the lady regarded me so disdainfully that I could practically hear her thoughts of how great but doomed America was. I couldn't disagree. We are doomed, and deep down everybody knows it. But I can't worry about that. I have to worry about the few people still in my orbit and whatever I can do to keep things spinning and tight, I will, including indulging a kid's whims.

Did my mother indulge me? All the time. I can't remember an instance when she ever, finally, flatly, said *no*. I'm sure sometimes the yes was just to gently tweak frugal ol' Clark. Otherwise she decreed open season. The ice cream truck guy could always count on me for a Bomb Pop. I had kickballs of every color. Christ, I had a shoebox full of pushpins, which for some reason I loved filling this big corkboard with. The irony is that aside from those few things I never actually wanted much, and even as a kid somehow understood that my asking was more about giving her the pleasure of bestowal than satisfying my needs. I had no needs, right up to the second she wasn't there anymore. Then, needswise, you don't quite know where to begin.

After our nail treatments we loitered around the downtown establishments in the summertime heat, poking through some racks of vinyl, then perusing porcelain figurines at the antiques store, and window-shopping the other places that were still somehow viable among the numerous storefronts long soaped up or butcher papered over. Yet there were signs of life; enterprising people probably not too much older than I was and drawn by the Third World rents had recently opened a variety of businesses, including a gourmet tea and cookie shop, and a store for skateboards and scooters, and the latest addition to the main street, a medical cannabis "wellness center," already popular with Stagnovites young and old. Whether this could be qualified as a civic resurgence was unclear, but at least Stagno was dying less rapidly. Val had been shopping at the consignment store across the street for some warm-weather dresses, as she was sick of sweating in shorts and leggings. In the meantime, Victor Jr. and I got a gourmet cookie, and then were looking at the display at the head shop next to the pot clinic, as they wouldn't let him inside. I was deciding whether I should upgrade to one of the ornate hand-blown water pipes, when a pack of four boys, probably rising seventh-graders, judging from the almost comical difference in their heights and the aspirational wisps on their upper lips, had stopped to check out the display while figuratively blowing smoke about their preferences and prowess, posturing and pissing at one another as boys will. They instantly reminded me of the squads of boys I never wanted to join but sometimes did out of boredom and loneliness, regretting most every minute spent with them. Val, now wearing a gauzy yellow summer dress, was coming back across the street when one of the boys noticed the earbudded Victor Jr. aiming his tablet to take snapshots of the sea creature–like bongs and hookahs.

"Yo, Bobby," a kid murmured to one of his mates, eyeing Victor Jr. He had a cheeky leprechaun thing going, one of those eminently punchable wiseacre faces. He fluttered his fingers. "He's going trans like you." The others snickered.

"You wish I was, you fugly lesbo," Bobby answered. "They could cut off half my dick and it'd still be twice as big as yours."

"At least Cooch says mine doesn't taste like shit," the kid said. Cooch, the gangliest one, gave him the finger, and Bobby did, too, all then reflexively exchanging another round of lazy birds. Although I was repulsed by their idiocy, VeeJ clearly hadn't heard a thing, and so I decided to just usher us on, when Val handed me a bag of the clothes she'd been wearing and stepped right over to them.

"Hey, can I?" she said, her voice strangely low and torchy. I realized I'd never seen her in a dress, this one for a fancy summer luncheon, the Marilyn Monroe kind that wraps around the neck, clingy and diaphanous and low cut but still classy, even if framing a silken valley of cleavage. Plus, she wasn't wearing a bra, because she never did, and, brother, she was glowing.

The boys couldn't stop staring at her, disbelieving that this undeniably gorgeous woman was talking to them, her stunning, more than apparent shape practically volatile in the humid air. Only the one named Cooch was slighter taller than Val, who had also bought heels, and she easily outclassed them in her physique and bearing, a primed lioness among scraggly dingoes.

"Will you show me?" she said, grasping the elbow of the leprechauny kid. "I bet your friend is just jealous." She nodded to the alley. "We can go over there. I bet you're massive. I don't want to just imagine."

The kid was trying to free his elbow from her, the others half laughing, if unnerved, too, as I was, for she'd gone from zero to crazy in nothing flat, and if anything, I was afraid for Victor Jr. and how confused and possibly disturbed he might be afterward. But Val wouldn't let the kid go, I could see the color draining from his already colorless face, he was undergoing a serious psychic shrinkage, and when she drew him even closer he chopped down on his own forearm to free himself from her grip.

"Leave me alone," he pleaded, nearly falling backward into Bobby, who was looking pretty shrunken himself, as if the gang-bang porno they'd screened had suddenly morphed into a teen-torture flick, *Drawn and Quartered II*.

"I'll leave you alone," Val said, still crowding him. I never saw her so bristling, so radiating, so seething and fleshed out. I was afraid she might actually tear his head off. "Just tell me you'll be kinder to people, including your friends. You don't know what a person might be aspiring to, or what they might be enduring. Just think of yourself, how others have no idea what you might be worrying about. So when you make comments like that it just makes the world a colder, meaner place. Is that what you want? For it to be more unwelcoming for everyone?"

There was an awkward pause, and the kid shook his head, and Val reached for his shoulders and said, "I'm sorry, too," and gave him a gentle hug. He hugged her back. I was glad, for otherwise VeeJ might have attacked him and the others with his tablet. Val embraced the others, too, and then so did VeeJ, and I made things even weirder by handing each of the boys a twenty (for how forlorn they looked) and they straggled off, nearly bumping into one another as they started to walk, unsure of where they should head. I knew, as I'm sure Val did, that they'd revert to bluster mode soon enough, but maybe one of them would recall her the next time he spoke too blithely, callously, and shut up a little quicker.

Maybe it was coincidence, but that night in bed, Val and I weirdly got down to it. We journeyed to the poles. She led the expedition and I loyally followed. We plumbed the core, pinning our own flesh-synchronous orbit, my axis and her axis aligned with such precision it felt like we grooved a new fault in the earth that we then dropped so far into we emerged on the other side, only to plummet back up again, every last patch of me plying every last patch of her. In the morning we could hardly look at each other, startled and slightly ashamed by how utterly frictional it had been, a purely material reaction.

After that, it seemed we were imperceptibly altered versions of ourselves, as if we'd been body snatched and placed back exactly where we were before, both of us trying not to notice how we'd been

Mr. Pibb'd. There was no tension but maybe that was the problem, Val and I content to drift on the mellowed flow of the days (now minus the rushing whitewater of 20 Whet), shepherding Victor Jr.'s intellectual and physical education, patronizing as many local eateries and businesses as possible, and zipping up the house at night so we could sleep more soundly, though I rarely did. My eyes would pop open and I'd turn to a slumbering Val and her drooped jaw— she was pouring herself more wine of late with dinner, or ordering a second or even third drink when we went out—and listen to the tides of her breath. I'd try to mimic her rhythm but the period was too long and steady for someone wide awake and eventually I'd be straining to quell my urge to breathe naturally. I ended up checking the windows and doors. Then I found myself perching for a while at the foot of Victor Jr.'s bed listening to him burble and mewl away in his dreams that I hoped were not of fantastical mayhem and fear but instead of delighting childish things, like climbing a huge mystical shade tree, or turning over a big flat stone to uncover all the wriggly, wondrous alien life.

It's funny, because one early morning not so long after my mother was gone, I half awoke to see Clark sitting on my half-sized kiddie desk, his head in his hands. When he looked up I loosely shut my eyes and watched him begin to cry; he was shuddering, clearly suppressing himself, and even then I knew I ought to rush and leap into his arms and wail myself, but I just closed my eyes tightly and stayed as still as I could so as not to embarrass him and make him feel even worse. I must have fallen back asleep because when I woke for real he was down in the kitchen in his weekend robe making us pancakes and greeting me with his customary kindly and dorky saying: "How 'bout some tea for the Tiller-man?" Like it had simply been a dream.

21.

CONSTANCE, utterly real in spirit and in body, kept us busy, narrowly and broadly both.

After she plucked me from my bizarre and dismal presentation at the yoga brunch, I would spend the next two days bivouacked with her in a room seemingly custom designed to elicit my most pampered princeling self. Of course I told her I needed to do my marketing duties for Elixirent but she insisted her father knew we were together and that he'd given his blessing that we "be friendly." He liked me a lot, she said, though surely he couldn't fathom what *friendly* could possibly mean. Or could he? Regardless, she told me he was intent on pursuing some high-level yoga work with all these experts and didn't want business talk disturbing the practice.

Constance had her own scenario. When she opened the door to her special suite it was the stuff of a Russian oligarch's wet dream, the sort of decorations and furnishings you might find on some mega-yacht in St. Barts; there were puffy oversized chairs and shimmery upholstery fabrics and amoeba-shaped black-and-white area rugs that looked like they were made from a waddle of penguins whose feathers had been wildly teased out. There were frilly shade lamps that were switched on low and the bed was a California king made up with a massing of black-cherry-red satin pillows with tas-seling that matched the tasseled black-cherry-red sheets and bed-spread. Various nude statuettes carved from elephant-tusk ivory were set on the bureau and desk and night tables, the female ones with asses so enlarged and protruding that it looked like they were backwardly pregnant, the males with upshooting dongs as long as their legs and twice as thick. I had to wonder what Constance thought of my barely arithmetically mean rig. What got me though was that the bedspread was littered with hundreds of freshly picked white and yellow orchid blooms, the extravagance of which tangled up my insides with equal guilt and glee. I was her bride, and al-though the standard operating procedure of romantically familiar-izing and wooing and consummating got wickedly reversed, I still felt like there was a caldera of mysteries yet to plumb between us.

To my surprise, we started slowly, innocently. Like fifth-graders figuring out the truly ornate weirdness of a first kiss. We didn't fully strip. Instead we fired up some choice Cambodian sativa she had in the night table and afterward sat and lay about listening to a track of nature sounds she had going, this while nuzzling and spooning, hugging and wrestling, rolling and sliding on the satin sheets until they got so staticky we had to literally ground ourselves on the floor to offload the charge. All that chaste rubbing got us both worked up, her décolletage flushed and damp, my earlobes fever hot (for some reason I get inflamed in a top-down fashion), our lower parts livid and trapped beneath our clothing and practically screaming to be freed. But according to her fixed plan she rang down to the kitchen and in the span of a few more suppressed moans and pelvic grinds, in through the door came a delivery of treats both savory and sweet, probably two dozen little plates of vittles and desserts and even one full of *luk chup*, which scared me but not enough to prevent me from recklessly cramming a few in my mouth, for how randy my soul was. *Damn the probes!* We lustily finished the trays

I wonder how Constance's talk story would go, about that first interlude of ours. I can't believe it wouldn't be with some fondness. Still, could she have been the slightest bit unnerved? The closeness was extraordinary; at times it was impossible to tell who was leading and who was being led. It was perennially night, as she closed all the blinds and illuminated our exertions only by candlelight. This suggests the atmosphere was crepuscular and romantic. In fact, it was as bright as the brightest dawn, and warm, too, because of the scores of tiny open flames, waves of flickers dancing on the walls whenever she or I stood up to fan ourselves and each other. For hydrating boosts we drank coconut water, before sleep we took shots of sweet milk tea with the scantest trace of Chilies' *luk chup* essence, which in that low concentration disabled only our dreaming. We were dreaming awake, moving from sensation to sensation. We didn't much talk. Constance was fundamentally a doer and I, well, I guess my fate was to be Tillered to and fro, to be a skin duffel of nerves and glands. Sure, we could have therapized each other via issues maternal, revealed the sheer wide hollows in our souls, but evidently we would rather bridge ourselves with the other, shrink any flesh space to nothing. I'm not referring to the typical parts and configurations. There was plenty of that, though to my surprise (and, even more shocking, my slight disappointment), no more battery-powered probings. We communed another way. It was an advanced tutorial in the varieties of carbon-based contact.

I would say we consumed each other, nonmetaphorically. Constance bundled her hair with rubber bands and stuffed the brushlike end in my mouth. I did vigorous calisthenics until I was dripping with sweat and she licked every last patch of me dry. We chewed on each other's clipped fingernails, ground our noses in the oily musk of our scalps. She hocked a loogie onto my tongue and I returned the favor. We skipped the toilet stuff because that was still a little too gross for essentially bougie kids like us. Friction was king; we rubbed our forearms, our cheeks, the spurs of our hips, all well past the point they began going sore. We lubed our eyebrows and let them go bangtime. That we were of similar size made our exertions feel gyroscopic, the force between us ever centering as it increased, like we'd fly apart if we suddenly stopped. I couldn't tell if the actual sex was a starter or a main or a dessert as we ended up going in a continuous loop, fueling ourselves with extra snacks and drinks Constance would call for with a few clanks on an ox bell as she leaned out the room's opening over the valley.

One time it was Pruitt who brought up the tray in the middle of the night and as he handed it to me through the door he said, "I've made up your side so whenever you're ready!" nodding gamely like I'd be done with this frivolity soon. Maybe I would be, but I knew I'd be long gone before ever sharing his dungeon suite. I rudely slammed the door on him and went back to Constance on the bed, bearing whatever the kitchen had prepared, this time a risotto with prawns, the heads of which she pulled off and made me suck dry. They were good but not as good as the scalding creamy rice she spaded on my belly and thighs and then portioned off, a spoonful at a time, feeding us in turn even as she wanked me, and despite how nice it felt I didn't think I would but very suddenly I simultaneously came and gagged from the sticky bolus that was halfway down my throat.

I began to see, too, that there was a design to our carnality: Constance was systematically assessing my reactions, my response to this or that stimulus, rhythm, order of operations, to particular matrices of bitter and sweet, of funky and nasty, gauging my proneness to pain and my tolerance for pleasure. She was testing my properties, psychic and molecular, pouring me from flask to beaker as she narrowed her Bunsen-burner focus to keep me on the cusp of volatility. She was assaying for the sake of assaying, pursuing pure research. All the while she herself was in the throes of an ecstasy, if a much cooler kind, her expression thresholding between anticipation and mania, and whenever I was able to bring her to climax—she professed she wasn't super orgasmic—it was a seismic event for us both. Glasses half fogged, she'd shudder terribly and claw whatever of me was in the way—mouth, ear, ass crack—until her grip relented and she started kissing me, with wild and unabashed tenderness, which glazed me with a dark joy. My few hookups to that point had happened mostly because the poor, unlucky girl and I had nothing better to do and no one more appealing to do it with, and while the lovey stuff proceeded it was essentially masturbation in parallel. With Constance it was a fundamental bondage, no need for cuffs or straps, we were the only moving parts of a mechanism whose sole purpose was to mark the limit of its own endurance. Patience. Persistence. What else is there, by way of all flesh? Is this what real love is? Maybe. What I do know is that my relationship with Val has been entirely different, for without my tenure with Constance I don't know if I would have been capable of being a worthy lover to her, and I don't simply mean in bed.

As noted, a span of days expired outside the mini-universe of Constance's boudoir, a period that I figured would have us become tight enough that my imminent departure (once Pong returned) would prompt our wistful wondering of what might have been, perhaps even some tears, certainly some quickened, knowing laughter for the cosmic serendipity of two young people from the far sides of the planet somehow aligning, dare I say it, eye to eye. Catch you in the next phase, my big chunk of sweet. Lying there listening to the steamy rasp of her breath as she slumbered, I imagined a scenario in which Drum was to be my father-in-law, decanting some precious nectar into my crystal goblet and reminding me to sip it slowly, as those who would possess much bounty need never make haste. Of course I didn't care a yuan about being welcomed into their riches; simply being welcomed was the thing, to be gathered up and kneaded whole into the larger batch until you happily disappeared, having no choice.

Maybe with Constance I secretly didn't want a choice. Maybe it had happened in the course of my time hitched to Pong, and was especially apparent now that he was absent, but I was starting to accept the fact that I had never quite developed a normal habit or need for choosing. Any amateur shrink can psychologize this deficit as precipitated by you-know-what, and who would disagree? I'm not special. This tough-shit thing happens to you and after that you either take up every rein with fury or else yield yourself, full feather, and pray you don't end up wholly plucked. But maybe chooser and choosee are in fact more similar than any of us think. In a wider view, we are all unwitting subjects in the shadowy laboratory of existence. We'll likely never know the ultimate chief investigator, or understand what he or she is seeking, or ever gain the wisdom of any solution that might arise. What we have is each other, to push and pull, to chafe and soothe, to huddle with in the darkness, and if we're lucky we'll get to ride this gig out together, brace each other as long as possible against the chill.

Craving some sunlight, I released myself from under Constance's hot, dense thigh and ventured out in her thick black terry-cloth robe and slippers—where my own clothes had gone was not apparent—sneaking down the stair past the level of Pruitt's dungeon quarters. As much as I wanted to avoid him, I also couldn't stop thinking about him; never having moved on from a gig he fell into, stringing himself along one lesson at a time, he was the embodiment of an ESL teacher's nightmare. I, on the contrary, had options, ambitions, manifold destinies. I was a dude possible, if not a dude complete. It was still chilly, being early in the morning, and I padded a short distance from the lodge, following the driveway that led down through the forest toward the megalopolis, which I could just barely make out on the horizon in the dishwater mist. It was not beautiful but it was real, and for the first time in a long time I felt utterly content, even as I was alone, for if I hadn't exactly found my place I'd at least discovered a new way to be while awaiting a more lasting situation.

I thought I heard a muffled wailing, a kind of wounded-animal plaint, but it stopped. Then I smelled burning wood, which might be as good a scent as there is to a human (short of burning meat), and saw some smoke curling up through the treetops around the hill. I noticed, behind a metal gate, there was a smaller paved drive-way diverting off the main approach and I followed it, hearing the strange sound again. The driveway led around the hillside to a ga-rage door set into the sloped earth, like the entrance to an armory or bunker. It was then that I saw the small wooden hut with a nar-row black-metal chimney pipe coming up through its shed roof. The hut was set on some terracing, its retaining wall the same gray-green rock that girded the skirts of the main building. Beside it was a small man-made pool of water, though it did take advantage of a natural brook that fed it. The space in front of the hut had been cleared so that the view of the valley was unimpeded, and as I gained a better angle I could see through its glass door none other than a naked Drum Kappagoda, sitting on the built-in bench with a towel draped over his lap. He caught sight of me before I could step back from view, and motioned that I come forward.

"Join me," he said, his words muted by the thick pane of the glass. I shed the slippers and went in, instantly enveloped by a stout heat in the cedar-lined sauna. The space was tight for the two of us, and Drum had to shift right up against the far wall to give me enough room so I wouldn't accidentally sear my leg on the small cast-iron stove, on top of which were piled chunks of granite.

"You caught me hard at work in my outdoor study," he said mirthfully, holding a thimble-sized porcelain cup. Beside him was a companion teapot, no bigger than a mug, from which he tipped a tiny gurgle of inky liquid into the cup. "Is it too warm for you in here?"

"It's fine," I told him. The sudden heat felt good, like an extra blanket does when first laid on. The scent of his tea was strong in the small quarters, its geological tang of something like dried clay and roots, mineral and bitter, making me think of an ancient apothecary, where some wild-eyed shaman in a headdress concocted a powerful brew. Naturally Chilies' tree bark–like complexion flashed in my mind. "I don't want to bother you. I can leave you alone."

"Please don't!" he said. He was about to take a sip. "I would offer you some of my drink, but it's not for a young and healthy person like you. Unless you're willing to take your chances . . ."

I brashly took it from him; why else was I out here, but to drink deeply of the realm? He raised his eyebrows as I made a show of sniffing, swirling, before drawing the demi-demitasse to my lips. But then he plucked it away before I could actually drink it.

"One must build up a tolerance," Drum said. He drank it down, shutting his eyes as he swallowed. He shuddered terribly. Then he took a restoring, yogic breath. "A tiny measure of poison, to ready the body for what Pong is making for me."

"The HG?" I blurted.

Drum's eyes sparked, but then he looked at me guardedly, as though a response any more animated might jinx something. "You know about it?"

I froze, instantly feeling callow and reckless for bringing up a subject I knew squat about, and that was clearly of great importance to him.

"That's all right. I'm sure he'll tell you when necessary. With Pong, everything is in its ready place. He's never in a rush. This is also why, although I have not known him very long, I trust him. A person like that endows you with great confidence. The feeling that almost anything is within your reach."

Drum was right; being with Pong made me feel the same. I was now more seasoned or brined or whatever, but what that experience really meant was that I believed I could handle anything thrown my way. This is not to say I was any braver than I was before, just calmer, knowing Pong had my back. Still, as cogent and rational as he was, I wondered if Drum's illness was affecting his mind. People in peril will grasp at any hope.

"You need to keep up your strength, I hear. My daughter has been keeping you busy, I take it?"

I didn't know what to say to this, just dumbly nodding while I tried not to meet his gaze.

"Don't worry, I don't know what's going on." He laughed, and perhaps even archly, as if it was all a fait accompli. In fact, I had to wonder if he knew literally what had gone down, which only made me more sheepish. I didn't want to ruin anything for our venture, or for Pong, or even, I was beginning to think, for myself.

"Constance can be a cosmic force, when she gets in a certain mood." He stretched his head in various directions, his eyes shutting tightly as he torqued past a limit. "You may now have an appreciation of this. It's this about her I have faith in. Her ferocious resolve. I know she'll be okay in life, even if she ends up alone sooner than is desired."

"I'm sure that won't be the case," I said, though noting the surprising prominence of his shoulder bones and clavicles. Whatever was afflicting him had drawn him down, made him frail. I wondered if the intense heat was to keep his blood warmed and flowing, to stave off a stiffening coil.

"Your energy is a different kind," he said. "So unassuming, and yet so irregular. Exceptional in surprising ways. You've always considered yourself to be nothing more than ordinary. Am I correct?"

I felt slighted by his supposition, but I could only nod, as it was true. I've always felt I was dipped in the River Mediocre just after birth, stained with the invisible ink of Just Okay. Certain people could see it immediately, most others eventually finding me out, *Oh, right* flashing across their faces. It was usually the prelude to my being shown the exit.

"I'm not criticizing you, Tiller. How can I? We're all ordinary in the end, as physical beings. Yes, even my precious Constance! We make everything of our distinctions, exceptions, working and pushing, convincing ourselves that we're not like everyone else. Yet at some point our cells slow in replicating, or else, as with my condition, the replication won't stop. You're young and have a long run of effortless regeneration ahead of you. The process, if you think about it, is a true marvel. Even magical, given the countless operations that are required on the molecular level. It's a coding native to us all, no matter our age. This dance of dying and living. It's in our makeup, always there. The question is, can it be reset, if it has gone awry? And if reset, continuously extend life? In the West, the alchemists were primarily interested in things like turning lead into gold. Gold! As if that is worth anything in the end. But if you read early Taoist texts in alchemy, people believed eternal life was possible. The first emperor of unified China, Qin Shi Huangdi, was one. Pong sent me many articles on him as well as Taoist alchemy and other related philosophical constructs. Qin had his doctors prepare remedies made with special herbs and minerals, including arsenic and mercury. He sent an envoy to a legendary mountain island to gather the blooms of a mythical immortality plant."

"I guess he didn't live forever?"

"Not that we know," Drum said flatly. I looked at him funny, but then he winked. "More famously, he had thousands of terra-cotta warriors made so that they could be entombed with him, as he would naturally need them in his long and prosperous afterlife. So he did anticipate a kind of deathlessness."

"One experienced in the mind."

"Quite wise of you, Tiller! Yes, he must have believed another existence was ahead of him. In Taoist alchemy, it is held that one can find a psychic elixir through meditative practice. I believe in this. A fully realized consciousness is the most powerful tool. But after reading the historical accounts, I can't help but feel that other measures regarding longevity still hold possibility. Do you know what I mean, Tiller? Do you know what I'm talking about?"

I nodded, but I didn't say a word, for what could you say to such an idea? And to a man who might soon be dead?

"You like it here, yes?"

I said I did.

"We can discuss it when Pong is back, but I am imagining that you could be his sales agent in this part of Asia, while serving as a manager for my investment in Elixirent. There would likely be travel to the yoga studios in Europe as well. Pong seemed fine with the idea of you staying on for a while." He paused. "I suspect someone else we know would be very pleased."

I could only nod, as this last notation about Constance—equal parts scary and exciting—momentarily overshadowed the totally cool prospect of working for Drum, plus being out here, in the ever-humming generator of Asia, where more and more I felt I should embed. Wasn't I a distant cousin returned, if now a few concentrations less removed, the tide of the Bardmon in me receding? Not to mention that manicured, enbubbled Dunbar seemed even more stifling and irrelevant, besides being galaxially distant, with the rest of America disordered and dilapidated, not to mention culturally mean and backward. The one brake was that although I'd not agreed to anything, a spike of guilt kebabed my heart vis-à-vis Pong, who'd uncovered for me the spangly ore veining through the mundane rock of this life, and I resolved that even if I signed on it would be a temporary free agency, just enough to nurture my necessary independence and competence and build new expertises to bring back to Pong's enterprises as enhancements and tribute and, most important, have us permanently cement our chemical bromance. And I was sure only delights and wisdoms lay ahead of me with the Kappagodas, if with periodic doses of highly unnerving stimuli.

Drum was quiet again, hung on a thought, sitting so absolutely still that it seemed he'd forgotten I was there. We sat baking in the heat, made hotter, no doubt, by the morning sun now casting its rays inside the hut, when he said, "Time for some cooling."

He ushered us out, ordering me to strip and take the first dip in the stream-fed pool. It was only large enough for one at a time. His mood had grayed and so I didn't hesitate. It was deeper than I expected. The water was so cold that for a microsecond my feet and ankles read it as lava-hot and I let out a little shout. But I couldn't expel another, the chill snatching all my breath away.

"Also your head," Drum said, and when I didn't comply he gently but firmly tapped on my skull, and I submerged myself. He tapped again and I practically jumped out, quickly bundling myself in the robe. "Go in the sauna but don't dry your hair. It's better for your health. Let the heat gradually evaporate the moisture."

Shaking miserably inside the hut, I couldn't follow his instructions and blotted my head with the sleeves of the robe. While I rubbed the blood back into my fingers I watched Drum step and then settle in the water. Maybe I'd misjudged his clothed frame, but in his nakedness he was much smaller, his chest not as rounded and jutting. The rest of him, his shoulders, his rear, his legs, still looked sturdy enough but all over him was a fine scrim of a rash, a lightly stippled redness that looked horribly itchy but that he didn't mind, or try to hide. He didn't react at all to the chilly water. He simply lowered himself, centimeter by centimeter, until he disappeared. When he didn't immediately rise I started counting, one one thousand, two one thousand, but after I reached twenty I stopped and stared at the barely rippling surface, my own breath suspended. I was about to go and drag him out when he rose from the water just as slowly and gradually as he'd descended. Then he went under again. When he finally came up his eyes were shut and he inhaled deeply, terribly. His face was wracked, not by discomfort, I thought, but from the effort of mastering that discomfort. This is not to say he wasn't experiencing pain, which I'm certain he was. When he climbed out he wrapped the meager towel around his waist and stiffly hobbled back to the sauna, his legs as if unjointed. I shifted over so he could be right next to the stove but he shook his head.

"You stay put," he said. He sat with his forearms propped on his knees, head bent. Water dripped from his nose, his chin. "I prefer to warm up more slowly. You're still a very young man, so it's impossible for you to know. I can feel the life in me waking, cell by cell. It's like rising from the grave every morning. It's the same feeling, when I sing. I'm revived."

"What were you singing before?"

"That? Let me teach you."

He started right in with it, immediately hitting the high, shrieky notes that I'd heard faintly. At Garbo he'd sung the tunes beautifully and melodically, but this song was entirely different, more like the snippets of Chinese opera I'd once heard on some NPR documentary, atonally screechy to my Western ear, plus rhythmically irregular, a sort of primeval yowl that you might imagine a witch doctor would sing to call forth powerful spirits. He said it was a boatman's song, something his great-grandfather and grandfather and father would croon as they oared passengers and goods up and down the tributaries of the Pearl River, this long before anyone even dreamt Shenzhen could be Shenzhen.

"I helped row when I was big enough, but my father didn't want the same life for me. It was extremely hard work in every season, but that wasn't it. There was no indication at all what would eventually happen to the area, all the massive development. That was still a decade ahead. But somehow he knew there was no future in it, and that I should make a different life for myself. He said he would probably die on the riverboat, just as his father and grandfather had, but he didn't want that fate for me. To be still floating at the end. He wished for me to have some ground to my name. My own land."

I repeated each of the verses after him, my mouth and vocal chords unaccustomed to the way they got wrenched and rattled, the sounds almost abrasive in my throat, but in a good way. I couldn't recognize a word of the dialect so Drum translated the verses for me, so I'd know the meaning of what I was singing.

> We must pull and pull
> Straining against the tides
> No rest until the last passenger
> Is brought to the far shore
> The full night brings quiet
> Waters, black and swirling
> Will the sunrise be kind?
> Will it wait for us to wake?

After a couple practice rounds together I sang it myself, more comfortable with the scale. I realized it was like any song, that there was no single right way to sing it, and I let the unfamiliar pitches and odd syncopations run a bit loose, naturally warp, expand into their own life. Again I don't know how I really sounded, I can never quite hear myself, but I tell you that hut shook a little when I hit certain notes, Drum bobbing his head with woeful recognition, and longing, and what seemed like a small burst of happiness.

"Your karaoke is just what I hoped," he said. "As I said, a song well sung can do amazing things."

I couldn't help but ask: "Did your father pass away on his boat?"

"Yes and no." Drum winced, though more from the chest, his shoulders subtly bracing. "I wasn't there but my mother told me what happened. I was already living on my own in old Shenzhen, buying and selling used radio and TV parts. That was my first real business. My parents were as always working the boat. One of the hired oarsmen was too sick to row so my father took his place, but he wasn't used to the exertion. It had been raining heavily, being monsoon season, but he made it through the day. That night he sat on the bow as always to smoke his pipe. My mother eventually called him to come in but when she looked out he was gone. She thought he must have had a heart attack or stroke and fallen into the fast-running water. He was a good swimmer, so she was probably right. A couple days later some fisherboys found his body stuck in a bank of mud. When we went to retrieve him his mouth was full of it and I did my best to clear it with my fingers. It wasn't for his dignity. I was not a child, but it didn't make sense to me that he was dead. I couldn't help but think that if I cleared his mouth he'd sit up and walk out with us."

He rubbed his face. We sat for a while in silence, drying ourselves in the slow way he prescribed. It did feel natural and right, like a plant taking in the full morning sun, steadily coming into one's being. We were comfortably dry when he said, "Come, Tiller. I would like to show you something now."

I followed him out of the hut. He stepped back on the path and at the garage door he flipped up a panel and punched a hidden electronic keypad. The door retracted like any suburban garage door, a rush of chilly, dank-smelling air streaming past our ankles. It was a tight antechamber, carved out from the earth and rock. There was a set of double doors and he opened these and even colder air immediately walloped us. But this air was sterile, strangely stripped of odor. He turned on the lights and I almost lost my balance, disoriented by how widely the space opened up; it was the same size as the main kitchen in the lodge, a huge high-ceilinged room full of vats and bins and tanks and fitted with industrial piping and ventilation hoods, the place looking like a cross between a high school science lab and a brewery.

"Pong had all of this set up," Drum said, walking us up to some large white plastic tanks with spigots on their ends. "Lucky hired a construction firm from Guangdong, and Pong consulted step by step on the design of the layout. He sourced all the mechanicals and raw materials."

He took a beaker from a cart and turned one of the spigots, releasing some clear liquid into it. He waved the beaker under my nose.

"This is sodium hydroxide in solution. It's a common ingredient around the home, such as in oven cleaners and detergents. It's critical in the paper-making process. One may cure olives in it as well. All of this I learned from Pong. It's fate, that my last business partner should be a chemist by training."

He placed aside the beaker and showed me the bins of raw materials they had for reacting with the sodium hydroxide: yellow sulfur, powdered aluminum, and in the last bin, what looked to me like ground red chilies. Drum stuck his hand in this and brought up a fistful, squeezing the reddish dirt until his knuckles showed white.

"This is cinnabar," he said. "Our source ore. Also known as Chinese vermillion. Using the other materials, we've unlocked what's inside. This could be achieved with heat and distillation but we used a simple chemical process."

Drum pointed out spouted basins made of inch-thick glass that could be tipped forward using the steel handles riveted into them on either side. "The work was done in countless small batches. We have plenty of manpower here so it's possible. The sodium hydroxide is mixed with sulfur. Then the cinnabar is added. Aluminum mixed in after that. The reactions release noxious gases throughout, hence the strong ventilation. After many cleanings and purifications, we yielded about two hundred fifty grams of material each time."

He gave me a set of thick black rubber gloves that came up to the biceps. He donned a pair as well. Before us were three identical iron vats about seven feet tall, and as wide around as small hot tubs, each topped with a hand-thick glass lid lined with rubber and affixed by a hinge on one side and secured by a folding wrought-iron lock on the other, like immense jam jars. We had to step up on a rolling metal walkway to be able to look down inside.

"What we've been able to produce is absolutely pure, as pure as from any high-tech industrial lab. You're assuming this is all for what Pong and I are exploring, and you would be right. But for that we need very little. It's enough to complement what Pong will be returning with soon. The rest of this, well, it's for something I'm working on."

"What is it?"

He needed my help to lift one of the lids.

"We keep it cold so it's less volatile," Drum said. "Still, one shouldn't breathe too deeply."

But I was hardly listening. The sight of it froze me, for I knew immediately what it was. A vat of quicksilver. Mercury. I remembered once playing with a dime-sized blob of it, tapping and watching it bubble apart and then bubble together. Here was an entire mirroring cauldron of it; I was rapt, peering at myself and Drum reflected in the slight curvature of its surface tension.

"Reach into it," Drum said, dipping his own gloved arm in. "Don't be afraid."

I did. It was far too beautiful to be afraid. Here was a pool of nirvana. A fount of heaven. I was startled, amazed, almost giddy for how incredibly difficult it was to push down into it. For a moment I thought my hand was getting crushed. But it wasn't that. It was more like I had finally found the one perfect lock to the long

22.

I CAN SEE THE MAIDEN . . .

This is what Drum Kappagoda would eventually whisper to me. He was of course referring literally to mercury. *Gong*, in Chinese. Scientifically known as hydrargyrum. *Hg*. You can look it up. Number 80 on the periodic table. But looking back on it, I realize now he was describing something even more elemental, and everlasting. Ever flowing.

The HG, as he and Pong coded their side project, was both a part and the whole of what Pong had promised him, if that makes any sense. Elixirent was a genuine business venture, but this was the venture that really mattered to him. HG was not just a cure for the cancer spreading unchecked throughout Drum's body. It was tasked with a much grander mission than killing rogue cells. It was to be the ultimate tincture. A drink, Drum said, that could grant unending life. I had to pause at his utterance, this the evening after he showed me the mercury room, when I was singing for him. Just as I did in the outdoor sauna, I let his words slip by, even as a part of me was certain that the disease had reached his brain. He was at least afflicted by overwishfulness, which, if you think about it, isn't the worst thing, and often enough, the only thing that a human being can do. It did make me wonder what Pong was actually saying to him, for if you knew anything about Pong it was that he was supremely realistic, supremely rational. The flip side of this was that if Pong said you could live forever, if he looked you in the eyes and plainly uttered those words, you might well believe him.

I would have, for sure.

Needless to say, Drum and I were bonding, for when Constance was done with me after our usual afternoon-to-twilight labors, I'd get escorted across the lodge to the karaoke room. Pong the chemist would have said that we amalgamated, the way silver or gold foil will disappear when added to mercury and instantly become one and the same.

It's when Drum said it again, this after we'd just finished a particularly felicitous and galvanic duet of "Islands in the Stream," when I took a bit too long in selecting the next song and prompted Drum to say, in the most measured and sane tone, how Pong was going to bring him back an elixir of immortality.

"Lucky Choi first brought me the idea last year," he said. "He connected me to Pong, and we eventually met at a conference, and then a few other times in the ensuing months. We decided to try making a formulation using some of the Taoist alchemical concepts we had been discussing. Reading more about it, it made so much sense to me. There is a so-called inner alchemy I already mentioned to you. The 'Three Treasures' of life—essence, vitality, and spirit, which we nurture in yoga—but also the so-called outer alchemy that employs raw materials of the earth, certain elements, plants, distillations. These are what Pong is using for me, in the hope of restoring the pure state of being we all had briefly at our very beginning, at the moment of diplosis, when each of us became the fusing of our parents. The perfect one, from two. Pong won't guarantee anything, and he never will, but I know he is doing his best for me."

Again I didn't question him. I just sang longer, and deeper, maybe more beautifully than I ever had. Drum was compromised of body and of mind but in a way I was, too, because the more I thought about what Pong was offering him the more I believed, or wanted to believe, Drum's calm certainty serving as a gyroscope to what should have been a cyclonic tumult in my head. His faith centered me such that I didn't need to revolve any further, and all I wanted was to pass this strange interlude until Pong returned.

After the karaoke, I'd get deposited back with Constance, both of us sleeping in until midday. Frankly, there was a depravity in alternating like that, daughter-father-daughter, daughter-father-daughter. Though once you stop resisting the situation, you see things with a new clarity. You catch glimpses of physical and psychological similarities, say, how they worked their tongues (if in very different activities), or the way they would very slightly wince, with a somberness, at certain moments of pleasure: a bull's-eye-hit middle G, a well-timed pluck of the belly button. With both of them it was serial intimacies, with hardly any pauses.

In the karaoke room, Drum and I ticked our way through the near infinite list of songs on his electronic tablet, songs from those riverboat days to just before he got rich (when he ceased, he said, living life like life), my choices from my mother's collection, and we crooned them fullheartedly. I sang the lion's share, as that was my role, but I'll tell you it was a job I wanted and fed on and lived inside nightly, my pipes trilling and lowing and larking and blasting until I was scratchy and mute. One night I actually started choking, the sides of the back of my throat so dry they adhered, and Drum had to slap at me to get me to buck and break the airlock.

It was funny, how Constance ended up slapping me, too. This was a few nights after my visit to the mercury room. Pong was now forty-eight hours past due. If Drum was concerned he didn't show it, and so I wasn't worried, either. Constance, on the other hand, was not eager for Pong's reappearance. Neither of us brought up the notion of my staying on but she knew it was a possibility and it hung over us like the particulate-rich haze that scudded the whole of the region, the matter osmotically tainting us such that at one fissile point of passion Constance actually backhanded me across the cheek, sniffing, "You don't know how fucking lonely it can get here."

I said she could slap me again, if she needed, but she just collapsed on my chest and cried herself into a postcoital coma, drooling a hot slick on my neck. She was a dead sodden weight. I lay there taking the shallowest breaths until I was sure I, too, was going to pass out, so I did a yoga bridge move for leverage in order to nudge her gently off. I checked her night-table clock. I knew from Pruitt that the finalists were being gathered—he'd whispered to me earlier as he dropped off a lunch tray—and I slipped out and went up to the great hall, where people had gathered.

Drum was there, along with Lucky Choi, both dressed in loose yoga pants and T-shirts. I was surprised to see Lucky, who, as noted, had shuttled to Shanghai right after Pong departed, and had returned sometime during the wee hours of my Kappagoda labors. He gazed coolly at me, and I gazed coolly in return, wanting to flex to him how well I was handling being here alone. The truth is that I also got a ripple of happiness with the sight of Lucky, even if I had come to realize that I didn't like him at all; he was an anchor to Pong, is what he was, and that was assurance for me.

I was happiest of course to see Shaundra, who along with that hateful, lithe Canuck, Alexandre, plus Lissy from Barcelona and another instructor who might have been a former Big 12 linebacker with his brick-silo frame, were Drum's finalists. Drum now called on each of them to demonstrate a favorite specialty position.

Lissy led off with a pretty wild variation of the frog, a belly-down position that looked as if she'd broken both legs at her knees in order to face her feet forward, which was plenty crazy except that her head was arched back enough that she was also looking straight up at the rafters. The mega-built dude did a firefly, though to me it seemed he'd taken it to a ridiculous level, a standing pose that had his upper body bent down and back between his legs so far that he could easily stick his tongue up his own fudgehole, which I noticed the self-loving Alexandre was particularly admiring. Alexandre then effortlessly wrapped one of his legs around his neck while standing, while Shaundra displayed stunning strength and balance with a one-handed flying peacock, making herself look utterly weightless. Everybody applauded, maybe I was the loudest. I describe all this also because with each pose Drum seemed to become incrementally vitalized, and it occurred to me that what he was obsessed with was the outer ranges of the human form, which was not simply about contortion, about normalizing the extreme, but becoming, through the tortuous process, a more beautiful idea.

"For fuck's sake, War Paint, you look like rat shit."

It was Lucky, with his smile-sneer, come up beside me.

"Looks aren't everything," I said, suddenly moved to tweak him.

"I hear you're working hard for us, on both fronts." He glanced across the array of folks at Drum, who was stretching. "So what's the Lady of the Lodge like?"

"Nothing you could handle."

He laughed at my cheekiness. "I wasn't convinced how you were going to be useful, even though Pong always thought so. Maybe you're finally there."

"I'm earning my keep. Are you?"

"Whoa there, young blood. Put it back in your pants. I just popped down for the day to check in with Drum before heading out again. I'll hook up with Pong in Seoul and then we'll both be back again."

"But Pong said I'd be going there, too."

"What, I thought you liked it here! Anyway, there'll be many more trips, for all of us. So just listen. Okay?"

"Okay."

"You're our guy until both Pong and I get back next week. Keep her contented. Be a filial boy to Drum. He was just saying how your voice makes him restful and happy. Simple stuff. So don't ever stop singing. You get it?"

"You hope."

He nudged me with his fist in the sternum before strolling back to Drum, around whom everybody was bidding one another farewell in a cozy scrum, as all the conferencees, save the finalists, would be leaving. I cursed him with the picture of his roulette ball dropping onto the green 0, over and over. Never the red or the black ever again! I went to Shaundra and she gave me an oven-warm, muffiny hug.

"Thought I'd never see you again! Then I heard you went on a trip with Mr. Kappagoda's daughter! Where'd you go? What'd you see?"

"I guess local sights," I said. "By the way, that pose you just did was pretty cool."

She shrugged with natural modesty. "We're going to conduct a special last session with Mr. Kappagoda. He wants to see what else we can do, all at once."

"Like a Mr. Universe pose down?"

"Something like that. But I'm not into competitive stuff. Especially yoga. To be honest, I'm kind of wondering if I should leave with everyone else."

"But you're already here," I said, suddenly anointing myself leader of the YOLO squad. Was this my new MO? Pong had plunged me into the wider world but for the first time I felt equipped on my own to quaff it fully, the stuff going to my head. This is not to say I didn't wish he was here. But maybe I didn't need him that way, beyond our excellent friendship. Maybe we had arrived at that inevitable poignant juncture when your mentor has become a kindly figment, a spirit guide who you know is sitting back somewhere and watching you, with delight and pride.

"Be honest. Aren't you a little curious about what the others will do?"

Her eyes sparkled. "I *totally* am."

"Well, how about just pretending you're there solo? Do your own thing and don't even pay attention to what else is happening."

"I could do that," she said. "Hey, you think Mr. Kappagoda will let you come watch? He mentioned you're hanging out for a while."

Seeing that he was out of earshot, I said, "He'd damn better! Plus, I'm super curious. If that pose you just did wasn't for the final demonstration, you must have even crazier stuff in reserve."

"I guess so . . ."

"C'mon, I'm not missing that!"

"Really?"

"Booking myself in the front row, baby!"

"You're a doof but you're a honey, too."

Shaundra, beaming, now leaned up closer. I thought she was going to lay a lush kiss on me right there, enfold me tightly and spread me thin like icing in her cinnamon-bun bounty, when I got a jab between my shoulder blades.

It was Chilies, wielding a wooden spoon. Behind him was Pruitt, who was easily two heads taller than the chef but was so hunched in his posture that they were nearly equal in height. His gaze was hooded and cast down to the side, and instead of his incessantly gabby self he was as mum as a cauliflower, although his sandaled feet minced with anxious energy.

"My favorite farang like yoga, too, ya?" Chilies was grinning but not in a friendly way. Pruitt, I thought, seemed pained by the "favorite" notation.

"I enjoy a variety of things," I declared, savoring the racy taste of my impudence.

"Chilies know that now, ya!" he said, with an alarming know-ingness. He perused Shaundra's heft like everyone did but with a clinical regard, like he was already sectioning her into bite-sized, well-marbled cubes. "You working so, so hard, ya!" He giggled, almost boyishly. "Ya-ha! But boss say you work for Chilies now. You like that, farang?"

"Work for you?" I wanted to tell him he was confused, under the mistaken impression that we were to make some new jamu blends together for the venture. But I thought, *Braise in your wish juices for a while longer, you fiend.*

I muttered, "I guess if that's what Drum wants, then great."

"What you think I just say! Work for boss, work for Chilies. Same, same, backward, forward!"

I went back to chatting with Shaundra when Chilies tugged me by my nape hairs.

"What the heck, Chilies?" I swatted his hand away.

"Playtime over!"

I waved across the room to where Drum was talking with Alexandre and some others and caught his eye but he didn't blink or waver even as Chilies, trailed by Pruitt, firmly nudged me out.

Shaundra mouthed, *Goodbye?*

I said I'd be right back, to which Chilies sniffed, and I began suspecting that this was a covert operation of Constance's, who, having somehow just surveilled my chatting up Shaundra, had decided to remind me of our fresh but abiding bonds, or else was just playing some prank for which she'd enlisted Chilies and no doubt her father, too.

"Where are we going?"

"Where you think?" Chilies replied, stiff-arming me toward the stairwell. "Ya, smart boy, make guess. No? You tell him, Poo-it!"

Pruitt shook his head, cowed enough that he could barely manage a titter. We went down one flight, and I thought we'd follow the long corridor to the other end where Constance's special suite was, but we descended one more, when Pruitt bowed quickly to Chilies and split off from us, presumably heading farther down to his miserable lair. I felt sorry for him but he was clingy and creepy and I was glad to be free of him. Besides, I was not a farang like him. Or in fact a farang at all, my other strain no longer only coming out sotto voce, now that I was fully welcomed into Pong's and now Drum's spheres. The smaller part was now the bigger part, if not the whole of me.

Chilies didn't need to march me anymore, as I was just following him. I could see we were headed to the kitchen, and I wondered if Constance had ordered a yummy surprise to be stewed up for us, maybe a picnic lunch we'd take away. Inside, the dimly lit kitchen was busy with activity, young workers stripping the outer leaves from stalks of lemongrass stacked high beside them, another fellow removing the papery skins from many baskets of shallots, the shelled ones a big pile of purplish-white lobes. The smell of them was sharp enough to make my eyes tear.

"Looks like another banquet," I said.

"No," he replied. "Chilies business."

"Oh yeah?" I snorted. "And what kind of business is that?"

"Farang will see."

"I'm sure I will," I said breezily, rooting now through a basket of galangal roots. I picked one up and scratched at its hide with my thumbnail, sniffing.

"Good enough for you?" Chilies asked.

"Quite fresh," I said, thinking back to the root that Getty had ground up in Lucky's mom's kitchen, the dark orange juice having permanently stained his fingertips. "This is a key ingredient for Elixirent. Actually, the lemongrass, too. And the ginger."

"That right?"

"Yes," I said, poking into each of the baskets. "Hey, you're not secretly making your own jamu, are you?"

Chilies cackled, showing his full set of broken-factory-window teeth. "No way. My stuff better for health, even for yoga people. But plenty sick of those, ya?"

"Yoga people? I'm not sick of them."

"Whateva! Boss like, too, I guess. Not Chilies! You know why? Care only about one thing! *Me, me, me!* Like good stretch make everything okay!"

If nothing else, I wanted to defend Shaundra against this ungenerous, small-minded attack, even if he had a point. For you did sometimes get the sense that all the purposeful bodywork and wellness visioning and special diets were just different means of damming off life's incessant shittiness. Was that what better living was? To put up a bulwark, a hard border? Wouldn't they eventually fail?

Chilies led us to the expansive rear section of the kitchen where they did the butchering and the dishwashing, but where a gang of men now pushed into place an immense stone basin on a hefty dolly base, the wheels of which they locked. The men secured the dolly with fat steel hooks they pulled from holes in the floor and then cranked them taut, the sound of the metal against the stone and metal deeply satisfying in a primitive way. The stone mortar looked just like the kind they cart out in fancier Mexican restaurants (like Zapata's in Dunbar), and make guacamole in right at your table. This mortar, however, was as high as I was tall, and as big around as a party-sized hot tub, its rim as wide as the length of my foot; it was almost comical to look at but when I touched its rough outer surface, and the cool, smoothed inside well, I suddenly felt flimsy and small. It must have weighed a couple tons at least.

"Where's the giant druggist?" I tried to quip, but Chilies wasn't laughing.

"Many night I have a dream, farang. Same dream every time. Grandma come to me and say, 'Chilies, why you forget me? You love me so much but you forget. How come, how come?' And I tell you, farang, I have no idea what she mean. What I'm forgetting? What

I'm losing? Chilies going crazy, crazy. Then I realize: I must do the way she does. No more make by machine. We must do by hand, the old-time way, make like Grandma."

"Make what?"

Chilies didn't hear me, or wasn't even listening. "So for many many month I plan. Draw this and that. Find quarry. Then have this cut from hardest rock. But when you know and believe, truly believe, nothing is too hard. You cannot understand, ya, farang?"

I shook my head, because I didn't understand, especially when Pruitt appeared and with his eyes lowered, murmured, "Ready, my friend?" He wore a hairnet, and was also shirtless and pantless; the only thing he had on was a patch of stained cloth tied around his waist by thick twine. Basically, a thong. I was confused, though I did feel a slurry of coldness calve off deep inside my colon: the knowing before knowing knows.

"What's going on?"

"I had to estimate your size," Pruitt said, ignoring my question. He handed me my own codpiece. "You might have to cinch the rope."

The bolt of linenlike cloth was meager and rough, a mean little junk diaper.

"Well, go ahead," Pruitt said. "Try it on."

I laughed heartily, and he laughed, too, if nervously, along with the numerous leverers and peelers around us. Chilies was now laughing as well, though with a different kind of joy.

"Hurry up, farang!" Chilies yelled. "What Koreans say? *Pali-pali!*"

"*Pali-pali!*" was now everyone's chant. *Pali-pali, pali-pali,* with Pruitt nodding to their rhythm. I froze, partly because I wasn't about to strap on Pruitt's dirty pelt rag, partly because I was freaking out. When I didn't move, Chilies chirped at a couple of the bigger men who had pushed in the mortar. One of them looked like he was going to shake my hand but instead punched me in the gut, the blow abbreviated but very hard, the other man half propping me up as he pulled my shirt over my head. If you haven't been punched like that in a while, or ever, I will tell you one's impression after the stun of the blow is of utter disbelief, which in turn gives way to a welling of anger at the profound injustice, before the knee-buckling pain. Though soon enough, compliance. For in the blur I found myself being lifted out of my house-issued slippers, and had the drawstring of my pajama-style bottoms loosened and then wrenched off me, with every last eyeball in the kitchen locked on my fast-shrinking shame.

Pruitt's handiwork—disconcertingly warm and damp when I put it on, as if he'd just taken it for a test run—actually fit me. He gave me a thumbs-up, to which I replied by cursing him blue, which I'm still sorry about. I was just trying to break through my confusion and figure out why things were proceeding this way and not via a less confusing and humiliating path. What had I done so wrong in the four short days and nights here? I'd only been a willing potential employee, not to mention a most obliging guest, freely offering my corpus to the young lady of the house for her complete discretionary disposal. I'd been the pure embodiment of *Yes*. Which is why I asked Chilies—well, practically shouted at him with sour spittle lacquering my lower lip—to get Drum, to bring him here, so he could set things right.

"I am your boss now. Big boss say so!" Chilies cried, his face screwing up with glee.

One of the kitchen staff prodded me in the back with a ladle and I miserably flared my hand, and Pruitt waved, too, though clearly Chilies didn't care if he did or not. Nor did he care when I insisted that he get Constance down here. In the meantime, the same gang of workers rolled in a small crane beside the basin and then secured its legs to the floor with metal bolts that screwed into inset housings. Others carted in what I thought was a huge turd, the same gray-greenish color of the mortar, but I realized that the turd was a pestle, which was confirmed when they looped a metal cable through an eyelet drilled through its narrower end and hoisted it over the stone basin.

Pruitt groaned from his gut. He breathed deeply in and out, in and out. "This is where it is, my friend."

"Where what is?" I asked, panicked by the depth of his tone.

"Don't you see?"

I shook my head. I looked desperately to Chilies, who was nonchalantly picking a sliver of gristle from his teeth. He flicked it high, this speck of meat comet shooting up into the dim vault of the kitchen, and as I watched it I shuddered with sudden, grave empathy.

Pruitt moaned. "The devil's workshop."

23.

WICKEDNESS, I LEARNED, doesn't come only from idle hands.

Sometimes it's the very opposite: compulsion, obsession, all the worse when you're the flesh algorithm for someone's undying pet idea. And whether you're up to the job or not, there's little else to do except perform each instruction without pause, for there's nothing more disruptive than dropping off the pace. Everything breaks down, it all falls apart, and you not so figuratively have to pull yourself out of your own muck and wipe your burning eyes and rev yourself up all over again.

What was my special sentence? One could blame Chilies but that would be wrong. Chilies is fearsome and diabolical but like most of us he is a prosthesis, an extension of a more committed consciousness that has reckoned the profound license he is bestowing and thus leaves the details to the forge of improvisation and chance. Drum was the big boss but he didn't deal with the smaller details like the disposition of me and Pruitt. He had no actual input into what we did or what would happen to us. We were like grains of sand he brushed off his elbow, crumbs to lick from the corner of his mouth.

For the first long stint I kept asking when I'd be invited back upstairs. Back to the relative gentility of Constance. I asked again to speak directly to Drum. I asked if I could call or email Pong, if I could call or email my dad. The terrified tourist in me even asked for the local American consulate. Each time the answer was a flurry of vicious strikes with the fat, ungiving end of a lemongrass stalk on my back, my legs. When I couldn't answer anything about Pong's return I got beaten again. The kitchen staff took turns as our minders, our punishers, including the younger ones, who mercifully hit me with the willowy narrow end. They would whack at Pruitt, too, even though he never asked for anything. They beat him worse than they did me. He didn't demand that I stay quiet, resigned as he was to our lot. He just shrank and took it, softly whinnying like a pony after each blow. I finally stopped because I couldn't bear to hear that soured pitch anymore. Soon after I relented, I have to admit, was when we got into a groove.

We worked through the full wheel of the hours. Poo-it and Titty. Titty and Poo-it. Caught up in the knotted innards of Chilies' kitchen. Mrs. Parnthong would never believe the scale of our task. Maybe Victor Jr. would, but he's a boy and still open to absurd and fantastical notions. Val would simply smirk at my preposterous imagination, and give me an endearing pinch on the butt. I've told them nothing of course. No need for such ridiculous things to live inside of them.

Technically, what we made was a curry, though I'm betting it wasn't like any curry that had ever been made before. It was Chilies' secret family recipe that he referred to as *ni*, which my rudimentary Mandarin training told me could also be the word for "mud." I thought back to what Drum had described of his father's mouth being full of mud, a haunting return to our origins.

I learned that we were making it for a business Chilies had been pursuing for the last couple years. One of the kitchen workers showed me a jar of it, which was packaged quite fancily like high-end jam, and featured a headshot of a smiling, bighearted Chilies on the label, which read UNCLE CHAISON'S ORGANIC CURRY PASTE, his teeth Photoshopped to a full set, perfectly straight and white.

Our tool was the monstrous mortar and pestle. His homage to his grandma, writ extra large. Wearing our skimpy togs and hairnets, he had us start immediately. First we had to wash our feet, soap and water and an ox-hair brush to start and then a lingering soak in lime juice, which began to burn after a while, puckering our feet and turning them pink. I got alarmed when the ruddiness then turned as gray as raw shrimp but at that point I didn't know the tenth of it. When we were sufficiently sterilized somebody prodded Pruitt and he stepped onto the wide rim of the mortar and extended his hand to me. But I shook my head; somehow it felt like I was being beckoned onto the capsule of that Apollo mission that never got off the ground, when the pure oxygen they were breathing instantly conflagrated with a single short-circuit spark.

Whoooomp.

Okay, perhaps not that dire. But when a ten-year-old boy spears you in the kidney with a wooden spoon the size of a canoe paddle, and then another one similarly armed jabs at you, too, you start moving, plus waking to the proposition that both these dear children look a lot like Chilies, you start appreciating the full measure of the situation. I glanced around, thinking of how I could manufacture an escape, somehow bribe somebody, but I began to notice that some other boys and girls and teens and young adults featured a certain wild, uprooted skew to their lower middle teeth, or a distinctive boomerang carve to their cheekbones, and that even one of the prettier young women displayed the subtle tic of flaring one nostril while snorting off the tickle of a phantom nose hair, all of which added up to Chilies' being the primary issuer of this cloistered ecosystem and that even when he was absent there was an army of his eyes and hands to secure me and Pruitt in place.

The rim of the mortar was pocked and rough, unlike the inside of its large bowl, which, as noted, was finished to a dull, matte smoothness and felt dry and powdery against my heels. Pruitt stood tall on the opposite end, locked on the task ahead, grabbing on almost rakishly to the arm of the crane just the way that in some alternate reality he might clutch the boom of a sailboat mast wearing those fugly deck shoes and I-am-a-drunkard Nantucket Reds shorts, and waved in the approaching bin of the wagon cart. It dumped a heavy load of peeled garlic and shallots that buried my leg and nearly pulled me down inside, nobody offering me any warning. Pruitt then swung the suspended pestle over the massing of cloves and with my help we attached a customized rig of curved bamboo bars with many cross struts so that the rig looked like a ladder balanced horizontally on top of the pestle, its ends arcing up to be higher than the middle. Actually it wasn't balanced, as Pruitt and I had to tippy-toe to hold it up in place from each end. I had to grab the second-to-last cross strut and on his end he grabbed a strut more inside to equalize our weight differential, and when he said *Now!* we'd simultaneously latch on and jump, our combined kilos bringing the head of the pestle chucking down on the garlic and shallots. I nearly lost my grip with the force of each blow. Then we bounded back up (I suppose from the fat coil on the elbow of the crane plus the natural upward bend of the "ladder"), and both of us niftily alighted on the rim again, our positions shifted maybe fifteen degrees clockwise. A Cirque du Soleil trouper would have been proud.

"Hey, you already got this!" Pruitt said.

"No, I fucking don't!"

"Ha! You're wrong. And no more Tiller! From now on I'm calling you Pale Cricket!"

"Okay, but can we be done now?"

"Ha ha, you are hilarious."

"I'm not fucking kidding!"

"I bet, partner! One and two and . . . go!"

"Fuck!"

So we went, and went, and went. I tried to wave my surrender but got immediately poked from below by Chilies' spawn, much harder this time; they knew just the level of necessary force. So we rode our Maypole of two, rode it hard as we attacked the defenseless aromatics. The first blows were muted but as we worked the massing you heard and felt the clash of stone on stone. It shivered the bones. The crushed bulbs also sent up a bouquet so sharp and powerful that I felt a convectional lift. My eyes were spitting tears, snot spigoting from my nose, and although Pruitt seemed unbothered his face had gone all red and puffy like he'd endured a couple brutal MMA rounds. I knew I looked much worse and may have started crying but it was impossible to tell if I was, which just made me cry even harder, I think.

Pruitt saw that I was trying not to spray so much into the mash and he said, "Don't worry, Pale Cricket, chef actually likes by-product. He says gives better flavor!"

They unloaded bins of galangal and lemongrass next, then the ground coriander seed and white peppercorns, the rehydrated red chili pods, the roots or leaves of about thirteen other plants, and finally clayey bricks of earthen-colored shrimp paste that smelled like some kind of prehistoric toe cheese, bits of everything flying up at us like antiaircraft fire. I sometimes lost my footing about the slickened rim, scooting and skirting the momentum of that unforgiving teardrop of stone. Flagging, at one point I lost my handle and fell in and luckily Pruitt instantly yanked on the ladder, just saving my foot from getting crushed. I paid attention after that. Of course with each ingredient the mash changed, becoming steadily curry-esque, which even through my wretchedness I could see was a marvelous alchemical process, but the true amazement was how every addition provoked a different physical reaction in me (if not

Pruitt, who was long immune). It was like the progression of an illness. Lemongrass: uncontrollable sneezing. Ground spices: groinal itchiness. Red peppers: lava spikes in the eyes. Kaffir lime leaves: a bolting sour sweat. As the curry became pasty it was a secret store of my drool that got tapped, my tongue knocking about like a race-horse in the gate and breaking out in hives, along with my entire back. This was some serious pharma, a funky, deep medicine that was juicing my nerves and keeping me upright even as I was certain it was also poisoning me, this chemotherapy à la Chilies, aka Uncle Chaison.

We made three immense batches. Even Pruitt noted the intensity of the run. He lowered himself down and cleared his eyes with the back of his hand and crouched on his own haunches, dead-eyed, very slowly chewing on an unripe apple banana, his hairnetted skull bobbleheading ever so slightly. I ended up temporarily half blinded, my hands blistered and raw, my sinuses now clogged shut, a couple kitchen workers helping me step down to the floor, where I col-lapsed. I must have looked like an afterbirth, my body streaked with curried slicks of sweat, snot, tears, and pee (I had leaked a couple times in utter exhaustion). I lay there cradled in some older woman's arms as she wiped my face with her sleeve, my breath shallow, my already meager bird-bone chest, I was sure, even more sunken and starkly ribbed out, like in the *Pietà*. I'm not suggesting I was a mar-tyr, either righteous or wronged, only that I was totally depleted, as spent as a one-ply sheet of toilet paper and useless for anything more.

Or so I thought. Afterward the woman gave me some tepid black tea and a slice of ripe mango, which made me shiver it was so good. I raised my hands but they were clawed up in a cramp and so she plucked the wedge out with her fingers. She held it and gently fed it back to me, one nibble at a time. Meanwhile Chilies had reappeared and was sampling our work, dipping his finger into several of the many clay tureens the kitchen workers had filled with our output.

He rolled the paste around his mouth, parsing the components, then gathered enough saliva to missile a fat wad on a flattish arc back up into the mortar. Some workers pulled me from the kind woman to my feet, Pruitt now standing beside me, both of us slumped of shoulder, heavy of chin, our grimy codpieces drooped low.

"First time not bad," he said to me, for once not emphatic. Then to Pruitt: "Teaching him right, English tutor."

Pruitt weakly saluted. He didn't dare look up. "Quit time, now, chef?"

"Quit time?" A sneer cut across Chilies' wrinkled face. "Farang always talk quit time, quit time."

"I thought because we managed to do a whole extra mortar—"

"You forget something?" Chilies scolded. "You forget again, ya?"

Pruitt thought about it and sighed, beaten. "Sorry, chef. My bad. I'm kind of tired today."

Chilies barked, "Why, Titty? Why! Why farang always look for shortcut!"

They gave us each a horsehair broom and then mops, and we climbed up into the bowl again to clean it out, first to scour and then wash. You'd think it would be way easier than the curry making was, as all we needed to do was scrub it and then hose it down with plain water (no detergents allowed, as that would taint the stone). But they didn't have a hose, or maybe they did but wouldn't let us use one, and after brushing and swabbing we had to pass up buckets of hot water to each other, which we poured down the sides of the basin while brushing and swabbing again, then bucketed the water back out, there of course being no drain. It took six passes to get the job done, and with a lot more fifteen-liter buckets than you'd think were necessary, for as Pruitt unhelpfully kept pointing out, relative volumes can be deceiving. The fresh nicks and abrasions on my feet and ankles lit up each time the spicy water splashed them, these fiery electric prods that at least kept me moving. By the end we'd gone through a bin full of mops. We knew we were done when our last one stayed clean and dry, and although I wanted nothing more to do with him, when Pruitt offered me his hand as we sat mute inside the barren mortar I had to clasp it, awed at what we had done.

I'd washed ten thousand dishes before, but never a dish like that.

"Who knows," Pruitt rasped weakly. "Maybe we do four batches tomorrow."

"Tomorrow?"

He regarded me with earnest wonder. "What, you think we should do one more now?"

I was about to grab his bony throat when one of Chilies' goons prodded me and motioned that we get out. I was crazed with anger, thinking of how I could marshal enough energy to charge through our minders and sprint down the hills to the main road and flag somebody, when who was standing there but statuesque Constance, looking amazingly clean and firm and fleshy in her signature white tank and yoga shorts, a flowing muslin wrap the color of saffron hitched about her sturdy hips. I stumbled forward and glommed onto her. I was damp, stinky, and stained, but I wouldn't let go, plus I was bawling, outright shuddering, the tears and snot melting the rest of me into a *ni*-y jammy mess, but Constance didn't budge, she didn't shrink, she let me get closer than I'm certain she could bear, which only made my pity party more satisfyingly miserable.

"I wanted to be here for you at the finish," Constance said, gently prying herself from my clutches. "You're fine now. Soon you'll feel better."

"I'm never going to feel better!" I whined.

"Pussy farang," Chilies literally spat, unable to abide another second of my petulance. He scoffed and left us, though his crew remained.

"Hush, hush," she cooed. "That's enough now. You made it through is what counts."

"Counts for what?"

"For my father, mopey dopey! Can't you see he's letting Chilies test you? To see what you're really made of? *I* know what you're made of. Now he'll appreciate, too, how much you can endure."

"I don't think I want to endure anymore," I said, trying to hide away in the smooth rope of her perfumed neck. "I don't want to endure anything."

"What about from me?" she said, gently raking her fingers on my scalp. I was too weak to answer.

"Well *that* makes me sad."

I mewled something about always being ready for her, though truly I couldn't take another poke or jab more. It was like how you feel after getting your fourth cavity filled on the same dental visit, when you're ground down and throbbing, the numbness dissipating, and all you can wonder is what you're so guilty of, to warrant such a fate . . .

The notion of which I flashed on as Constance led us not up the stairwell but down to the rear hallway, where Pruitt lived. He accompanied us, though he didn't say a word to Constance, who ignored him not simply as if he weren't present, but as though he had never existed. Pruitt, his posture shrunken, seemed in tune with this reality.

Awaiting us were two ancient, shirtless, prune-faced men in rubber sandals, perhaps semiretired veterans of the kitchen crew. They wielded the same thick-bristled horsehair brushes we had used on the stone bowl.

"After they're done you can rest. Maybe I'll call for you later."

"Don't go," I pleaded, eyeing the old men, one of whom had begun tugging at the twine rope of my thong. I slapped his hand away.

"Be respectful, Tiller," she said. "They're just doing their job. They're going to help wash you. I want you totally, totally cleaned of that stuff. I don't want to get a rash."

"They do a pretty decent job," Pruitt muttered to himself. He padded into the dingy bathroom.

"But I don't want them to!"

"I don't want certain things, either, buster," Constance snapped, suddenly ice-cold. I tried to cling to her again but she sloughed me off. "I don't want my father to be sick. I don't want him to suffer. I don't want to be alone."

Uttering this last sentence almost made her lose it. She caught her breath.

"But now maybe I will be, because your boss Pong took all that money from him and still won't help!"

"What are you talking about? You mean the Elixirent deal?"

"No, you dummy! You think my father really cares about some yucky-tasting smoothies? He's *dying*!"

My hands felt instantly icy, as I flashed on the mercury room, the inner and outer yogic alchemies Drum mused about. The Hg. "I'm sure it's a misunderstanding. Pong always does everything right. He'll do everything he can for your father."

"You mean by not coming back?"

"Of course he's coming back!" I cried. "Why wouldn't he?"

She grabbed me by the throat, her nails biting in.

"You tell me."

24.

How I wish I could have told her. But I had no story to tell, either true-life or made-up, and in fact had been subject all along to the turns of someone else's tale.

In that one, Pong didn't come back in a few days. He didn't come back in a week, then two. When it became clear he was not returning anytime soon—Lucky Choi was completely out of contact as well—my status at the Kappagoda Mountain Inn quickly devolved. The fall was precipitous, from where I started as VIP lodge guest, to boy-toy princeling, then to trial kitchen staff, and now to something else altogether. I kept assuring myself that my pitiful situation was temporary, my abandonment unintentional, and that Pong had simply left me to fulfill certain critical roles, namely, to keep singing for Drum, and offering my body to the dark sciences of Constance, and marketing Elixirent to the yogis and whoever else might listen, but the reprise calling to me in a supercilious chorus was that I had become fodder for a diversionary and perhaps totally bogus campaign.

Had I been played in a long confidence game? From the initial mention of Drum in Pong's study, to his investment group's discussion of the venture at the Chop Station, to the jamu blending at Lucky's mom's house, had it all been a wondrous, cynical production? I could see how I'd been asleep to my own sleeper self, a ready and unwitting actor that now got woke in the rudest way, here in the fiendish bowels of the Kappagoda lodge.

Whenever I had enough strength, I cursed him. Oh my friend, my mentor! It wasn't the standard blight-upon-your-house variety. I didn't wish ill on his businesses, his girls and Minori, Lily Zhang. I cursed him in the way you curse a brother, with blind and self-wounding fury, ending up batting myself in the ears, abrading my knuckles against the rough stone wall. With the various deprivations some of my toenails began falling off and I'd pull them before they were ready. Eventually, however, when a true trial befalls you, you forget the original sequences and causalities, and exist in the enclosing twilight world of your misery.

Chilies was our jailer, our weather, our God. He put us on subsistence-level rations, which along with the rounds of incessant labor only made me more crazed and desperate, my panic welling and pressurizing and, when seeing an outlet, geysering. Without provocation I verbally lashed out at Pruitt. I yanked on my own hair, taking alarmingly big clumps. As loud as I could I started singing Drum's father's boatman's song, in the hope that Drum might hear me. Chilies had me whipped when I wouldn't shut up. I went on a hunger strike and in response they stopped giving me anything to drink. Soon enough, I lost track of everything.

"He break deal with big boss," Chilies told me, after tickling me conscious with his sharp-nailed big toe. A kitchen worker dripped milk tea on my lips. "His special medicine all lies! No exist, never!" He rasped with disgust: "So we got nothing but you, farang."

"Pong will bring it!" I cried, the last few grains of my hope not yet pulverized. "He'll come back!"

"Because of you, Titty?" he wheedled. "I doubt, ya!"

Of course I begged to see Drum, entreating Constance, Chilies, even asking Pruitt to have one of his staff friends have Shaundra lobby for me, but he had no real staff friends. And Shaundra and the other yogis had long departed. I was shut out. It was as if I alone had caused Pong to stay away, and not the hard fact that he and Lucky had banked a breathtaking sum of Drum Kappagoda's money, which, according to Pruitt, was merely a down payment. He'd overheard whispers that it was twenty million USD, or that much each, though whatever the amount was, what could it mean to a man who was terminal?

Still, I couldn't believe that Pong would con anyone. For what? He lacked for nothing, including respect and admiration, each new day another enterprise to be engaged and surmounted.

"Nobody likes being cheated," Pruitt said, during a break from our mashing, futilely picking the spiced grit from his fingernails. "No matter if you're a king or a pauper."

But of course paupers have much less to buoy themselves with. I sank lower and lower. I went through most of the typical stages, cursing Pong, then pretending it was all a mistake, a grand misunderstanding, and when nothing changed I cursed him more, along with myself, for being so pitiful and helpless. I whimpered myself to sleep each night, the pickled taste of my tears a comforting ointment. I bargained with some craven deity but realized a superseding deal had already been done. And a funny thing happened after that. Maybe it had to do with the physical duress, in combination with my personal history of sudden abandonment, which brought out the burrowed little creature in me, but I relented, wanting any connection; I fully submitted myself to Chilies' cottage enterprise. As if in some casino, I was locked into a steady, preoccupying rhythm of very particular activities and people, where before you know it the moon and stars have transited without you, as they always have and always will.

We worked from dawn to midafternoon, with a meal break late morning, and then got cleaned up, hosed down and scrubbed and scoured by our old-men washers. They were as strong as longshoremen, exfoliating me with the stiff bristle brushes and scalding water spray until I could smell my own raw placental freshness as I passed out on the sheetless cot in the dungeon cell opposite to Pruitt's. One night, I awoke in the pure blinding black and frantically shielded my head, sensing a figure looming.

Who's there? I squealed, or thought-squealed, desperately enough for a voice to reply: *Me.*

It sounded like Drum. He just hovered, I couldn't tell how close, the cavey, draftless pitch rendering everything immeasurable.

Calm now, he said. *Slow your breathing. I won't hurt you.*

The assurance only made me cower more.

I would like you to sing.

I couldn't answer, the disembodied words not quite sticking.

Will you do that for me? Maybe one you sang at Garbo.

"Which?" I finally squeaked. There was a long pause. Long enough that I wondered if I might be hallucinating.

"Without You."

The Nilsson. A few trusty, plaintive notes. I needed them, too. I sat up, clearing my throat of the curdled fright-bile, and opened out my chest the way Shaundra had in her mountain pose, to invite the breath. Even in the perfect darkness I closed my eyes and pictured that old LP spinning, a slight warp rippling its edge, my mother's slender fingers letting the needle touch down and release the sonic crackle. And I'll tell you in those last few turns of static your little-boy heart, poised for the song to begin, can practically stop.

What happened next? I must have really sung, clobbered it clear out of the park, onto the neighborhood street, kids and dogs chasing it past the stoop of the sawdusty Irish bar. For immediately after I finished Drum said, *Same again.* I complied. *Again,* so I sang it once more, and then another time without his requesting, craving the sensation of succor from my warming lungs, after which I asked why he was bringing this misery upon me. There was no reply. I combed the black with my hands, shuffling and murmuring, realizing that Drum had probably left in the middle of the second go-round and that I'd been as usual performing for myself. Or maybe he had not been there at all. I felt a seam in a wall and found a handle lower down and pulled, the harsh coils of the single LED bulb momentarily blinding me. There was a God-killing stink. Through my squint I saw a crouching Pruitt, straddled comfortably over the inset porcelain shithole, elbows hooked around his kneecaps and peering up from his reading glasses as he held a tattered paperback western.

"You didn't wake me," he mumbled, flipping a page. "This happens to be my showtime. By the way, you sing very nice."

You sing very nice. The refrain of my sentence. At first I didn't count the passing of time, because you only do that when you've given up and are resolved to leave a record of your marooning. We each do this in our own way, bracket our existence by crosshatching ourselves onto some slab of driftwood that will get dissolved anyway by the indifferent sea of the universe. Paraquoting my favorite movie moment, *We are but tears in rain.* Yet we still insist; I ended up using the disturbance of Pruitt's three a.m. flushes to etch the aluminum leg of the cot with my little folding knife, his peristalsis metered like a Teutonic train timetable despite the hellish toil his body was put through, another testament to the mind-boggling tolerances of our flesh.

I saw Constance, too, though not as before. If it was her wish, I was delivered to her, never sure of what mood I'd find her in. She could be chatty and gracious, serving jasmine tea and red-bean mochi, or furiously impatient, pulling off my clothes as soon as I stepped across the threshold and incinerating me in the raging firestorm of her need, only in small part sexual. Mostly it was as if I wasn't there; she might lie in bed and flip through a thick Victorian novel; or take a long, slow bath, humming to herself; or even just sit at her undersized childhood desk and cradle her face in her palms, no doubt in sorrow for her father. I'd stay an hour, or two, sometimes mere minutes, and like Pruitt I didn't question her or even make a peep. I began to understand the secret joy of a volitionless existence. I was a lone mussel attached to a tidal rock, in turn marooned, submerged, pounded by rough surf, and if I was to be detached, let me be detached. I didn't care. I was fully seeing, hearing, feeling, tasting, and no longer terrified of being locked in a *luk chup*ped–like state. For there was nothing to be locked; the contours of my former self had fallen away and evaporated into the ether.

In the vacuum, Chilies provided a new framework. He conducted a seminar, of sorts, and if I was a poor pupil at first, eventually I caught on. I'm not talking only about the task of curry making, with which Pruitt and I kept on. We had to keep on, as the evidently popular brand of Uncle Chaison's Organic Curry Paste demanded product, and a lot of it.

Yes, the forced labor in the mortar was a key factor in the process. But even after all the motions and exertions became rote, even after I became as technically expert as Pruitt, Chilies furthered my knowledge. For it's never simply about mastering technique. He would watch from what was essentially a very high chair (that may have been an actual tennis umpire's seat), not so he could observe and offer critiques of our work—as noted, we had serious game— but to maintain a privileged position. So he wouldn't have to speak *up*, as it were.

He was talking to me, but Pruitt didn't seem to mind hearing the lessons again.

"The man has a deep worldview," Pruitt whispered, keeping his eyes averted. "Ideas worth listening to."

I was dismissive at first. Who wouldn't be, in the face of a sadistic pidgin-speaking chef who'd never attended school. In fact, he was barely literate, as he freely disclosed to me, and had to have his helpers write out lists of the foodstuffs and ingredients he couldn't get locally. What he was endowed with was a knack for language, and although you wouldn't say he was orally fluent in any of them, he understood English, French, Thai, Finnish and Russian, Uighur, Korean, and Japanese, plus of course the five main Chinese dialects. And it was through this faculty that he got his learning, which was exclusively through online videos and college-level courses. All his free time went to this. I assumed that he'd ply me with the data-heavy information download that marks an autodidact, spewing stuff about cooking science, or the cultural origins of his diabolical recipes, or some other suitably food-related area of study, like a topic in anthropology, botany, maybe even a link to what Drum and Pong had discussed at the bioenhancements conference.

Instead he went on about such things as labor-power, and money-forms, and use-value, vaguely familiar terms from a reading module assigned in my Western Thought and Theory class that I remembered vaguely understanding, and that was all about capital. Chilies, it turned out, was a booster of Marxism, at least intellectually, if not in practice. Or maybe he was. I can't be sure because in college I was a skimming kind of reader, and Chilies had simply watched a ton of videos, and besides, as my section leader would point out, theory is an extremely complicated thing, as varied and mixed-up and contradictory as life itself.

Regardless, Chilies lectured as we worked, and you got the sense that he was freewheeling, fine-tuning his own interpretative and conceptual frameworks as he spoke. He started with basic questions, propositions.

"What you think you doing?" he asked me, and being fatigued and thirsty and splattered with the burning juice of pounded aromatics, I earnestly answered, "Making curry?"

"That's what you think!" he shouted. "You are a tool in the superstructure!"

I took him to mean that we were all slaves to a more dominant actor, as I was to him, and he was to Drum, and Drum was to someone else, but he spat, "Up in fucking commanding heights! But we go too fast. You must see whole story!"

So Chilies backed up. Together we reviewed how our civilization had developed, vis-à-vis production and labor, from tribal societies to feudalism to the birth of the proletariat and protocommunism and finally to capitalism, which was now so unquestioned and powerful and insidious in its reach that it was, in his words, "in the blood and bones, a disease people think is cure!"

I didn't consider it a cure or not, or much think about capitalism at all, which of course to Chilies substantiated his citation of the Jamesonian view of capitalism's all-pervasive and yet imperceptible power. He asked me to describe in detail Dunbar and my family home and what my father did for a career and some of the vocational coursework I'd taken in my supposed liberal arts education (Coding Basics 10, Emerging Markets Marketing 202), and to Chilies' mind every aspect of my unexamined farang life was a highly developed and sophisticated component in globalist corporate and banking and technology mechanisms, mechanisms that worked to reinforce the social and economic structures that prevailed simultaneously outside and inside of me. That my soul had become the soul of the machine.

"And for what, farang?" he hollered at me, his spittle burning my eye. "To sell your bourgeois-flavor jamu? It is what? Just juice! *Juice!*"

Chilies, however—being a savvy teacher—allowed that he, too, was subject to these "goddamn hegemon forces," although he did excuse himself by slyly bemoaning the fact that he was poor and illiterate to begin with and would be poor and illiterate to the end, as all proceeds from his jarred paste were supporting a string of riverside villages in rural Guizhou province, where his people were from.

To be honest, I believed him. He had no reason to lie. It wasn't as if he jetted off to some luxe island aerie to splash about in an infinity pool of profit. He was obviously and contentedly heading nowhere, these high stone walls of his kitchen and the ragtag army of his familial worker tribe and his fealty to Drum Kappagoda constituting his universe. He required nothing more except perhaps the "use-value" of me and Pruitt, labor he could have drawn from anyone but more satisfyingly drew from us farang, and in that sense we held a special abstracted value for him, a certain charm that could not otherwise be effected. We were his Pale Crickets, to toy with in a shoebox zoo, our every groan and wail a minor but still dulcet recompense for the profound disasters our farang culture and ideology had wrought upon what he saw were purer forms of human community.

"Kinship is only thing, Titty!"

He treated Pruitt rougher, with long hours and random unwarranted beatings. In Chilies' mind Pruitt was a farang's farang, his ESL backpacker profile the very picture of soft Western imperialism, spreading the Anglophone contagion, bedding native women, and corrupting the local economies. But every so often he'd put aside his earphones and the tablet screening the lectures he was viewing and motion for Pruitt to climb out from our great bowl and approach his chair. He'd place his bare foot with its dingy, gnarled toes on Pruitt's hairnetted forehead—Pruitt would tightly shut his eyes—and give one good push to offload his dilating intellectual rage and discontent. Pruitt would stagger backward a bit too theatrically, which Chilies nonetheless appreciated. He'd grunt and flit his hand, the signal for Pruitt to get back to work.

His abuse of me was subtler, and thus perhaps more penetrating.

along a driveway lamppost that had a screwhead exposed and deeply gouged the entire length of those pristine metallic-blue panels. Clark was his best self, sublimating any anger into his usual nerdy consternation, the dollar tally ticking in his eyes as they traced each inch of the perfectly straight scrim. My mother was silent but furious with herself and kept testing and trying to push in the sharp screwhead until her fingers bled, which only made her more enraged. Chilies took a dark delight in this, particularly my detail of her smudging the car hood bloody as she stormed inside the house. I was calling these things up for him but of course his aim was to narrow my focus, train me on my natal origins in order to tease out what my "project" was in coming here, in contrast, according to Chilies, to Pruitt's "naked Orientalism." I insisted my only project was to help Pong, but Chilies dismissed this out of hand, saying my project was me, to find myself by erasing myself and connecting up with something irreducibly real, which was forever gone, none of which I could follow but still kind of understood when Chilies unmelodically crooned, "Back of her knee, farang, back of her knee!"

I hated the man, for sure. You can't help but despise your jailer, your slaver. Though in truth I couldn't deny that something began to butterfly in me each morning when I sat beside Pruitt to get our feet scrubbed in the shadow of the stone crucible. Like footballers slowly pulling on their cleats, we knew the hours ahead would be a fierce battle, a beastly enterprise in which we'd engage the earthly and primal that would at some breaking point give way to a moment of clarity. Chilies was the nudge, prodding me with the hot pokers of his myriad theoretical constructs, coaxing out more early childhood impressions, all while peppering us with some well-timed and flagrant physical punishment, to impress upon me the belief in a destiny that placed me here and only here. It was an insane notion, I know, especially from my coordinates thigh-deep in ochre-hued mush, but that's what I truly thought and felt, right down to the miserable bones of my miserable spice-scalded feet. Chilies had pounded into me the idea to marshal whatever was at hand in my body and psyche, to be, as he howled, "a bricoleur, farang! Fucking improvise!"

Which is what I did. I didn't know what I was seeking but instead of simply trying to endure I gave myself over to the work with all my human and creaturely capacities. I got Pruitt to change the way we hung on the "fire ladder" and refocus the blows of the pestle so that it'd be more random and dispersed in its strikes, which in turn cut down on our time spent remixing and repiling the material in between each stage, and more quickly made a more uniform paste. We figured out a tweak to the hinging as well, which allowed the pestle more play. It worked beautifully; we made six batches in the time it previously took to make five, then five rather than four, four instead of three, the rapidly accelerating efficiency rendering Chilies wordless. We already had a surplus inventory of Uncle Chaison's Organic Curry Paste but he wanted more, despite our having run out of jars to put the stuff in, if only to see how far we could take his Stone Age lab.

I learned that they had other pestles of differing sizes and shapes and we hooked those on the new rig, though we had to alter the play of our weighting. We went back to the original. Pruitt got into it, too, proposing a minor reordering of the ingredients as they were dropped into the basin, which Chilies instantly considered heretical and another instance of the innate colonialist farang contempt for ancient cultural traditions, and had him thwacked a few times with the lemongrass switch. Later I lobbied Chilies to let us test Pruitt's idea and I got thwacked, too, but before our last batch he muttered, "You can try," and we revised the order of operations and, as Pruitt posited, it made for a smoother and earlier integration, which didn't make the process demonstrably quicker but did result in a finer texture and perhaps a more volatile bouquet and flavor that Chilies wouldn't admit he preferred but that did prompt him the next day to say, "Run it new way."

After that nothing obvious was different between him and us. Yet you couldn't help but feel a new sense of mutual identification and trust, if not empathy or warmth. Call it Shenzhen syndrome. We labored and sweat and bled; Chilies harangued and sermonized, mocked and criticized; his henchpeople and henchkids doled out punishment, both condign and gratuitous. The project was intense, it was alive and real, and it was ours alone, all of us and our contributions representing its peculiar, thriving culture.

Constance, on the other hand, had begun to flag, and whether it was because she was tiring of me or our relations, or grieving about her father, who, Pruitt had heard from whispering staffers, was doing poorly, I couldn't be sure. Certainly I was not who I was; I knew because I had long ceased mourning that self anymore. All I knew was that she hardly touched me, and was a zombie whenever I touched her. She was distracted, moodier, even more laconic and self-involved, and she summoned me less and less, and then not at all for what must have been a long stretch.

Finally, a staffer appeared after scrub-down one day; he was to escort me to her. I quickly dressed in actual clothes instead of a robe, as the man indicated. Pruitt gave me a game if utterly wearied grin. I thought, *Okay, she needs a reset*. I needed one, too, as I was feeling pulverized again, infinitesimal, a scant dried leaving in a rut. There was our scullery camaraderie, busy with exertion and activity, but a profound loneliness was gaining on me. At times it was breathtaking. Other than Clark, who probably (and happily) assumed I was traipsing along Las Ramblas or across the Ponte Vecchio with a buoying Negroni buzz, not a soul in the world was expecting or missing me.

To be honest, I'd begun to think about doing something drastic.

Not to Chilies or Drum, but to myself; how, if I could somehow get Pruitt to hang full weight in the middle of the rig, I could fall to the bottom during his upward bounding and spot my skull directly in the path of that huge teardrop of stone. It'd be a brainy mess, plus ruin a perfectly good batch, and in my head I preapologized to Pruitt, who I knew would have to clean the whole thing up.

When we went up past the corridor that would have led to Constance's lair, and crossed the expanse of the main hall shimmering with the daytime, I got excited; could she perhaps have a new beginning in mind, say, a smoothie on the sundeck, maybe even a picnic? There was no one out there. In fact, there was no one about at all, the sparse furnishings looking all the more forlorn. Yet just being in all that warm natural light hollowed me out with a gratitude. I must have faltered, because the staffer had to buttress me by holding my arm, and even though he wasn't especially big or burly he seemed inordinately strong. That was when I caught a ghostly reflection of myself in the pane of the sliding porch door and saw how shockingly thin I'd become, how pointed of elbow and shoulder, and suddenly I thought I was seeing Pruitt, except a Pruitt who was revealed to be Asiatic: my cheekbones now more pronounced, the set of my eyes seemingly angled higher with how drawn I was, my hair looking positively black against my kitchen cave-dweller skin, which was paler than ever. Was this part of Chilies' custom reeducation program, his aim to stoke my own private cultural revolution by breaking me down into rudimentary units?

We kept going, the staffer dragging me by my stringy biceps. I had to bear down to keep pace. He knocked on a door that I knew wasn't to her suite but it was Constance who answered, her natural, slightly confectioned scent a heartrending welcome. I would have thrown myself into her bosom but the firm, placid set of her face, and her pinpoint stare, buffeted me.

"You look different," she said, and not as a compliment. "Stronger, in a way. We'll have to fatten you up again. You're too lean for me, the way you are now. I'd break you in two."

"As long as I can be with you, I won't care."

"You're so dramatic." I stepped into the tight vestibule and she gave me a hug. I fell into her then, trying to hide myself in her flesh. It didn't matter that I could hardly breathe. I was willing to quit breathing, given that it only led to more toil. She leaned back to peer at my wracked face.

"But you don't want to be with me." She was speaking more coldly now, almost whispering. "I know that. It can't be forever. Forever is for other people, I guess. Not for me."

"I'm so sorry," I said, unable to help but fluff the downy pillow of my self-pity. "I'm sorry for everything."

"It's all over now," she said, leading me into the rest of the suite. "We're done."

"Do whatever you want with me," I moaned into her neck. "Just keep me here. Please."

"If I did, dummy, it wouldn't be *here*."

For a moment the dimness of the room proper disoriented me. All the blinds had been shut, random shards of daylight poking through the slats. When my eyes adjusted I realized we were in Drum's study, and that Drum himself was seated in his low-slung armchair. He looked thinner, almost spindly, especially in contrast to the stout, squat figure standing beside him. It was Spideyface, from the robata and Garbo. He wore a radio earpiece, like the Secret Service. He regarded me but flickered with nothing. Drum was sitting awkwardly, sort of perched up and leaning to one side with his legs stiffly fused, as if holding them together made something else in him hurt less.

"Come," he said, his voice threadbare, abraded. "You missed this."

There was a tablet A-framed on the coffee table, which Spideyface tapped to life. On screen was a still shot of Shaundra and Al-exandre, both lying supine in a line on their mats, their hands extended.

"It's a repeat for me," Constance mumbled, sloughing me off. She grabbed a novel from atop Drum's desk and started reading it in a corner easy chair. I stepped around the coffee table and sat on the sofa beside Drum. Of course I should have asked him why I'd been assigned to Chilies, what wrong I'd ever done him, but with the fragile way he was reposed, it felt like another existence when we'd sung his father's boatman's song. Which of course it was.

"Shaundra was disappointed that you couldn't be there for the final pose. I assured her you would see it."

Spideyface leaned in and pressed the arrow. You could hear murmurs in the background, a hollow white noise. Both held their position, their arms reaching out in alternation. Alexandre, much longer, vigorously extended his hands, almost reaching Shaundra's feet. Shaundra moved more easefully, stretching her bulbous length. She took slow and even breaths. Then a bell rang softly off screen and they curled their hands underneath and pushed upward while simultaneously lifting their torsos as well, arching belly-first to the ceiling. Now both were in a relaxed upward bow, the wheel.

"Such ideal form," Drum said, entranced.

It looked pretty perfect, though even I knew it wasn't a super-difficult position for them, and nothing happened for a few moments, both of them settling into the pose. The bell rang again and Alexandre moved his hands and feet notably closer together. Shaundra did the same, though not as quickly. Alexandre shifted again, his belly rising higher; there were hoots of approval. He moved his hands some more and indeed it was special, his rangy frame arched in an astoundingly steep parabola, which made me wince. Shaundra's hands and feet were traveling inward as well, steadily drawing herself up. Her position matched his, then surpassed it. I wanted to close my eyes, but couldn't. Alexandre was watching her and he literally dug in his heels, his jaw tensing, but then he bucked with a spasm in his back and he cried out. Others rushed to gird and release him from the pose and help him walk off screen. But Shaundra kept going, narrowing the arch of herself until she wasn't an arch any longer, instead bending herself back toward parallel, into the bow of a trombone, her hands and feet practically touching. It was an old-time circus freak show, a Vegas-style magic trick, ridiculously good CGI. People were shouting. I was biting my lower lip, feeling the torque on her vertebrae. She eased out of it slowly, resetting to a more normal wheel, and then deftly flipped herself smoothly up into a handstand before coming down again on her feet like a gymnast. She was sweating profusely and shuddering a little but she was fine, weakly smiling. She mopped her brow with a self-effacing *whew*.

"Will she have her own studio now?" I asked.

"Many more than one," Drum said, still watching Shaundra, who was getting hugs from the others. He backed it up to her near-ultimate position, playing it again. He leaned forward, elbow on knee, a momentary lifeblood rising in his face. "She pushed herself. For me, yes, and for the prize, too, but I believe for the sheer possibility. It is astounding, what a person can achieve. When one sees something like this, one can't help but feel a burst of hope."

Spideyface touched his earpiece and murmured something in Japanese to Drum, who tapped the screen, switching windows. The new image was in black-and-white. It was clearly one of the lodge rooms, though mostly emptied out; the only furnishings were an improvised worktable, the rough plywood slab supported by two sawhorses, a folding chair on either end. Drum peered grimly at the screen.

"Hope is a most humbling emotion."

I had to agree, as I'd been desperately hoping all my life and sopped with a constant and serious humility and so in my case it aligned, but I was distracted—there was movement on-screen; three men entered what I thought was a still picture. The one in front was slouched, his hands bound before him as he was pushed and forced to sit by the other two. There was no sound. I asked why but neither Drum nor Spideyface said a word. It was Lucky Choi, or so I thought; his smooth boyish face had been badly pummeled, his bottom lip brutally flared and exposed, torn up like road meat. He didn't appear to be in pain; his head was lolling, ponderous, like he'd been drugged. His white dress shirt was darkly stained on the shoulder and sleeve, and he was shoeless on one foot, the other still shod with a loafer, the asymmetry of which made him look even more abject, vulnerable. Yet the absence of color made everything seem distant and wan, and somehow academic, as if the scene had already transpired, but when Constance stepped forward to get a look I realized that the feed was live.

"And yet the feeling doesn't last," Drum said. "One reverts to small thinking. Focusing on the little ache, despite the immense scale of things. We're all imprisoned in this way."

Another man was being shoved forward toward the opposite chair. My breath caught. For before he even turned to the camera I knew it was Pong. It was the hair, that amazing helmet of hair, always lifted, kinetic, which made me think despite the circumstance that he was his primed, apt self. But when he looked up I could see everything was skewed. He was unshaven, and grimacing, disheveled even in his sleek traveling clothes, though he hadn't been beaten, at least not in a way that was evident. If anything he looked shuttered in on himself, receded far inside, his gaze vaguely cast somewhere past Lucky.

"We must break out," Drum said, measured, calm. His eyes flickered with the glow of the screen. "If not on our own, then otherwise."

One of the men beside Lucky stepped forward and took hold of the edge of the plywood. Something in me landslided, flashing on what might happen on that table. But he lifted it and shoved, toppling the board onto the floor. I didn't get what had made him angry or frustrated. All of this coming to me in absolute silence. The other man pulled Lucky to his feet and backed him up against the sawhorse, his partner going behind and wrapping his forearm around the front of Lucky's chest and neck. His partner then knelt before Lucky and wrapped his arms around his thighs, as though he were in a tackling posture, and suddenly the horror of what they were about to do to him became clear. They were going to bend him the wrong way, or maybe the right way. I had to stop looking, at least at Lucky. I just kept trained on Pong, who was trying to scrabble and kick his legs but he was being held down. He was shouting, you could see, at the top of his lungs, and though it was perfectly silent, I swear I could hear him.

25.

HERE IN STAGNO, I invite dreaming too readily. As noted, I thought Val and Victor Jr. and I were rolling along okay, and even if we were somewhat flatlined in our domestic practice, I was still all about nurturing a good everyday rhythm. That Val was maybe running at a slightly elevated rpm seemed fine to me, especially given how pleased she was that VeeJ and I were now constantly doing stuff together. Aside from the hoops—VeeJ had developed a surprisingly deadly set shot from downtown—he and I decided simultaneously that we were going to spruce up the yard. I had been mowing the lawn whenever it got calf-high but otherwise the property stayed mostly a wild, beardy mess. So I took inventory of the yard gear and got us protective glasses and work gloves and we surveyed the unruly plot like it was a load of raw foodstuffs awaiting transmutation. I dusted off some power tools that were hanging on the walls of the garage, equipment that one wouldn't normally allow a kid Victor Jr.'s age to ever touch. But given his kitchen skills, I let him get trigger-happy, with me usually trailing with the rake or blower. We trimmed the sun-scalded hedges so they looked at least somewhat dignified; we uprooted a rash of opportunistic blackberry bushes and fed them into a rented chipper; we edged both sides of the driveway of the marauding webs of crabgrass. VeeJ liked the electric Weedwacker best and attacked the entire yard every few days, ranging as far as the extension cord would let him. His favorite site was the abbreviated section of sad, paint-chipped picket fencing that bordered the street, on which he unleashed the whirring head. "I'm just like a dentist!" he shouted, his ears corked with orange foam protectors, *ziz-zizz*ing the stubborn weedage around each picket with ruthless focus, right down to bare dirt.

Val sometimes watched from the living room, cheering us with a raising of her coffee mug or glass of wine if it was later in the day, and when we finished she had some ice-cold drink for us or often slices of watermelon, the first fat bite of which after a couple hours of dusty, gritty toil beneath our ever angrier sun was like getting a mainline of nectar straight to the heart.

"You boys are doing an amazing job," she said, this after we'd been at it a full week. VeeJ and I were chomping and slurping with our heads down, building a stack of rinds. "Maybe we don't have the nicest yard in the neighborhood, but at least we're no longer the eyesore."

"Are you suggesting that a random person driving by wouldn't even notice?" I said.

"Exactly."

"Does that mean we're *mediocre*?" VeeJ said, his chin glazed with juice. Among the various podcasts and web articles he was taking in were unavoidably too many about self-optimization, which had you catching him doing a Sudoku puzzle or leaning into an overhead warrior pose, supposedly to stretch the critical psoas muscle; apparently people sat too much in wealthy industrialized nations, which made the muscle too tight and led to chronic back and hip issues.

"In this case it means we're flying under the radar," I told him, a phrase he clearly didn't understand. "Which means we're fine."

He assented, if looking a bit skeptical. Val, I was happy to see, was grinning, her teeth tinged carmine from the inky red wine she favored. It wasn't that she was drunk a lot, or even drunk at all, just always cueing up some steady background cushiness, that feeling akin to having soaked maybe a bit too long in a hot tub and then perching on the rim, your body unwound from any rigors, your thoughts unlatched and floaty. Nothing wrong with a cabernet buzz, right? I also wasn't so worried because in parallel with my and Victor Jr.'s attentions to the yard, Val had begun a new beauty regimen, or should I say started one, for in our time together she was content to let her hair naturally dry after a shower, apply some sunscreen on her face, and if we were slated to meet Courtney's crew, maybe break out a lipstick. These days her routine was much more elaborate, and brought a whole city of paraphernalia to our bathroom countertop, a crowd of palettes for the eyes and cheeks, blush compacts, mascaras and lip liners, not to mention all the lotions and tonics and gels. She bought a hair dryer and curling iron and a minibasin for soaking her feet. Early on I made some comment about how I'd always loved her style, to which Val said, "That's because you never saw how I was before. I looked in the mirror last week and realized I didn't look like me anymore."

This struck me as odd, as I was thinking she didn't really look like Val now, even if she was very skilled at the practice. I did recall that photo of her and Victor Sr. on the Golden Gate Bridge, so maybe it was true that she used to be more cosmetically inclined. To me the layered makeup and done hair made her appear both older and younger, and people definitely noticed her more readily wherever we went, which she didn't seem to mind. Courtney got all excited about this new Val and was inspired to get gussied up herself, and while the ladies had an afternoon-long session experimenting on each other like teenagers, Keefer and I had a smoke-out and munchie fest, both of us more than psyched when they emerged looking as spangled and glam as high-end strippers, frosted high-lights in the lazy curls of their tresses, a hint of glitter *dans le décolletage*, their midnight eye shadow making the late Saturday afternoon dilate and feel even more glacial in its passing. I don't know what went on with those two that night but Val and I got busy in a most agile manner after not getting together for a while, our ministrations cinema worthy, which was amazing of course but lacking something critical, at least for me. Skin stuck on skin, my limbs ached and shuddered, but no matter how good it felt neither of us was making much, if any, sound and I was still desperately missing her.

So when I got word from Mrs. Parnthong about the annual charity cooking competition at the YWCA, including a category for kids twelve and under, I found out more about it and went ahead and signed up Victor Jr. without telling him or Val. It wasn't the cooking per se that I was interested in but rather the fervor and groove we'd enjoyed while doing it, our crack team that got sweaty and stressed and sometimes seared and scalded, staying in constant motion, full-court pressing, to come up with something good and maybe even great. An item sublime. One evening when we were eating at the Chicken Hut with Courtney's crew I casually mentioned the Y thing and Keefer asked if there was a special theme for the kids' contest.

"There is," I said. "Sandwiches."

"*Sandwiches?*" was the group groan. But I didn't need to do any further promotion, sensing what everybody was undoubtedly thinking, and that Liam neatly verbalized for us in his matter-of-fact way: "A sandwich for Victor is a piece of cake."

Val asked VeeJ if he had any interest.

"Maybe," he said, intently nibbling the cartilaginous end joint of a drumstick. "But I don't want to do it alone."

"Why don't you enter, too, honey?" Courtney said to Liam. "You love making sandwiches. You made yourself a nice salami-and-cheese the other day."

Liam sat up, intrigued by the idea, but the light in his eyes dulled when he glanced at the wunderkind of 20 Whet sitting across from him. He murmured, "I'm not terribly confident, Mother."

"Don't worry, my little Einstein," she said to him. "You'll figure it out. And look, maybe Victor Jr. will even give you advice."

I think we were all bracing for a less than ideal response—he was still eight years old—but VeeJ did one better than simply agreeing and said, "I'd want to do it together, if that's okay with you?"

Victor Jr. raised the drumstick and Liam toasted it with his chicken wing, and we all shouted huzzahs, though maybe Val was a little quieter, suitably awed, I'm sure, by her son's ever-unfolding human decency. She kissed him on the head, her lips lingering against his hair, maybe tasting the not-yet musk of his fleeting boyishness, and I got the feeling she was as happy as she'd ever been, at least since I'd known her.

The contest was less than a week away, so the next day Victor Jr. and Liam got down to work in our kitchen developing ideas and testing them. We rehearsed and rehearsed, and by the time the contest came around, we were ready. It was a bigger deal than I expected, a large white party tent set up in the parking lot of the YWCA. The kids' competition was first so we left the boys at the kitchen inside with the other contestant kids and their helper/guardians (I could only convince the dubious coordinator that VeeJ was capable of serving the role by having him open his leather knife fold and flex his pro speed-dicing skills), then went outside to get seats. The tent was already filling with family and friends of the kid competitors, and there was a heady pregame buzz in the air, muscly beer-bellied dads in baseball caps jawing one another with friendly taunts, the moms faux complaining about the messes their kids made in practice runs, the feeling being of a junior sports travel tourney where the stakes were infinitesimally small relative to the unbounded parental aspirations. Keefer and Courtney knew one of the judges (the fire chief) and immediately lobbied him, Keefer with the appropriate chill laconicisms, while Courtney played it upbeat flirty and cute. Val and I found seats in the third row as volunteers unfurled tablecloths on the long dais at the front, where the entries would be displayed.

"My gosh," Val said, placing her hand over mine. "Look where we are."

"In a tent in a parking lot in a long-forgotten boonie?"

"Well there's *that*," she said, with an easy smile, though I could tell she wasn't feeling super jokey. "I was talking about Victor Jr. How amazing it is that we can now actually leave him inside there, with full responsibility for another person, and not be concerned in the least."

"The idea is kind of mind-blowing."

"It's not just that. The most amazing thing is that I totally believe it. I'm not worried at all about Liam. I know he's in capable hands. To be honest, I'm anxious only about Victor Jr. and how disappointed he'll be if he thinks he's let down his friend. Now, isn't that crazy?"

"I think I'm worried about that, too," I said, because I realized I was. Maybe this is an inflection point you eventually reach as a parent, when you can see that your offspring is suddenly at the helm of his or her life, and there's not much use to shielding anymore because you know from this point on, the most hurtful slings and arrows will likely come from within.

Val hugged me but then also kissed me on the mouth, if dryly, firmly, so I could almost feel the press of our teeth.

"Victor Jr. is so lucky to have you."

"I'm lucky to have him."

"You must have a good father," she said, rebreaking one of our rules.

"He is," I replied, not wanting to call her out. Maybe this was the onset of a new beginning for us, when we'd disclose the stuff most people do, not so much to understand each other better but simply to share because you cherish them. I was actually having the urge to mention Pong, too, to start unwinding the infinitely complicated coils of that still very fresh part of my still-young life. Yet there was something that continued to pester me, maybe all the pretty makeup on her pretty face, and I thought to hold off on Pong for a more settled time.

Val said, "I wouldn't call you lucky exactly, but that's okay. He adores you, you know."

"Oh yeah?" I chuckled, instinctively sloughing it off, just as Clark would.

"Yes," she said. "There's no getting around it. Victor Jr. loves you."

We sat in silence, everything suspended by the full stop of Val's words, which were clotting up my heart. All I could do was stare down at our clasped hands and feel the disembodiment I'm stricken with whenever a truth is uttered.

She squeezed my hand and said, "Thank you, T," her answer to the answer I would have gladly given.

Courtney and Keefer now came and sat on either side of us, clearly eager for the contest to begin.

Keefer said, "The chief is an old bud of my dad's, and also coached me in Pee Wees, so I think we're good."

"There *are* two other judges," Courtney pointed out, and these were being chatted up by other audience members as well. One was a buxom, wholesome-looking young woman who was last year's Tri-Counties Fair beauty contest winner, the other the middle-aged hipster owner of a newish kitchenware shop in town, who was giving her store-logo'd aprons to the other judges. "Unless you're friendly with the fair queen."

"Don't know her yet," Keefer said, leering at the young woman, who was giggling about something as the fire chief helped tie the apron strings behind her back.

Courtney stuck her tongue out at him and he filthily flickered his in return, and it was nice to see that they were on better terms. Our family outings had been beneficial to all of us, I think, for how they'd provided us simple activities to have fun with and be silly about, like our now regular bowling and arcade night and the dock fishing we'd started on Sunday afternoons at one of the many picturesque little lakes we'd discovered that dotted the area. Stagno should have been named Lago, so just add that to this town's high stack of missed opportunities. But looking around at all the cheery people I was beginning to realize that this wasn't such a futile, backward place, or if it was futile and backward the citizenry hadn't totally given up and, whether from denial or defiance, kept at their labors.

And if the kids' entries were any indication, there were plenty of creative reserves in Stagno to be tapped. The YWCA director, a mousy, slim guy with a bullhorn, introduced the competitors and the kids filed in, each carrying a plate of his or her sandwiches and squeezing together along the length of the dais set with folded tent cards, each with a descriptive title and numbered. They were fourteen in all, Liam was number five, with Victor Jr. the sole kid of the helpers standing behind the contestants. The judges went down the line and took an evaluative bite (one of each entry sandwich had been cut up), the beauty queen and kitchen-shop owner taking extensive notes on the pads drawn from their apron pockets, while the fire chief, a portly, wattle-necked guy you could never imagine sliding down a pole or climbing a ladder, simply relished the eating, even popping the partly eaten nubs left by the other judges. And why not? There were tasty-looking hoagies, po' boys, sliders, gyros, paninis, melts, and several submissions from the more-is-more school of nearly foot-tall Dagwoods that only a hippopotamus could actually take a bite of, though you could bet the fire chief would have tried. There was only one frankly unfortunate entry, at least in appearance, a sliced-turkey-roll "Thanksgiving Wrap" filled with cranberry sauce "catsup" and brown gravy that oozed syphilitically from one end and like any street-food-eating tourist in Mumbai from the other.

I could empathize, because when I was VeeJ's age, I was the Cub Scout at the Pinewood Derby contest with big aspirations. I showed up all excited about my crudely shaped Indy car that was matte green with white and yellow striping and a Snoopy head glued in the driver's position. Clark had done the basic whittling of the wood block's corners and I followed with a full hour of sanding and together we did the painting (he was originally from Eau Claire, thus the Packers colors) and when we finished we were feeling optimistic about our chances in either the speed or the style category.

But once at the derby we might as well have been wielding femur bones, for the Neanderthal tech of our vehicle. It was like an international design expo, with maybe just half the cars actually being *cars*. The invention, the craftsmanship! The paint and decal work! There was a manta-ray car and a wedge-of-Swiss-cheese car and a car that was a blocky old-fashioned cell phone and, maybe the coolest one, a mini Pinewood Derby track with mini derby cars racing down its slope, with the mini derby track car winning in a kind of meta-infinity-loop statement.

The other entries ranged from perfect replicas of a Ferrari Daytona and a Shelby Mustang to fantasy rides like the Batmobile and the *Back to the Future* DeLorean and the one I wanted to smash I was so covetous, a Nathan's hot dog truck. Like all kiddie competitions it was primarily about the capacities of the parents, in this case the dads: the can-do working-class dads who still had wood and metal shops in the basement, and the rich-guy dads who ordered elaborate kits and/or hired consultants, and finally the professional engineer and architect dads, the sons like-constituted, who had legit skills and inexhaustible creativity. Needless to say, my turd-shaped racer was eliminated in the first heat, beating only a bikini-clad chick hanging ten on a longboard with starfish-spoke wheels, whose father-son makers (in matching Hawaiian shirts and sunglasses) clearly didn't give a loco moco about optimal aerodynamics or weighting. Everybody crowded around their ride, ogling the curves of the surfer girl's smoking three-inch-tall body. They won Best Design.

We losers got yellow ribbons—I know, I know, pathetic millennial and Gen Z emotional welfare—which is still what I hoped they'd award today's contestants, all these earnestly excited, hopeful kids. Given VeeJ's extensive and hands-on counsel, I was confident that Liam's entry had a serious shot at contending; their "Thai-Dixie Brioche Banh Mi," featuring curried duck breast with deep-fried green tomatoes, shallot-and-mango relish, and spicy basil aioli on a made-from-scratch brioche bun that VeeJ had baked early that morning, drew bug-eyes from all three judges as they munched on their samples of it, the fire chief even reaching for the intact demo model to get another bite before the kitchen-store owner shooed his greedy fingers.

"They're loving it," Keefer exclaimed, noticing this, too. "The chief can't get enough!"

Val now said, "They're about to announce the finalists."

We all rose from our seats and edged toward the dais in anticipation of the decisions, the Y director holding the bullhorn in front of his face. Val was wholly focused on Victor Jr., who had slung his arm around Liam like a big brother would, tapping him gently in the chest as they awaited word. The Y director ran through the usual acknowledgments and thank-yous for the food bank donations and started in on a bromide about encouraging the talents of the town's young people when some lady hollered, "Gas attack!"

and soon enough he cleared his throat to explain that all entrants would receive honorable-mention coupons for a free one-month trial family gym membership, along with a commemorative shot glass courtesy of a local car dealer, which struck a funny tone given the kiddie contestants, but whatever. The winners would receive gift certificates to the judge's kitchenware store. Finally he handed the bullhorn to the fire chief, who named the three finalists: a tall, pig-tailed Amish girl and her vegan gluten-free bagel with fava bean hummus, golden beet sprouts, and roasted red peppers; a cherubic Latinx boy who'd made a truly delicious-looking fried torta filled with pork *al pastor* and cotija cheese and a cactus-jalapeño slaw; and, to no one's surprise, Liam (and VeeJ).

There were hoots and guffaws and claps, the three of us girding Courtney, who was beginning to hyperventilate. The chief then caught the whole tent off guard by suddenly announcing the third-place winner: "Veggie Bagel!" After the Amish girl got her prize certificate, however, the fire chief heightened the drama by inviting Liam and the other boy, whose name was Jorge, to the front of the dais and asking them to talk about the inspiration for their creations.

Jorge went first, talking about watching his grandma (the digni-fied white-haired lady beside him) prepare dinner each night be-cause his parents worked late into the evenings, and that he wanted to make something they would be happy to eat when they came home, which pretty much made everybody want to rip their hearts out. The chief asked Liam for his thoughts and Liam, holding the bullhorn, started to say something but trailed off, all too aware of the scores of eyes staring back at him. You'd think that being on the spectrum maybe would insulate him from such sensitivity but in-stead he was oystering tightly, hibernating in a place safe and dark and silent. The chief kept nodding, waiting. The tent went dead quiet, except, I thought, for a very faint pained whistle that seemed to be coming from Courtney, and we might have all stayed like that had Victor Jr. not stepped forward and taken the bullhorn from his friend and said, "Liam would like to honor his parents, too. Without their support, encouragement, and love, he would never have found this outlet for his creativity."

"Yeah, Li-AM!" Keefer hollered, and I blurted, "Fuck, yeah!" the Y director and fire chief and the other judges and pretty much everyone else glaring at me. But I didn't care. Neither did Val. Hearing VeeJ say those words—even if they were cribbed from a food-foundation award ceremony he'd been watching on YouTube—instantly broke me into crumbs, for it was then that I understood how a parent might feel when his child did something undeniably and purely decent and good, which is that you were happily vanquished, that you could willingly disappear.

But now was decision time. The three judges huddled; then they flanked the Y director, and with the two boys standing to the side with surprising nonchalance, the director bullhorned the verdict: "And the winner is . . . Terrific Torta!"

Val and I immediately looked toward Victor Jr., just in case, but there he was, high-fiving with Jorge, and then graciously shaking hands with the judges, with Liam bouncing up and down with glee as he waved the second-place certificate and then threw himself into the arms of Courtney and Keefer, who had already rushed to the dais. The director invited the audience to come and sample all the now sliced-up sandwiches, and Val and I alternated with Jorge's grandma in being the first to taste our boys' work. The banh mi was pretty spectacular, a three-ring circus in the mouth, though I must say that the torta was righteously satisfying, visceral and comforting, definitely a last meal kind of thing. Victor Jr. clearly concurred, staring bug-eyed at Jorge as he chewed, and soon enough the two of them were talking shop about braising techniques, the spices they'd used, and I proposed we have a celebratory dinner, hosted by me of course, and afterward the McDonoughs and the Cuellars and we Aliases agreed to meet that night at the Spaghetti Depot for an all-you-can-eat shrimp and pasta blowout.

We went home and promptly took a nap, or at least Victor Jr. and I did, dozing together on the sofa while Val tidied up the kitchen (the boys had pre-prepped in the morning and we'd left in a rush); at some point I feel like she planted kisses on our heads, blessing her exhausted men. Or perhaps she regarded us for an extended moment and I dreamt it. Regardless, when I awoke she wasn't inside and I stumbled around for a few seconds until I heard the *zuzz*ing. From the picture window I saw Val going at the fencing in the front of the yard with the Weedwacker, the long orange extension cord running to the back of the house, where there was an outside outlet. Her posture was a mirror of her son's, those same rounded-in shoulders, the slightly bowlegged stance, and I was content simply to watch her until I realized she wasn't wearing any eye protection. So I stopped by the workbench in the garage and ran out there with a pair of safety glasses.

"Oops," she said, taking them from me. Her hair was stuck to her temples, her nose and cheeks damp with sweat in the August heat. "I totally forgot."

"Understandable oversight," I badly joked.

"Clearly not for long," she less badly joked back.

"So what's with the wacking?" I asked. She'd not done it before.

"It looks fun whenever you two do it, so I wanted to try."

"Well?"

"It's okay," she said, not terribly excited. "I'm just enjoying being you guys."

"You should try the trimmer next. It's like cutting hair."

"Maybe I will."

She put on the safety glasses and motioned that I step back, then revved the head with the trigger. I watched for a moment but she was intent on blasting away what paint was left on the bottom of a picket and I went back inside the house. Victor Jr. was up mixing a special malt-powder beverage that he'd read aided recovery after workouts, as we had basketball on the daily agenda, sometimes a pickup game forming with some neighborhood kids around his age, in which case I refereed. VeeJ and I had fine-tuned our fitness regimen, cross-training with core work and lifting barbells in addition to intensified treadmilling and hoops, and I was feeling like we should stick around the house, maybe even get out there to assist Val. He was keen on practicing hook shots and floaters in the lane, and so I said fine. As we dribbled down the driveway Val had already switched to the trimmer and was shaping our one sad, threadbare, asymmetrical hedge. I waved and she gazed up at us with the trimmer still going and even though I waved again she blankly let us go by. I sympathized—those sawing trimmer teeth can be mesmerizing—and yet there was something to her lack of acknowledgment that kept flashing me while I was rebounding the ball for VeeJ, a silent notification that I tried to tap away but couldn't. It was warm enough that I wanted to quit anyway, and I was lucky that some of the usual kids had appeared. I went one versus all for a couple games until I told them I was done and left VeeJ to play.

Not another person or pet was outdoors along the whole length of Whetstone, nor was Val in the yard anymore, and it felt good to step inside our lair with the central AC gently rattling away and let the chill pacify the hot coursing of my blood. I went to our bedroom with the sexy idea of maybe finding Val in the shower—we still weren't tangling enough—but it was vacant. I came out and realized the hall bathroom door was closed and I rolled my knuckles against it.

"Val?" I said softly, leaning on it.

"Hey," she answered, her voice muffled and distant. "You're back so soon."

"It was boiling out there."

"What about Victor Jr.?"

"He wanted to keep playing with the other kids."

"Okay."

I said, "How come you're in *there*?"

She didn't answer.

"Val?"

"I felt like a bath."

Our bathroom had a shower stall only. I said, "May I come in?" gingerly trying the knob. It was locked.

"I'm already in the tub."

I let a few beats pass before I said, "Okay, I'll go shower," stepping away, if still craning for an answer. But as I was about to undress in our bedroom I heard the pipes belch and shudder—the walls are extra flimsy, like everything about this house—and listened to her very slowly filling the tub. Our water pressure, unsurprisingly, was also third-rate, a pissy drip coffee machine. I wondered why she pretended the tub was full, why she wouldn't let me in. Sure, sometimes, out of the blue, you get shy about your body. Sometimes you simply prefer to be alone. Sometimes you crave an enclosure, a kind of crèche, a bathtub as good for that as anything. Okay. But then I pictured some naked dude shimmying out the half-sized bathroom window and falling into the bed of mulch below, a seriously idiotic notion, though soon enough I had drifted out the front door, telling myself I was curious about her yard work. Of course there was no bare-assed Lothario. In fact, the front yard was especially neat and clean; she'd left zero clippings by the fencing, not even finely cut bits of grass and weeds. The only thing was the pair of safety glasses, which I found on the lawn.

Mostly I was startled by what she'd done with our lone hedge, no longer a teetering hunchback. It was still parched and bare but now it was almost straight-shouldered, its freshly cut ends white-green in the blaring light, as if the poor thing still held the promise of vitality.

Yet nothing else felt much alive to me. The afternoon was wildly hot and bright but it might as well have been Norway in winter. And I kept hearing this funny refrain in my head. *For what,* it said. *For what, for what, for what.* It wasn't a philosophical lament, more my response to something I couldn't put my finger on despite how much I tried, like when you wake up and can't quite remember what you were dreaming of so intensely mere moments before, only your body knowing if it was ecstatic, or scary, or sad. If anything I felt depleted, like I was missing an important part, and for a second I panicked that Chilies had somehow secretly excised an organ. I came back in through the side door in the garage. All seemed to be in order, the trimmer and wacker, redolent of fresh-cut vegetation, leaning in their places along the wall, the pegboard festooned with its array of hand tools. I put the safety glasses back on the workbench top, my fingertips grazing the ever-proliferating nailheads, maybe a couple dozen more of them now.

I could hear Val's bath faucet still running. It made me thirsty and I went to the kitchen and poured a glass of Victor Jr.'s malt health drink, which tasted like sawdust soda. I was pouring it down the drain when I noticed the orange extension cord. The window above the sink looks across the nook of the small back deck to where the bedrooms are, and I could see the cord snaking along the edge of the house and up from the mulch bed into the hall bathroom window, where it disappeared beneath the sash. Without a thought I flicked on the disposal and it ground on itself, metal on metal. *But the power is on.* And it was then that I awoke to the strange song in my head. *For what, for what?* And suddenly I pictured the pattern now, the inlay of the nailheads on the workbench top, the message finally coalescing.

SORRY

I ran to the hall bathroom and banged on the door, hollering, "Val! Val!" When she didn't answer I kicked it, the cheap jamb partially splintering. I was sure I'd broken my foot. I tried battering it with my shoulder, but nothing. I had my little knife and worked it against the latch, levering it furiously, and I was going to get something much bigger in the garage, when the door creaked free on its own.

You never think you'll see what you'll see, and then you do. There was Val, sitting in the filled tub in her clothes, her dark T-shirt wicking up the water, which must have been cold. She was shivering terribly. In her hand was a curling iron, its black cord plugged into the female end of the thicker orange one dropping down from the window. There was an outlet by the sink but by building code it was the safety kind.

"Hey," I whispered, barely able to call up enough breath from my chest. The curling iron's switch glowed red.

"Go away," she grunted through her teeth. "Get out of here."

I sloshed forward on the wet tile, practically feeling the tickle of a charge.

"Stay there!" she shouted harshly, miserably. "Stay the fuck back!"

I said, "What do you think will happen?"

"What are you talking about?" she said, waving the appliance, her eyes incredulous.

"Not to you!" I said. "Not you! To your boy! Your wonderful boy!"

Val kind of shivered, the loop of the black cord now contacting the water. "You'll take care of him. You already do so well, better than his father. Better than I ever could."

"It won't matter what I do for him! Don't you know what it'll be like? What he'll have to feel in his gut forever? Have you thought about that?" I took a breath. "You think it's enough to leave him with some stupid message? I mean, come on! *'Sorry'*? What the hell is that? You can hardly even read it!"

She bit her lip, the curling iron stiff in her hand.

"If you don't want to be here, let me propose something else," I said. "Take a trip. Go someplace nice. Or awful, if you really need to torture yourself. Stay for as long as you want. I'll tell Victor Jr. you went on a humanitarian mission. Or I'll say I hit you like Victor Sr. did and you freaked and had to escape. I'll tell him whatever story he needs to hear. I'll let him hate me. Better for him to hate me than to hate you."

This made Val begin to cry. Her hand was dipping and I moved closer and she leveled the curler at me. "Don't!"

I took another step anyway. "But I'm not going to be the one to tell him that you're dead. Some poor cop or social worker will have to do that. I'm not going to stick around and have to look at his face every morning for the second he's still sure you'll appear. So I swear, you do this and I'm getting in the car. I'll drive away right now."

"You wouldn't . . ."

"Why not? He won't have a real life anyway. Not from this point on. He'll keep looking for something to hold on to, but it won't be there. He'll try to fill himself, to no use, with any little sweetness. He'll pretend all the time, like sad losers do. Like I do."

"You're not a loser!" Val yowled miserably. "Please don't ever say that!"

"It's the truth. You're dooming him," I said. "You're doom-ing him."

"But your mother's out there somewhere, right?" Val said. "One day she'll come back to you . . ."

"No!" I yelled, booming. "No!" I shouted, with everything I had, my throat hurt by the ugly sound. I think it broke my voice, and maybe something else, too. "She's gone. *Gone*." I said this like I'd never said it.

"Oh, Til . . . I thought she . . . oh no . . ."

Val started to reach for me, rising from the water, but I could already see exactly what would happen: how her free hand slipped on the wet tub edge, how the other involuntarily extended, to break her fall, and plunged the live iron into the killing water.

26.

T RY AS I MIGHT, I couldn't keep hating on Pong. I had every right, every reason; I wished him ill, but in the end I couldn't stop thinking of how badly he was suffering. They had pummeled and kicked him about the torso, the bruising of which he wouldn't show me; this made me feel the pain of them even more, for having to gaze at his ever-undisturbed exterior. For a while he stood leaning against the wall, his arm cradling his middle. Then he had to sit, breathing audibly through his teeth, because standing made something stretch in him that wouldn't be stretched any more. By the end he lay on the floor on his right side, one knee slightly drawn up, his body stiff but no longer tensing. This was a day and a night after what they did to Lucky Choi, whose body had been taken away before they put me with Pong.

The sawhorses still stood sideways in the middle of the stripped lodge room, the plywood tabletop left where it had been tossed to the floor. I couldn't bear to move or even touch its terrible array. What had happened to Lucky happened in complete silence on the video but sometimes even now I'll shiver with what must have been the bright report of his vertebrae, the sound like tree limbs snapping in an ice storm. He can't have died instantly; the breaking was well below his neck. Or maybe he died because the pain was so great. Or else, the worst case, he'd lingered like that, his bottom half dead, until one of Spideyface's guys finally put him out of his misery.

Or so I hoped.

They had snagged Pong and Lucky in Kowloon, where the two had just made their final deposit, and ferried them here by power yacht, cruising up the Pearl River past the very banks where Drum's father had fallen in the water and drowned. If Pong had intended to go back to Dunbar and see his wife and daughters, he had not done so. Instead, he and Lucky had been shuttling by leased private plane from Manila to Jakarta, and to Phnom Penh, for meetings with other bankers willing to accept large and undocumented cash deposits, their rolling duffels densely lined with the softened, pocket-worn, smaller-denomination yen, and renminbi, and rupees, and baht, all accrued from the various Kappagoda enterprises. I got this from Pruitt when he came and snuck a leftover *bao* to me soon after I was locked in.

"Big boss hurting," Pruitt whispered; his speech had become distinctly Chilies-esque. He'd been ground down so long, his assimilation, which he'd been working years toward, was now complete. But it was an assimilation to his Man, a mode of both veneration and self-protection. He'd even styled his hair like the chef's into a jagged, razor-cut crew. Collapsed his shoulders, to be that much shorter. "Hurting in his feeling most. Your boss bad, bad man. Did you know? Why he and Lucky have to betray? Why mess up everything?"

I shook my head; Pong was surely hearing him but still not saying a word, just staring down into the floor with his brow knitted as he braced his belly, his ribs.

"I don't know, Pale Cricket. Boss just so low now. Right to bottom of his heart."

Clearly Pruitt was broken up, too, with glum, canine eyes, and he gave me a dingy, sticky Pruitt hug, though it felt like he was giving succor as much to himself as to me. "Watch out," he said, glancing coldly at Pong as he left. "Do not trust."

This was what I was telling myself as I gripped the stale *bao*. By then I should have been famished but I'd lost any savor, which only deepened my sense of doom. I threw the *bao* into the corner, where it settled with a new fur of dust, and seeing it forsaken like that made my chest buck, my eyes so dry and itchy that I couldn't even cry. I'd had nothing by mouth and so there was nothing in me to leach out. It was maddening, too, that despite his condition, Pong didn't once moan or weep. He wasn't trying to be stoic. It was simply who he was, even in his misery, ever composed to the end. I think now that it wasn't for the sake of appearances, whether for others or for his own self-view. His was a much greater conceit. For all along, the idea about Pong was that he—and whoever of us was (un)fortunate enough to tag along with him—was always exactly where he was meant to be, regardless, pinging in his coordinates as if in a divined GPS, and so confirming some elemental harmony of the world. Now it was all laid bare as simulated, and badly misaligned, and the frightened, grasping creature in me wanted him to suffer, to rue, to taste the welling bile in his mouth and tremble at the horrid sum of his deeds. The flagrant waste of it all.

And yet the more I ran him down in my thoughts, even as my insides screeched with ire, I couldn't help but mostly turn on my wretched, useless self. I was the serial latcher, after all, the mad clinger-on; and in my craving I had sought out and found what I needed to become the person I wouldn't otherwise have become on my own. Trouble is, that person turned out to be a useful idiot, or a ready piece of interference. Someone to be expended, whether by others or by circumstance. I had to retreat to the bathroom and curl up in the cold, dry tub, pressing my knees as tightly as I could to my chest, trying to ball up like one of those armored bugs and somehow negate the larger sphere of reality, which at least calmed me.

But when I came out Pong had turned pale, breathtakingly pale, his head lolled back against the wall beneath the meager bulb from the ceiling fixture—the windows had been shuttered and nailed shut from the outside—and I shook with dread for both of us. I couldn't help myself and asked if he needed some water. He didn't reply. He wasn't going to make me do anything for him. But when he slid down in a crouch, looking even more wan, life-sapped, I went to the bathroom and found the only thing there was, a faded plastic soap dish, and filled it for him.

He sipped from it slowly, as if it were very hot tea. The swallowing made him wince and shudder and he accidentally spilled it. He clearly wanted more and shifted to get up but wasn't able to. I watched him for a while, but then couldn't stand it. I took the dish and filled it again. But he first offered it back to me, then he drank a little, and we shared the rest of the slippery, soap-tinged water.

"You know, I never finished saying what happened with Ling and her son," he said, surprising me with the mention of the restaurant owner. I sniffed, asking why that mattered now.

"There's no great consequence," he said. "But I wish to tell you. Will you let me? It won't change anything."

"Nothing ever can be changed," I said. "Isn't that the truth?"

He didn't reply. Then, as if there had been some interlude of conversing, he said: "Do you remember what I was saying about them?"

"I don't know," I said, though this was wholly false. After a while I said, "You were debating if you should move into their house, or go off on your own."

"Yes, that's right," he said. "You always pay close attention, which is what I immediately understood about you that first day at the yogurt shop."

"I guess I didn't pay close enough attention to you," I said bitterly.

He let my spiteful words absorb into the moment, and I realized that I'd never seen Pong directly disagree with anything or anyone. This, somehow, without being a yes-man. But maybe this was more contemptible, maybe this was the worst kind of lying, to make it seem to others that whatever they felt or thought or hoped was possible, and even right. Especially when there was no hope, no chance at all.

After a pause he continued.

"I began living in Ling's immense house. In the basement bedroom at first, but her son was having some seizures then and she needed my help at all hours. So I moved upstairs into the room adjoining his. He shook severely enough that he sometimes fell out of his bed and I set up rails on one side and also installed padding on the wall, as he nearly broke his nose while thrashing. Eventually I set up my own bed in his room so I could monitor him throughout the night. Perhaps it was coincidence, but he mostly stopped having the seizures after we started sharing the room. We were around the same age, and although he was cognitively very limited and could hardly communicate, he was clearly pleased that we were together."

"Like brothers?" I spat, though the words came out much less caustically than I intended. I wanted to shout him down, to tear into him, but even then I was drawn into what Pong had to say, and I couldn't help but imagine myself as Ling's disabled son, peering over at the figure in the bed across the dimly night-lit room and happily knowing Pong was my sentinel.

"Yes, I think so," he replied. "He did appear to improve once I got settled in. He was less stiff physically and had more control over his bodily functions. He had always eaten well. Ling appreciated all this. In the daytime she watched him so I could look after the restaurants, and when I returned at the end of the day she had dinner ready. I could have easily brought back food from one of the restaurants but she insisted on cooking. Her son preferred it, and she knew I did as well. Fried rabbit was a specialty. She also made her hometown Chengdu-style hot pots, very herbal and very spicy, which her son enjoyed, even though it was a difficult dish for him to consume. Ling and I took turns picking pieces of meat and vegetables from the boiling pot and blowing on them before feeding him."

"I've never had them," I mumbled.

"You will," Pong answered, his face momentarily brightening. His accent, I thought, seemed slightly more pronounced to me, the warbles and shushes somewhat stouter, rounder, more like when we'd first met. "You may not believe me, but I am certain of it. None of this trouble is your doing. This is merely the beginning for you. You have just begun to unlock your talents. Who you truly are. I know you will live your best life."

My best life. I was certain I was already living it, going around with him. And okay, the trouble might not have been mine but it had risen right up to my eyes. Yet the way he spoke sounded so natural and sure, so tender and brotherly, and even as I figured it was some sort of con, I understood at last that it was a con I needed. Now and from the beginning. For maybe your favorite teacher or coach or best friend conned you, too, into believing in a version of yourself you hadn't yet imagined, a person many factors more capable, a person who might not have otherwise bloomed.

I couldn't help but ask, "You never said if you actually liked them."

He took another sip of water. "It is funny," Pong murmured. "What you just said. It makes make me realize I don't think of people in such terms. So I don't know if I did 'like' them. I grew close to them, certainly. We came to trust and respect one another. Ling loved her son, but it was clear that my living with them also made her think about the child she might have had, one without such severe handicaps. Who could have pursued his own full and vigorous life. Whose time here would not be cut so short. In this way I believe my presence made her both grateful and sorrowful at once. It was none of my doing, but I think she grew to love him even more."

I sat with this notion for a while, Pong maybe with his daughters on his mind, and I definitely thinking about my mother. I wondered if this loving kind of sadness made her depart for good, which instantly gutted me, and I caught myself about to tell Pong about her, tell him everything she was before she was gone, but it was far too late for us and it would only have made me more miserable for having uttered it. I guess if you think about it too much, if you acknowledge the true fullness of your feelings like Pong said, the loves of our lives are so precious that it's impossible not to mourn every waking moment, even as it's happening. In certain cases, you can't help but flee.

"I felt a genuine devotion for Ling and her son. I had many aspirations but strangely, I was not thinking about the future. I was most content to be there with them, in the day to day."

"You could have stayed like that for a long, long while."

He nodded. "You know then what I mean. I was working, learning everything about running a small but growing business, and making good money. We were helping each other, appreciating each other's company. I felt very much at home. No one would consider it an ideal scenario for a young man starting his life but in its own way it was ideal. We had our own little world, and I felt fortunate to be in it. It was often draining, dealing with her son's needs, but nothing was beyond us. We always managed. The one unsolved obstacle was my immigration status. My application for a student visa had just been rejected, and my tourist visa had already run out, and I informed Ling that I would have to leave soon. She was very upset by this. She called several immigration attorneys she knew but there was nothing to do. They all confirmed that I should leave the country as soon as possible, as there are strict guidelines, depending on length of overstay, that delay any future return by three or even ten years. Or forever. I could not take a chance on that kind of jeopardy. At the same time, her son's health degraded. His seizures had resumed, and after each one he seemed to weaken a little more. He had to be hospitalized for a full week. When we brought him home we fed him in bed and gave him sponge baths. He still possessed a lively spirit, even though he could hardly sit up. I hated to leave them but there was nothing to be done and so I bought a plane ticket to Beijing. The morning I was to depart I was packing my bag when Ling asked to speak to me down in the kitchen. She had made me her scallion pancakes, which were always very good, and when I had my last bite she broke down. She threw herself at my feet. She had not told me what the doctors informed her, but her son's defective heart was finally failing. Likely he had no more than a year, though it could happen anytime. You would think that this would make my leaving easier, as she wouldn't need me for very long, but in fact it made her keener to keep our life together intact. For as long as she could. She was sure her son would be happier and live longer with me there. Ling was a smart and practical woman, and she came up with a solution. A way that I could stay."

"She was going to adopt you?"

Pong could barely half chuckle, needing to press at his gut. "If I had been young enough, I am sure Ling would have made that happen. I would have been glad. My father was still an official nonperson, and for my sake he stayed clear of me. Ling was a good person. A good mother. She faithfully endured her late husband. Her generosity was boundless. No, she didn't adopt me. But I did become her son."

I learned then what he meant by that, literally speaking. For Ling gave him the most valuable thing she could offer. It was simple enough, and made perfect sense, given that she had no other immediate family or heirs, and had already entrusted Pong with the full run of her business and personal finances, and of course the welfare of her child in his waning days. Like Ling, her son was a naturalized citizen, and so she had him and Pong swap identities, this verified by a folder of impeccable documentation generated by crack forgers in Chinatown.

Instantly, they became each other.

When Ling's son died in his sleep one night four months later, it was Pong who was taken away by the funeral director and cremated, his ashes placed in a compact bronze urn that would sit on the night table beside Ling's bed, and surely still does; a few months after his death, Ling decided to return to her hometown of Lishui, in coastal Zhejiang province, where a cousin lived. She sold all the restaurants except the one in Leonia, which, as agreed, she deeded to him, and he ran that successfully with the help of Minori after they became a couple. Once he began graduate school they sold it to some other newcomer entrepreneur, in turn buying and renovating a couple rundown rental apartments on a direct commuter train line to the city, the first investments of his varied portfolio, which led to more rentals, followed by the service stations, the event halls, the eateries, the light industrial and laboratory facilities, the senior centers and car washes, and the rest of his prosperous homespun empire that was now, in this ultimate venture, the final rooting of the ignominious tick of me.

How depleted it all was, how empty and bleak.

I asked if Minori knew.

He shook his head. "We first met just before Ling returned to China. I told Minori I had purchased the restaurant from her. There seemed little point in saying otherwise, which would only cause needless complication. We were dating then, and also working non-stop, and there was time for little else. Soon enough we were married and were to have a baby and it became just another item of many items of the past. This may sound strange to you, Tiller. But to me, it was less than nothing in the scheme of things. Two young Chinese men in a small town in New Jersey exchanging names and birthdates. It was like trading a set of clothes of the same size. An infinitely trivial happening. Who would ever care, or notice?"

"What about your father? Didn't he wonder why people were calling you by a completely different name?" Then I said, "If that's who he even is."

"He *is*," he said. "He is my father. Everything I told you about what happened in China is true. He suffered it all. When I was finally able to bring him over, the life I had set up in Dunbar was comfortable and safe, so to him, what did it matter what my name was? By then he had become a very simple man. After that final exhibition, he never picked up another paintbrush. The artist, the husband, maybe even the father he was, they all died. By the time we were reunited, he had long ceased asking questions of any kind."

"But he still knew," I said. "And somebody asked questions."

"That is right," he said gravely.

And then it dawned on me, finally, the reason for this telling.

"Lucky . . ." I said.

His expression darkened. "One night, my father let it slip. Lucky had stopped in for some drinks. He was often arguing with his then wife, and he would come by regularly, before heading to his all-night poker game in Atlantic City. My father offered to make us some fried dumplings but there was a sudden flare-up in the pan, and he shouted my name for help. He didn't repeat himself, and he never made the mistake again. The moment passed. Lucky said nothing. That was many years ago, but he noted it, as a card player naturally will. He noted it and kept it."

"Until he could use it," I said, recalling what Drum had told me about Lucky introducing him to Pong. "He was going to expose you. Destroy your life."

"It was not exactly that way," he said, his eyes narrowing. "Still, I do not know why he looked into it. Perhaps just curiosity. He had contacts at the USCIS and Social Security offices in Newark. It is not so difficult to determine such things when you have material to cross-reference. My identity was simply something he knew. But this last year was terrible for Lucky at the gaming tables. He was over-reaching at poker as well. His debts became huge. He was, I know, in real danger, and not just financially. I offered to remortgage my house, even sell the eateries in Dunbar, but it was not nearly enough. In Drum he saw a way, and proposed a deal to him."

"So was Elixirent bullshit, too, all just a sham?"

"No, no," he coughed. "It was a genuine venture. It still can be, for you. In fact, here." He unzipped the chest pocket of his warm-up jacket and withdrew his leather card wallet. "The dark metal one links to the account we set up for the business. You can use it for expenses, for supplies, for whatever you find necessary." His face took on some color with the talk of commerce and he told me the passcode but I wouldn't take the wallet when he tried to press it in my hand. I was done. I had no stomach left for swallowing any more line. Or better, I couldn't bear to disbelieve him for another second. I didn't have to say anything and he put it away.

"I know Drum showed you what I set up for him here," he said, a bit weary. He was sitting on the bare floor now, pitched awkwardly to one side. "But that is separate from what you were helping me with. What Drum and I discussed exploring from the beginning, about erasing boundaries between mind and body through meditation and yoga and our venture of Elixirent, that was all real. But he began to focus on the most extreme possibilities. He became obsessed with the historical practices we were reading about, including the mixtures for extending longevity."

"The mercury tea you were making for him."

"I did not make that," he said. "I formulated the base, to which Drum himself decided to add mercury. They were herbal, alkaline tinctures with trace inert metals, like silver and gold. But he insisted on the mercury, the concentration of which he had me specify. He knew what he was doing. They were infinitesimally small concentrations, yet harmful nonetheless, just as they were to the Chinese emperors."

He explained how Lucky delivered Drum the bases in rounds, with each round prompting another cash payment. This way it would be drawn out. It was a classic scam, bleeding the mark dry, dram by dram, right up to the moment of the largest final payment, which Lucky moved up, because of Drum's worsening condition. He received it just before he and Pong both disappeared.

I asked how he could do this to anyone, much less to someone who'd only been a trusting partner, a trusting friend . . .

"There is no justification. I tried to tell myself we were simply giving him what he wanted. And what Drum wanted was that we simply keep trying. He didn't care about the money. Just that I keep returning. To help guide him through. To help him keep believing in the idea of deathlessness. Perhaps the idea most of all."

I had to laugh, if only because the notion struck me as so squarely true.

"But I found I could not do that any longer."

"Was all this in motion when I first met you at Bags' golf club?" He nodded.

"But why involve me? Was it because I'm worth nothing? Did you see that from the start?" I had grabbed him by the shoulders, jostling him, my sight blurred by a rush of tears. I could have killed him, or hugged and kissed him, or hung myself to his star forever, all the above, I didn't know. I let go.

He murmured, "That is wrong. You are a substantial young man,

Tiller. Everything we did together was real. I enjoyed those times. I just wanted you to see the world."

"I wanted to see the world!" I cried, unable to utter the last, truest part: *with you.*

We fell silent. I didn't know what to think, whether he was telling me another story, or telling himself one, or simply, finally, losing his grip. Regardless, he was exhausted, his face turned the wrong shade, and for the first time since knowing him I could hear a key of wavering in his voice, which, as much as anything else, made whatever hope or courage or delusion still girding me shake and crumble. I hated that I still needed him to forge the way. I asked if he thought all this was an excuse for what he and Lucky had done, for promoting a fantasy of eternal life to a desperate man, for ruining everything he'd built and nurtured and shepherded, for throwing away his family, his friends and colleagues. Me.

He didn't respond. We sat for a long while, only the sound of his frail, shallow breaths marking us. He lay down then on his side. Soon he closed his eyes. I thought he had fallen asleep but he murmured something about feeling too warm, constricted. His legs got suddenly jittery. Working gingerly, I peeled his light warm-up jacket off of him and rolled it up and put it under his head. He seemed to rest better, but after a long while of his being very still and very quiet I began to fear the worst. That maybe he was gone. In a panic I blurted the oddest word: *watermelon.* Without pause he opened his eyes and replied, "No, thank you," this as blithely as if we were sitting at a terminal gate and awaiting the boarding announcement for our flight home, and I knew then that he was in a dire way.

I got him some more water, and he cradled the soap dish like a peasant child, his hands trembling. He gamely tried his best to drink it, if only to show me his gratitude.

I said: "You haven't told me your real name."

He almost smiled. "I have not spoken it since Ling and I made our arrangement. Or even thought of it very often. But I will tell you now, if you wish."

It's funny. I must not have wanted to hear it, because I didn't answer.

So we left it at that.

We left it as Pong.

HE FINALLY SLEPT. It was unclear how much time passed; it could have been an hour, or a few. I'd left the ceiling light burning because otherwise it would have been pure blackout in the room, but the bulb merely cast a dull, soupy glow and I must have fallen dead asleep myself, for rousing me was Pruitt, his breath rank and hot in my face.

"You will come now, okay?" he moaned, his face ruddy and puffy, as if he'd been crying.

"What for?"

Pruitt just shook his head miserably, and Spideyface appeared from behind him and tugged me to my feet. I balked and with one stout hand Spideyface grabbed me by the neck and shoved me toward the door. In my mind I had wheeled around to deliver a Bruce Lee hammer punch and free us from this prison but somehow he was already corkscrewing me down to my knees, his ferocious grip clamping my elbow.

"You will re-lax," he grunted, squeezing the joint so hard I thought I might wet myself.

"Please, Pale Cricket," Pruitt pleaded beside him. "Boss want you now."

I raised my free arm in surrender and Spideyface let me up. He was out of sorts, too, a certain hunch to his meaty shoulders, and I realized that I wasn't in imminent peril. Maybe Drum simply needed a kindly song. As they led me away I glanced back at Pong. All of a sudden it felt terribly wrong to be leaving him alone. But he lay there undisturbed, snared in the depths of his unconscious, his eyes shut tight, his lips faintly working, and I wondered if he was dreaming his name.

We went down the stairwell, down past the other floor of rooms, past the vaulted main hall and its long wall of high windows, where I saw it was raining, a cool, overcast afternoon in the surround of these darkly verdant hills. Inside the lodge it was peerlessly quiet, with even some of the furnishings covered in sheets, as if the place had been closed down for the off-season.

"Where is everybody?"

Pruitt woefully rubbed the shorn crown of his head. His accent was even more Chilies-like, gone even deeper into its cadences, its colors. "Miss Constance in bad shape. She make pretend big boss not sick. Just stay in bed, no food, keep reread novels of Victorian lady going loco. Oh, Pale Cricket! No can be right, like this."

We had descended farther, past the kitchen that was unsettlingly empty and odorless, and I asked where Chilies was, why he wasn't helping her.

Pruitt's eyes swirled with hurt. "He in Bangkok, to sell curry brand to big multinational. He saying sick of exploitation, try for buyout, and become big boss, too. I tell him, I love dignity of work, but he just take my hand and say, 'Love this, farang,' and spit in it. Then he leave."

We stepped past the level of Pruitt's dismal lair, and out through the drive that led down to the valley, the clouds seeming to hang just above our heads in a drooping vault of sky. The lodge and the trees and the grounds were going *tock-a-tock* with raindrops that felt too dispersed and too big to be real. You could see each one tinsel and trace it right down to the fat splash on your face, like the world was weeping for you. Or maybe it was plain spitting, à la Chilies. Pruitt was now full-on whimpering, huffing and gasping like a kid will when the thought of the hurt is worse than the actual hurt itself. And I realized why: here I was, caught in the classic movie-gangster pretext of "taking a walk," with Spideyface trailing us wordlessly, the midnight-blue ink of his web tattoo seemingly turning chillier and bluer with every step, the back of my skull feeling as tender as a soft-boiled egg as I pictured him drawing an ice pick from his suit jacket. Something in me cued up Drum's boatman's song and I started to sing those doleful atonal bars in the hope that wherever he was they'd strum a clement note in his chest and somehow magically herald my commutation. Spideyface shoved me in the back with his stony knuckles and growled, *Damare*, which I somehow knew meant shut the fuck up. But I only crooned louder as I shuffled forth down the path that led to Drum's outdoor sauna, squealing like a possum I once unintentionally cornered in the backyard shed, and Spideyface wheeled in front and grabbed me by the windpipe and practically lifted me onto my toes while grunting almost kindly, "No more, okay . . ."

I went mum and though he let go before I fully passed out, I needed propping up by Pruitt while I watched the garage door to Drum's cave lab slowly retract upward. The gush of frigid air cleared my wooziness. Pruitt's inconsolable mug suggested that he and I were headed for another horrid labor. Or was this my final act? Suddenly I thought of Clark, whom I hadn't thought of for weeks, not for any lack of loving but because we loved each other in the way that was least potentially hurtful, by which I mean we loved purely but tacitly, via a mutually understood transmittal that has always been comforting and sufficient. But I would have given anything to hug his meager chest tightly, break out from our tidy emoji-set life. And I couldn't help but think of Pong then, too, the soft wreckage of his insides, and how I should be with him now, and simply serve as his girding, no matter if we were doomed.

"Go, go," Spideyface ordered, nudging me forward through the double doorway into the bright expanse of the lab. The ventilation system was blowing steadily and it seemed even colder than when I was here before; I could practically see my breath. I sensed a padding of footfalls receding behind me and I saw Spideyface stiff-arming a hunched-over Pruitt, who was craning back and weakly waving, his face stricken. Spideyface shoved him out the doorway and cast his eyes miserably at me before shutting me in.

I started for them but I heard Drum's voice echo, "Please, Tiller. Over here."

I couldn't see him at first, as he was obscured by the iron vats, their hinged tops unbuckled. He was standing beside their triangular array in his striped robe, the tops of his bare feet and ankles spindly and dark. Although his face was unshaven, his chin and cheeks splotchy with salt-and-pepper growth, he didn't look so sick anymore, his eyes sparkly and alert, his posture upright.

"It is good you are still here," Drum said, as if my fate were somehow not completely in his wide, rough hands, which had now taken firm hold of mine. There was something roiling about him, or within him, a charged flow of vitality that conducted through his icy grip and practically made me leap. "No one is willing. My poor Constance of course. But not even faithful Ji-Ji. It is just as well. I would have asked Pong to be here but I know he is not able."

I could only nod. It was clear now that the man was in a very distant, faraway place. I tried to shake free from his grasp but his hold was unrelenting, if seemingly effortless, his gaze most placid and fair.

"I had originally pictured a chamber carved out of the rock," he said, walking us between the vats. "But I think it is right this way." There was a low wooden bench with a fat bundle of black cloth neatly folded and placed on top. He had released me by then and I should have run, but I was disarmed when suddenly he shed his robe. The sight of him froze me. His nakedness was terrible. The rash I'd seen before had spread and thickened, with angry patches of fresh outbreak on his lower back and rear and flanks and then streaks of darker, purplish sections on his shoulder blades that were scarred over and cruddy, as if they'd been scratched at obsessively.

"Here," he said, tapping the bundle. "Help me put this on."

He turned his back to me and winged his arms slightly, as you might for a tailor, or a personal valet. He stood there patiently and was shivering now and there was nothing for me to do but heed him. I hefted the black bundle but it was startlingly heavy, like a small but dense body, maybe thirty kilos, if not more, and when it unfurled I had to heft the top part over one shoulder to be able to hold it. Some kind of hard weighting had been sewn into the banded panels of the garment, which had three-quarter sleeves and reached almost to the floor, like a vestment some judge or priest or royal might wear, if they also required a flak jacket.

Drum threaded one arm through, and then the other, his frame at first sagging with the full load. But he was now standing tall. There were small buckles running the whole length in front and he had me fasten all of them, right up to his chin. He gestured down at our feet. There was an iron ring inset and riveted to a wooden trapdoor in the flooring, the rectangular seam of which I hadn't noticed. He asked me to pull it up, but I wouldn't, scared of what it might reveal—a bloody, broken corpse—but he said, *Tiller*, with a soulful weariness and insistence that made it clear that I was not the one in peril. I tugged and swung the door up and over and I let it drop to the floor, exposing an iron trough filled to just shy of its rim, a shimmering, coffin-sized pool of mercury.

Without warning he clutched my hand and with one foot stepped down into the liquid metal. Had I not been there to brace him he would have fallen, for it was amazing to see how the mercury resisted him. It was like a magic-show trick. His bare foot kept popping to the surface, so buoyant that he had to force it down. It was only when he stepped in with his other foot and centered the extra weight from the garment that he could stand there solidly up to his knees, though the pressure must have been excruciating. His face was contorted, tears now wetting his taut cheeks, but I could see they were tears of straining and elation. He let go of me and crossed his arms, hugging the black robe to his body.

"This may be the most valuable piece of clothing in the world." He gave a wayward little laugh. Then he slowly lowered himself. He was breathing shallowly, faster now, as he began to lie back in the stunning metal liquor, and it was only later that I realized what he meant: the robe was filled with gold, a substance dense enough to sink in mercury. Now it was sinking him. His bottom half was already under, his chest and elbows dipping, but his hands, as yet unsubmerged, were clenching tight against the immense pressure and the cold.

"I can see the maiden," he said, gasping. His eyes were closed. There was no blood left in his face. "Keep me down . . . yes?"

He pitched backward and opened his mouth. He let it be filled. Then his head disappeared. A fat bubble rose up from the terrible, beautiful liquid and his chest bucked and rose. I knelt and pushed down on his body with my bare hands, not letting him come up again until he was completely still. By the end he'd sunk inside and there was nothing to see but the gently flowing mirror of his waters.

When I tried the outside door it swung open on its own. It was raining ferociously now, the skies unleashed. I ran up to the lodge and called out. But there was only the hard rattling of the rain against the roof. I called again, afraid Constance would appear and I'd have to give witness of her dead. Though now I wish she had, if only to feel her sturdy clamp on me one last time. But there was nothing, no one, not even a babbling Pruitt. The great hall darkened. Then I sprinted to the room where they'd held us, my heart suddenly afire with how we were unbound, free to go home. But here, too, there was only emptiness. Pong was gone. His spot on the floor still shiny, free of dust. His rolled-up jacket was all that was left. So I put it on, running out of that place, running as fast and as far as I could.

27.

W E HAVEN'T MOVED YET, and may never.

It turns out we are not simply biding our time here in Stagno, our newer friends becoming older friends, the process both incremental and sudden. The September heat has been briefly dissipated by the first cold front from the north, and when I woke up this morning I felt like making something warming for the gang. So, an early Sunday supper. Mrs. Parnthong, whose beaming round face lit up from the scent of my work the second she stepped in the house, happily accepted a glass of the fresh lime-and-mint tonic VeeJ had made and sat with Liam and his folks in the living room, where everybody was playing a board game. She didn't need to see what I was cooking, though she did ask what brand of shrimp paste I used, nodded politely, and wrote down a different one for me, saying she thought it had more "goodness." I knew what she meant. A moodier, fishier clay. More essence, more stuffing. With the simple and honest you can keep packing it in; the vessel will not fail.

Pruitt would have been proud, and maybe even Chilies, of everything I tossed in the mortar, mine just a normal-sized white marble one I got at the sandwich judge's kitchenware shop with VeeJ's second-place gift certificate. I definitely made too much; chin down, my headphones grooving with my classic rock and folk favorites playlist, I pounded all morning, not measuring anything, the recipe now part of my muscle memory, and if the curry had none of my blood, it sure had plenty of my actual sweat and tears, which when mixed up is like a blood, the best evidence that you're still alive.

When my lady popped in—yes, my Val—she noticed my wet cheeks and made worried eyes but I simply gestured to the pile of shallots I was pulverizing. She dabbed my face with her sleeve, kissed me on the nose. I didn't want her to know that I had indeed welled up, which I have been finding myself doing at certain moments when I'm alone, like sitting behind the wheel while tracking through a car wash, or in the restroom of a fast-food joint, or like yesterday, while I was showering after playing hoops with VeeJ and his neighborhood playmates, when all of a sudden I broke down and had to clutch the shampoo caddy to steady myself. I'll be perfectly fine, my head running through the chores I need to do, errands to be run, and then without warning I'm tsunamied by a rushing tide, this wallop of mixed-up fear and joy, for what happened and didn't.

It was this close.

This.

A knife's edge, in fact, between Victor Jr. riding out this time line and an alternate one in which he fended for himself. Tilting solo comes naturally to him, and he'll surely subjugate the world soon anyway, but in his case being orphaned would have only made his innate hardness that much more invulnerable. He'd become this flinty, armored young man whose inner reaches stayed forever unsullied. I remember an old dead poet's line from a freshman writing seminar about the heart leaping at seeing a rainbow in the sky, not just when you're young but all through your life, because if it didn't you might as well tap out; the notion seemed quaint and gassy to me then but now feels utterly modest, so very simple that it hurts to think how desiccated you'd have to be not to cherish life in that way. I'd never want VeeJ to grow up like that, and as long as I'm around I won't let him. And I won't let myself, if I can manage. I may grow haggard and stooped by the heavy duty of the complicated and sad. I might too soon get crushed to nothing, but please, as the poet said, let me remain the child to keep becoming the man, over and over and over again.

This, unfortunately, won't prevent that last moment in the bathroom from playing in a regular loop in my head. How, in the ruthless trajectory of natural law, our end was clear: Val pitching sideways toward the water, the heated curler in her hand about to firework. My sole thought was *Such rampant hazards in a house*, a curiously dry and toothless gripe that paradoxically, I believe, freed my body to react in full. Did I secretly want to perish, too? Was this an impromptu suicide pact, now presenting its best chance? What I am certain of is that only those joined power cords came into my vision, the orange and the black, and that I was instantly hurtling toward them.

Your eyes are working but you can hardly see. It was all murk and crud, a stickiness webbing my vision. For a second I was terrified with the thought that this was how it was to be dead: everything obscured to you for an eternity. But then Val shouted, "Tiller!" and she was holding me as I was bellied over the tub edge, frantically wiping my face with her bloody hand. I tried to check her hand for injury but she cried, "It's you, it's you," and I pressed against my scalp where it met my forehead, where bright blood was freely flowing. She curled herself out from the water and we lay splayed for a few breaths on the wet tile floor. She had me keep pressure on it as she searched the medicine cabinet for a bandage, and when I looked over I saw the cleanly cut end of the black cord dangling a few inches above the now pinkish water, the curling iron sedately nestled on the tub bottom. Submerged beside it was my little knife, glinting like some sea treasure. As Val battle dressed the gash—I'd receive stitches at the Stagno Community Clinic soon thereafter—she described how I stumbled forward and thumped headfirst against the tile wall and accidentally jabbed myself. Somehow, in the lurch, the cord got in the way of the blade, its edge ever magnificent, ever sublime.

I called Clark later that night. Though there had been the periodic emails and texts, we hadn't actually spoken, we both realized, for half a year. He assumed I was still work-studying somewhere in Western Europe, and I didn't dispel the notion, even making a lame joke about craving ice in my cola, which he knew I never drank anyway. He hoped I was staying healthy, and I hoped he was keeping busy, and we made a tentative plan to have Thanksgiving with Aunt Didi, if not necessarily back in Dunbar. He didn't need to know that I was hardly a day's car trip away. Why wound the man? There's no good reason, just as he saw no use leaving a bruise on me with some sorrowful comment about my scarceness. He knows I love him, and I know he loves me, but this is how we operate, no matter how unideally ideal it is. He offered to send some spending money but I told him I was panhandling just fine, which was the sort of goofy turn our chats took when they were about to end, when, surprising us both, I asked what he thought was my mother's favorite song.

There was a silence, but knowing my dad, I could practically see him quickly getting it back together, marshaling all his considerable goodness, to mull what I'd said in earnest.

"She loved so many songs," he said, his voice sounding almost enchanted, as though he were remembering the very best of times. "It's difficult to say. Is it one of those she played most often? Or the ones she put on when she was feeling a certain way?"

"Up to you."

He didn't answer for a while and I thought he might just give up and say goodbye. I must not have been able to hear myself humming, just like how you can't hear your own snoring, because he said: "I guess you know the song."

"I guess I do," I said, realizing how painfully transparent I was being.

He let out a chuckle. "I miss her music," he said. "I should play it more."

"Me, too."

"Let's do that, then," he said.

"Every day?"

"Well . . ." he said, maybe now appreciating the full weight of what he was actually suggesting. "Whatever works."

"Okay."

"Talk to you soon, son."

"Sure thing, Dad," I said.

And that was that.

The tune, of course, is on my playlist, and it'll probably drop by the time we're clearing the dishes. It's one of the songs I sang at Karaoke Garbo, then as a wink at Constance. Except for Mrs. Parnthong we're all too young for it to be familiar (it's not a super-famous song), but she's a recent immigrant and so likely won't know it, either. Most of my mother's favorite records were oldies for her then, and like this one had the sort of sound she liked, scratchy and full of soul. Those horns will herald in the background and maybe arouse a good twitch in Courtney's feet or hands, or make Liam and Victor Jr. groove and shimmy in their chairs. Keefer will unconsciously head bop. That's fine with me. No one needs to sing along. Truth is, it probably wasn't her favorite song. She had way too many to narrow it down to one. It was more like our favorite, mine and Clark's, the refrain both too easy and too hard for us to play: *I can't quit her.* It literally brakes the heart, stopping it right in place.

Mercifully, for just the length of a song.

I sometimes think of what VeeJ and I would be doing, had things gone differently. Of course I had lied to Val about abandoning the boy. That was the most vacant of threats. I would have adopted him, though I'm sure no one would have allowed that, and not just because the magic card is now kaput. We would have had to bug out together, orphan brothers on the run, squatting wherever we could, doing odd jobs to get by, perhaps eventually rolling out a food cart on the main street of some unsuspecting town, to start our empire. I'd have christened it *Val's*, the letters stenciled in fat script on the side, and even though our customers would constantly ask who she was, we'd smile and quell ourselves and just say, *A great lady we knew.*

Still, we should probably get the cart anyway, to supplement the monthly allowance from the feds, which is all we have coming in to refresh the donations we've saved. I didn't say anything to Victor Jr. after the incident, just fibbing that I'd slipped in the shower and cut my head. We were making grilled cheese and tomato sandwiches for lunch, and I casually said something about his keeping an eye on his mother.

"Is that what you did?" he asked, some instinct firing.

I was a pinned cricket. Of course he knew nothing about it, at least consciously, and I pipped: "I always tried."

Not that my trying made any difference. Still, maybe I'm more okay with this now after everything that's gone down, here and abroad. I won't switch to those old automatic modes. I don't want to be that default boy again, that default soul, thinned out in blood and in his loving, that boy who could only sing inside his own head.

VeeJ flipped our grilled sandwiches, seemingly oblivious. Afterward, though, he's stuck pretty close to his mother, padding after her room to room like a faithful dog who's picked up a sad portent in his nose. Now, I see them folding laundry together, or doing planks side by side to streaming yoga videos. He even has her shooting baskets with him. Val is purposefully staying active, which is great, but you can flip that, easily turn it around and interpret her doings as quietly desperate treadmilling, a grinding of the gears. You can spend the days cataloging the impending hazards of your loved ones, whether self- or world-inflicted, but where does it get you? Vigilance is a static mode of living.

I'm trying to move us forward in a different way. Unwitting, even comfortably blinkered, until the moment of encounter. Like letting life place a sharp mint on your tongue. Or, if you're open to any kind of fortune, a die-sized cube of the crispest, juiciest watermelon. My hand will pause, as it did the other day, whenever I slice some up. To know what's contained in a scant mouthful! The hoping, the wreckage, the passion. I sometimes shudder with the picture of those folks, Pruitt and Auntie Choi, Lily and Minori. My dear dread block of Constance, newly orphaned to the world. I'm afraid for all of them out there, drifting, alone.

And him? I don't know where he went, whether he has a place in this world or the next. Sometimes, when we're out at the shopping center or supermarket, I'll catch a glimpse of some dark-haired figure and drift in that direction, my tongue caught, my lungs bucking, and try to call forth his name. But I can't, and it won't be him, it most likely never will be, and I only hear it in my head like I do my mother's, these endless echoes in the cave of my heart.

With Val, I'm practically breathing her name. I call it out whenever I can, through the rooms of the house, in the yard, on the street, hoping that the very sound of it will fix her to this spot. The song is not a wish; the song is not a dream. It is what I have left, a savor I can live in. In the most practical terms this has meant liberating the more hazardous garden implements (not to mention the orange-extension-cord wheel) from the padlocked shed and placing them back along the garage wall; preparing food regularly at home again, the knife block be damned; or blithely tossing her the car keys whenever she feels like going shopping alone. I can't track her with our cheap burner phones, though I admit my mind's satellite-map view will open onto the bright, hard topography of the quarry. Instead of retreating to the back deck to blaze off the fear, I grab a hand rake and go hard at the beds we've dug out from this rocky patch of ground, weeding between the rows I tasked Val and VeeJ to seed with various autumn vegetables. I don't give a crap about healthfulness, at least not that kind. We need not munch a single stalk of chard. I simply hope that their first wonderings of the morning will be of how much sprouting might have happened overnight. In fact, I'll sneak out there and damage some of the leaflings and stay silent when Val complains about some pest eating our babies. She'll sigh over the bed with her hands knuckled on her hips and then squat and pluck out the ones I've mauled, then spear her trowel into the loam and tap in the tiny seeds from one of the dozen packets I bought at the hardware store. I want to keep us planting and not worrying about a harvest. Let it jungle. The bounty is here already. It's in our joint earth tilling, our basketball dribbling, in our melodic low-down humming and in our vigorous eating and drinking, and it finds sudden contour in random, lovely things, like the meringue Victor Jr. can froth to a Himalayan peak, or the warmed dent Val leaves in her pillow, the buttery smell of her hair threaded deep in the flannel.

Then, as if in reverse alchemy, they're gone, all this vital gold dissipated to nothing.

Still, this is the world I want to shape myself to; this is the world that I want to shape me.

Val, maybe sensing a funny cast to my stance, asked the other day in the bathroom if I was doing all right. This shot me with joy, if only because in the previous cloister of her mood it was impossible for her to break out and ask anything. I just said, *Sure, I'm fine*, even though I wasn't feeling so hot, and wanted to stand there like I sometimes would after walking home from the school-bus stop to the shuttered emptiness and lingering outside for an extra minute or two before keying in, even in a steady rain. Especially a rain. I'd let it soak my head until the trickles became rivulets streaming down my back, and I'd look up and think, *This rain doesn't know who I am, or what happened to my family, and never will. It will stop when it stops and not a drop before.* Val leaned in for me to hug her and she whispered, *Tighter*, and then, *Tighter*, again, and I knew it wasn't herself she meant to comfort.

Now the curry pot simmers on the burner. I shiver at it, every cell. Noodle and salad platters are set out on the counter. Sweet skewered meats are stacked in a pile. I have begun to deep-fry. VeeJ pops in and asks if I need help, the furry brushes of his eyebrows disquieted with how much I have going. I assure him I'm fine; like any apprentice I'm banking on surplus to fill deficits in quality. He refills Mrs. Parnthong's glass and leaves. Soon Val comes in and dips a spoon into the pot, the taste straightening her spine.

"Yow," she says, the sound, to my ear, like an inflection of Pong's.

"Too strong?"

"Nearly," she says, sampling again. Her eyes seize momentarily, half closing. "But good. It's a little better every time. You're growing into a mastery."

"Really?" I laugh.

"Definitely," Val says, her spiced lips grazing my cheek. A tiny burn. She hefts a platter to carry out. "Someday soon."

Truth is, mastery is beyond someone like me. Val, too. We'll leave that to people like our special boy. The rest of us, as capable as we are, as earnest, have enough burden simply becoming. We figure our way in halfway bounds, eternally not getting there. Yet we keep on. Eyes open, mouths wide. Ready.

Acknowledgments

A great shout of gratitude to Sarah McGrath, with special thanks to Alison Fairbrother, for their expertise, kindly wisdom, and endless patience.

To Amanda Urban, for her peerless faith and counsel.

To the creative writing programs at Stanford and Princeton, and to the Civitella Ranieri, for generous support during the writing of this book.

And as ever to my loving family, for indulging my silly songs.